STORM SURGE

AUTHOR'S EDITION

D0868970

By

KATLYN

Storm Surge
A BookEnds Press Publication
Printing History
First Printing August 2002
Author's Edition May 2003

Cover design by Sheri

For information address:
BookEnds Press
PO Box 14513
Gainesville, Florida 32604
1-800-881-3208

For distribution information:
StarCrossed Productions
PO Box 357474
Gainesville, Florida 32635-7474

So

Dedication

I would like to dedicate this, my first novel,
to my family.

To my mom, God rest her soul, who
always accepted me for who and what
I am, and never tried to change me.
I miss you terribly.

To my dad, who has always provided
a strong shoulder, and a warm heart.
You are the best father in the world.

And last but certainly not least,
To my wonderful sister. You have always
been and will always be my hero,
my mentor—my best friend.

I love you all, very much.

Acknowledgements

I could write another book acknowledging all of the people who have assisted, encouraged and supported my efforts during the writing of Storm Surge. I owe a special thanks to those individuals who encouraged me to revise and resurrect this story.

I will be forever indebted to all the members of the KatLynFic group for your support. Many of you have been with me from the first web posting and I will never forget the faith you have had in me.

KK, Pam, and Liz, thank you for never allowing me to abandon my dream of bringing this story to life once again, for being patient with my many absences as I worked on this revision, and for *always* showing me what true friendship is really all about.

Radclyffe, my colleague, my friend. You always knew this day would come, and I thank you for believing in me. You are an inspiration but most of all, a true and treasured friend.

My eternal thanks goes to Stacia Seaman for accepting the challenge of editing the author's edition of Storm Surge. Your professionalism is exemplary, and I could not have made this journey without you.

A very special thanks to BookEnds Press for providing me with a truly wonderful experience in publishing this story and to Bob and Pete for allowing me the opportunity to live my dream.

Denise, how can I ever express my gratitude for all of your hard work, encouragement and not so subtle nudges along what has become a wonderful journey into our future. You are truly an awesome Aussie and I love you with all my heart.

Chapter One

The wind blew softly in the darkness, caressing her skin like gentle fingers. It was soothing, reassuring, and hopefully would be healing. The air still held the heat of the day, as did the sand sifting between Alex's toes. It was after midnight, and all of the tourists had long since retired for the night. This was the time of day Alex liked to walk the beach. Something about the darkness and the unending roar of the surf calmed her. Maybe it was the simple fact that the ocean never slept, never tired. Or maybe it was because she felt so comfortable in the darkness. Who knew, who cared, as long as the peace came?

For Alex, peace had been a distant friend for far too long. The last six years had been hard, mentally and physically. However, Alex knew that if life were to move forward, she would have to find some sort of peace within herself. She had spent too many days and nights running from the past. Now she was here, back where it all started, to face the demons, exorcise them, and hopefully move on.

Alex Montgomery, at 35, had been an FBI agent for 10 years. Now as she walked on the beach, she wondered if she wanted to return. Her life had reached a crossroads and she had choices to make. Choices that not only affected her, but everyone she cared for. The last few years had proven to Alex that she didn't live in an encapsulated world within the FBI.

Every day her life was in danger, but more terrifying than anything else was that the people around her faced danger as well. Her last case had proven that the best way to get to an agent was to get to someone they loved. The academy had drilled this small but important aspect of being an agent into them, and Alex had always been careful to keep her family and friends well away from her work. However, somehow her enemies had found the one thing she loved most dearly in her life, and extinguished it like a match. They not only destroyed the only person she had ever allowed herself to love, they had destroyed her heart and darkened her soul.

As she walked through the darkness, Alex vowed that they would pay. *I will come for you, Malcolm, and when I do you will pray for an escape to hell.*

Alex walked up the steps toward the warm lights shining in her house. She sat on the deck awhile and had a glass of the wine and one of the sandwiches Sam had left for her. Laying her head back against the cushion of the deck chair, she was instantly asleep.

Around 2 a.m., Alex awoke to the sounds of the tide coming in and crashing on the shore. She shivered in the cool breeze and pulled herself up to a standing position, groaning at the aches her body felt, then slowly made her way into the house. She locked up and went to bed, falling into a restless sleep filled with dreams of times past.

The room was dark, and the air conditioning provided the only noise in the house. Conner Harris rolled toward the middle of the bed and felt its emptiness. How long had it been since she had awakened to find someone there? Lately, the only encounters she had allowed in her life were not even one-nighters—they were half-nighters. Once the sex was over, she made sure she disappeared into the night and was gone.

She never brought anyone to her lair, instead suggesting they go to her latest conquest's apartment, house, or hotel. It was a protective mechanism that allowed her to remain aloof, and alone.

Conner threw the covers back and felt the cool air flow across her naked body. Wishing she could relax in the comfort, she sighed, rolled, and sat on the edge of the bed in one graceful motion. Running a hand through her hair, she stood and headed down the hallway, anticipating the smooth full flavor of that first cup of coffee, the only thing she needed at the moment.

"Damn, damn, damn," she mumbled to herself as she looked at the still-sleeping automatic coffeemaker. She stumbled to the freezer and retrieved the coffee beans, ground up three scoops, poured in the water, and watched the pot boil.

"You would think in this age of technology, someone would invent a damn coffeemaker that you could put a pound of beans in, connect to a source of water, program, and miraculously have a cup of java each and every morning without this daily ritual of grinding pouring, waiting," Conner complained to the empty kitchen.

She trudged back down the hallway to the bathroom, having decided to shower while the coffee brewed. Stepping under the spray, she allowed her muscles to relax and the warm water to wake her. As she stretched out her arms toward the wall, she tucked her head and let the spray wash the shampoo from her hair. She was surprised to find not only the warm water from the shower but also tears gliding down her face when she raised her head.

"What the hell is wrong with me this morning?" she fumed as she stepped out of the shower. Counting the days, she assured herself that it wasn't a bad case of PMS, so what the hell was it? She thought back to the loneliness she had felt upon waking—and now this. Surely she wasn't going to start falling apart like this on a regular basis. She didn't need anyone in her life; she had her job, and there wasn't enough room in her life for both.

Conner looked sideways at her reflection in the mirror and chastised herself for the emptiness that she saw on her face. "Okay, snap out of it, shut it out, and get moving...this is no time to be losing it, I have to go to work." She dried her body and pulled on her silk robe, then headed once again down the hallway toward the kitchen.

As she reached into the cabinet for a cup, she felt a presence in the room, and all of her senses went on full alert. She thought longingly of her Sig Sauer 9mm under her pillow. Not turning, she grabbed a knife from a drawer and spun around to face the intruder.

"Meow."

Conner slumped against the counter and cursed. "What the fuck do you mean sneaking up on me, you little shit? If you weren't the owner of my partner, I would de-fur you right here." The tiny cat just meowed again and stared at Conner.

Conner returned the knife to the drawer and poured a cup of coffee. Throwing her most vile look at the cat, she leaned back and took a sip, trying to ignore the stares of the furball at her feet.

"Okay, okay, already. Geez, you're just like Seth, always hungry, and always vocal about it too. How did I let him talk me into keeping you for a week while he went traipsing around the country?"

Seth had dropped Magnum and his luggage off the night before, and Conner had stared unbelievingly at the huge backpack that contained the cat's personal belongings.

"He'll miss me," Seth said with an embarrassed look on his face. "I just thought he might get along better having some of his toys and stuff."

"Damn, Seth, what's that smell? Don't even tell me that I have to feed this cat sardines and other rotten shit for the next week."

With an even more embarrassed look Seth pulled out an obviously well-worn, seldom-washed piece of cloth.

"No, it's not sardines, Conner," he said a little harshly. "It's just an old t-shirt. I thought he might feel better if he had something that had my scent on it while I was away."

"Please put it away," Conner said while pinching her nose, failing in the attempt to hide her teasing smile beneath her hand.

After a few more minutes of playfully arguing over Magnum's routine, Seth left for his long-awaited vacation. Once Seth had gone, the cat had cried unmercifully until Conner dug through the backpack and, using only two fingers, brought out Seth's dirty t-shirt and tossed it in the farthest corner of the room.

"That's fine, Seth, spoil the damn cat, but did you have to bring the dirtiest thing in the hamper?"

Magnum immediately ran over, curled up in the shirt, and went to sleep. "Well, I'll be damned," Conner mused. "Who'd have ever believed it?" That was the last time Conner thought of the cat. She had turned and headed for bed, falling asleep almost as quickly as her head touched the pillow.

Now she opened a can of cat food and spooned it into the cat's personalized bowl. Magnum curled around her legs, rubbing his scent on her, marking his territory. "Damn men, you're all alike. Spend one night with a woman and you think you own her. Well, I've got news for— okay, Conner, you are really losing it now. Conversing with a cat, what the hell has my life come to?"

She finished her second cup of coffee while reading the morning newspaper, then went to the bedroom to dress for work. She pulled on a pair of faded Levi's and a white cotton tank top, strapped on the shoulder holster, and pulled the Sig from under her pillow, tucking it nicely under her right arm. She topped it off with a brown leather jacket and her Doc Martens.

Conner glanced in the mirror, not vainly, but checking for any cracks in the façade that she called her cover. Nodding in approval, she headed back down the hallway to the living room. She picked up her keys and walked out into the cool early morning, heading for her Jaguar. The car started with a roar, and she pulled quickly out into the street. This was really her home—the streets.

It was a thirty-minute drive to downtown Jacksonville from Amelia Island. The drive gave Conner the opportunity to transform herself into her undercover persona. Living on the island also provided her with the anonymity she needed. She didn't converse much with her neighbors, nor did she have any close friends on the island. That didn't mean that she had no close friends; she did. They all lived inland and came over for an occasional weekend of barbecuing, sailing, and beachcombing.

Stuck in traffic, she drummed her fingers on the steering wheel impatiently, then picked up her cell phone and dialed.

"Hey there you sexy thing. Got any clothes on at the moment?" she asked in a low, sultry voice.

"Yes, and even if I didn't, I don't think I could ever drag your attention away from work long enough to get you to do anything about it. How the hell are you, Conner? It's been way too long."

Conner smiled and pictured Sam's face on the other end of the line. "Well, I was wondering if you wanted to get together for dinner tonight. It's been a while and we have a lot of catching up to do."

"Oh my God, something terrible has happened, right?"

"Ha ha, very damn funny, Sam. If you're just going to heckle me, I'll just find someone else to spend my evening with," Conner said.

"Like hell you will. Meet me at Mike's at seven sharp, and make sure you're driving that cool machine you call a car. I may just feel the need for a drive up the beach and I want to feel some power under my body tonight."

"You're insatiable, you know. Always thinking about getting laid. If I were smart I'd take advantage of that by getting you drunk and—"

Sam's teasing voice cut her off. "Well, Conner, hanging around all those drug heads must have mushed your brain; if I remember correctly you've already been there, done that—and walked away. I don't give second chances to just anyone. And anyway, Kelly loves you like a sister, but I think she would draw the line at you providing that kind of comfort while she's out of town."

"Well, lover, or maybe I should be politically correct and say ex-lover, I'm not just anyone. However, you're probably smart by denying me the pleasure. I'd only screw it up like the last time," Conner said with more than a little sadness in her voice.

"Okay, enough heavy stuff. I'll see you at seven, and don't be late." With that, Conner heard the line go dead. Sam hadn't hung up on Conner; she had simply hung up, a trait that Conner had grown to know well. Sam never was good in uncomfortable situations and chose to avoid them whenever possible. That in itself had made their pairing difficult. Conner always believed in spilling everything out and dealing with problems head on. Sam, on the other hand, tended to let everything simmer until it one day exploded.

Their kidding and jesting was their way of letting each other know that the love they had shared still remained, even though neither would ever do anything to rekindle the flame. Sighing sadly, Conner headed into the River City.

Walking into the police station house, Conner headed for her desk, but Buet, who always had a cheerful word, stopped her before she could sneak past the front desk. Mack Buetford was the in-house archive for gossip and politics in the department. At 56, he had come to the hard realization that too many days on the beat had worn out his knees. Everyone in the department knew Buet missed the street, so they always included him in their after-shift get-togethers at one of the local pubs.

Conner was resting her elbows on the counter, casually chatting with Buet, when she heard a quiet "excuse me" come from just behind her. She stood and turned just as Buet spoke. It was a good thing he still had his voice, for Conner's was buried somewhere in her stomach.

A chill ran up her spine as she looked into the bluest eyes she had ever seen, although she couldn't figure out if the chill was due to the beauty of the irises looking back at her or the danger that lurked just beneath.

"Can I help you?" Buet asked.

Holding Conner's gaze, the woman handed her identification to Buet. "Yes, I have an 8 a.m. appointment with Captain Peterson."

"Sure. If you'd like to have a seat, I'll let him know you're here," Buet said while looking at Conner.

"Um, well, see ya later, Buet, I've got a ton of paperwork waiting." Conner barely got the words out of her mouth, afraid she would choke on them as they came out.

As she walked toward her desk, Conner could feel the heat of the woman's eyes on her back. Turning the corner into her cubicle, she dared a glance back and sure enough, the woman was sitting so her line of sight was directly down the corridor Conner had just walked.

Conner pulled the first of a stack of papers from her in-box. On orders from Captain Peterson, she was taking a desk day to get her paperwork done. "I hate this damn paperwork shit," she grumbled. "I need to be on the street doing what I do best, not in this damn cubby-hell-hole pushing a pencil."

From behind her she heard a sultry voice say, "Think of the collar as a great date with the paperwork being a good-night kiss. Together they pack quite a punch."

Spinning around in her chair, Conner watched as the woman from the front desk walked purposely into Captain Peterson's office. She sat for a moment looking at the closed door wondering why the mystery woman was. *I hope it has nothing to do with anything I'm ever involved in, since I just made a complete ass of myself*, she thought.

As the blue-eyed woman sat in front of Captain Peterson's desk, she couldn't help but smile at the reaction from the officer outside. She also couldn't believe that she had allowed herself to relax long enough to tease the other woman; it was so against her style. *Oh well, I'll never have to see her again, what harm could it possibly do?*

Peterson relaxed and rested his elbows on the desk. "Well, Shadow, you seem to be in a good mood for a change."

The woman's eyes turned a deep blue, showing the danger that such a comment ignited within her. Peterson shifted back slightly in his chair and raised his hands in a gesture of peace. "Ease up, Shadow, just happy to see you're still among the living."

The woman relaxed her shoulders. "Sorry, Jack, I had a long trip and I'm still a little tired. Give me a few days and I'll be back to my old jolly self."

Peterson looked at her and knew the words were hollow. She would never be back to her old self, not after the hell she had endured over the past year. "If you want a few days before you jump in the game again, just say so. I've waited a long time to have you back in the city. A few more days won't make me change my mind."

"Really, Jack, if you don't mind, I would like a few days to get settled. It's been a long time since I've been home and I would really like to get the house in shape and a few good nights' rest before I get started. I was thinking of next Monday, if that's okay with you."

"Take all the time you need, Shadow. We'll be here waiting." With that said, Peterson stood and extended his hand across the desk. The woman shook it firmly, and when she began to pull hers away, he held it a little tighter. "It really is good to see you again. I'm glad you decided to come home where you belong." He then released her hand and led her across the room, opening the door for her to leave.

Halfway out the door the woman turned and looked Peterson in the eyes. "One more thing, Jack. The Shadow died the last time she was in town. She's not coming back—ever. If she's what you want, maybe you should do some thinking yourself between now and Monday morning. Give me a call if you change your mind between now and then." She turned and started walking away.

From behind, she heard Peterson say, "See you Monday, 8 a.m., and make it sharp."

As she walked past Conner's cubicle, she couldn't help but glance inside. Conner was buried elbow deep in the paperwork before her. Stopping, the blue-eyed woman turned around and stuck her head in the cubicle in one quick motion, startling Conner and making her spill her coffee.

She smiled the most blazing smile Conner had ever seen. "Must have been one hell of a date, Officer." And just as quickly as she had appeared, she was gone.

Chapter Two

*D*amn, *how do I let Sam talk me into these things?* The last thing Alex wanted to do was spend the evening sitting in a bar talking about old times. Most of the old times Alex could remember since the raid were times she would love to forget. Plundering through her closet searching for something to wear, she selected a pair of tan linen slacks and a white silk shirt and laid them out on the bed before heading to the bathroom to get ready for the evening.

After showering, she thought about calling and making some excuse not to go, but placed the phone back in the cradle, deciding that she couldn't put off the inevitable. She had to get out and see people. She at least had to go through the motions of being recovered and ready to face the world again.

Pulling on a blue blazer that complemented her eyes, she gave her reflection one last look in the mirror, mentally preparing herself for the coming evening. She headed out the door and got in her Jeep, hesitating only for a moment before turning the key and hearing the engine roar to life. Only after a few moments did Alex realize her knuckles were white from the death grip she had on the steering wheel.

There was a thin sheen of perspiration on her face, and her hands were damp and clammy. Taking a deep breath, Alex shook off the memories that would forever be frozen in her mind. This driveway, Feryle leaning out the window of her Camaro on a cool Monday morning, smiling and waving good-bye as she left for work after their weekend together. Then came the blast, the pain, and the knowledge that her life, along with Feryle's body, had just been blown to hell.

Alex and Feryle had bought the beach house for their fifth union anniversary. Located in a lush area south of Jacksonville, on the ocean side, it was a gift of love, commitment, and promise. It had also been a contractor's nightmare, most shaking their heads in disbelief after finding out how much the couple had paid for the house. But Alex and Feryle had been determined. They had depleted their savings and devoted countless weekends to demolishing, scraping, painting, and hammering—loving every moment they spent together creating their new home. Feryle, an architect, had drooled over the vaulted ceilings and the sharp angles offset by smooth curves.

Finally the house was complete and they had the time to enjoy it. The effort Alex and Feryle had put into the house had not gone unnoticed by local developers, and soon new homes appeared all around them. Feryle had even designed some of those homes; it was almost as if this neighborhood were her creation. Feryle and Alex spent many nights sitting on the deck, watching the waves, while Feryle told Alex about the houses she had designed that were visible from where they sat drinking wine and gently caressing each other.

Now looking at those houses only brought an emptiness that Alex knew would never be filled again. She sat for a few minutes, letting her heart rate return to normal. Usually she could control the memories, at least while she was awake. The nights were different. There she had no control, and the ghosts and darkness haunted her on a regular basis. She backed out of the drive and headed north into the city.

Before she realized it, she was at her exit to JT Boulevard. Rolling down the window for some fresh air, she focused on the drive to the restaurant. As she pulled into the parking lot a few minutes later, Alex spotted the familiar car. The vintage 1964 1/2 Mustang was in mint condition. Smiling at her friend's love for old things, she entered the restaurant.

The bar was dark as she entered, and it took a few seconds for her eyes to adjust. She immediately recognized the voice screaming from across the bar.

"Alex, over here," the woman yelled as she practically crawled over the table to get out of the booth. Alex looked around rather self-consciously. Several eyes had found their way to her, and she met them with an apologetic look, stepping a little quicker to quiet her friend.

Sam barreled into her and immediately clamped Alex into a bear hug. "My God, you are skinny, woman. If it weren't for all those muscles, you'd be nothing but bone." Alex groaned as Sam hugged her tighter. At the sound, Sam quickly released her. "Oh damn, Alex, I'm sorry, did I hurt you? I'm just so glad to see you."

"I'm fine, really. Just a little stiff still, but I'll get all the kinks worked out soon. Let's go have a seat and quit making a spectacle of ourselves, all right?"

Alex stopped dead in her tracks when she spotted the woman sitting in the booth Sam led her to.

"Alex, I'd like you to meet a friend of mine. Alex Montgomery, Conner Harris." The two women didn't speak, only stared at one other for what seemed like an eternity before turning to look at Sam, who was looking very confused, and once again back at each other.

"Um, hey guys, everything okay here? Did I say something wrong?"

"About two years. My work was the reason we broke up. She couldn't deal with what I did on a daily basis, not knowing when or if I would come home, and I was too stubborn to ask for a transfer to something a little less risky."

"Do you really think that would have saved the relationship?" Alex asked cautiously.

"No, not really. One of us would have eventually ended up resenting the other and it would have come apart anyway," Conner said sadly. "I love her and I always will, but thankfully our friendship has reached a level that I can be happy for her and Kel. We have a great friendship, all three of us. Kel knows how I feel, but she also knows that I would never do anything to hurt Sam again, and she respects that. I'm really lucky, when you think about it. Not many people are fortunate enough to remain in contact with old lovers, much less become best friends. What about you, do you have a partner waiting patiently at home?"

When Alex didn't answer immediately, Conner turned toward her and saw the pain in Alex's eyes. "Okay, here I go again, putting my foot in my mouth. Sorry if I'm being nosy."

"No, you didn't upset me, it's just that...well...um...no, I'm not with anyone," Alex said in a whisper so low, Conner almost couldn't hear her.

"Damn, I always seem to say the wrong things around you." Conner ran a hand through her hair.

Alex grabbed Conner's arm. "It's all right." She told Conner of Feryle's death, the raid on the drug lab, and her resulting injuries. At some point during the story, Conner reached out and placed her hand on Alex's, gently caressing it as Alex relived the hell that that had consumed her last year. The pain in Alex's eyes was so raw, it hurt Conner to see it, and all she wanted to do at that moment was take Alex in her arms and help soothe the pain away.

When Alex finished the story, there was a moment of uncomfortable silence before Conner gently squeezed Alex's hand. "I am so sorry for your loss, Alex. I can't even imagine how you feel. We've all lost people in our lives that we have loved, but each loss is unique in its own way, so I won't even pretend to understand what you're going through. But I will say you have a new friend, and if you ever need to talk, you know where to find me."

Alex listened to Conner and was amazed by her compassion. For the first few days after Feryle's death, a bombardment of friends and colleagues had come to the house expressing their condolences. They all said the same thing: "I know just how you feel." Alex had heard it so many times she wanted to scream. No one knew how she felt—no one. How could they? Not one of them had set the scene placing their loved one in harm's way and then had to stand there and watch them die. None of them had been so careless as to allow the darkness into their home.

"Thank you, Conner. Thank you for not making this just another death. So many people kept telling me that they knew how I felt, but they didn't. You're the first person that has ever recognized that, and I appreciate your thoughtfulness."

Conner gently squeezed Alex's hand once again and then released it. She picked up her wallet and pulled out a few bills, laying them on the table. "Well, I guess I had better get going, I have quite a drive, but thank goodness tomorrow's my day off and I can sleep in."

Alex searched for her wallet but felt Conner's firm grip on her arm. "No way, lady. Tonight's on me. Consider it a welcome back, here's to new friends, evening."

Slightly embarrassed, and a little surprised, Alex nodded and smiled. "Okay, Conner, but only on one condition—you allow me to treat next time. Got it?"

Conner chuckled. "Okay, okay, you win. Next time's on you." Sliding from the booth, both women contemplated the last few comments and the expectation of the next time.

As they made their way to their cars, both women realized that neither wanted the evening to end just yet, but they knew it had to. The outing had turned out to be very entertaining and uplifting—something unusual for both of them.

On impulse, Alex turned to Conner. "You know, I was just thinking, It's been a while since I've had a good meal, and, well, um, I was wondering if you aren't doing anything Friday night, um...maybe you would, um, like to get something to eat, and...ah...maybe catch a movie or something?"

Conner, her stomach once again fluttering, could only manage a garbled, "Sure, sounds like fun. Follow me to my car and I'll give you my number."

Alex followed Conner to the Jag and looked at it with envious eyes. "Wow, maybe I should apply to the JPD; they sure seem to pay better than the FBI."

Chuckling, Conner explained that the Jag was really an asset of the JPD. Her only privilege was getting to drive it off hours to keep up her cover, and more importantly, to have it close by in case she had a meeting somewhere.

She reached in the sleek Jag and pulled out one of her cards. Alex looked at it and back at Conner, who was smiling. "Another part of my cover, I'm afraid."

The card advertised a personal courier service. Alex smiled and shook her head in acceptance of the double lives they both had to lead in order to do their jobs. *Welcome home, Alex,* she silently said to herself.

Conner wrote her personal cell phone number on the back of the card—just in case Alex needed to get in touch with her when she wasn't at home, she told herself—and handed it back to Alex. Their hands brushed lightly during the exchange, and each woman unconsciously jumped as the heat radiated between them.

Alex recovered first. "Just how far of a drive do you have tonight?" she asked in a slightly nervous voice.

"Not that far, maybe 45 minutes. I live on Amelia Island," Conner replied.

"Well, if you don't feel like driving all the way home tonight, you're welcome to the spare room at my house. I don't live very far from here, maybe twenty minutes." *Geez, Alex, what are you thinking, asking this woman to go home with you? You only met her today, and although she probably isn't a serial killer...*

Conner interrupted her thoughts, explaining that she was keeping her partner's cat for the week and needed to get home to check on him— or more importantly, check on her house. There was no telling what Magnum had gotten into.

For some reason Alex felt a little disappointed, but hid the feeling well. "Okay, then, I wouldn't want to be the reason for starving your partner's cat, so I guess I'll see you on Friday." They said their good-byes and headed off in opposite directions. They both drove into the night, each wondering just what to make of the evening and the mysterious woman she had met.

Chapter Three

Alex realized she was humming along with the radio as she pulled into her driveway. The contrast of feelings overwhelmed her for a moment, and she sat quietly in the car staring out into the darkness. *The house*, Alex thought, *looks almost as it did that cool October morning, just before the blast.*

The trees bore new foliage, covering their scorched and scarred limbs. The large area of burnt grass, replaced with new sod, was now green with new growth. The day after the blast, a demolition crew had shown up, completely stripped away the blackened concrete, and replaced it with a freshly paved drive. After two days of endless questioning from Alex, the men had finally told Alex that Sam had sent them to do the work. A few weeks later, when Sam still had not mentioned the new drive, Alex had quietly questioned her about it.

Sam looked at Alex, tears running freely down her cheeks, and explained. "Alex, I'm sorry if I overstepped any boundaries, but I just couldn't let you come back to the house and face the carnage that those people inflicted. I knew there was nothing I could do to bring Feryle back home to you. All I could do was what I did."

Alex was openly crying by the end of the explanation, and Sam gently pulled her into her arms and rocked her. Alex's mournful howls and primal moans echoed off the walls as she finally crumbled against the force of her pain. For what seemed like hours, Sam held her as she cried, softly speaking her name and encouraging her to release the pain that was so evident in her heart—the pain she had refused to acknowledge lest it weaken her in some way to the evil that threatened to consume her. "It's okay...let it go...I've got you...come back to us, Alex, get it all out, and come back to us." Until that moment, Sam had not seen Alex cry. Too consumed with anger, Alex had refused to allow any other emotions to surface.

Finally, Alex had calmed and her breathing returned to normal. Sam held Alex in her arms until finally their bodies screamed for relief from the cramped positions in which they had been sitting.

"Jesus, Sam, I'm sorry," Alex whispered with a look of total exhaustion on her face. "I don't know what happened, but...I—I just couldn't hold it together any longer. I'm really sorry you had to see me like this."

"Like what, Alex? Human?" Sam gently asked. "I know you're hurting—no, dying inside. You don't have to hide the pain from me, Alex. I'm your friend, and I was Feryle's friend too. I'm sure I'll never know the depth with which you loved each other, but I do know how much she meant to you and you to her. She was your world...the only light that could take you away from the darkness you have to face every day."

As Alex sat in the car, she remembered that night and knew that the new, deeper friendship she had formed with Sam would last a lifetime. She slowly got out of the car and headed into the house. Too keyed up to go to bed, she grabbed a beer from the refrigerator and walked out onto the deck.

Sitting once again in the darkness, she thought about the past few hours and realized that meeting Sam at the bar had been a good idea after all. Maybe Alex was beginning to heal, not only outside but inside as well. She couldn't remember the last time she had smiled, much less laughed, as she had that night.

Sipping her beer, she thought about Conner and their surprise meeting at Mike's. Both had been shocked, to say the least. Alex wondered if she would have been as openly playful with Conner that morning had she known they would see each other again.

What possessed me to ask Conner out Friday? Well, I didn't really ask her out on a date...just a meal and a movie, right? Alex ran her hand through her hair as she always did when frustrated or confused. She stood up quickly, as if trying to escape the question, and felt the muscles in her back scream against the sudden movement. "Damn," she muttered as she headed to the kitchen.

She tossed the bottle in the recycling bin and hobbled off to the bedroom, holding her back, feeling like an old woman. She thought about and then decided against taking a hot bath to soothe her muscles. "Damn right I'm not taking a hot bath. Next thing I know I'll be scooping Epsom salts in the water and knocking back Geritol shooters," she murmured as she eased herself into the bed.

For the first time in weeks, sleep came easily to Alex, and for the first time in months, the ghosts and demons of the night stayed outside.

Conner arrived home to find almost everything not attached to the walls or floor scattered throughout the house. "Freaking cat, you're a visitor in my home, not out on some adventurous scavenger hunt. Where the hell are you, you little beady-eyed furball?"

Stomping down the hallway and into the bedroom, she stopped short. There, curled up on her pillow, was Magnum. He was obviously awake because she could see his eyes peering at her expectantly. She crossed the room and scooped the cat up in one swift motion. "No one, especially a man, sleeps in my bed without an invitation...got it?"

She dropped the cat gently on the floor, trying her best to stay mad at the creature. She went into the bathroom, removed and tossed her clothes into the hamper, and got ready for bed. Walking back toward the bed, she heard a quiet meow coming from the hallway. "Damn, now I remember why I don't have any pets or kids—always wanting something."

She trudged back to the kitchen and plopped some food in Magnum's bowl. He immediately started gobbling it down. "Slow down, kid. You're just like your dad, never chews, just swallows everything whole," she growled, and headed back down the hallway.

She crawled into bed, turned out the light, and lay in the darkness thinking about the evening. Conner had been stunned, embarrassed, and, to her amazement, excited to see Alex again. After the initial shock had worn off, they had fallen into comfortable conversation. Of course, having Sam there as a buffer helped ease things along. One thing she could always count on around Sam was conversation. It seemed Sam never ran out of things to talk about, unless of course it was something serious like their past relationship.

Conner had thought the evening would quickly end when Sam left, but the easy rapport between her and Alex had continued. They had both been surprised to realize that two hours had passed since Sam went home. She was a little surprised that Alex had opened up to her; she didn't seem like the kind to trust another so quickly. *Maybe it was the beer, maybe it was just time.*

A soft thud on the bed interrupted Conner's thoughts. Rolling over, she saw Magnum sitting—and staring—at her, half ready to bolt at her first move toward him. She couldn't help but smile. "C'mere, you little shit," she whispered as she gently reached for the cat.

"You're a very lucky little guy, because I had a great night," she crooned as she sat him on her chest. "Just this one time, you can stay. Tomorrow, you go back to the stinky shirt. Got it?" Magnum just snuggled between Conner's arm and torso and went to sleep.

As Conner listened to the purring cat, she sighed. "Damn, you're getting to be a real softie, Harris." With that, she drifted off to sleep, dreaming of dark blue eyes and warm soft hands.

Alex woke with a start. The sun was shining brightly through the wall of windows. She sat for a moment, allowing her mind to catch up with her body. For the first time in almost eight months, she had slept through the night without dreaming. She glanced at the clock to see that it was past 10. With a sigh, she lay back on the pillows and looked out over the ocean. *Oh well, half the morning is gone, might as well not rush things*, she thought, deciding to enjoy the comfort of the cool sheets against her body.

The waves crashing to the shore were hypnotic, and soon Alex was reminiscing over lazy mornings like this with Feryle. They always seemed to wake up almost at the same moment, perhaps they were so in tune with each another's mind and body. Whatever it was, they always treasured the rare mornings that they could lie in bed together, watch the sun slowly rise over the horizon, and make slow, gentle love until a different hunger drove them from the bed.

Alex closed her eyes, remembering Feryle's touch. She had been the gentlest lover Alex had ever been with, often driving Alex to near-insanity with her slow caresses and feather-light kisses. Feryle only provided the relief Alex needed when she begged for release from the sweet torture. Making love to Alex like that was Feryle's way of pushing the darkness and evil from her life.

Sometimes, though, Feryle could sense a deep primal need within Alex to purge her body of demons through cold, hard sex. Alex was always surprised that Feryle could tell exactly what she needed and how she needed it. During those times, their bodies came together with a fierce and powerful need that only they could understand, a need so strong that, in the end, it left them sweating, exhausted, and gasping for breath.

Alex felt the heat spread through her body, a heat that had been absent since that last lazy Sunday morning. Hugging a pillow to her torso, she buried her head in the soft down. The tears were gentle, not like the ones she had shed so long ago with Sam but slow, tender tears for the loss of the love of her life. She drifted off to sleep and did not wake again until almost noon.

As she awakened for the second time that day, she remembered the dream she had just had. Strong yet gentle hands caressing her face; tender, full lips gently kissing her neck; and it was only when her dream lover lifted her head to claim her lips that Alex realized it wasn't Feryle but the mysterious and intriguing Conner Harris.

Alex pulled the covers off her body and slowly rose from the bed. She had learned by now that mornings were the hardest part of the day for her body. After lying in bed for hours, her muscles would get cold and stiff, and only gentle persuasion would get them to cooperate.

As she made her way through the house to the kitchen, she thought about the dream. *It's only because I was thinking of Feryle and our making love. Conner was the last person I spoke with*, she argued to herself. "It's only a brain thing going on. It has nothing to do with her holding my hand last night," she mumbled to herself. "Sure, it felt good...hell, it felt great...but...oh hell, woman, pull yourself together. It was a dream, for God's sake, just be thankful it wasn't like all the others," she said as she walked into the empty kitchen.

She poured herself a glass of juice and walked out onto the deck. Leaning against the railing, she let the warm breeze wake her up. Just as she was about to step off the deck for a walk down to the water, the phone rang.

"Hello."

"Good morning, sunshine," Sam's voice beamed over the line.

"Good morning to you too. I'm surprised you're out of bed this early. It's only noon, and I know you didn't go right home and go to bed," Alex playfully replied.

"Hell yes, I did. Didn't get a lot of sleep though, and I'll have you know I've been awake for hours." Sam laughed. "Haven't gotten out of bed yet, but I have been slinking about."

"Enough," Alex cried. "God, woman, you're a maniac. How's Kelly? Did she survive the night?"

"Yes, she survived, my dear Alex. But hey, I didn't call to chat about my sex life, good as it is, though," Sam snickered. "I was calling to see how your evening went last night after I left. You and Conner stay for a while and talk?"

Alex could feel the heat rise in her cheeks. "Yeah, we stayed for a little while after you left and finished off the beer."

"Hmm. Well, I just got off the phone with Conner. Seems she just drug her lazy ass out of the bed, and she told me she didn't get home until almost 2 a.m. Must have been quite a party, but I'm not sorry I missed it."

Great, you were just busted, and good, Alex thought. "Okay, okay, maybe we did stay just a little longer than a little while, but—hey, don't you have more important things to be doing on a Thursday morning than ragging on me? Don't you have to go to work or something?"

"Settle down, girlfriend. I'm just giving you a hard time," Sam said with a little bit of sincerity. "Okay, now for the real reason I called."

"Gee, Sammy, I don't know if I can handle any more of your reasons for calling today."

"No, really," Sam started, "Kelly and I were thinking about doing a little grilling out on Saturday and wondered if you were game for a nice fat steak."

"Come on, Alex. I haven't seen you in ages," Alex could hear Kelly pleading.

"Enough already. Okay, I'll bring the wine and dessert," Alex said in a tone of surrender. "What time is my presence expected?"

"Come early, say 4-ish, that way you and Kel can get caught up, and then we can concentrate on getting sloshed and going skinny-dipping in the ocean," Sam said.

"No way; been there, done that, ain't going there again." Alex laughed, remembering the night the beach patrol had the group cornered in the surf. It had taken a lot of smooth talking on her part to get them out of an indecent exposure charge.

"Okay, well, we'll see you on Saturday. Oh and Alex, you'd better make that two bottles of wine—two large bottles."

"Hey, I'll take care of the wine; you take care of the steak. See you Saturday. Bye." Alex couldn't help smiling to herself. *Damn that woman. Always up to something sneaky. I cannot believe I let her trip me up like that.* "You're out of practice, Montgomery. Better shape up, and quick."

Suddenly she felt a surge of energy and decided to go for a long run on the beach. She quickly changed clothes and was out the door. She hit the sand running and was a half-mile down the beach only moments later when her phone rang.

Chapter Four

Having slept in, Conner felt refreshed and relaxed. She was a bundle of energy and what she needed was some hard work to burn off some of the excess vigor she felt.

When she walked in her room, she spotted Magnum curled up on her pillow. "Hey, furball, only a few more days and Papa will be home to take you away. Aren't we happy?" She sat on the bed and petted him. "Okay, so you're not so bad after all. Just don't get too comfortable."

While taking her shower, she decided to head over to the marina and check on the *Shady Lady*. It had been a while since she had taken her out for a good run. She had bought the boat when she and Sam were together. Sam loved to go out for long weekends of island hopping and clam digging, and they had spent some of their happiest days on the boat. Sailing away from the shore gave them both a sense of freedom from the stresses of their jobs. Out on the water all they had to concentrate on was each other and an occasional squall that blew up.

Conner had not taken the boat out in a long time and sometimes thought of selling her. She deserved a proper owner, one who would care for her and treat her like the sleek sailing vessel that she was. Conner sometimes did not feel worthy of owning the *Shady Lady*. However, today she was not going to think about selling her. She was ready for a long hot day of scrubbing the decks, checking the lines, and getting the engine serviced. Maybe one day soon she would take her out.

She pulled into the marina parking lot and was instantly eager to get to the boat. As she walked down the pier, several of the weekend warriors she used to sail with were loyally tending to their vessels. She spoke to several, but did not linger. Climbing onto the deck, she could see how much she had neglected the boat and knew she had a long, hard day ahead of her. The lack of attention was even more apparent below deck. Dust bunnies flew off the captain's table as she walked past into the aft cabin. "Well, my lady, looks like I have my day cut out for me."

Conner decided to start below, and soon the deck of the boat was littered with trash. After several hours of scrubbing and polishing the teak woodwork, she stood back and admired her work. "Not bad. Not bad at all," she said, smiling at her reflection in the brass metalwork. She closed and secured all of the hatches and moved to the part she always liked best—scrubbing the deck.

She pulled off her shoes and t-shirt, leaving only her sports bra and shorts. Although she was naturally dark, Conner never could get enough of the sun. After moving the dinghy, bumpers, and other movable parts over the side to the pier, she went to work, starting at the bow. Before she had reached the beam, her muscles were screaming for a rest. She rinsed off the deck and headed to the cooler for a beer.

Sitting near the bow, she looked out over the marina and wondered if Alex had ever sailed. "Hey, *Shady Lady,* if tomorrow night goes okay, I just might see if the pretty lady wants to go out for a sail one day. I think the two of you would get along fine. She's sleek and sexy, and has the bluest eyes...damn, *Shady Lady;* I think I've been in the sun way too long today."

Conner finished off the beer and started on the aft section of the deck. She had just soaped up the deck when she heard her cell phone ring. She dropped the scrub brush and turned to reach for the phone. Just as she hit the send button, her feet slid out from under her and she went sliding toward the port side.

"Fuck!" Conner shouted as her chin hit a cleat. "Son of a bitch...Hello!" she barked into the phone.

"Um, Conner, this is Alex. Ah, did I catch you at a bad time?"

Oh, damn. Great, Conner, humiliate yourself again, will ya. Conner thought to herself.

"Conner, are you there?" Alex heard a groan from the other end of the phone. "Hello, Conner...are you okay?" She became a little concerned when Conner didn't immediately answer her.

"Oh yeah, I'm fine...just had a little accident getting to the phone, that's all," Conner replied.

"Are you hurt? Do I need to call someone? Do you need help?" Alex, though trying to stay calm, was on the verge of panicking. All she knew about Conner was her phone number and that she lived on the island, which was enough information to deploy the EMTs.

Conner broke into her thoughts. "Yes, Alex, I mean, no, I'm not hurt." She groaned loudly. "Actually, I'm at the marina, on my boat. It's been a while since she had a good scrubdown and I decided today was good day to get it done. I was scrubbing the deck when the phone rang and I slipped in the soap as I reached for the phone, that's all. It was nothing exciting or daring, just a stupid accident."

Alex let out a sigh of relief, relaxing for the first time since the conversation began. "Are you sure you're okay? No broken bones, no stitches needed?"

"Well, actually, my chin did stop me from going over portside by grabbing onto a cleat. I haven't looked at it yet, but I think it will be okay." Conner chuckled.

Alex let out a laugh as she imagined Conner sliding chin first across the boat. However, she stopped short when she realized that her phone call was the cause of the entire accident. "Jesus, Conner, I am so sorry. If I hadn't called, none of this would have happened."

"Don't even think about it, I'm fine...um...and I'm glad you called." Conner finished almost in a whisper. She had now crawled over into the cockpit and was leaning against the console. Using her discarded t-shirt, she attempted to stop the flow of blood dripping off her chin. "Actually, I needed a rest. It seems I have neglected my *Shady Lady* for way too long. I'm sure somewhere deep in her hull she got a kick out of my slip-and-slide act." Conner winced again as the smile that came to her face pulled against the gash in her chin.

They talked a while longer, confirming their dinner plans for the next night. "I really am sorry I caused you to hit your chin, Conner. You can have your choice of desserts tomorrow night. Maybe that will make you feel all better."

Conner tried to find her voice, but only managed a mumbled, "Ah, sure, dessert's always my favorite." She couldn't believe she said that and threw her head back in exasperation, banging it on the console. "Fuck!"

"Excuse me?"

"Oh no, I wasn't talking to you. I just hit my head," Conner said, feeling like a total klutz.

"Sounds like you need to abandon ship and head for higher ground, mate," Alex teased.

"Aye, Captain, I'll be heading into port soon."

"Conner?" Alex hesitated. "Will you give me a call when you get back home, um, just to let me know you're okay?" Alex asked in a quiet concerned voice. "Between your chin and head, I just want to make sure you don't end up dangling off the lifeline using your body as a human bumper."

"Ha, ha, ha, very funny, Agent Montgomery. One day I'll get my chance to get the last laugh. Just you wait and see."

"Well, will you call me, then?"

"Sure, Alex, I'll give you a call. I'll probably be here another couple of hours, so it'll probably be around six. Don't send out the cavalry until then, promise?"

Alex laughed. "Okay, sure...no cavalry until half past six. But not a minute later, got it?"

"Aye, Captain, I'll talk to you soon then."

They said their good-byes, and Conner remained sitting on the deck for a few minutes nursing her chin. She was surprised that Alex had called; she had rather expected her to call the next day with some reason not to go to dinner, and she smiled when she finally realized that they would be going out after all. *Okay, Conner it's not a date, for God's sake. We're having dinner, that's all. Hell, the woman just lost the love of her life, not even a year ago. She couldn't possibly be ready to start going out again.*

She crawled out of the cockpit, glanced at her watch, and knew she needed to get moving if she was going to get home by six. Somehow, she had a feeling Alex would dispatch the cavalry if she were a minute late.

Alex set the phone down and wondered what had possessed her to call Conner. Sure, she needed to confirm their plans for the next evening, but even as she dialed the phone, there were questions in her mind about going through with dinner. She had not been out with anyone since Feryle, and the thought of actually having to carry on a personal conversation with someone made her stomach hurt. Still, she had called, and now stood smiling over the conversation.

Conner certainly did not seem like the tongue-tied, klutzy woman who had been on the other end of the line. Experience told Alex that in order to survive the rigors of undercover work, a person had to be quick-witted and agile. Maybe it was meeting someone new that made Conner nervous. Sam had mentioned in their conversation earlier in the day that Conner had not dated anyone—well, more than once anyway—since their breakup two years before. Alex chalked it up to nerves, just like the ones she herself was feeling.

Alex did some work around the house, frequently glancing at the clock, waiting for Conner to call and say she was safe at home. She smirked when she thought about Conner's chin slide. *Being home and being safe are not necessarily synonymous considering how accident-prone Conner seems to be lately*, she thought. She finally decided to have a nourishing dinner of wine and cheese out on the deck.

The sky began to turn subdued shades of gold and purple as the sun began its nightly descent. Alex watched as two women, oblivious to everything but each other, walked hand in hand down the beach. How many times had she and Feryle walked that same path, making plans for their house, and for their future? She acknowledged that those days were long gone as a tear slowly crept down her cheek.

Today, Alex decided, it was okay to feel the pain. She almost welcomed the raw, heart-wrenching feelings that her memories evoked. Today she would allow the pain, for it reminded her why she was back.

Monday she would turn the pain into the hate she knew so well, the hate that would bring Malcolm Hernandez to his knees.

She ran a hand through her disheveled hair. *Damn, if I keep this up I'll be bald.* The habit was one that always gave away the fact that she was frustrated. Feryle had noticed it right away and used it often as a means of getting the upper hand in some of their heated discussions.

Walking through the house to her office, Alex decided to read back over some of the files she had compiled on what she called "Feryle's Revenge." She had painstakingly categorized, cross-referenced, and catalogued hundreds of files, interviews, and case notes that pertained to the elusive Hernandez. As she reviewed them, she relived the fateful night of the raid. The night that she found out someone on the inside was a traitor; the night she had almost been killed because of that treason. She remembered the warehouse, the explosion, and the searing heat that radiated throughout her body as flying shrapnel imbedded itself in her back. Flinching at the memory of the pain, she jumped out of the chair, knocking the phone on the floor as its shrill ring broke into her thoughts.

Conner heard the receiver clattering to the floor, and a colorful array of exasperated curses as Alex picked up the phone, followed by a breathless "Hello." She was not sure how to respond, so she simply told Alex that she was home and safe.

"Good, I was about to dispatch the cavalry and the Coast Guard."

"Alex, is everything okay? I mean, you sound a little upset," Conner asked, hoping not to offend Alex with her questioning.

"Yeah...sure, Conner, I'm fine. I was just reviewing a case file, and I was startled by the phone, that's all."

"Okay, if you're sure. Well, I'll let you get back to your reading."

"Hold on a minute Officer," Alex almost ordered over the phone. "How's your chin, your head, and the rest of your beaten and bruised body?"

"Chin hurts like hell, I now look like a conehead with this goose egg I have, and the rest of the body, well, it's not going to be very nice to me tomorrow, I can tell already," Conner said, laughing into the phone.

"I'm sorry I caused your, um, accident. Maybe I should just page you in the future; maybe that will be safer and easier on the body."

"Ha ha. That damn thing usually scares me worse. I have to keep it on vibrate, especially when I'm on the street, and it always feels like a stun gun when it goes off. Most people probably think I'm having the DTs or something when they see my reaction."

Alex laughed and said, "Well, maybe I'll just start e-mailing you, then."

"Oh no you don't, I hate damn computers. They make me feel so incompetent. Last time I checked my e-mail at the precinct, I had to get

Buet to get me into it. I had something like a hundred e-mails, dating back six months. So my suggestion is if you want a timely response, just call me. I promise not to do any more swan dives."

"As you wish. It's your body, after all," Alex replied.

"Hey there, I can get this treatment from the crew downtown." *I'm sure I will tomorrow morning,* Conner thought. "I thought you liked me."

"I do, Conner. I like you a lot. Why else would I give you such a hard time? I don't treat just...anyone like this." Alex's voice took on a dark and sultry tone as she chided Conner.

Conner found herself searching for her voice somewhere in the depths of her gut. Not knowing just how to respond to Alex's statement, she uttered a simple, "Oh, okay."

"I usually just body slam and cuff the ones I don't care for. You might want to watch out that you never make me mad. I just might come at you with an evil look on my face and cuffs in my hand."

Conner could feel the heat radiating in the lower parts of her anatomy. She could easily imagine what Alex could look like with an evil look and handcuffs, but the image evoked lust and not anger. "Well, if you're not careful, Agent Montgomery, I just might think you're daring me here. It's been a long time since I've had a woman come after me with handcuffs," she said in an equally sultry voice.

Conner could almost hear Alex swallowing. She did not know if the silence on the other end of the phone was because Alex was angry or if she was speechless as Conner had been just moments before. She knew the conversation had turned toward dangerous ground, and she didn't want to frighten Alex away before she really got a chance to know her.

Alex was trying very hard to find her voice when she heard Conner screaming from the other end of the line.

"You little shit! I'm going to kill your furry ass in about two seconds if you don't get out of my face."

Alex broke out in a hearty laugh. "Conner, how is it can you take down drug dealers, but can't seem to control a tiny little kitty?"

"This isn't just any tiny little kitty, I'll have you know. This is the cat from the depths of hell. You should have seen my place when I got home last night. Almost everything in the house that wasn't nailed down was scattered in the middle of the floor. When I left, he was doing that cat thing, licking himself and looking all innocent, but when I walked out the door he apparently found other things to take up his time." Conner finished her raging with an audible growl.

"And if that's not bad enough, my living room smells like a dirty shoe. Seth, Magnum's daddy, decided he needed to have something that had his scent on it so the poor little thing wouldn't be frightened in his absence. Now I have an old dirty t-shirt lying in the corner of my living room, and from the stench coming from it, I think it's been worn daily and not washed in years."

Alex laughed as the other woman recounted her experience with the cat. At least the conversation had veered back toward safer ground. They talked a while longer, deciding to meet the next evening at six. Alex gave Conner the directions to her house and her phone number in case anything came up or she got lost, and they said their good-byes.

Conner glared at the cat. "Well, I guess you did get me out of a tight situation. At least my scream broke the heavy silence that had made its way into our little conversation." With a growl, Conner gave the cat a pat on the head and walked down the hall to the bathroom, to the next order of business, a nice hot bath.

As she let the warm water soothe the aches and pains that were quickly beginning to settle throughout her body, Conner let her mind drift back over her conversation with Alex. She had already felt what those blue eyes could do to her heart. The visible pain in Alex's heart when she had spoken of Feryle had shown deeply in her eyes, turning them into pools of deep blue. Conner wondered just what shade they turned when want and need was the emotion she felt.

The heat she felt drifting through her body was not from the water but from the thoughts that raged in her brain when she thought of Alex. She thought of the strong muscles she knew were hidden under the other woman's clothes and how they would feel pressed against her naked body. Conners had felt the strength in Alex's hands the previous night, hands that she knew could not only fire a gun or disable an assault, but were also capable of great tenderness. She let out an involuntary groan as she thought of Alex's full, soft lips begging to be kissed.

Realizing that she was not helping her muscles relax, she pulled the plug in the tub and stood to rinse off under the shower. "Cold water...gotta have cold water," she growled as she turned the spray on full force. Although the icy spray was doing its job in cooling off her libido, it was wreaking havoc on her already tense and sore muscles. Stepping out of the shower, Conner grabbed a towel and began to dry her body. The nerve endings in her skin were on full alert, and she felt the heat begin to stir once again. Throwing the towel on the floor, she pulled on her University of Florida t-shirt and headed into the bedroom. There, curled up in what was now his pillow, Magnum had settled down for a good night's sleep. She silently swore at her unwelcome house guest and crawled into the other side of the bed.

Chapter Five

Alex woke up early on Friday morning. After a quick shower and a pot of coffee, she headed to the office. One thing she hadn't yet figured out was who on the inside had turned. There were many reasons a cop would be tempted, money being top on the list. Agents were always being offered bribes, payoffs, drugs, almost anything to keep them off the criminals' backs. Most agents had the resolve and dedication to resist the temptation; however, the occasional rogue agent succumbed, not thinking twice about risking fellow agents' lives. Alex had given herself migraines trying to think of any agents or cops involved in the case who had shown any weakness, and so far she had come up empty-handed.

As she sat and read the files, she made a mental note to ask Conner about her fellow officers, as the FBI and the JPD had worked closely on the case. She wondered how Conner might react to such a question. Alex decided to see how things progressed during dinner and decided she would not bring up the issue unless the opportunity presented itself.

When her body started screaming for relief from sitting in the chair, she glanced at the clock and realized it was almost one o'clock. She decided a little fresh air and a long walk were what she needed to limber her up. A few minutes later, she was walking along the shoreline, the cool ocean water lapping at her bare feet. She thought back to the two women she had seen the day before and a sudden feeling of sadness flooded over her. "Stop it, damn it, just stop it," she chided herself as she felt tears well up in her eyes. "We had some great years together. Maybe one day, Feryle, when this is all over, I can focus on those times, and not hurt so bad...maybe."

Alex knew she must look ridiculous, walking on the beach alone, talking to herself. She looked up and realized she had walked a lot further than she intended. Looking back over her shoulder, she could barely see the house beyond the dunes. She turned toward home and jogged at an easy gait, thinking about all she had to do before Conner arrived that evening.

Conner tried to look inconspicuous when she walked into the precinct. Buet, being a jokester, did not let her even get by the front desk before he was looking her over with a gleam in his eye.

"Thought you had the day off yesterday, Conner?"

"Morning, and yeah, I did, Buet," Conner said, trying to sound casual, knowing he had spotted the gash on her chin and the bruises on her arms.

As she rounded the corner, she could hear him yelling, "Must have been one hell of a date, Conner. Didn't know you were having problems fighting them off. Let me know if you need a big stick." At the commotion, all the other officers within earshot looked up and wanted in on the action.

"Hey, Conner, you can borrow my stick anytime," Frank Bivins, one of the more repulsive cops in the precinct, yelled to her.

"Give your wife a break, Bivins, and go fuck yourself," Conner snapped back as she headed into her cubicle.

Being taunted was something Bivins hated, and he headed toward Conner with a macho stride. He sat down on her desk, making his presence known, to not only Conner but also everyone in the squad room.

He leaned over so close Conner could smell the bacon he had eaten for breakfast and growled, "So was your hot date with the legs that came in to see the captain the other day? I noticed how much she flustered you when she stuck her head in here. Made you spill your coffee all over the desk."

Conner sat forward, effectively pushing Bivins away with her movement, and stood up looking him squarely in the eyes. In a voice that could easily be heard by the crowd outside the cubicle, she snarled, "You know, Bivins, I'm not like you, fucking anything that walks. When and if my private life becomes your concern, I'll send you a memo."

Bivins's face turned so purple, Conner thought for a second that he had stopped breathing until he leaned to whisper in her ear, "Better watch out how you talk to me, Harris. One day I might have to cover your ass, and I don't think you want me pissed off when that day comes."

Conner stood her ground, not flinching when she could feel the whiskers on Bivins's face brush her skin. She turned her head just enough to hide her mouth from the onlookers and whispered, "That's true, Bivins, but you also have to remember that it might be your slimy ass I'm covering one day, and I think you want me to be a real happy camper when that moment comes." Leaning back, she raised her voice. "Now if you don't mind, get your ass off my desk, I have work to do."

Conner sat down at her desk, turned her back to Bivins, and started searching through her filing cabinet, thus dismissing him. "Watch your back, Harris," was all Bivins said as he turned and stormed off toward his own desk.

Conner was sick and tired of the abuse doled out by the macho boys of Precinct One. She had heard almost every insult she could think of since her assignment here. *I guess it's not their fault*, she thought to herself. She was in the middle of the Bible Belt. Most of their belief system was so ingrained in them that their DNA had mutated to reflect that fact.

She knew the danger of alienating her fellow officers. Undoubtedly, some of them would side with Bivins against her. However, when she dared a glance beyond the cubicle, she saw a few respectful looks coming her way. She even saw Sonny Henderson, one of the hardest cops on the force, give her a slight nod when she caught his eye.

Conner had been working on an unusual case. There had been some bad cocaine floating around the streets all over the north Florida area. Typically when a load of bad drugs hit the street, the affected area was small and confined to the customers of the neighborhood dealer. This time, however, the dealers, when busted, had rolled over on their suppliers. All the fingers were pointing to a man the JPD, FBI, DEA, and ATF had been drooling over for years. A man covered by layer after layer of protection that no one had ever been able to penetrate—Malcolm Hernandez.

Malcolm Hernandez began living on the streets when he was twelve. He had never known his father, nor had he been interested in finding out who he was. Malcolm's mother was a junkie; the only work she did was the occasional robbery or petty theft to feed her habit. On the days her body hurt from the need of her next fix, Maria sold whatever she had in her possession for a hit. She was not above trading sex for her drugs, either, and Malcolm had spent countless nights listening from the next room. Finally, after one of her friends, as she called them, had come to his room after his mother passed out, he decided the streets were safer than his own home.

He had fit in well on the streets. He made his rounds from store to store, sweeping the sidewalks for the owners in trade for food. He had always considered himself lucky the day the long black car pulled up outside of Mr. Stone's market. He had watched as three big men stepped out of the car. One walked into the store, another stood on the street with his right hand in his coat pocket, and the third man calmly opened the car door for the man Malcolm would come to call Pop.

Mr. Stone sent Malcolm on an errand when the man walked in the store. Feeling like he was being shooed away, Malcolm snuck around to the back door of the store and crept inside, hiding behind the large boxes in the storage room. Mr. Stone begged as one of the men held a gun to his head. "I promise you, Mr. Gonzolas, I sent the money with my usual boy. I don't know what happened to him. I haven't seen him since yesterday morning, I swear."

Malcolm could see the sweat sliding down Mr. Stone's face as he shook with the terror of knowing he was about to die. Malcolm knew something had to be done or they were going to kill him. Slowly, he slid out from behind the boxes and eased his way toward the men. Gonzolas looked up casually as if he knew Malcolm had been there all along.

"I seen him yesterday after Mr. Stone gave him the bag. Don't know what was in it, but Joey went around the corner, got in a big car just like yours, and drove off. I promise, mister, don't hurt Mr. Stone, he didn't do nothing."

Gonzolas looked hard at the boy. "What's it to you, kid? Afraid you're going to lose your meal ticket?"

"No, sir, I just don't want to see Mr. Stone hurt for something he didn't do."

"So how you know they didn't plan this thing together, kid? Maybe Joey is hanging low for a while, until things settle down. Then the two of them are gonna split the money and run," Gonzolas countered.

"Don't think Joey wanted Mr. Stone to know nothing 'bout it, mister. He would always look around real nervous-like whenever that car would come around, like he didn't want Mr. Stone to know."

Gonzolas laughed deep from his belly. "Well, Stone, looks like this kid saved your sorry hide today. I'll keep you around, but only on one condition. From now on, the kid is your courier. Do I make myself clear?"

"Yes sir, yes sir, anything you say, Mr. Gonzolas." Stone knew he was sentencing Malcolm to a life of darkness, but as usual, greed and his will to live won over his conscience.

Gonzolas, calmly walked toward the front of the store, removing himself from the sound of shattering bones as the guard brought the gun across Stone's face.

Malcolm watched with blank eyes. It was not his first taste of violence, and it certainly would not be his last.

At five o'clock, Conner decided to wrap up her day. There was a lightness in her step as she walked into the precinct and spotted Buet.

"My, my, we must have had a productive day. I haven't seen you smiling this big in—well, never, actually. What do you have up your sleeve, Conner?" Buet was probably the only person that could tease her about her private life and walk away unharmed.

Conner grinned and headed toward her cubicle, chuckling over her shoulder. "Well, Buet, if I told you that, it wouldn't be a secret, and I'm sure it wouldn't be nearly as juicy as what you're imagining."

She grabbed a few files she knew she wanted to read over the weekend, dropped her notes in her filing cabinet and locked it, then headed toward the door. Bivins was on his way in and effectively blocked her exit as he stopped in front of her. He leaned down and whispered. "You have a good weekend, Officer Harris. Don't do anything that might make those bumps and bruises any worse."

Conner shoved past Bivins and stormed out the front door. "Damn, what a fucking bitch of a day," she growled as she headed to the parking lot.

Well, at least it's over until Monday, and I'm sure the night will be an improvement. She rounded the corner and saw all four tires of the Jag flat against the concrete floor.

"Bivins, you mangy piece of shit," Conner fumed as she walked over to the car. She glanced at her watch and knew she would not have time to get the tires replaced. It was five-fifteen already, and she had to be on the road by five-thirty to be at Alex's on time.

Alex saw the taxi pull into the driveway and wondered who it could be. A few seconds later, the doorbell rang. Alex opened the door to a clearly frustrated Conner Harris holding a hanging bag in one hand and a duffel bag in the other. Alex invited her inside.

"Sorry if I'm late. One of my esteemed colleagues decided to flatten all four of my tires this afternoon," Conner explained.

"Whoa, you mean another police officer slashed your tires?"

"Well, I can't prove it was him...yet. But I have one of my famous gut feelings that he is the one who did it," Conner offered.

"Here, let me take that for you. Do you haul around luggage in your car on a routine basis?" Alex laughed as she helped Conner by lifting the weight in her arms.

"Well, actually, no, I don't. I didn't think I would look presentable going to dinner in my street clothes. I also didn't want to change at the station, especially after the hassle I got when I walked in this morning." Conner tried to growl but could not hide the smile coming through her voice.

Turning toward the hallway Alex said, "Let me put these in the bedroom. Looks like you could use a drink and a little time to settle before we go out. There's beer in the refrigerator. Grab a couple and I'll meet you on the back deck."

Conner looked around. The house was absolutely amazing. She had never seen so many windows in one structure. Combining oak hardwood floors and high vaulted ceilings, the house was both energizing and refreshing.

She walked toward the fireplace, noticing a collection of photographs on the mantle. Several had captured Alex in an amazing smile, one that was set off by the twin dimples that usually hid within her cheeks. Her eyes were a clear sparkling blue, emitting a happiness that only love could generate. The other woman could be no one else but Feryle, Conner surmised.

Alex hesitated as she entered the room. It had been a long time since anyone else had been in her home, and she wasn't quite sure what she felt having a virtual stranger examining her private moments with Feryle.

"Ah, everything is in the bedroom whenever you're ready to change. I don't know about you, but I'm ready for a drink. What would you like, Conner?"

Conner turned around quickly and faced Alex, surprised by the contrast of expressions she saw. She wasn't sure if it was anger, sadness, suspicion, or all three that swept across Alex's face. One thing she knew for certain, it wasn't the happy face she had just observed in the photographs.

"Ah, beer is fine with me, unless you'd prefer something else."

"Beer is fine with me, too. I just thought you might need something stronger, considering the kind of day you've had," Alex offered. As she stood in front of Conner, she reached out and gently took her face in her hand, lifting her chin for a better view. "Ouch. Bet that hurts like hell."

Conner froze at the contact. She silently cursed her voice for turning tail and hiding in her stomach every time Alex was near. "Um, well, it does kind of smart a little."

"Have you put an antibiotic on it this afternoon?"

"No, Mom." Conner laughed. "I haven't been anywhere near a first aid kit, out on the streets."

"Well, you get the beer, and I'll get the first aid kit. See you out back," Alex said as she headed back down the hallway.

Conner found her way into the kitchen, where she got two beers from the refrigerator, and headed out to the deck. When she stepped through the sliding glass doors, what she saw was remarkable. The view to the ocean was completely unobscured except for the natural dunes lying peacefully between the house and the water. The saw grass swung lazily in the evening breeze and the water...the water was the most beautiful azure blue Conner had ever seen.

She looked down the beach in both directions and saw nothing but the pure undisturbed environment for at least a hundred yards on each side. The few houses she saw dotted on the landscape fit in perfectly with their natural surroundings. Conner could not believe this home sat close to one of the largest cities in the state. It felt more as if she was on a deserted beach somewhere on a far-off island.

"Well, I see you're admiring the view," Alex said as she walked out onto the deck.

"Admiring. That's an understatement. This view totally blows me away, Alex. How did you find this place?"

"I will tell no secrets until your chin has been seen to, so don't even try and change the subject," Alex said, motioning Conner to a deck chair.

Conner could not move. She thought for a moment that she might pass out right there on the deck.

Laughing at the look on her face, Alex grabbed Conner's arm and pulled her toward the chair. "Geez, and I thought you were a tough cop, Harris. You look like I'm about to perform major surgery here. Relax, it's just a little peroxide and some antibiotic."

Conner took a deep breath and sat in the chair, nervously putting her hands in her lap.

"You're pathetic, Harris. I've seen kids braver than you," Alex said, kneeling in front of Conner. Touching her chin, Alex gently lifted Conner's head to get a better view of the gash. She could feel Conner trembling beneath her hands and wondered if she had also felt the jolting shock when their skin had met.

Closing her eyes for a moment to regain her composure, Alex became aware of the delicious scent of the other woman. The clean, spicy scent that radiated from Conner made Alex want to lean in for more. When she finally opened her eyes, staring back at her were Conner's sea-green eyes, and she caught herself in mid-gasp at what she saw in that instant. Desire and confusion, those were apparent, but also a hint of uncertainty.

She felt as if the air was being squeezed from her lungs. Taking a slow deep breath and nervously licking her top lip, Alex broke eye contact first and looked down at Conner's lap. "Um, let's get this, ah, cleaned up, so you can go get changed for dinner," she said in a ragged voice as she reached for the first aid kit, giving them both a moment to recover.

Both women had to focus to control their reactions when their skin once again touched. Conner tilted her head back and stared at the sky, trying to think of her flat tires, groceries, anything but the gorgeous woman touching her. The heat that radiated through her body threatened to consume her.

Alex gently cleaned the broken skin on Conner's chin, taking great care not to inflict any more pain than necessary. Her hands shook as she dabbed the peroxide on the wound, and she hoped it was not too apparent. As tenderly as she could, she applied the antibiotic, and as she was beginning to sit back saw a faint scar running under the length of Conner's jaw. Unconsciously, she reached out and ran her hand down the scar, wondering how much pain this woman had endured.

Conner could not control her quick intake of breath as she felt Alex's hand stroke her jaw line. She lowered her head and looked deeply into the dark seductive eyes, asking her a wordless question. She knew that if nothing else ever happened between them, she would always remember this moment. If only she had a clue as to what Alex was thinking, maybe she could make a reasonable choice as to how to respond. Taking the safe way out, she curled her lips into a smile and said, "Bernie Fromboiskie."

Conner's comment broke through Alex's thoughts, and she sat back on her heels looking a little confused. "Excuse me?"

"Bernie Fromboiskie," Conner said dryly. "A ten-year-old nightmare." The spell was broken and now Conner sat back in her chair and laughed as she remembered the night.

"My partner and I got called to a domestic dispute. When we got to the residence, this woman was beating the crap out of her kid. Seth went for the boy, and I went for the woman. Together we managed to separate them, and everyone chilled out. Seth had the kid a few feet away trying to distract him, showing the kid his billy club. I was in the middle of questioning his mother when out of nowhere this kid whacked me in the jaw with Seth's stick."

Alex was not having much success in holding back her laughter, her entire body shaking as she tried to keep the grin off her face.

"Hey, you're supposed to be feeling sorry for me. That kid almost killed me." Conner pouted.

"Okay, okay, go on with your story."

"Well, anyway, as I was saying, the kid whacked me. The mom, obviously used to the brat's reactions, decided to take advantage of the situation and jumped on Seth. Next thing I knew I was calling for backup and bleeding like a stuck pig."

By this time, Alex was on the deck laughing so hard her sides were threatening to burst.

"Hell, it only gets worse from there. The ass that I suspect slashed my tires today was our backup. He and his partner, riding in like white knights, broke the whole thing up, carted me to the patrol car, and sent me off with Seth to the hospital for a few stitches. By the time we got back to the precinct, the entire squad had heard Bivins's blown-up story about how a ten-year-old kid beat the shit out of me. I don't think I'll ever live that one down," Conner whined.

Alex sat up and reached her hand out to stroke the scar once again. She looked into Conner's eyes for a moment and wanted nothing more than to pull her close and hold her in her arms, basking in her scent. Alex took a deep breath and smiled as she looked deeply into her eyes.

Conner saw Alex's lips part just enough for her to see the glistening tongue that teased those inviting lips as Alex whispered, "Looks like that's going to get you a double scoop of ice cream for dessert," then let flow the most enlightening smile Conner had ever seen. Had she not been sitting, she would have surely fallen flat on her face.

"No way am I settling for ice cream tonight. You already owe me big time for my chin slide. Now, since you have found so much humor in my painful experience with Bernie, it's really going to cost you," Conner said as she raised an eyebrow.

"Okay, okay, whatever you say. Now go change so we can get moving. All that laughing has worked up an appetite in me, and I'm famished."

Alex led Conner back into the house and down the hallway to her bedroom, asking herself the entire way why she'd chosen to put Conner's things there and not in the guest room. She showed Conner the bathroom, and after a moment of uncomfortable silence, left her to get dressed.

She immediately headed to the kitchen and pulled a fresh beer from the refrigerator. Feeling the cold beer flow down her throat, Alex ran her hand through her hair. *Damn,* she thought. *What am I doing? You would think I was some adolescent teenager with raging hormones.*

She walked into the living room and sat down on the sofa, wondering just what it was about the woman in her bedroom—*No,* Alex thought, *not my bedroom...Feryle's and mine.*

A few minutes later, Conner came into the room. She had changed into a pair of brown slacks and a tan silk blouse. She had let her hair down, and it now flowed freely across her shoulders. A small gold chain adorned with a tiny locket hung around her neck. The tough street cop who had sat on the deck a few moments before had transformed herself into a stunning and seemingly fragile woman.

Conner tried to read Alex's expression, but all she could do was fall deeper and deeper into the sultry eyes staring back at her. Breaking the silence, she asked, "Well, do I clean up okay, Agent Montgomery?"

"Yeah, I'd say you clean up pretty well, Agent Harris. Now let's see if I can do the same. Make yourself comfortable, I'll be right back." Alex headed back toward the bedroom. She had not intended on changing clothes, but needed a minute to let her thoughts, and body, settle down. Seeing Conner had set flames coursing down to her soul. Grabbing another blouse and a vest out of the closet, Alex quickly changed.

Conner was strolling around the living room, looking at bits and pieces of Alex and Feryle's life together, when Alex reentered the room. This time, though, Alex's protective shield did not come up; somehow, she knew Conner was not a threat to Feryle's memory. It was as if the more she knew of Conner, the more she could remember of Feryle without hurting.

The drive to Antonio's took only a few minutes. Alex had made reservations, so she knew that they would not have a wait. As she and Conner walked into Antonio's, she was overwhelmed by the smell of Italian cuisine. She was telling Conner that this had been one of her and Feryle's favorite restaurants when a booming voice broke into their conversation.

"What do you mean *one* of your favorites? You always told me it was your favorite."

A grin broke across Alex's face, and she was swept up into a warm and fond embrace. "Maria, of course it's my all-time favorite. I can't imagine what I was thinking." Alex placed a tender kiss on the woman's cheek.

Alex and Maria spoke for a few moments, Alex nodding while Maria chastised her for staying away for so long. Conner knew there was a history here, one that involved Feryle, and didn't know exactly what she should do, so she strolled over to the displayed menu and pretended to read.

A few moments later, a warm breath caressed her ear, breaking into her thoughts. "I was wondering where you got off to."

Conner turned her head slightly, only inches away from tantalizing lips. She hesitated for a moment, and then almost whispered, "Well, I had a feeling that you hadn't seen each other in a while and wanted to give you a few moments to talk."

Alex tilted her head and looked at Conner with an appreciative smile. "Thanks, it has been a while. Actually, I haven't seen Maria or Antonio since Feryle's memorial service. It's really good to see them again, but..."

"Alex, you don't have to explain," Conner broke in, her eyes telling Alex that she understood and that everything was okay. "I know it must be hard for you, coming back here, reliving all of these memories." She was about to ask Alex why they had come here when Maria called that their table was ready.

Maria took Alex's elbow and led the way through the dining room. She stopped at a very private table by a window overlooking the garden. Conner could see the strain in Alex's face as she sat down, and her trembling chin as she stared out the window.

"Alex, if you're not comfortable coming here tonight, we can go somewhere else. I really won't mind. I like Mexican, Chinese, Burger King..."

"No, Conner, it's okay, I just didn't think Maria would seat us here, at this table, not tonight. Not my first time back." Alex ran a hand through her hair and let out a ragged breath. "Anyway, if we left now, it would only upset Maria, and I wouldn't want to do that."

"Okay, if that's what you really want, but..."

"Conner, it's fine. Really." Alex smiled. "And furthermore, you can't find better or bigger scoops of ice cream anywhere else this side of the Mississippi."

Conner saw a slight twinkle in Alex's eyes and knew that she had dealt with the first, probably of many, demons, and everything was going to be okay, at least for that night.

Maria hovered over them most of the evening. Alex, finally able to get a word into the conversation, introduced Conner to her old friend. The sideways glance, the raised eyebrow, and the small smile Maria gave Alex did not escape detection by either woman. Alex handled it well, and they ended up having a wonderful dinner.

They talked about the house and the months it had taken Alex and Feryle to get it livable. They had completely gutted the kitchen and had to look elsewhere for nourishment; thus, the friendship with Maria and Antonio had begun. Alex went on to tell Conner that the last night she and Feryle had spent together was having dinner at that very table.

Conner suddenly felt like an intruder. Alex picked up the signs of Conner's uneasiness. "It's okay. If I didn't think I could deal with it, I would have taken you somewhere else for dinner."

By the time they had finished dinner and shared the biggest bowl of ice cream Conner had ever seen, it was almost midnight. When Maria came back by the table, Alex asked for the check, and what ensued was the funniest sight Conner had seen in a while. The two women arguing over the check had her in stitches. Maria finally won, of course, saying it was a welcome-home gift. Alex feigned a pout when she realized the battle was lost.

As they slowly made their way back to the car, both women felt stuffed from dinner and a little light-headed from too much wine, so the drive back to the house was refreshing. Alex had taken the top off the Jeep, and the cool ocean breeze swept though their hair. Once back at the house, Alex led Conner around back. There was a peaceful and easy silence between the two women as they walked toward the dunes, lost in her own thoughts until after a few minutes, Alex finally spoke.

"I really enjoyed dinner with you tonight, Conner."

"I'm really glad you did, Alex. I was afraid that you weren't going to when—"

Alex broke into Conner's words. "I did, too, at least for a while. Somehow, it was almost surreal going back there, the memories that flooded my mind when we sat down at that table...the pain...the—the loss." Alex almost said "loneliness," but realized that she had not been lonely. Conner had made the trip back into Antonio's bearable. Although a sad veil had enveloped her spirit, Conner's presence had lent a peaceful ambiance to the evening.

They had stopped walking and were facing each other in the darkness with only the light of the full moon on each woman's face. The smell of the sea, mixed with Alex's scent, was almost more than Conner could bear. She reached out and pulled Alex into her arms.

Alex tensed at the touch, then let herself relax, relishing the comfort of Conner's embrace. Conner's arms surrounded her, letting Alex know the strength of the other woman's feelings. She slowly let her arms circle Conner's waist, and the two women stood for a long time, taking pleasure in the warmth of the other, lost in thoughts they were both too frightened to utter aloud.

Pulling Alex closer, Conner let out a small, quiet sigh as she tucked her head into the soft tresses of her hair, inhaling the scent of her shampoo and the essence that could only be Alex herself. Conner could feel the rapid beat of Alex's heart in her neck. Turning her head slightly, she planted a small kiss over it.

Conner felt more than heard the quick intake of breath. She lifted her head and looked into Alex's shaded irises. What she saw was a barely concealed look of want and need; what she felt was a deep burning heat that ached to find relief.

Alex was completely overwhelmed by the warmth and tenderness in Conner's embrace. She could feel her pulse pounding in her chest, making her light-headed. The quiet moan she heard from Conner as she kissed her neck was almost as powerful as the sensation she felt coursing through her body. Slowly she lifted her head to meet Conner's eyes. There, in those eyes, were passion, lust, and need.

Conner's lips were but a breath away from Alex's, and her own lips parted, just slightly, in anticipation. She slowly bent her head to kiss those delectable lips when suddenly headlights engulfed them in a bright circle of light.

Both women jumped as the four-wheel-drive truck pulled up beside them. Alex and Conner spun around and faced the offending lights.

Stepping out of the truck, the driver let out a robust laugh. "Scared you there, didn't I, Harris?"

"What the hell do you want, Bivins? You could have killed us, driving up on us like that."

"Easy, girl." Bivins smirked. "You're just pissed 'cause I messed up your little party here."

Alex could tell that Bivins had been drinking. She could smell it on him from five feet away. The more the man derided Conner the angrier Alex became.

"Do you mind telling me what you're doing on my beach?" Alex asked in an equally hostile voice.

"Whoa there, sweetie," Bivins responded. "Hey, Conner, why don't you introduce me to the legs." He made no attempt to hide the fact that he was admiring Alex's body from head to toe.

"I really don't think she cares to meet you, Bivins, and I think she asked you a question," Conner said.

"Well, to answer your question, legs," Bivins leered at Alex, "I don't think you own the beach, lady. I'm a law enforcement official in this county, and I do believe this is a public beach." Bivins now stood inches from Alex's face, the stench of his breath threatening to force her backward.

Alex returned his cold glare, not allowing him to intimidate her. She regarded him as she would a suspect. "I believe you should go back and do a little reviewing, Officer. According to the law in the state of Florida, the public beach area begins at the wet/dry line. If my estimate is correct, you would now be standing approximately ten feet within my property line, and I'm asking you very nicely to leave."

Even in the darkness, Conner could see the veins in Bivins's neck almost explode. His breathing ragged, he growled, "And what if I don't feel like leaving, little lady? What if I feel like sticking around and getting in the game you and Harris were starting?" Grabbing Alex's arm, Bivins tried to pull her toward him.

Before Conner could react, Alex lifted her left elbow and rammed it into Bivins's nose. Stunned by the quick movement, Bivins released Alex, grabbed his nose, and stepped back a couple of feet. Alex did not waste any time taking advantage of the distance. She pivoted on her left foot while bringing her right leg up and delivered a brutal blow to Bivins's chest.

Alex never slowed, and as Bivins lay on the ground gasping for air, she flipped him over until his broken and bloody nose pressed into the sand. She twisted his arm around behind him, rendering him defenseless as she pressed her right knee into his back. "Well, if you don't leave on your own, you just might piss me off, Officer, and I don't think you want to do that," she growled into his ear.

"You fucking bitch," Bivins screamed as Alex twisted his arm higher on his back. "Conner, tell this bitch who I am, tell her I'm hauling her ass in and taking you with her as an accessory."

Even the severity of the moment could not diminish Conner's amusement. She slowly circled him and knelt down close to his face, openly laughing at his predicament. "Well, asshole, before I do that, maybe I should make some formal introductions here. Alex, meet Frank Bivins, a slimeball cop I have the misfortune of working with downtown." Conner's voice was full of contempt for the man. Looking toward Alex for approval, she saw the other woman's slight nod. "And, Frankie, I'd like you to meet Alex Montgomery, or maybe I should make things a little clearer and say Special Agent Alex Montgomery of the FBI."

Bivins strained to turn his head to look at Alex, but she kept him pinned firmly to the ground. Leaning forward so she could get closer to his ear and pressing her knee further into his back, Alex spoke. "I'll make a deal with you, Officer Bivins. I'll let you up and you can get back in your truck and get the hell off my beach, or I can charge you with not only trespass and destruction of a natural resource, but with assault on a federal agent. I think the first choice would be the wisest, unless of course you don't have any plans for the next couple of years...or five." Twisting his arm once more, she asked, "What's it going to be, door number one or door number two?"

"Let me up, now," Bivins growled back.

"Remember what I told you. Leave like a good little boy, or I'm coming down hard on you, and I promise you won't like it." Alex released his arm.

Bivins stood quickly, rubbing his shoulder. Alex and Bivins glared at each other for a moment, each testing the resolve of the other. Finally, Bivins broke the stare and turned toward Conner. "Next time, I'll make sure you don't have your pet feebie with you, Conner, and then we'll see what a tough girl you really are." Bivins stalked to the truck, got in, and sped away, showering the two women with sand.

Not realizing she had been holding her breath, Alex let out an exasperated sigh and ran her hand through her hair. Looking at Conner, she could tell Bivins had gotten to her. She took Conner's hand and pulled her down to the sand.

"God, Alex, I'm so sorry. I had no idea he had followed me out here tonight." Then with a sudden realization Conner turned and faced Alex. "He must have been watching us all evening, or at the least lurking somewhere in the shadows waiting for us to come back to the house." She suddenly felt guilty. Alex had already been through enough the past year, and now Conner had somehow managed to drag her into her undeclared war with Bivins.

"It's not your fault, Conner. You can't take responsibility for someone else's actions. He doesn't seem to be a very stable man," Alex said in a soft, soothing tone. "If I were you, I think I would avoid him as much as possible, at least until he calms down a bit."

"Yes, I know what you mean. I think it's a good thing we have the weekend before I have to see him again...at least, I hope." Conner was frustrated, scared, and tired. Looking at her watch, she saw that it was one-thirty in the morning. "I need to go. I wanted you to have a good time tonight. I didn't mean to practically get you assaulted and keep you up half the night."

Not knowing exactly how to express herself, Alex took Conner's hand. "Conner, I really don't think it's such a good idea that you be out on the road tonight. I'm sure he's halfway back to the city by now, but you can't be too careful with people like him. I would really appreciate it if you would stay here tonight," she said softly.

"Alex, this has already been too much of a hassle for you. I'll just go call a taxi and get out of here so you can enjoy the rest of your weekend in peace."

Anger flashed through Alex's eyes, and her lips formed a very thin line as she took a deep breath to calm herself before she spoke. "Conner Harris, you must think I am a cold bitch if you think for a moment that I could go in and go to sleep, knowing you were out there on the road, not knowing where Bivins is at the moment."

Conner's eyes registered her shock. She opened her mouth to speak, but Alex cut her off before she could say a word. "As for enjoying my weekend, well, I thought I might get lucky enough to get an invitation to, um, meet the other terror in your life."

"You mean you want to meet Seth's cat?"

"No, silly," Alex said, laughing at the confusion she saw on Conner's face. "I thought you might let me meet the *Shady Lady*. After all, she worked in concert with me to bang up that cute chin of yours." Alex gently stroked Conner's face with her hand, not knowing if the trembling she felt beneath her finger was from her fright moments before or from her touch.

Laughing quietly, Conner nodded in agreement.

"Okay, then; it's settled. You'll stay here tonight. In the morning, we can see about getting your tires fixed, then I'll follow you to your little island and we can spend the day as far away from Bivins as we can get. Does that sound like a plan to you?"

"Sounds like a damn fine plan to me, Agent Montgomery, a damn fine plan."

Standing up, Alex reached down and offered her hand to Conner. Stumbling from the uneven terrain, Conner found herself once again in Alex's arms. As she hugged Alex, Conner whispered a quiet "thank you" in her ear. Pulling her face away, she looked into Alex's eyes.

Alex was disappointed when Conner began to pull away, until she felt the gentle kiss Conner deposited on her temple. At that moment, she felt a welcome warmth spread through her body. The two women held each other's eyes for a moment, and then they reluctantly released each other, turned, and walked slowly toward the house.

As they walked up the steps to the deck, both women realized that they needed to wash off the sand Bivins had sprayed in his heated departure. After showing Conner to the guest bedroom and bath, Alex said good night and left Conner alone.

Alex showered and slipped between the cool sheets of her bed. The chill she felt was in contrast to the warmth she felt when she had slipped into Conner's arms. Laying there, thinking of the evening, Alex fell into a fitful sleep, filled with dreams of Feryle...and of the woman who lay sleeping in the next room.

Conner needed the cool water of the shower to wash away the heat that had threatened to overtake her body. She quickly dried off and curled beneath the sheets, holding a pillow close to her body. She soon slept, dreaming of what might have happened had Bivins not made his unwelcome appearance on the beach.

Chapter Six

Conner woke with a start, confused until she remembered the events of the night before. She lay back down against the soft pillows and listened for sounds that would indicate Alex was awake. A few moments later, the alluring aroma of coffee crept into the bedroom, pleading with her to get out of bed. She quickly brushed her teeth, dressed, and headed in the direction of the tantalizing smell, knowing Alex would be waiting at the other end of the journey.

Quietly walking into the kitchen, she could see Alex sitting on the deck, coffee in hand, gazing out at the receding tide. After getting a cup of coffee for herself, she opened the sliding door and stepped into the cool ocean breeze.

"Good morning, sleepyhead."

The sound of Alex speaking startled Conner. She thought the roar of the ocean had drowned out her entrance. "Good morning back. Have you been up long?"

"About an hour. I just couldn't bring myself to wake you. You looked so tired last night, and I thought you needed to sleep." Alex looked at Conner as she sat down next to her. "Actually, you look like you could use a little more. Didn't you sleep well?"

"No, I slept fine."

A knowing looked crossed Alex's face and Conner realized she had been caught in a lie. "Well, I did wake up a few times, here and there, but overall I think I got enough rest."

"Well, I was thinking that after we both shower, you might want to get some breakfast and then go see about your car. I would cook for us here, but I only returned to town on Tuesday, and I haven't shopped for groceries yet," Alex said sheepishly. "Anyway, it gives me a great excuse to expose you to another fine dining establishment that I frequent." Alex had a sneaky gleam in her eyes as she informed Conner of their tentative plans.

"I have a feeling maybe I should be frightened here, no?"

"If you think you were full last night after dinner, just wait until we finish breakfast. I know I will be feeling like a beached whale." With that, Alex puffed out her cheeks and made a face at Conner, trying to get her out of her quiet mood.

Conner spilled her coffee as she laughed. "And just where are you taking me this morning?"

"Sal's."

"Sal's?" Conner raised an eyebrow, imagining a greasy spoon diner.

"Yes, Sal's, it's—it's, well, indescribable. You'll just have to see for yourself. I'm famished just thinking about it, how about you? You hungry yet?"

At the question, Conner's stomach growled, which prompted another outburst of laughter.

"Well, maybe we had better go get ready, before that thing comes to life," Alex said, rising from the chair. "I'll meet you back here in a few minutes," and she turned and went inside.

She showered quickly. She pulled on a pair of white shorts and a dark blue tank top that was very form fitting, accentuating her firm breasts. She spent a little extra time with her hair and makeup. Looking in the mirror as she smoothed in her blush, she wondered why she was being so meticulous about her looks that morning and snarled at her reflection. "Okay, I like her, all right? It doesn't mean anything is going to happen. I just want to look good today." She ran a hand through her hair and immediately swore. "Damn, now look what you've done!"

A tentative voice came from outside the bedroom door. "Alex?"

"Oh yeah, I'll be right out."

"Are you all right? I heard you talking and..." Conner suddenly realized that Alex had been talking to herself and smiled. *Wonder what that was all about*, she thought, heading down the hall to the living room. *Maybe Alex isn't the calm, cool, and collected woman she wants me to think she is. Maybe she's just as nervous and warm as I am*. She was contemplating the question when Alex walked into the room.

"What are you smirking about in here?"

Rising and walking to the table to get her wallet, Conner snickered. "Oh nothing, just...stuff." As she walked toward the door, she looked back over her shoulder. "You coming, or am I going to have to introduce myself to Sal?"

Sal's was a local institution that Conner had somehow managed to miss in her years in Jacksonville. The breakfast bar, as the regular patrons referred to it, was located on a side street in Atlantic Beach, close to Mayport Naval Station. It was a gathering place for many of the naval and civilian personnel of MNS and the Port Authority. Although it was close to ten by the time they arrived, Sal's was still packed with people eating huge plates of eggs, bacon, grits, toast, and other things Conner couldn't discern.

After a twenty-minute wait, the server seated them at a table overlooking the St. John's River. The women ordered coffee first, wanting to take their time and look over the menu. Conner noticed that some of the people eating breakfast had obviously not been home yet, but were nourishing their bodies after a night out partying. The place seemed like an unusual place for someone like Alex to frequent. *Maybe this is Alex's way of letting me know she isn't the prim and proper woman she appears to be*, Conner thought.

"There you go again. Am I going to have to push bamboo shoots under your nails to get you to tell me what you've been smirking about all morning, or are you going to 'fess up?" Alex asked in a raw husky voice that sent shivers all through Conner's body

"Well, right now I was thinking about how this place doesn't quite fit your personality."

"Well, I do have several personalities." Alex smiled and sat back in her seat.

"Oh, okay. Well, just make sure the nice ones are out and about when I'm around."

"I'll try, Conner, but sometimes I just can't control one of them. She's always trying to get into some kind of trouble." Alex gave Conner a sly smile.

Conner could feel the heat surge through her body, and she knew Alex could see it as well. Taking a moment to regain her composure, she took a sip of her coffee. Determined not to let Alex get away with the tease, Conner leaned back in her seat and draped her arm out and over the back of the booth. "Well, then, Agent Montgomery, I wonder what would happen if both our alter egos surfaced at the same time? There might be a lot of trouble lurking in the shadows for us to find." Giving Alex a dark, sultry look, she slowly licked her lips, waiting for Alex's reply.

Alex knew Conner had called her bluff, but decided to play it out a little further. "Well, when my alter ego comes out, it's sometimes hard to get her to go away. She isn't allowed out very much and sometimes—"

"Oh. Well, that's great," Conner broke in. "I've never been one who really enjoyed one-night reviews." She hoped Alex couldn't see the half-truth in her eyes. She had certainly had her share of one-night stands the past couple of years, but she had never really enjoyed them; they were more of a purging of pent-up anger and tension.

Their eyes locked and held as each tried to read the hidden message in the other's words. Alex knew she was playing with fire, but couldn't stop. There was something about Conner that got through her protective shield, and a fire stormed through Alex's body as Conner bit her bottom lip and smiled a knowing smile.

"Can I take your order?"

Feeling relief at the interruption, Alex picked up the menu and began studying the various choices. "Is Sal in the kitchen?"

"No, not until later. Said he had a meeting or something."

Alex nodded, and she and Conner placed their orders and continued talking as if whatever passed between them had never happened.

They ate quickly and efficiently, anxious to get on with their plans for the day. Full of nervous energy from all the caffeine, they headed toward the parking garage to tend to Conner's car. Conner had called the police garage before they left the house and asked that they send someone over to replace the tires. Since it was a Saturday, she hadn't really expected them to be there when she and Alex arrived, much less there and gone already.

Happy that they had just gained a couple of more hours of playtime, Conner quickly drew directions to her condo. As she closed the Jeep's door, she smiled at Alex.

"I'm really glad you thought of going to see the *Shady Lady*, Alex. I have a feeling we're going to have a fun day." Conner strolled over toward her car, then asked, "Wanna race?"

"I wouldn't stand a chance against that hot machine of yours. I think I'll pass and be a law-abiding senior citizen...just for today."

Conner got in the Jag and leaned out the window. "Party pooper," she pouted, then stuck her tongue out at Alex and laughed. She started the car and they headed for what both women felt would be a day filled with fun and a lot of sexual tension.

It took Alex a few minutes to realize that Conner intended to take the ferry over to the island. Once they arrived, they discovered there was a fifteen-minute wait. "Conner, this is great. As long as I have lived here, I've never taken the ferry." Alex's twin dimples popped in as she let out a glowing smile.

The women leaned against the Jeep and Conner told Alex about the history of the ferry. Alex listened with interest, but soon the line began to move and the two women headed toward their respective cars. After they drove on, they once again got out of their cars and leaned against the railing as the ferry crept across the St. John's River. It was only about a ten-minute voyage, but it left Alex invigorated and eager for their day trip to continue.

Conner led the way past breathtaking scenery. Soon they were on the island and headed toward Conner's condo. Although there had been a major influx of tourists and residents over the years, Alex could tell the developers had taken great care to preserve the natural landscape as much as possible. They turned onto Ocean Avenue, and Alex could see the beach a few hundred feet to her right. Conner pulled into a wide double bay garage, waving Alex into the adjacent space.

As Alex followed Conner inside, she was struck by the beautiful space that Conner called home. Looking a little bewildered, Alex turned to her. "I thought you said you had a small condo on the island. Conner, this is absolutely breathtaking." She walked over to the floor-to-ceiling windows that spanned the entire room and looked out at a private walkway leading to the beach below.

"Well it is small compared to some of the other places on the islands, sort of....ya know?" Conner replied sheepishly. She saw Alex eyeing the expensive artwork and furnishings in the condo. "Okay, I'll confess the whole story, but you have to promise not to hold it against me, okay?"

Alex's eyes narrowed and she smiled. "Well, I'm not sure I can promise that I won't hold anything against you. I kinda liked holding me against you last night."

Conner took a ragged breath and moved closer to Alex. "You'll get yourself in a lot of trouble if you don't watch that teasing, Agent Montgomery—or is your alter ego trying to come out and play?"

Alex felt a rush of heat course through her body as Conner's eyes melted her soul. Deciding it was too early to start playing, she redirected the conversation. "Well that depends on if you're going to tell me the story about your mini-mansion and then take me sailing."

"Oh, we're definitely going sailing, but I need a drink if you're going to make me spill my guts. What so you want? I have sodas, beer, wine..."

"Beer is fine with me, if that's what you're having."

"Make yourself at home, I'll be right back," Conner said, heading to the kitchen.

Alex looked around the room. There were personal pictures sitting discreetly among the works of art. She moved closer to get a better look at a photograph hanging on the wall near the fireplace. The man in it looked vaguely familiar to Alex, but she couldn't place him.

"Ah, I see you've met Pops."

"Pops?"

"Yes. He is the reason for all of this." Conner spread her arms to indicate the house and its contents. "Geez, I can see you're not going to let me get out of this, so have a seat and I'll explain the whole outrageous story." She sat down and propped her feet up on what had to be a Chippendale coffee table. She stole a look at Alex, noticing her surprise.

"Prop 'em up there. I'm sure if we scratch this one, I have a few more just like it in the warehouse somewhere."

Alex's eyes widened. "Conner, are you mad? This furniture is worth a mint. I suppose Pops has something to do with your disrespectful attitude toward fine furniture."

"Actually, yes and no. See, Pops was my paternal grandfather. He was one of the pioneers of the modern shrimping industry. He worked hard and bought land here on the island. Several years later, he, along with a few other men, began developing the land that is now known as the Plantation." Conner pointed to an aerial photograph hanging on the wall close to her grandfather's picture.

"Anyway, after that, he moved on to other projects and finally, in the early '60s, moved to Hilton Head, South Carolina. He was obsessed with developing new areas while preserving the natural environment. He was one of the old-timers, like Frank Lloyd Wright, who built around the natural landscape."

Alex immediately remembered why the man looked so familiar. "George Winfred Harris," she said, to Conner's amused surprise.

"You and I are almost the same age. How could you possibly know my grandfather? His peak was way before either of us even knew or cared about the environment, or good architecture."

"Feryle was an architect. She loved the challenge of designing around the landscape. I remember seeing his books in her office. She was an ardent fan of his work."

Conner beamed with pride. She immediately removed her feet from the table in a subtle display of respect.

"Do you remember the houses close to mine at the beach?" Alex asked

"Yes, very well. I remember commenting on them. They reminded me a lot of Pop's work."

"Well, you should be pleased to know that Feryle had a hand in creating those homes. She was the architect for many of them and used your grandfather's ideals and philosophy for her designs."

"Wow," was the only word Conner could think of in response.

"Okay, finish your story, I didn't mean to interrupt."

"Hmm, well, okay. Anyway, Pops spent the rest of his life in Hilton Head and Savannah, developing the area and making obscene amounts of money. My father followed Pop's example and is a developer in his own right. When Pops died twenty-something years ago, Dad decided to put all of his assets in a trust for me, and when I turned twenty-one, I got it all."

Conner looked a little embarrassed with the entire story, and Alex decided not to tease her any longer about it. "Well, you sure haven't let the wealth go to your head. Most people would, but I could already tell before this story that you're not like most people," she said.

"Thank you. Okay, you've heard the whole gruesome story, can we go sailing now?"

"Yes, dear. Let's go see if you can do an encore chin slide."

Chapter Seven

On the short drive over to the Amelia Yacht Basin, Conner told Alex a little about the *Shady Lady*. The boat had been seized during an arrest on the open sea, and after the case was tried, the Coast Guard auctioned off the boat. Conner had heard about the auction and immediately registered as a bidder. It had been a tough auction, with many interested parties, but in the end, she had won out and now the *Shady Lady* was hers.

As they got out of the car, Conner told Alex about the boat. "She's a Morgan 41 Classic, has a center cockpit, wraparound seating. Below there are two cabins, two heads, a salon, a U-shaped galley, and a captain's workstation. She has a 13'10" beam and a 4'6" draft. She's powered by a 27 horsepower Yanmar diesel engine...what?"

Alex could not contain her laugh at Conner's excitement over her boat.

"Okay, I guess I do get a little carried away talking about her. Although I haven't paid much attention to her lately, she is my pride and joy...much like a child, I guess."

As they stopped before the *Shady Lady,* Alex thought of how majestic she looked. The boat had a gleaming white hull, with sparkling cleats and stanchions, and the companionway and grab rails were made of very fine honey-colored teakwood. There was a dark blue stripe circling the craft at the deck line and a Bimini of the same deep color. On the transom the boat's name was written in a bold script.

Climbing aboard the boat, Conner continued her narrative. "She was named the *Shady Lady* when I bought her. It's supposed to be bad luck to rename a boat, so I decided to leave it as it was. I sort of think it's appropriate. I do live and work in the shadows."

She turned to help Alex down the ladder, gently placing her hands on Alex's waist in case she needed some support. At least, that was how Conner defended her actions to herself. "Be careful, it's a little dark down here until I get the hatches open."

Alex descended the ladder, then turned to take in her surroundings. The salon was paneled and floored in the same honey-colored teakwood as the upper deck. The hatches were covered with floral curtains and complemented with matching pillows and cushions on the benches and chairs.

"Conner, this is beautiful. Did you decorate it yourself?"

"Yeah, you should have seen how bad she looked when I got her. The previous owners used her for nothing more than a transport boat for their drugs. The outside was sparkling, so that she wouldn't draw any unwanted attention. However, the area down below was in shambles. It took Sam and me almost a year to get her presentable."

They stowed their supplies and went back up top so they could get underway. Conner expertly maneuvered the boat out of the slip and they were soon motoring down the channel to the intercoastal waterway. Alex sat back, watched, and listened as Conner provided a guided tour of the area and the structures that they passed.

"On the Sunday morning of the festival, all of the local shrimp boats are decorated like floats in a parade. They line up and pass the end of the pier, where a local priest sprinkles holy water on the deck and blesses the boat and its crew. It's a symbolic gesture for a fruitful and safe shrimp season. I'll have to bring you back out next March for it. I think you'd really like it, Alex."

"I think I would, too, Conner. We'll have to plan on it, then."

"You bet," Conner said, smiling.

Alex and Conner sat in comfortable silence as they watched the inhabited landscape fall away, and the unspoiled and lovely landscape of nature took its place along the Amelia River. Alex asked a few questions about the area as they made their way through the St. Mary's channel, finally reaching their destination off the shores of Cumberland Island.

Conner cut the engine and dropped anchor. "This is the place I want to come to when I die." She spoke quietly, looking off toward the shoreline.

"What do you mean, Conner?"

"I mean this place is so peaceful and serene, I can't think of any other place on earth where I would want to be for eternity, so it's written in my will that I want to be cremated and my ashes spread here, where we sit."

Seeing the look in Alex's eyes, Conner regretted bringing up the topic of death. "Okay, on to lighter subjects. Want a beer to go with all this sunshine?"

"Yeah, a beer sounds great, but let me get them. You've been doing all the work this morning; it's time I earned my keep here."

When Alex climbed back on deck, she noticed Conner's contemplative expression. "Penny for your thoughts?"

"Oh, deep ones, I'm afraid. You know, the ones contemplating life. Can't let those go cheap, I'm charging a quarter for those," Conner teased, letting Alex decide if she wanted to pursue the question further.

"Mmm. Well I just happen to have a few quarters, and a good ear— that is, if you want to talk," Alex said, handing Conner her beer and sitting down close beside her.

Conner looked back out toward the shore and spoke in a quiet voice. "Well, I've sort of got a problem. See, I've met someone recently that I think I really like and want to get to know, but I'm not sure if she wants the same thing." She ran a hand through her hair, then took a long pull from her beer.

"The thing is, I'm afraid if I let her know and she isn't interested, then she'll just disappear."

Alex's heart fell a little at the thought of Conner having feelings for another woman. "That's kind of a tough place to be. Does this person have any idea how you feel?"

Conner rolled her eyes and blew out a long breath. "Not likely. It's not like I have much experience in putting words to my feelings. I guess it's the thought of being rejected, as well. I sometimes think the pain of rejection would be harder to take than the pain of not knowing. You know what I mean?"

"Well, what is this woman like?" Alex asked, wanting to learn more about the woman who was about to take her chances with Conner away.

"Well, she's probably the most beautiful woman I have ever met." Conner's eyes lit up. "She's about my age, a little taller than me, and a great body. It's all I can do when I'm around her to keep from reaching out and touching her. She has dark hair, deep blue eyes, and a mouth you just want to devour." Her eyes had turned dark. "And the cutest dimples I've ever seen pop out when she smiles." She smiled with the last statement.

Alex felt her heart skip a beat. *Could it be true that Conner is talking about me? The description is pretty accurate—well, all except the great body part.* "Sounds like an interesting woman. Where did you meet her?"

"Um, sort of through work." Conner realized she had offered a much too detailed description to Alex and was sure she was about to be busted.

"Well, I can only advise you to be patient, and maybe things will work themselves out the way you hope."

"Yeah, I know, I'm just afraid I'll lose my chance if I wait too long. I mean, she's a gorgeous woman, and I don't think she will be available long, if I know the women in this city." Conner felt her frustration rising, running her hand once again through her hair. She finished off her beer and stood to get them fresh ones from below.

When Conner left, Alex took a deep, exasperated breath. She could only wonder if the woman Conner was referring to was her. She hoped it was, in a way; then again, she was also afraid of the possibility. She felt guilty for having these feelings so soon after Feryle's death. Although it had been almost a year, she still felt like she was betraying what they had had together.

She suddenly realized that Conner had been gone for a while. "You okay down there?"

"Yes, I decided to make us some sandwiches. I thought we could dinghy over to the island and have a picnic on the beach." Conner stuck her head through the companionway. "Um, if that's okay with you, or we could just stay here and sun on the boat."

"No, that sounds like fun. Need some help down there?"

Although Conner wanted Alex close, she also knew the galley was small and she didn't think she could handle being so close to her at the moment. She had decided to make the sandwiches as an excuse to give her more time to settle her nerves and heartbeat.

"No, I'm almost done. Why don't you change into your suit while I'm finishing up?"

"Okay, if you're sure you don't need any help," Alex said as she climbed down the ladder.

"I put your things in the forward cabin," Conner said, pointing the way for Alex.

When Alex walked into the cabin, she again noticed the attention Conner had paid to the décor. It was a very intimate and sensual arrangement in dark greens and burgundies. Built into the walls were bookshelves, and several pillows were thrown on the bed, inviting long sensual evenings of reading and cuddling when it was too cool to be topside. The overhead hatch provided a perfect view of the sky above. Alex felt a warm heat pulse through her as she envisioned herself there with Conner. Shaking her head to clear the thoughts, Alex changed into her swimsuit and headed back toward the galley.

Conner looked up, and her eyes immediately went dark as Alex appeared from the passageway. The boiling heat Conner felt raging through her body threatened to overcome any patience she had promised herself regarding Alex. She knew that Alex could see the need in her eyes, and for once, she didn't care.

When Alex's eyes met Conner's, the naked truth was exposed. The look of ragged need was so apparent on the other woman's face it gave Alex courage as she stepped closer and closer. She could see Conner's barely controlled breathing and as she moved even closer, she could see the pulse throbbing in her neck.

Conner put the knife down on the counter and reached for her. Alex walked gently into her arms, and both women gasped as their bodies responded to the sudden contact. They held each other for a long moment, not knowing exactly what should happen next.

Conner was trembling as Alex finally pulled away and looked into her eyes.

"How did you know?" Conner asked.

"I wasn't sure until just now. I can tell you, however, that I was getting very jealous up there, hearing you talk about another woman. I'm surprised you couldn't tell from my reactions. I didn't think I was hiding them too well."

Conner smiled and pulled her closer until their lips were only inches apart. "Well, you don't have to hide them any longer, Agent Montgomery." She pulled the other woman down and gently brushed her lips.

The heat from the brief contact surged through Alex's body. As Conner slowly pulled back from the embrace, Alex tightened her arms around her, urging her closer, letting Conner know with unspoken words that the brief kiss was not enough to sate the desire surging through her body. She took Conner's face in her hands and lowered her head to taste her once again. Her thumbs gently massaged Conner's cheeks as their lips tenderly explored each other.

As the moments passed, the women felt the heat move lower in their bodies, and when Alex gently parted Conner's lips with her tongue, both women moaned. Conner's hands moved slowly up and down Alex's naked back and circled around to stroke her stomach.

Alex gasped as the nerve endings in her abdomen responded to the touch, and pulled away to look into the dark sensual eyes of the other woman.

"God, Alex, I want you so bad right now, but I know you're not ready for any kind of—"

Alex placed her finger over Conner's swollen lips. Having quieted her, she leaned down and gently kissed the inviting lips again. "Conner...God, you taste so sweet. It's not that I don't want you. I do." Smiling and almost shyly looking down into Conner's eyes, she continued, "I've felt the same way almost since I met you in the precinct. I don't know what it is about you, but I do know I want to explore whatever it is we are feeling for each other."

She pulled back a bit, but didn't break the embrace. "I think we need to take things slow and see where they go from here. I know I have several unresolved issues in my life right now, and I don't want those to come back to haunt us later."

Conner listened as Alex spoke, knowing that what she said made sense, even though her body argued the contrary. Letting out a teasing growl, she smiled. "Yeah, I know you're right, but if I'm going to stand a chance of not imploding right here, I think we need to head out for our picnic. Like now."

Alex snickered and pulled her close for one more kiss, then reluctantly backed away, breaking the sweet and torturous contact. "Okay, why don't you go change and I will take this feast you've prepared for us up to the dinghy."

"Deal," Conner replied, leaning in to steal one more kiss from Alex before sliding past her and disappearing into the cabin.

At the ranger's hut on the island, Conner bought a map as a souvenir for Alex. After looking it over, they decided to hike to the ocean side of the island, about two miles away.

During their hike, Alex listened as Conner once again became a tour guide.

"The island is about three miles wide and roughly eighteen miles long. The National Park Service limits the number of people allowed on the island to help preserve the environment and reduce the exposure of some of the island's natural inhabitants to the public. People can come and camp here at a variety of campsites. Some have electricity and showers, while others are located in the remote areas of the island for those who like to rough it. It's is such a popular place that you have to make reservations six months in advance to stay here overnight."

Conner looked at Alex, smiling sheepishly. "I know, I get a little excited telling people about this area, so let me know when you want me to shut up and I will."

"I don't want you to shut up. I like hearing you talk about the things you love, and obviously you love this island." Alex threw her arm around Conner's shoulder and gave her a hug as they walked. She reluctantly dropped her arm as she remembered they were in a public place. Clearing her throat, she said, "Now, continue with your tour, Ranger Harris."

"Very funny. Remember, you need my help to get back to Amelia. Don't make me mad. I just might leave you stranded on this not quite so deserted island." Conner laughed, poking Alex in the shoulder.

"Okay, as I was saying, in 1972 the island was established as a national seashore, and since that time it has been left to return to its natural state. We don't have time today, but maybe one day I'll take you over to the Dungeness ruins and you can see for yourself. Dungeness was built in the early 1900s and was later abandoned. Sometime in the late '50s it burned to the ground, and about all you can see of what remains is stones covered with vines."

"What was it before it was a national seashore, just a deserted island?"

"No, it was originally settled by the Timucuan Indians. Over the years, it's taken on many other faces. It's been a fort, the main hub for the first interstate railway, and in more recent times it was responsible for making the shrimping industry what it is today."

"Okay, you're really on the payroll here, right?"

Laughing, Conner attempted to punch her in the shoulder again, but this time Alex was ready for her and moved too quickly.

"No, I just really love the area. It fascinates and bewilders me at the same time."

They had been walking for about 30 minutes when, through the tunnel of trees, Alex saw the first waves of the ocean crashing to the shore. As they cleared the trees, Alex was astounded with the beauty of the shoreline. As far as she could see, there was nothing hindering the natural flow of the environment. The dunes were unencumbered by fences or beach bars. The sea grass swayed in the wind as sea gulls lazed easily on the beach.

The women walked about a half-mile further down the beach to a completely deserted area. Alex spread out a large beach blanket as Conner removed her backpack and began setting out their feast. Though Alex had kidded Conner earlier about the amount of food she had prepared, she was now glad, because the hike had worked up an appetite for both women.

Conner pulled out a thermos and poured dark red liquid for each of them. "Sorry about the plastic, but glass isn't allowed on the beach."

Alex gave Conner a teasing glare. "Well, it's nice to know you follow some of the rules."

Conner took on an innocent look. "What do you mean *some*?"

"Well, if my memory serves me correctly, and I know it does, I believe alcohol is not only prohibited on the beach, but on the entire island." Alex tried to give Conner a stern look, but it was totally broken up with her next comment. "I guess we'd better drink up. I wouldn't want to have to arrest you."

After a relaxed lunch, the women went on a long walk further down the shoreline, sometimes stopping to look at shells that had washed onto the wet sand.

Before either woman realized it, they had walked well out of sight of their blanket, and they decided to head back. As they turned around, Alex placed her hand on Conner's arm, stopping her so they were facing. She stroked Conner's face, gently looking into her eyes.

"I can't remember the last time I had as good of a time as I have today, Conner, thank you." Looping her finger in the neckline of Conner's t-shirt, Alex pulled Conner to her and placed a gentle kiss on her lips. Conner whimpered at the contact, and Alex wrapped her arms around Conner's waist. She spent a long moment savoring Conner's bottom lip as she sucked it gently into her mouth, tasting it with her tongue.

Conner ran her fingers through Alex's hair, feeling the soft silkiness of the tresses, trying to pull her closer still. She pulled back suddenly, taking a ragged breath and looking at Alex as if trying to comprehend what was happening. She suddenly pulled Alex close again and kissed her, her tongue probing, opening her lips until their tongues were dancing in unison.

A deep yearning groan escaped Alex's throat as she felt Conner's tongue join hers, savoring the warm sweet flavor of her mouth. Conner tasted like the warm sweet wine they had drunk with lunch, and Alex found herself probing deeper in search of more.

Lost in a passion she did not want to stop, Alex broke the kiss. Breathing heavily, she leaned her head against Conner's so they were touching noses. Eyes closed, she whispered, "I think we had better take this somewhere a little more private, or we're likely to be arrested."

Conner stepped back quickly, completely breaking the contact. She looked disheveled and a little disappointed as she tried to compose herself and stop the rampaging heat boiling through her veins. She felt like she might have gone too far, too fast for Alex, but she had been so overcome with her need she couldn't contain her desire.

"Um, yeah. Sure, we probably need to get back to the boat anyway. It'll be getting dark soon, and I think I might have a couple of running lights out." Taking a deep breath, Conner ran her hand through her hair and turned to head back toward their blanket.

Alex could see the frustration and uncertainty in Conner's face. Taking her arm, stopping her mid-stride, Alex could feel Conner tremble. "I didn't say I wanted to stop, Conner," she said, looking hesitantly into her eyes, "just get somewhere a little more, um, private." She looked out over the water before bringing her eyes back to Conner's face. "I want you so much right now, I hurt. I want to make love to you Conner, here. Right now."

Alex looked around as if trying to determine if there was a possibility of just that happening. Releasing a torn sigh, she added,

"However, I think we would be a lot safer, and more comfortable, back at your house, okay?"

Conner smiled and pulled Alex close for a tender hug. Both women relaxed, knowing that this break in their touch was going to be tolerable, but only because they knew that soon they would not have to stop.

Conner pulled back and looked at Alex with a mischievous gleam in her eye. "Race ya." She laughed as she sprinted toward their forgotten blanket.

"No fair, you got a head start," Alex yelled at the running woman's back as she shot into a sprint of her own. "Cheater!"

To Conner's surprise, Alex quickly caught up with and passed her. Alex ran with the grace of a long-distance runner, and Conner held back, taking the time to appreciate the flowing figure gliding like a gazelle in front of her. She almost tripped several times as she watched the muscular body of the woman she had so recently held in her arms—a body she intended to hold again before the night was through.

By the time Conner reached the blanket, Alex was already pulling the cap off a bottle of water. Conner bent over, hands on her knees, gasping for air, while Alex leaned back on her elbows and grinned up at her. "Looks like you need a little PT, Officer," she said and took a big swallow from her water bottle.

Conner felt the remaining air in her lungs escape as she watched Alex's lips encircle the mouth of the bottle, glimpsing a hint of her tongue as it met the hard edge of the plastic.

"Y-Yeah, I guess...I could use a little more...exercise." She plopped down on the blanket, knowing that if she did not get off her feet she would end up on her face and in another humiliating situation.

"Well, I happen to know a very good personal trainer," Alex said, grinning, showing the dimples that turned Conner's body to mush. After taking another long pull on the bottle, she wiped her mouth with the back of her hand and passed the water to Conner. She watched as Conner took a long pull from the bottle, then poured what was left of the cold water across her stomach. Alex bit her bottom lip hard, trying unsuccessfully to stifle a deep groan.

Conner's lips turned up at the corners. "Oh yeah, and just how much does this *very good* personal trainer charge for her services?"

Leaning up on one elbow, Alex reached out for Conner. Drawing her fingers through the now-warm water pooled on her belly, she drew arcing designs on the woman's skin. Conner gasped as the muscles in her stomach respond to the soft touch of Alex's fingers.

Alex glanced up at Conner and, seeing the dark cloudy expression, decided to make her suffer just a little longer. "Hmm, let's see. I could probably negotiate you a good deal, but only if you throw in a few sailboat trips and maybe a romantic walk or two on the beach."

"Well, um, I think I might be able to afford that." Conner was still breathing hard, both from the run and subsequent bout of lust for the woman next to her.

Alex rolled over on her stomach so that she could see Conner better. "I was hoping that it was an offer you couldn't refuse." She wiggled her eyebrows and laughed.

"Damn, woman, what did they feed you at the FBI Academy?"

"Hell, they didn't feed us anything, woman. Once a week they would drop a ham bone from a helicopter, and whoever reached it first got to eat. Makes for a good reason to run fast."

"Hmm. Well now, Agent Montgomery, just what prompted the fast run today?" Conner added, grinning as she sat up on the blanket close enough to Alex to feel the heat from her body and smell the sweet musky scent of her glistening skin. "Looks to me like all the food was eaten a long time ago."

Alex gave a low growl and leaned in, capturing Conner's mouth for another kiss, letting Conner use her imagination to answer her own question. She gently bit Conner's lower lip, savoring the taste, a mixture of the salt from her sweat and the sweetness of her skin. Taking her time, she sucked Conner's lower lip into her mouth, gently running her tongue over the surface, only releasing it when she heard the guttural moan she was waiting for.

She placed her hand on Conner's face and gave a mischievous look of her own. "I'm waiting on dessert."

It was all Conner needed to hear. She stood and reached down to help Alex to her feet. Together they walked back toward the ranger station, each woman lost in her own thoughts of what was yet to come.

It was getting dark when they arrived, and as they made their way down the long pier, a ranger looked up from Conner's dinghy. "I was just about to send someone out to look for you two. I hope you enjoyed your visit to the island."

Alex and Conner grinned and stole looks at each another.

"We sure did. A very memorable trip," Alex replied as she stepped into the dinghy.

Conner handed Alex the backpack and climbed in beside her. They said their good-byes as Alex untied the lanyard, then headed the short distance back to the *Shady Lady*.

"Why don't you go change into something dry while I get her started and headed for home," Conner said as she handed Alex a dry towel.

"You sure you don't need any help?"

"Nah, I could do this in my sleep. Go ahead, get changed, you look like you're freezing."

Alex headed down as Conner climbed into the cockpit. She once again found herself in the warm, inviting cocoon Conner used as her cabin. As she began to dry her cold body, the nerve endings in her skin screamed at the contact and she knew she was close to becoming completely unwound from the desire she felt. The only thing that had kept her from tearing Conner's clothes off and making love to her right there on the beach was the fact that they were both law enforcement officials; the thought of getting arrested for indecent exposure was enough to keep her raging hormones in check. Now, though, there was nothing holding her back, and her body was screaming for relief.

Conner attempted to engage the motor, but each time she turned the key, the engine only sputtered and growled its refusal to cooperate.

"Damn, *Lady,* come on. I know I haven't treated you very well lately, but, God, I need to get home—like now. I'm dying here."

Alex heard Conner swearing up on deck and smiled. *Must be as frustrated as I am*, she thought. She looked up through the forward hatch and saw that the moon was going to be full that night and the weather perfect, thinking it wouldn't be so bad if they found themselves stranded.

"Damn, sonuvabitch, start, damn you!"

"Well, if you spoke to me like that, I just might give you the cold shoulder too." Alex laughed as she climbed up the ladder.

"Sorry, I'm, um, just sort of, ah, in a hurry, ya know." Conner's face turned crimson as she looked at Alex's knowing expression.

"Well, I was just thinking that it wouldn't be too bad if maybe we, you know, got stranded out here for the night." It was now Alex's turn to redden as Conner's eyes lit up in comprehension.

"Hmm, you know, you may have a point there, Agent Montgomery. I seem to recall seeing a couple of steaks in the freezer below. I know I have a couple of bottles of wine on board. You think you might like to grill the steaks and dine with me under the stars?" Taking to the idea immediately, Conner formed a great evening in her mind. *The* Shady Lady *just might be doing me a big favor tonight*, she thought.

"Well, if I remember correctly, you haven't been on the boat in quite a while. Just how old are those steaks? I'm not sure I want to get stranded out here if I have food poisoning."

"Cute. Benny, the mechanic at the marina, left the steaks. I let him use the boat sometimes and he gives me good deals when I need something repaired. He used it a couple of weeks ago, so I'm sure that's when he left them." Conner strolled very slowly over to Alex and stopped only when she could feel the heat radiating off her body.

"Anyway, the last thing I want to do to you tonight is give you food poisoning." Smiling and bringing her lips so close to Alex she could feel her breath, Conner whispered, "I have much, much more interesting things in store for you tonight." She could hear the intake of breath as Alex's body responded to her words.

Alex's eyes turned a deep blue and as her hand found Conner's face, she bent slowly and took Conner's warm lips between her own. Their tongues fought for control. Alex slid her hand down to the hollow of Conner's neck, stopping to fist the cloth of her shirt. She pulled Conner closer, and as their kiss deepened, she felt herself lose all resolve, and she fell into the chasm of her desire.

Conner gasped as Alex's hands inched their way down her chest. Using only her index fingers, Alex traced a burning path between her breasts. The muscles in Conner's abdomen went into spasms as Alex spread her hands to gently caress them and play circles around her navel. Electric shivers ran up her spine as Alex slowly took her hands in her own and brought them up to lay flat against her chest.

Alex broke the kiss and looked intently at Conner, her lips swollen from the long, consuming kiss. She could feel Conner's hands tremble beneath her own and knew the other woman was as lost to the passion as she herself was.

"Can you feel how fast you make my heart beat?" Alex asked in a low husky voice.

Conner could not find words, only nodded and pressed her hands closer against Alex's chest.

"I want you so much." Alex did not know how much longer she could keep standing on the deck. She didn't know if the rocking was from the ocean or her equilibrium, but either way she knew she had to get Conner below...in the cabin...in the bed...inside her.

Conner took Alex's hand and turned toward the companionway, stopping at the opening to sate her need again for the sweet taste of Alex's lips. She climbed down the ladder, then turned to take Alex's waist as she descended into the salon. She wrapped her arms around Alex and pressed herself against her back, slowly caressing the firm, taut muscles of Alex's stomach, then playing with the sensitive skin just below her breasts.

Alex leaned into the touch, holding the rungs of the ladder for support. Her legs shook from the adrenaline surging through her body, and every nerve in her skin was on alert as Conner's hands teased and stroked. When Conner bent to tenderly bite the back of her neck, Alex released a pent-up primitive growl, urging her on. Conner slowly moved her hands up and took a breast in each hand, gently squeezing.

Alex was shaking so much Conner thought she might fall. Shifting her weight, she brought her right leg forward, placing it into the hot, wet vee of Alex's legs.

"Oh my God," Alex cried as Conner's leg made contact, only the fabric of her shorts separating them. Her knuckles white from griping the rungs of the ladder and losing the fight to remain standing, she allowed some of her weight to settle on Conner's thigh.

"God, Conner—I need...oh yes." Alex completely lost the ability to speak as Conner gently pressed her nipples between her fingers while once again leaning in to nip at her neck.

"You feel so damn good, Alex, so soft." Conner's breath came in ragged gasps as she tried to remain in control. "And you taste even better." She wanted this first time to be slow, special, and unforgettable. She knew she had to fight hard to keep from taking Alex right there on the floor.

"I want you, Alex, now—naked, in my bed," Conner whispered hoarsely as she pulled on Alex's hard nipples, "where I can touch you." She nipped at Alex's earlobe. "And taste you." She pulled her fingernails across the sensitive skin of Alex's stomach. "And feel your entire body pressed against mine."

Alex used all the strength she could gather and turned around to face Conner, her eyes dark, her skin glistening, and her breath ragged as she passionately devoured the other woman's lips.

Conner's lips parted to allow Alex's tongue to hungrily search out her own. Her hands entwined themselves in Alex's dark silky hair, pulling her closer, deeper. After a long moment, Alex broke the kiss and slowly opened her eyes, eyes that pleaded for mercy.

After a few moments, she finally found her voice. "Conner, please...I need you."

A slow smile spread across Conner's face as she took Alex's hand and led her into the forward cabin. She turned and again took Alex's lips in her own, tugging lightly at her bottom lip.

"Ahh...Conner."

Conner pulled away and smiled gently. "Don't move," was all she said as she stepped to the port hatches and opened them. She came back to stand in front of Alex and reached up to release the forward hatch above them, letting the cool night breeze glide through the cabin. The only light came from the full moon, which cast a gentle shadow over the two women.

Conner pulled Alex forward for another kiss as her fingers searched out the buttons of Alex's shirt. Conner felt Alex's hands join hers to quicken the chore, but she gently pushed them away.

"Let me, Alex, please." She slowly unbuttoned Alex's shirt and very slowly pushed it off her shoulders, exposing the small firm breasts she had caressed just moments ago.

"I want to undress you very slowly," Conner whispered as she leaned forward and bit Alex's collarbone. "Very slowly."

She feathered kisses down Alex's chest, stopping to appreciate the beautiful curves of her breasts, but careful to avoid the ultrasensitive nipples, instead placing tender bites and licks on the hot skin around them.

Alex put one hand on the bookcase and one hand on Conner's shoulder as she knelt before her, and Conner could feel the uncontrollable trembling of Alex's hands as she steadied herself. She let out a low hungry groan as she left a warm wet trail, kissing and licking her way down Alex's stomach. The flavor was like no other Conner had ever tasted—a hint of saltiness mixed with what could only be the liquid fire of Alex herself. Conner growled hungrily as she slowly circled the small indention of Alex's navel. She felt Alex's hips thrust forward in an urgent need for contact as she nipped the skin just above the waistband of her shorts.

"Conner," Alex rasped. "Woman, you're killing me. I need you, baby, I need to feel you touch me. Please."

"Soon, love. Very soon." Conner undid Alex's belt, then tore open the snap of Alex's shorts, feeling her strength weaken as she neared the wet heat that she yearned to taste. Grasping the sides of the shorts, she pulled them down to Alex's feet, exposing the soft, clipped curls lying at the juncture of her legs. When Alex stood before her totally nude, Conner slowly ran her hands up Alex's body, starting at her feet and not stopping until she was once again standing and facing the most beautiful dark eyes she had ever seen.

"You are so beautiful, Alex."

Alex's eyes closed as Conner leaned in and kissed her neck, nipping lightly on her earlobe. "Oh, God, Conner, please...I need you. I need to feel you next to me." Grabbing the tie of Conner's swimsuit top, she pulled until it came undone, then she released the tie in the back, letting the top fall between them to the floor. Placing her hands flat on Conner's back, Alex slowly brought them around in a gentle caress until her hands cupped Conner's small breasts.

Conner closed her eyes, threw her head back, and let out a deep moan as Alex massaged her nipples with the pads of her thumbs, watching as they hardened into small peaks. Her entire body jerked as she felt Alex take one nipple in her mouth and circle it with the hot, wet smoothness of her tongue.

She dug her fingers in Alex's hair as she felt her bikini bottom being lowered and kicked it aside as it hit the floor. Lifting Alex's chin with her fingers, she urged her to stand so she could fully press her body against Alex's. The women stood quietly in their embrace as they each explored the other's body, placing tender kisses on the smooth hot skin of the other.

Conner shifted, bringing her leg between Alex's, and released a hungry moan as she felt the hot wetness. She kissed Alex deeply while gently turning her toward the bed and laying her down, never breaking contact with Alex's mouth. Climbing up and straddling Alex's leg, she settled against her.

"God, you feel so good, Alex," she whispered as she feathered kisses on her face and brow. Raising herself up on one arm, she lowered her lips to Alex's neck, tasting the sweet skin before exploring her way down Alex's torso. She finally came to Alex's breasts and kissed circles around each nipple.

Alex entwined her fingers in Conner's hair, pulling her head where she needed to feel her, and her hips bucked as Conner blew a gentle breath against the nipple, then ever so slowly enveloped it in the warm soft cocoon of her mouth.

Alex had not allowed herself to feel any physical pleasure in a long time—not since Feryle. Now that she had finally permitted Conner to release the pent-up fire, she felt as if she would explode from the overload of emotions. She clung to Conner as if she were her lifeline, holding on as Conner revived feelings she thought were lost forever, taking her over wave after wave of rolling passion. Alex threw her head back in the pillows and let out a mournful cry as she pushed Conner's shoulders, pleading for her to travel farther down her body.

Conner let herself be led, allowing Alex to tell her with her cries and urging hands what she needed. She prolonged the sweet torture, knowing the release would eventually be worth it to Alex.

When she finally reached the juncture of Alex's thighs and felt the soft curls against her cheeks, Conner could hardly contain her hunger. Inhaling Alex's sweet musky scent made Conner long to taste her, knowing the explosion that followed would consume them both.

Alex's skin was indescribably smooth, flawless, covering toned muscles. Conner nestled herself between Alex's legs, feeling the long, sensuous limbs as they wrapped around her shoulders and pulled her forward in a silent plea. Conner teased Alex's outer lips with her fingers, and gazed, for the first time, at the object of her desire. The small hard bundle of nerves was reaching out for contact, pleading for a touch, a kiss. Instead, Conner turned her head and gently bit the inside of Alex's thigh.

Alex bucked wildly at the sweet pain and tightened her grip on Conner's head, pulling her toward her center, to the hot wetness that could only be cooled by Conner's mouth and tongue.

Conner let herself be pulled in and kissed the outer lips, tasting the warm sweet need flowing from the other woman. She groaned in anticipation and felt her own hips press against the bed as she drew closer and with a tender touch kissed the core of Alex's being.

"Oh, Conner—yes, yes!"

Conner was overwhelmed with desire as she felt Alex's hips thrust up to meet her mouth and heard her cries. She moved closer still and tucked the bud between her lips, feeling spasms throughout Alex's body. She spread the outer lips wider and slowly licked the entire length of the shaft as Alex bucked beneath her.

"Conner, I need you. Please." Alex's voice was almost a growl as she reached down and led Conner's hand to the entrance to her sex.

Conner had an uncontrollable need to grind her hips against the bed beneath her. She could feel the wetness seeping from the folds that held her aching clitoris. She reached down, moaning as she felt the wetness between her own legs, and heard Alex whimper as the contact was broken. Delving deep for one luxurious moment, Conner felt the contractions as her body responded to her touch, then she pulled her fingers back out and up and slid them into the slick wet opening that was the core of Alex's being.

"Conner...oh baby, that feels so...good." Alex's breaths were torn and uneven as she rode the wave higher and higher.

Conner pressed deeper and upward. Slowly but firmly sliding her fingers in and out of Alex's womanhood, Conner stroked her to the peak. She slowed her movements and held Alex there, allowing her to linger, basking in the heavenly torture.

Alex's face glowed with desire. Eyes closed and her head thrown back in ecstasy, she waited, pleading for the rapturous release she knew was sure to come, if Conner would only permit it.

Drawing one arm under and around her leg, Conner gently opened Alex, completely exposing the small bud she knew would take her over the edge with just one touch. She eased closer, brushing her cheeks against the soft skin of Alex's thighs, hearing her moans of desire rise with every inch she traveled. Very slowly, she licked the swollen shaft in one long luxurious stroke, taking Alex over the edge of the abyss and holding her close as she fell into her orgasm.

"Oh, Conner, I'm—it's coming." Alex gripped Conner's head and pulled her closer. "Yes...don't stop...oh my God...Conner."

Hearing Alex's cries of release and feeling the contractions around her fingers sent Conner over the edge, and they both fell into a uniting orgasm. The surprising release shook Conner to the core, and she probed deeper, lapping up the liquid fire that flowed from Alex as her own body shuddered.

Alex had never had an orgasm rack her body like this one. Every cell in her body screamed and the blood surged from her brain to her core as Conner's tongue slowly caressed the screaming bud of nerves.

Conner gently licked and kissed the ultrasensitive nerves and felt the muscles contract as the orgasm overtook Alex's body in a long slow wave. She continued to gently press in and out as Alex's hips lifted to meet her thrusts, and after what seemed like a lifetime of rapture, she felt Alex's body relax into a satisfied exhaustion. Slowly licking and kissing the pulsing shaft, Conner let Alex settle quietly back to earth. She rubbed her cheeks against the inside of her thighs, savoring the aftershocks of her own release.

When their breathing slowed, Conner began to slide out, but Alex caught her, hand urging her to stay. "Don't leave me yet. I want to feel you inside me."

Conner could still feel the contractions as she pressed back inside, and Alex let out a slow moan as she pressed her legs against Conner's head. "Stay inside me and come up here. I want to feel you inside me when I kiss you."

Conner released a groan of her own and moved up, placing warm kisses on Alex's body on the way. When she reached Alex's face, she lowered her mouth to her lips, letting them both savor the lingering remnants of Alex's essence.

"You are so beautiful," was all Conner could say. She did not have the words to describe what Alex had just made her feel as she came beneath her lips and around her fingers.

Kissing Conner gently, Alex told her what she knew words could never convey. Her hands trailed a light path from Conner's shoulders down to her hips, where they pressed hard against her. They lay pressed together, their bodies glistening from their passion, taking pleasure in the warm glow that surrounded them. Alex began to draw small, invisible circles on Conner's back with her fingers. Hearing her ragged breaths suddenly stirred a need in her to taste and feel the woman that had brought her such pleasure.

She shifted and slid her leg between Conner's, watching the surge of heat in Conner's eyes as Alex's thigh made contact with the fire between her legs. In one slow motion, Alex rolled over, taking Conner with her, until Conner was pressed firmly beneath her body. Alex gently kissed her, pressing her tongue against the warm lips until they parted and she found the warm sweet tongue that had just brought her so much joy.

Alex could taste herself on Conner's mouth and felt her own body stir again as she remembered the orgasm that had racked her body only moments before. Surprised that she was already aroused again, she pressed herself against Conner's leg, relishing the sweet sensation.

Sliding down Conner' s torso, Alex paused at the hollow of her neck and placed a light kiss there before continuing her slow descent, savoring every inch of her body on the way. Pushing herself up on one hand, Alex slowly bit Conner's nipple.

"Oh, Alex," Conner moaned and wrapped her legs around Alex's waist, pulling her closer.

Smiling at the effect she had on Conner, Alex slowly took the nipple into her mouth, flicking it with her tongue until it was hard and she heard ragged gasps from Conner.

"God, you taste good." Alex's eyes were hooded with desire as she looked at Conner, wanting to devour all of her in one mouthful.

"Um, no, you taste better. I can still taste you. I want to taste you again, now," Conner growled, the need apparent in her dark eyes.

"Soon, love, soon. But right now, you're all mine," Alex said as she slid further down Conner's body. She leaned in to kiss the taut stomach and lick a small circle around Conner's navel. "You're all mine, and I don't want any distractions." Sliding further, she blew a light breath on the light curls between Conner's legs.

"I want to see your face when you come for me." She nipped at the soft skin of Conner's inner thigh.

Conner let out a long slow moan and reached for Alex's face. Cupping her cheek in her hand, Conner smiled and lifted her hips, silently telling Alex what she needed.

"Don't think I'm letting you off that easy," Alex said with an evil smile and bent to kiss the moist outer lips of Conner's sex. "I seem to remember you making me beg, and now it's my turn."

Alex's throaty growl sent shockwaves down Conner's spine as she felt Alex's lips graze her lower lips once more.

Alex caressed Conner's small firm breasts as she continued to tease her unmercifully. Using her free hand, she massaged Conner's lower legs, wanting to taste, feel, and touch every inch of her at once. Slowly, gently, and with featherlike touches, she caressed the soft skin beneath her fingers, finally reaching the hot, wet center of Conner's desire. She lifted Conner's legs over her shoulders and lowered her face to drink the sweet nectar that was, and could only be, Conner.

Alex inhaled the sweet musky scent and dove deeper as she ran her tongue beside the hard bundle of nerves, careful not to make contact.

Conner thrust her hips higher, urging Alex lower. Alex smiled and pulled back just enough to make Conner think she was leaving. Turning slightly upon hearing Conner's agonized whimper, she gently bit the swollen lips of Conner's sex, then slid her tongue across the wet slick folds, sending Conner to a new, more potent summit.

"Alex, oh God, please...touch me. I need you so much. Please." Conner's fingers were intertwined in Alex's soft mane. She pulled her closer, imploring, demanding a reprieve from the agonizing pleasure. Alex teased, licked, drank of her until Conner was begging for more.

"Alex—Alex, please...I-I need you inside me now...God, Alex, please." Conner succumbed to the passion, passion she had not allowed in her life for too long. She let herself fall, knowing Alex would keep her safe, would watch over her as she rode the waves of her desire.

Alex felt the change as Conner shed her protective shield. Having Conner allow her to experience this vulnerability made Alex tremble with a new desire for the woman beneath her. As Conner lay naked beneath her, her emotions and passion raw and exposed, Alex pulled her closer—embracing, nurturing, and encouraging the transformation from protector to protected. She celebrated the freedom their joining had brought and felt the passion of her rebirth rise to new heights.

In one swift movement, Alex dove her fingers deep into the fire and placed a long, slow kiss on the swollen bud, enveloping the warm, wet core with her lips.

The sudden overwhelming change in sensations drove Conner to the edge of the cliff and the muscles in her back convulsed, bringing her to a half-sitting position. Resting on her elbows, she opened her eyes and met the dark, penetrating gaze of the woman commanding her passion. The look in Alex's eyes conveyed the words she would not stop to utter, words that encouraged Conner to let go, to free herself, to feel the passion, to fall into arms that would protect her and not let her fall.

Alex felt the hot walls of Conner's core pulse as the first waves of the orgasm gripped her. Conner tucked her feet beneath herself, lifting her hips, trying to get the other woman deeper.

"Oh God, Alex, yes, harder, baby...I need you deep."

Alex curled her fingers, searching for and finding the spot she sought. Plunging hard, she lifted Conner higher and higher. Gently, almost reverently, she licked the hot, hard bundle of nerves, sucking it between her lips, feeling the spasms as Conner fell into the flood of her climax.

"Alex...oh my God...don't stop. Yes...oh yes." Conner gripped the back of Alex's head, pulling her deeper as she rode the waves of her orgasm.

As Conner floated peacefully back to earth, Alex moved upward, leaving her fingers buried in the wet, sweet core, and captured Conner's lips in her own, sharing the nectar of their joining.

Conner wrapped her arms tightly around Alex's shoulders and her legs around her firm hips. Holding each other close, the women let their breathing slow, lingering in the afterglow of their lovemaking, astounded by their awakened passion and need for one another.

Alex had not known desire this fierce in a long time, and the emotions had her spinning. For a fraction of a moment, Feryle's face flashed into her mind, and she felt a surge of disloyalty. She and Feryle had shared the same kind of intense passion in the first few years of their relationship before their passion changed from sexual lust to loving contentment. *Am I being unfaithful? No! Would Feryle want me to live life alone and lonely? Certainly not!* At that moment, Alex felt herself set free, not from the love they had shared—she never wanted to be free of those memories—but from the pain, the loss, the loneliness. She felt the weight of the last months lift from her shoulders as she held tight to the magnificent woman beneath her.

Conner could feel Alex trembling and reached to lift her chin. As she looked into the eyes of the woman she had just made love to, Conner saw a solitary tear slide down her cheek. She used the pad of her thumb to wipe the tear away.

"What's wrong?" Conner's heart lurched as she tried to interpret the reason for the tear. Frantic to know the reason, she asked, "Are you okay? Did I hurt you?"

Alex only swiveled her head to place a tender kiss on Conner's neck.

Letting her head fall to the pillow in frustration, Conner tore a hand through her hair. "Oh God, Alex, you hate me, don't you?"

Alex tried to speak but was cut off as Conner continued.

"Damn, I knew we should have taken things more slowly." Taking an exasperated breath, she cupped Alex's face in her hands. "God, Alex, don't push me away." A tear slid down the side of her face toward her ear. "I'm sorry, so sorry, I knew you weren't ready for this, but I just couldn't stop. I nev—"

Alex stopped the words with a deep kiss, one that took Conner completely by surprise. Alex's tongue pushed and probed, opening Conner's lips, and with passion, not words, she made her lover feel what she felt at that moment: peace, tranquility, the beginning flames of love.

As Conner realized that the tears Alex shed were tears of joy, not anguish, she wrapped her arms tightly around her and let herself flow into the warm embrace of their newfound love. Tongues probed, hands searched, and senses mingled as they once again took each other to the other side, only this time their descent was long, slow, warm, and in complete harmony with one another.

As their breathing slowed and they lay peacefully content within each other's arms, they slept.

Chapter Eight

The boat rocked gently in the changing tides. The moon was in full view through the hatch and cast a warm glow over the woman lying next to Conner. Conner watched as Alex slept, taking advantage of the chance to unself-consciously gaze at the perfect face and those perfect lips. She had never noticed how long and silky Alex's lashes were, but now with Alex's eyes closed she could appreciate their beauty. Conner smiled as she realized that she had never watched any of her previous lovers sleep and leaned down to place a feather light kiss on Alex's forehead as she recognized that she had never wanted to—until now.

For Conner, waking up early was rare. She was usually the last one awake, and certainly the last one to get up. She had never been a morning person. However, she thought that things just might change if she found herself waking up next to Alex on a regular basis. She could not resist the urge to reach out and trace a gentle line down Alex's jaw. As she did, Alex stirred, snuggling in closer to the warmth of Conner's body.

The cool morning air had drifted into the cabin from the open hatch. Careful not to wake Alex, Conner pulled the sheets up over their naked bodies. Gently nuzzling her face into the crook of Alex's neck, Conner breathed in her scent—the natural spicy scent of Alex herself and the aroma of their lovemaking. Pulling Alex closer, their bodies fitting together in a perfect spoon, Conner fell back into a gentle slumber.

When Conner next woke, she reached out for the warmth of the other woman and found nothing but a cool, empty bed. Opening her eyes, she looked around the cabin trying to ascertain if the weekend had all been a dream. Strewn on the floor were the clothes she and Alex had removed from each other the night before. Searching through the sheets for her shirt, Conner was startled when a naked Alex strolled into the cabin, smiling and holding out a cup of hot coffee.

"Good morning, sleepyhead." Conner took the coffee as Alex bent down to place a tender kiss on her lips. Conner curled her fingers behind Alex's neck and eagerly returned the gesture.

Crawling into the bed beside Conner, Alex snuggled close to steal some of the warmth radiating off her new lover. "It's a little chilly out there without any clothes on."

"Damn, and I thought you were just glad to see me." Conner laughed as she gently pinched one of Alex's hard nipples.

"Ah, God, woman, you'd better be careful, or I'll make sure that coffee gets cold before you get a chance to drink it."

After taking a long swallow of the hot liquid, Conner bent and captured the hard nipple in her mouth. The contrast of sensations sent Alex soaring, her hips involuntarily thrusting from the sensual assault.

"Conner," Alex whispered, "do you have any idea what you do to me?"

Conner continued with her early-morning exploration, capturing the other nipple in her mouth and gently biting it.

"Ooh, yes." Alex curled her fingers in Conner's hair and pulled her closer, leaning back to give her an unobstructed path to other regions of her body.

Conner released Alex's nipple with a slurp and a quick kiss. Raising her head and flashing a mischievous grin, she straddled Alex's hips and continued off the other side, landing lightly on her feet beside the bed.

"Hold that thought. Me—morning breath—gotta have toothpaste, toothbrush. Now," Conner said as she ran into the head.

"Damn, woman, you're killing me. Get back here."

Alex could hear the water running and the sounds of her new lover brushing her teeth. She smiled at the intimate closeness and realized just how comfortable she felt lying there naked in the daylight with Conner. She had not been that bold when she and Feryle had just gotten together. Somehow the thought did not bring her distress, just added another factor to the equation. She burst out laughing as she heard the other woman gargling in the other room.

"Woman, get out here now before you drown yourself."

Conner stepped though the door, wiping a mixture of toothpaste and mouthwash from her mouth. Throwing one leg across Alex, she once again straddled her, pressing her legs together tightly, forcing Alex's together as well.

"The only thing I plan to drown in this morning, Agent Montgomery, is you." Conner's husky voice hushed as she bent to take Alex's nipple in her mouth.

Alex lifted her hips, aching to bring Conner closer to her, needing to feel her inside. She lifted Conner's chin with her fingers, and as mouths parted, tongues dueled, and hands searched, their passion reached a new height.

Conner pulled away quickly, dark eyes focused on Alex's face. "I want to make love to you, Alex, slowly. I want to learn your body, I want you to tell me what you need, what you want me to do, where you want me to go, and how you want me to go there." She leaned in, sliding her tongue along Alex's bottom lip until she moaned.

"Oh, Conner," Alex sighed. "I want you...want you to—to..." She closed her eyes and bowed her head in embarrassment.

Conner gently lifted Alex's chin and placed a tender kiss on the tip of her nose. "I want you to talk to me. I want to know what you want...what you like...what you need. There's no reason to be embarrassed, love. I want to make you happy and give you what you need."

It was now Conner's turn to hide her eyes. "Anyway, it really turned me on last night when you talked to me." She gave Alex a sidelong glance and saw the dimples appear as she broke out in a grin.

The tension-filled moment now broken, the women continued their exploration of one another's bodies. Hands once again met flesh, mouth met lips, and soul met soul, as they felt the heat melt their hearts.

"I love the way you smell." Conner traced small kisses down Alex's chest. "I love the way you taste." She ran her tongue in circles around her nipple.

Pressing her hand against the back of Conner's head, Alex pulled her closer. "That feels so good." Her hips lifted in a silent plea.

Conner lifted her eyes to Alex's. Dark, half-closed eyes relayed to Conner what her touches were doing. Parting Alex's legs with hers, and lifting up on one hand, she leaned in for another kiss.

"You drive me crazy, Alex. It's all I can do to keep from ravishing you in an instant. Talk to me, tell me what you need."

"Ah, oh Conner, I need all of you...everywhere." Alex took Conner's hand and gently pushed down, taking Conner to the hot, wet heat below. Using her own fingers, she pushed Conner's inside.

"That's what I need. I need you inside of me."

Conner gasped as she felt the immense wetness. Taking Alex's hand, she turned it so Alex's fingers were inside along with hers.

"Do I do this to you? Make you this wet?" Conner's eyes were dark, her voice husky.

"Yes. Oh God yes, you do." Alex's hips bucked.

"Show me what you like, Alex." Conner slowly ground her hips, pressing their hands deeper.

Alex's eyes widened. She tried to move her hand, but was stopped by Conner's fingers intertwining with hers. Conner slowly turned Alex's hand until their fingers rested on the hard bundle of nerves and slowly moved Alex's fingers, making slow circles around the bud.

"Is that what you like?" Conner moved their hands in the slow circular motion. "Or do you like it like this?" She pressed their hands harder.

"Oh yes, like that."

Conner could feel the trembling in Alex's legs as she thrust her hips higher. She gently placed soft kisses along Alex's jaw line, then moved up to capture the warm lips that were parted, waiting for her. Running her tongue lightly over Alex's bottom lip, Conner smiled as she felt her respond to her kiss.

"See, Agent Montgomery, that wasn't so bad. Now tell me more," she demanded in a sultry voice.

Letting out a long sigh, Alex ground her hips harder into Conner's. "You're so, so bad, Officer Harris."

"No." Conner chuckled as she matched Alex's thrusting hips with her own. "I'm good, very good, and you're going to make me even better."

Conner moved her hand lower and slid two long slender fingers inside the other woman. When she felt Alex once again attempt to remove her hand, Conner held her there with her hips. "No I want you there. I want to watch you make yourself come for me."

"Ah, Conner," Alex growled. She bit her lower lip as she continued massaging the hard nub.

Conner slid lower on the other woman's body, planting light kisses along the way until she once again found Alex's nipple. She took it in her mouth, teasing it with her tongue and tenderly tugging with her lips.

"Yes. Damn, you feel so good inside me." Alex's hips were now moving in rhythmic motion with Conner's hand.

Conner continued her southward journey, stopping only for a moment to lick small circles in and around Alex's navel, causing Alex to moan again in her dark desire.

"God, Conner, please, I need to...need to feel your tongue. Please."

Settling between Alex's legs, Conner teased her more by placing soft kisses along her thigh and then moving up to kiss the warm lips of her sex. She slowly licked the swollen lips and could feel Alex's fingers brush against her tongue as she pleased herself, which sent Conner's hips into a frenzied thrusting of their own.

Pulling back, Conner laid her cheek against Alex's thigh and watched her rub her swollen bud as she continued to slowly pump her fingers. Conner had never seen anything as beautiful as her lover caressing herself, giving in to the passion she felt.

"Harder, baby. Go inside me deeper." Alex gasped as she rubbed her clit faster. "Now, Conner. I need you...please."

The contented moment was now replaced with a determination to please the woman beneath her. Conner pressed her fingers harder inside Alex, curling them until she found the spot she knew would send Alex over the edge.

"Ah, yes...oh God, Conner, don't stop."

Alex's hand was moving faster now, with a determined need. Conner joined Alex's fingers in their ministrations, licking Alex's clit and fingers and gently biting the swollen lips of her sex.

"Yes, oh, Conner, yes!" Alex screamed as she felt the first surges of the orgasm overtake her body.

Conner continued to lick Alex, now fighting for possession of the hard nub. She attacked the tender shaft, flicking her tongue in quick jabs.

Alex arched her back, bringing her hips closer to Conner's probing tongue as the first contractions started. Moving her hand and grabbing the back of Conner's head, she pulled her closer, burying Conner's face in her sex.

"Oh Conner...I'm coming, baby...don't stop."

Conner pushed her fingers into Alex in long deep thrusts, licking the shaft of her clit in long slow motions. Conner felt herself on the verge of an orgasm as she ground her hips into the mattress.

She almost lost control when she felt Alex's long soft leg slide against her wetness. She growled as she continued licking Alex, never slowing the rhythmic thrusts of her fingers into Alex's core.

Feeling the wetness between Conner's legs sent Alex over the edge. Thrusting her hips one last time, she felt her body convulse in the rapture of her orgasm.

"Ohh, Conner, yes—oh God...Conner."

Alex's head, once thrown back, now tilted forward so she could watch Conner pull the orgasm from her. She had never felt such intense pleasure and needed to look into the face of the woman giving her such a gift.

When their eyes met, it sent Conner over the edge in her own orgasm, and together they rode the waves, knowing something magical had just happened between them.

Finally, Alex's contractions slowed and her hips settled back onto the mattress. Conner continued nurturing Alex, careful not to hit the ultrasensitive nub, instead running long strokes along her swollen, now satisfied lower lips.

"Mmm, you taste so good," Conner growled. "I could stay here all day, tasting you, licking you." Conner looked up into Alex's half-closed eyes as she placed a long gentle lick along the slowly receding shaft.

Alex ran her fingers through Conner's hair and cupped her face in her hands. "And I could let you stay there, but I want you here holding me." Alex pulled Conner's shoulders, bringing her up against the length of her own body.

Conner lay against Alex for a few moments, her body warm and still trembling from the aftershocks of orgasm. She raised herself up on both hands and captured Alex's mouth in her own, delving deeply with her tongue as she shared the juices of their lovemaking. Alex took advantage of the distance Conner had created between them and cupped both of Conner's breasts in her hands, rubbing her thumbs lightly over the hard nipples.

"We're never going to get out of this bed if you keep that up."

Pinching the nipples lightly, Alex bit Conner's bottom lip as she responded in a throaty whisper. "I didn't intend to get up anytime soon."

Alex tucked her legs under Conner, forcing her to straddle her hips. In a slow, light caress, she ran her hands down Conner's side until she reached the taut muscles of her hips. Cupping one in each hand, she pulled Conner forward until the short curly hair of Conner's sex was mixed with hers.

In an attempt to keep her balance, Conner sat up straighter and grabbed hold of the built-in bookcases that served as the headboard. Alex once again took advantage of her movement, sliding her hand between their bodies and plunging into Conner in one swift movement. Conner's gasp of surprise lit a smile across Alex's face as she slid another finger into Conner.

"Ah, Alex," Conner screamed, as she tried desperately to hold herself upright. She pushed her hips forward, melting into the rhythmic thrusting of Alex's fingers. Not thinking she could stay in that position any longer, Conner began to lean, trying to roll them both over. Alex noticed the motion, and reached out to hold Conner on top of her.

"No way." Alex licked one of Conner's hard nipples. "You wanted me to tell you what I wanted. Well, this is it." She switched to the other nipple and gently bit it, sending another surge of heat through Conner's body.

"I want you sitting here on me, looking me in the eyes, while I make love to you."

Using her free hand, Alex wrapped her fingers in Conner's hair and pulled her head down so she could capture Conner's swollen lips in her own. Alex matched her thrusting fingers with her tongue, sliding it in and out of Conner's mouth.

Breaking free for a breath, Conner stared deeply into the other woman's eyes, saying, "God, you're beautiful," as she ground her hips harder against Alex's fingers. "So beautiful."

Alex flattened her hand and let Conner's weight press her clit against the palm of her hand. Seeing the lusty look on Conner's face and hearing her moans spurred Alex's courage.

"This is what I want." Conner's dark eyes stared into her own. "I want you to come for me, like this." She grasped Conner's hips with her free hand, pulling her harder and faster against her fingers. "I want to see your face, and you to see mine." Her fingers moved deeper. "And I want to hear you scream my name. I want to know I'm who you're thinking of when you come."

Conner's knuckles were white from gripping the bookcase. The blood boiled though her veins as Alex talked to her and told her what she wanted. Conner had never been this turned on by anyone, and she felt the hot juices of her desire as she slid over Alex's hand.

In one ravishing moment, Conner bent down to engulf Alex's mouth with her own, pushing her tongue deeply into her mouth, as she ground herself harder against her probing hand. Alex firmly rubbed Conner's nipple between her thumb and forefinger, sending Conner over the edge.

Conner arched her back, thrusting harder against Alex's hand, trying to get her fingers deeper. Her eyes locked with Alex's as the first spasms of her orgasm shook her.

"Alex...oh my God...baby, I'm coming...oh, do you feel it?"

Overwhelmed by Conner's words, Alex cupped Conner's face in her hands. "Yes, baby, I feel it. God, you're so tight...give it to me. Come on, let it go, I've got you," she whispered.

At Alex's urging, Conner let the rush overtake her and gave in to the torrent of spasms surging through her body. Looking into Alex's eyes, she saw warmth there like she had never seen before. Alex's eyes told her what she was not ready to put words to, told her what only making love could relay, that there was hope, there was a future for them, that there was at least, on some level, love wanting to break out of her long-protected heart.

"Ah, yes, it's yours, Alex, all yours. Take it...take it, baby."

Alex did, and plunged her fingers into Conner until she felt the muscles finally begin to relax. Conner's eyes never left Alex's as the spasms slowly receded and she came back down to earth. Still holding onto the bookcase, Conner slumped forward, breathing hard.

Alex sat up, sliding between Conner's outstretched arms, and held her, supporting her weight. Nuzzling her face into Conner's neck, she placed light kisses along her jaw line, slowly making her way to capture Conner's lips with her own.

"Thank you," she whispered. "You're so beautiful when you come."

With a shy look, Conner smiled and kissed Alex on the nose. "Why are you thanking me? I should be thanking you. I, um, think I got the best end of that deal."

"Hmm. Don't think so, I love to watch your face when you come. It's so intense, so—so intimate." Alex traced the scar under Conner's chin.

They lay in each other's arms, relaxing with the lazy morning. Soon, Alex's stomach growled its protest at being neglected, which made both women laugh.

"Well. I haven't been a very good hostess. I think we need to get some food into you before your stomach gets really pissed."

"Yes, well, I am a little hungry, not that I've noticed before now."

"Well, why don't you get some clothes on so I can concentrate, and I'll call Benny to come tow us in. Then we can go back to my house and make some breakfast."

"Sounds like a good plan to me. I'll bet Magnum will be ready for breakfast, too."

"Magnum," Conner groaned. "Damn, I'll bet that little shit has shredded everything in the house by now." She smiled sheepishly. "Actually, I hadn't even thought of him. I'm a baaad cat sitter."

"Well, as much as I hate to, we better get going. What time is it, anyway?" Alex asked as she slid out of the bed.

"It's just a little past six." Conner said, sliding out of the bed and reaching for Alex once again.

"Not a chance, missy. You want more of me, I need nourishment first." Alex slid from Conner's grasp, only to wrap her arms around her from behind.

Not being able to look in Conner's eyes made her next words easier to say. Nuzzling her face into Conner's hair, Alex breathed in the spicy smell of her shampoo.

"Conner, I don't know how to say this, and maybe I shouldn't at this point." Conner tensed as she anticipated Alex's next words. "But I just need to tell you that, um, I don't know what it is about you, but, um, anyway, I just want you to know I've had a great weekend, and I want you to know that—well, I don't usually, um, actually I've never, um...slept with someone on the first date, and, um...."

Conner felt Alex's uneasiness and turned in her arms. "Alex, it's okay. I feel the same way too, and, ah, although I can't say I'm as noble as you about the first date thing, this isn't just another one-nighter for me, Alex." Looking at anything but Alex's eyes, Conner continued. "I want to see more of you, Alex—a lot more, actually. I know things have been crazy in your life the past year, so I want you to tell me if I push too hard. Okay?"

Alex smiled and cupped Conner's face in her hands. "Okay, I want to see more of you too, and yes I will tell you if things get too intense too soon." Biting her bottom lip, she gave Conner a sidelong glance, then her eyes moved to the rumpled unmade bed they had just vacated. "Although I don't know if my body can stand anything more intense than what we just experienced."

Conner's face relaxed and her slight frown was replaced with a raised eyebrow and slanted smile. "Oh yeah? Well I have a whole lot more of that intenseness, whenever you're ready." Conner pulled Alex into her arms for a slow, tender kiss, and as their tongues explored, their breathing got heavier. Alex placed a hand on Conner's chest pushing her away and offered a bright dimpled grin.

"Food, you promised me food. Now go, call the tow boat, or whatever you call that thing, and get me food."

Conner radioed Benny at the marina and went below to make a fresh pot of coffee. She could hear Alex running a shower running in the forward cabin. Pushing away the temptation to join her, Conner searched for something solid for them to snack on while they waited for Benny. Finding some frozen bagels, she thawed them in the microwave and retrieved plates and cups from the cupboard.

Her mind wandered back to their morning together. In her wildest fantasies, Conner had never imagined that she and Alex would have spent the night making love. Yes, she was interested in her, but she had decided to take it slow and see what happened. *Maybe,* she thought, *it was just the romantic setting of the island and the boat. Set away from the rest of the world, we could pretend real life didn't exist.* Sighing heavily, she prayed that had not been the case. Hopefully, Alex would not get back to the city, back to what was once her and Feryle's home, and decide she had made a terrible mistake.

Seeing Alex step into the galley, Conner held up the plate of bagels. "Food, as I promised."

Alex had seen Conner's frown as she rounded the corner, and wondered what she was thinking. Although Conner's mood seemed to be jovial, Alex noticed a thread of strain in the smile.

Shaking off her curiosity, she mock-snarled, "Food? You call that food? I want eggs, bacon, toast, and juice. I want the works."

"Hey, it's all I could come up with in this tub. I'll get you food when we get back on land, but for now, nibble of these meek offerings, and quit snarling." Conner laughed. "Are you always this grouchy when you're hungry?"

"Actually, no; I'm usually worse. It just happens that I woke up in a great mood this morning, so the hunger didn't irritate me so much." Huffing and chuckling at the same time, Alex grabbed a bagel from the plate.

"Hmm, well I'll have to remember to always make sure you wake up in a good mood, Agent Montgomery." Conner was busy putting jam on her bagel but stole a glance at Alex, who was now in a full blush.

"Uh-huh, I guess you just might have to do that, Officer Harris."
Alex moved closer to Conner and bent to kiss a spot of jam off her lip.

"Um, maybe I do like this kind of breakfast. Quite tasty."

Just as Conner was about to take advantage of Alex's closeness, she
heard Benny pull up alongside them. Sighing hard, she moved to the
ladder to go above. "Damn his timing," she growled.

Alex chuckled and climbed up behind her, taking the opportunity to
admire Conner's muscular legs as they disappeared through the
companionway.

Conner and Alex helped Benny tie the boat up in preparation for the
tug back to the marina. As they got underway, Conner went below to
retrieve their pre-breakfast snack. The women sat lounging in the
cockpit, enjoying the scenery and chatting about their weekend.

"I'm a member of the local sailing club. Sometimes we have
weekend cruises to different islands and towns up and down the coast.
There is one in a few weeks, and, um, well, if you're interested, I could,
well, put us on the list."

"Hmm," Alex almost purred. "Sounds like a relaxing and fun trip.
Why don't you tentatively write us in, and when you have the dates and
all the other information, we can make a decision then, 'kay?"

"Great, I'll have Benny pencil us in when we get back to the
marina."

Conner spent the rest of the short trip telling Alex about the Naval
Submarine Support Base at King's Bay, adjacent to Amelia and
Cumberland Islands. Benny's tug had been forced to give passage to an
incoming submarine, and both women had been struck by the contrast
between the unspoiled natural environment and wild horses feeding in
the marsh off Cumberland on one side and the passage of a nuclear
submarine as it made its way through the channel back to St. Mary's on
the other.

"Wow, talk about coming back to reality," Alex said in a quiet
voice.

Conner was not sure if Alex was speaking only of the ending of
their weekend escape, or if she was referring to her entire life. She placed
a hand on Alex's back. "You know, coming back to reality doesn't mean
we have to forget the last couple of days. We can take them home with
us."

"I know, I didn't mean what you're thinking. I'm sure I'll not forget
this weekend." Alex kissed the tip of Conner's nose, gently tracing the
line of her jaw with one finger. "After all, you'll probably have a little
scar right there on your chin to always remind us of this weekend."

Conner rolled her eyes and smirked. "All right already. I know I've
been a klutz, but it was only because you had me so stressed."

The two women laughed, leaned back in a relaxed comfort with one another, and soon they were back in the marina. Conner had Benny write them in for the sailing trip and asked him to check the engine and have the *Shady Lady* ready to sail the next weekend. Although she had not asked Alex, she was silently hoping for another weekend getaway.

Raising the garage door, Conner could not help but smile at the Jeep sitting in the other stall. *Looks like it belongs there*, she thought.

"My Jeep seems to like the luxury of your garage," Alex mused. "She just might have to come visit more often...doesn't get this kind of treatment at home."

"Well, she's welcome to come visit anytime she wants. Oh yeah, and by the way, you're, um, welcome to tag along, too, if you want." Conner added the last part with a teasing grin as she hit the button to lower the garage door, then took Alex in her arms. Placing a gentle kiss on Alex's lips, she sat back and let out a satisfied sigh. "I've wanted to do that since Benny showed up."

The women headed into the house and were met by a very attention-deprived and very energetic Magnum. The cat pounced on Conner just as she cleared the door, causing her to scream and fling the bag of groceries she held in her arms to the floor.

Plucking the cat off her shoulder, she held him just under his front arms and dangled him in front of her face. "Jesus, you little shit. You trying to kill me or something?"

The cat meowed and swatted Conner on the nose, and she shrieked with pain as the tiny needle-sharp claws contacted her skin.

The sight had Alex almost in tears, and she held her stomach as she laughed. "God, Conner, I hope I never see the day some big bad drug dealer sneaks up behind you." She could not keep from grinning as she watched the staredown Conner carefully staying out of the swatting range of Magnum's claws.

Conner dropped the cat gently to the floor and wrinkled her nose at Alex. "Har har. Drug dealers I can handle, cats—well, at least this particular one has managed to get the best of me."

The women picked the groceries up off the floor and headed to the kitchen as Magnum trailed behind, being very vocal about his hunger.

"Well, I think he's just precious," Alex said, bending over to scoop up the cat. "See, he's not a bad boy; listen to him purr." As if the cat and Alex had conspired against Conner, Magnum raked his rough tongue against Alex's face, then nuzzled her neck.

"Damn cat. Well, you can feed the precious little baby while I go get cleaned up," Conner growled as she tried to hide her smile. "I'll be back in a few. Make yourself at home. There's juice in the refrigerator if you want some."

As she entered her bedroom, she noticed the blinking light on her answering machine. She hit the play button and listened to the messages as she turned on the shower and got clean clothes from her closet. The first message was from Seth, telling her he would be by Monday night to pick up Magnum.

"Couldn't be too soon for me, pal."

The next was a message from someone wanting to sell her vinyl siding.

"Go stick your vinyl siding up your—why am I talking to the damn machine?"

The next message got Conner's full attention. "Conner, this is Peterson. I wanted to let you know there has been some progress in the Hernandez case and we are having a task force meeting tomorrow at 8:00 a.m. I want you there, so be prepared to give a complete update on all you have so far. Oh, yeah, I almost forgot. We have some new people coming in on this case, and I'll need you to provide them with copies of everything you have. Uh, Conner, I—well, just get a good night's sleep. Looks like it's going to be a long week."

Conner stood and stared at the machine. Peterson rarely called her at home unless it was important. He knew how much this case meant to her. *That monster murdered one of my ex-lover's best friends.* Running her hand through her hair, she realized there was yet another important factor involved that made this case even more important to her now: Sam's friend, Feryle Hughes, was also the partner of the woman Conner had just spent the weekend making love to.

"Damn, Harris, you always have to go and complicate things, don't you?" Conner said to herself as she hit the erase button on the machine. Heading for the shower, she was glad for a few minutes by herself. She was going to need it before facing Alex again.

Standing in the shower, Conner thought about what this could mean for her and Alex. She was sure Alex would not be thrilled about Conner's involvement in the case. *Maybe, just maybe, I can end this thing without Alex having to know.* She quickly finished her shower and headed back to the kitchen.

Conner stopped short and her frown turned to a pleasant smile as she spied Alex lying on the sofa, asleep. Magnum had crawled onto her chest and was nestled between her breasts in a peaceful slumber.

"Damn, cat. She better not have a scratch on her when you two wake up, or you'll be needing all of your remaining lives, got it?" Conner whispered as she scratched the top of the purring cat's head. She quietly headed to the kitchen to fix breakfast.

Alex woke up to the purring cat on her chest and lay there stroking his head as she listened, laughing at Conner in the kitchen. Magnum quickly tired of the bouncing and jumped down. Alex stretched, thankful for the power nap, but felt guilty for leaving Conner to do the cooking. It was obvious from the grumbling and clanging that culinary traits were not in the woman's genetic makeup.

"Ahem. You need some assistance, Chef Harris?" Alex leaned against the doorframe, attempting to hide her amused look. Conner was on her hands and knees searching through a cabinet; for what, Alex was not quite sure.

"No thanks," Conner said defiantly, self-consciously brushing flour off her sleeve. "I can manage."

Sitting back on her haunches, she growled, "Just because cooking isn't one of my favorite pastimes doesn't mean I can't fix a simple breakfast."

Alex walked over to the stove and looked at a very interesting concoction in the skillet. "Mm-hmm, and just what are you preparing for this glorious meal?"

"It's a old family recipe called Sailor's Sunrise. It's one of my favorites." Conner took Alex by the arm and led her toward the door. Giving her a little nudge, she ordered Alex out of her kitchen. "You need to go outside on the deck and enjoy the morning and get out of my way, so we can eat before midnight."

Alex let herself be led out onto the deck and placed in a chair. "Okay, okay, but call me if you need any help."

"Thanks, but I won't. Just relax and enjoy the fresh air. I'll have everything ready in a few minutes." Conner retreated to the kitchen to fight the culinary demons.

Alex sat on the deck, thinking about the weekend she and Conner had spent together. She knew Sam and Kelly had been disappointed when she'd called Saturday morning to cancel their cookout. However, both women did seem to shrug off their disappointment when they found out Alex and Conner were going sailing together.

Leaning her head, Alex smiled. "Boy, would they ever be surprised to find out what I've been up to this weekend."

"Hey, I didn't mean to bore you so much you started talking to yourself." Conner walked out into the warm sunshine and sat on the end of Alex's deck chair.

"Not bored, just thinking about Sam and Kelly."

Conner looked out over the ocean, a frown crossing her face, causing a thin line to crease her forehead. "I take it they didn't approve of you going sailing with me."

Taking Conner's hand, Alex gave Conner a reassuring smile. "Not at all. They were not happy I called to cancel. However, when they found out what I had planned, they were more than happy to reschedule. Sam loves to play matchmaker, so you should probably be warned that she'll most likely call to have you over next weekend."

Conner couldn't read Alex's expression, so she decided to just jump in and see if there was any water in the pool. "And what do you think of that? Would that be okay with you?"

A deep frown crossed Alex's face; her lips pinched tightly together. "Well, Conner, you know, I'm not sure. I mean, if you had to choose between facing Sam and Kelly all alone, getting drilled to no end, or having someone there by your side to protect you," Alex broke out in a grin, "Which would you choose? Of course, silly, I want you there. I'd ask you myself—actually, I will now. Let's keep it our secret, though, so Sam and Kelly can enjoy their scheming."

Conner's shoulders noticeably relaxed. "'Kay. Now, my lady, time for breakfast."

Alex was pleasantly surprised at the breakfast Conner had prepared. The interesting concoction she had earlier spied in the skillet was now a delicious mixture of eggs, bacon, mushrooms, onions, cheese, several ingredients that she did not recognize, and of course shrimp. This was set on a bed of fluffy white rice and accompanied by what tasted like homemade buttermilk biscuits and jam.

After stuffing themselves, both women sat back, rubbing their stomachs. "I think I'm going to explode," Alex groaned. "I have to correct my previous observation. You certainly didn't look like you were very astute in the kitchen when I walked in, but you just proved yourself to me. I stand corrected."

Conner blushed a bright red. "Well, I have to admit, it's probably the only thing I do cook well, but thanks. I'm glad you enjoyed it."

"I did. And since you cooked, I get to clean," Alex said, standing and picking up the empty dishes.

"No way. My house, my kitchen, my mess," Conner countered.

After a few minutes of friendly arguing, Alex won out and sent Conner on her way to the deck.

As Conner sat on the deck listening to Alex move around in the kitchen, she could not help but think of how natural it sounded and felt. She knew she was setting herself up for a big disappointment if things did not work out between them, but she decided to just enjoy the experience and worry about the fall later if it came.

Once the dishes were done, Alex wanted a tour of the island. They climbed into Alex's Jeep, so they could enjoy the open top, and headed out with Conner at the wheel.

Conner took Alex down to the city marina. They spent a couple of hours strolling through the various shops along the brick-paved streets, moving easily among the other tourists. Then they drove to Fort Clinch State Park, a Civil War-era fort that overlooked Cumberland Sound, where they enjoyed a leisurely walk. Before they realized it, the day had swept by and dusk was settling over the island.

Walking back to the Jeep, Alex thought of how much she had enjoyed the weekend and realized that she was not ready for it to end. However, she did have a busy day the next day; it would be her first day back at the local FBI field office, and she knew it would be stressful in many ways. She had not been back in the building since the warehouse raid, and she knew that just walking through the door would stir up a flood of emotions.

Conner watched as Alex's face took on a dark mask. She walked silently beside her, deciding to let Alex talk if she wanted and be content to just be with her if she did not.

"It's getting dark, and as much as I don't want to, I guess I had better be heading back to the city."

"I know. I've enjoyed it too." They were simple statements, but carried a lot of meaning for both women.

When they arrived back at Conner's, the women quietly began to gather Alex's belongings. After stowing everything in the Jeep, Alex returned to the house to say her good-byes to Conner.

Conner was standing at the window, looking out at the receding tide. Alex eased in behind her and embraced her before planting a kiss on her neck.

"Mmm, you taste so good." Alex continued to kiss Conner's neck. Moving her hands in small circles, she caressed the taut muscles of Conner's stomach. Alex could feel an excited tension building in Conner's body that caused her own body to react.

Deciding to toss all caution to the wind, Alex nibbled on Conner's earlobe and whispered, "You know, it's only about an hour's drive from here to my house, and it's really not that late. What do you think about giving me another tour of your bedroom before I go?"

Conner let out a primitive growl as she turned in Alex's arms. She pressed her lips against Alex's forehead in a tender kiss, and without saying a word, took Alex by the hand and led the way down the hall.

The room was dark, only the fading light seeping through the blinds, as Conner reached for Alex.

Alex gently took Conner's arms, placing them by her side, and then took hold of the top button of Conner's shirt. "You have made me feel so good this weekend, made me feel so many wonderful things I never thought I would feel again. Now it's my turn to make you feel some of the same things. I want to make love to you like you did to me this morning. I want you to talk to me, tell me what you want. I want to be the one to take you there."

Conner gasped as she felt Alex slowly unbutton her shirt. She felt electric shocks each time Alex's fingers met her skin. After what seemed like forever, Alex gently pushed the shirt off Conner's shoulders and nipped the tender skin in the hollow of her neck. Conner shook her arms to shrug off the shirt and reached up to wrap her arms around Alex.

Alex quickly grabbed Conner's arms and once again placed them by her side. With a quick bite to her collarbone, hard enough to get her attention but not be too painful, Alex locked eyes with her lover.

"I want you to be very still. Don't move, understand? The only thing I want you to do is talk to me." With a mischievous grin, she added, "I'll do all the work, you just lay back and enjoy the ride." She reached between Conner's breasts and unhooked her bra. In one fluid motion she pulled it off Conner's shoulders, leaving her naked from the waist up.

By now, Conner's breaths were coming in shuddering gasps. Both women could feel the heat radiating off her. Conner's knees gave away just as Alex gave her a slow push, effectively sitting her on the side of the bed.

Standing over Conner, Alex gave her an evil grin and pushed her shoulders back, sending Conner into a prone position with her feet hanging off the side of the bed.

Conner moaned as Alex leaned over her body to suck on one of her hard nipples. Resisting the urge to pull Alex closer, she tucked her hands behind her head and watched as Alex continued undressing her.

Alex unbuckled Conner's belt and opened the snap. Letting her hands roam freely, she caressed the hard tight muscles of Conner's stomach before grasping the zipper of her jeans and pulling it down slowly. Conner's chest rose and fell in quick thrusts as she tried unsuccessfully to control her breathing. Alex let her gaze completely flow over Conner's upper body as she hooked her fingers in the jeans.

The only movement Alex allowed the lifting of Conner's hips as she pulled the jeans down. After removing Conner's shoes, Alex pulled the jeans off her legs and stepped back to admire the beautiful woman lying before her. She felt a rush of heat surge down her as she let her eyes fall on the trimmed hair between Conner's legs. Slowly, she lifted each of the long slender legs and placed them on the edge of the bed. She gently pushed Conner's knees apart, allowing her an unobstructed view of Conner's sex.

Alex stepped back and, never breaking eye contact with Conner, slowly removed her clothes, piece by piece, until she stood completely naked. In the back of her mind, Alex could not believe her own actions.

She still could not understand what it was about Conner that made her want to be this daring. She shook off her inner self and stepped between Conner's legs. Conner let out a ragged breath at the slight touch of their skin.

Placing one hand on each inner thigh, Alex slowly stroked the sensitive skin. As she reached the juncture of her legs, Conner whimpered and thrust her hips out to meet Alex's hands. Alex ignored the silent pleas and continued up her stomach until she reached the small mounds of Conner's breasts.

Planting her hands on each side of Conner's head, Alex bent in and captured her lips as Conner reached a hand behind Alex's neck. Grabbing her hand and pushing it back down, Alex nipped Conner's neck.

"Looks like you're going to be uncooperative." Putting on her best interrogation face, Alex asked, "Am I going to have to handcuff you to the bed to keep you still, Officer?"

"Oh God." Conner's eyes were dark and hooded as desire swept through her body. No one had ever made her feel what Alex was making her feel at that moment, and her body responded with an almost violent need to be satisfied.

Alex knew she was driving the woman crazy with her teasing, and it only spurred her on for more. "Are you going to be good, or am I going to have get mean?" Alex ducked once again and bit Conner's neck.

The passion driving Conner had sent her imagination into a frenzied state, and she decided that two could play this game. "Looks like you're going to have to get mean, Agent, 'cause I have no intention of being good tonight." Conner watched Alex's face as her eyes turned a deep blue and closed halfway. In a surprise attack, Conner slipped a hand free and pinched Alex's hard nipple, rolling it between her fingers.

Alex took in a shuddering breath before recovering and grabbing Conner's hand, once again pushing it above her head. Keeping Conner's hands pinned, Alex captured her lips and plunged her tongue deep into Conner's mouth. Tongues dueled for control as Alex slid up and straddled Conner's body, rendering her helpless.

Breathing hard, Alex finally broke the kiss and stared into Conner's eyes.

"Do you feel how wet I am for you?" Alex growled as she slid across Conner's stomach, each stroke teasing the hard bud buried between her swollen lower lips.

"Yes."

"Do you want to taste me, Conner?"

"Yes." Conner was now grinding her hips up in an effort to make contact, although Alex had purposely positioned herself out of reach.

"Well, if you want me, you had better behave, or I'll stop. Do you understand me?"

Conner's eyes turned dark, and she growled in agreement.

"Do not move, not a muscle, unless I say you can—got it?"

"Yes." Conner would have agreed to anything as long as Alex kept touching her.

Alex removed one of her hands and caressed the side of Conner's face. With intense tenderness, she placed light pecks across her forehead, eyes, nose, and cheeks, and finally captured her mouth in a long, passionate kiss. Conner felt her senses reeling as Alex's tongue explored her mouth.

As Alex continued her exploration, she dropped her hand to Conner's side and traced a light path up her ribs, sending tremors through her body. Smiling through her kisses, she eased down further and released Conner's arms. To her surprise, Conner left her arms above her head and allowed Alex full access to her body.

Feeling more certain of herself, Alex slid off Conner's stomach and again stood between her parted legs. She bent and continued trailing a path of kisses over Conner's body, stopping to suck on first one nipple, then the other. Raising her head, she saw Conner watching her and noticed that she had grasped the sheets in her fists.

In the boldest move Alex had ever made, she lifted one leg and placed it on the bed, allowing Conner a full view.

Conner stared at Alex's hot, glistening core, and thought she would die from her need to reach out and touch her. Instead, she gripped the sheets tighter, wanting and needing to experience every second of Alex's fantasy.

Alex saw Conner swallow hard, and unconsciously licked her lips in anticipation. She pinched Conner's nipple, just enough to get her attention. When their eyes met, Alex reached down and buried her fingers inside herself.

Conner's moan was indescribable. Her face had turned a dark shade of red, and for a moment, Alex thought she had pushed her too far. Finally, Conner took a deep shuddering breath and her natural color returned.

"You like it when I do this, don't you?"

"God, yes. Please, Alex, let me touch you?"

As she continued to stroke herself, Alex smiled and spread her legs further apart. "Not yet, lover." She slowly removed her fingers and leaned over Conner, parting her lips with her wet fingers. "I will, however, give you a little taste."

"Ahh, Alex." Conner greedily licked Alex's fingers, sucking the warm juices off them and quietly whimpering as her need to be touched increased.

"Do you want me inside you?" Alex asked as she let her fingers trail down Conner's body, stopping just at the hairline of her sex.

"Yes." Conner lifted her hips, her need now reaching a point of desperation.

Alex slowly let her fingers fall until she felt wetness. Kneeling between Conner's legs, Alex gently traced the folds of Conner's lower lips, gently parting them with her thumbs. Beginning at Conner's left knee, she placed slow, torturous kisses along the length of Conner's thigh. When she reached the tender cleft, she paused for only a second before gently enfolding the hard nub between her lips.

Conner's hips bucked wildly as the contact sent tremors throughout her body. "Oh my God, Alex." Her words came in shudders as Alex's tender lips rhythmically squeezed and her tongue placed feathery touches directly to the tip of the ultrasensitive nerves.

Alex continued her slow movements while watching Conner's face. As Conner bucked, Alex plunged three fingers deep into her, sending her into a frenzy of motion.

"Alex, God, I need to touch you, please. Alex, please...come here."

As Conner screamed her name, Alex felt her own body spasm and knew she could no longer deny Conner's need. Remaining deep inside, she slid her body up onto Conner's and felt the electricity surge through her body in response.

Conner released the sheets and wrapped her arms tightly around Alex's neck. Their tongues dueled in their united passion as Alex felt her body cry out for relief.

Conner pulled her mouth away and took a shuddering breath. "Alex, I need to taste you now, please let me...I've done what you wanted, now I need this...please."

Alex smiled and placed a warm kiss on Conner's lips, and then she slowly rolled off her body and sat up, looking down at Conner. For a moment, Conner thought Alex was going to make good on her threat and quit. Just as she was about to protest, Alex bent and placed a trail of kisses down Conner's stomach. When she reached the soft line of hair leading to Conner's sex, she lifted her leg and straddled Conner's face, allowing full access to her desire.

Conner wrapped her arms around Alex's legs, and just as she was leaning in to kiss the swollen folds of her outer lips, Alex plunged her fingers deep inside of Conner once again, sending her into another passionate whirl.

Conner buried her face in Alex's sex, raking her tongue the length of the hard, swollen shaft. The muffled moans of both women continued as they matched each other stroke for stroke. They held on as they soared higher and higher until at last they fell in unison into their orgasms.

After a few minutes, their breathing slowed and Alex turned around to face Conner. When their eyes met, Alex saw a smirk on her lover's face.

"Hey," Alex said before placing a warm kiss on Conner's lips.

"Hey yourself." Conner maintained their eye contact. She wanted Alex to squirm a little, so she just lay there quietly looking at her.

Squirming was exactly what Alex was doing, and a lot of it. She ducked her head, breaking the eye contact, and gently bit Conner's jaw.

"Hmm, you really know how to make a woman feel good, you know." Alex tipped her eyes up and gave Conner an innocent grin.

"Uh-huh."

Alex, nervous that she had taken things too far and not quite knowing what to do next, placed her hand on Conner's chest. As she was pushing up into a sitting position, Conner pounced.

In one smooth quick motion, Conner flipped Alex over and somehow managed to straddle her, pinning Alex solidly to the bed. Grabbing Alex's hands, she shoved them above Alex's head and held them there.

"You will pay, and pay dearly, for that little stunt." As Conner grinned, Alex let out a relieved sigh. "However, I will require at least an entire night, and considering the late hour, I'll reserve my revenge for another time." Conner nipped Alex's earlobe. "So be prepared, my dear," she kissed her nose, "for a night of sensual torture."

Alex laughed as she threw her arms around Conner's neck and hugged her close. "I've had such a great time this weekend. I don't want it to end." Turning her head and glancing at the clock, she groaned. "As much as I hate to, I need to get going. My first day back is tomorrow, and I have an early meeting."

"I know. I don't want it to end either, but we have lots of time. We'll be together soon." Conner nuzzled Alex's neck and took in one last breath of her scent. She slid off Alex and they began to dress slowly, neither wanting to, preferring to crawl back into bed to hold each other as they fell asleep.

They made small talk until they reached the door to the garage. Alex turned and pulled Conner close, kissing her deeply, trying to satisfy her need until they could be together again.

"Will you be at the precinct in the morning, or out on the streets?" Alex asked.

"I'll be in until around ten or so, then I'll probably head out."

"Good. You mind if I give you a call sometime in the morning?"

"Actually, I'd be upset if you didn't. I want to know how your first day back is going. Maybe we can, uh, maybe get together for lunch. That is, if you have the time."

"I'll make the time for lunch. I'll call you and we can decide where we want to go, okay?" Leaning in for one last kiss, Alex held Conner close for a few moments before straightening and turning to climb into the Jeep.

"Please drive carefully, okay?" Conner said, as she leaned in for another quick kiss.

"I will. Sweet dreams, Officer Harris. I know mine will be." Alex grinned as she started the Jeep and backed out of the garage.

Conner watched Alex drive off until the taillights disappeared into the night. She slowly turned and went back into the house, realizing for the first time how quiet and empty her condominium seemed.

She fed Magnum and headed for bed. As she lay there, she could smell Alex's perfume on the pillows and sheets. She tossed and turned for an hour before getting up and searching through the kitchen until she found a bottle of scotch. She poured herself a large shot and knocked it back in one swallow. Turning, she saw Magnum staring at her curiously.

"Yeah, hotshot, I'm miserable. Go to bed and leave me alone."

She turned and headed back to her room. She lay on her side and hugged the pillow. After what seemed like forever, she fell into a peaceful sleep, dreaming of the mysterious woman who had swept into her life and stolen her heart in just a few short days.

Chapter Nine

The alarm broke rudely into Alex's dreams, and she slapped impatiently at the snooze button. She rolled over onto her stomach and buried her head beneath the pillow, determined to get another few minutes' sleep. She had not arrived home until almost midnight, and by the time she got her briefs and files organized for the morning's meeting, it was almost 2 a.m. Now, at 6 a.m., she was wishing she had gotten to bed earlier. *On second thought,* she decided, *no,* because that would have meant forgoing the previous night's lovemaking. Just the thought of their last hour together sent a tingle down her spine.

Rolling over, she stared at the ceiling, remembering the heat, the passion, and the explosive orgasms they had shared. Without her knowledge, her hand drifted up and began rubbing a nipple that was quickly coming to life. Alex became aware of her roaming hand as a surge of heat rolled through her body.

"Damn, you're hopeless, Montgomery," she mumbled as she threw the covers back and sat on the edge of the bed. Shutting off the clock, she eyed the last photograph she had taken of Feryle. Picking it up, she stared down at the woman she had thought she would spend the rest of her life with. She traced a finger over the glass, outlining the smiling lips of her lover, and wondered if Feryle would approve of her budding relationship with Conner.

"I do, and will always, love you, Feryle." Alex often sat and talked to Feryle's photograph. Somehow it made her feel closer, and more alive. Now she was looking at the photograph, asking for acceptance, for understanding. As she sat and watched the face smiling back at her, a tear gently splashed across the glass. Wiping the moisture from the frame, she reverently placed it back on the nightstand and stood, not sure if she was ready to face the morning. Her muscles screamed as she straightened, and although the pain was uncomfortable, she smiled. "Guess I'm getting too old to be romping around the bedroom," she said as she headed for the kitchen.

After a quick cup of coffee and a bagel, Alex headed for the shower. Dropping her robe on the bed, she moved to the bathroom and turned the shower on. She brushed her teeth while waiting for the water to heat. As she stood, she caught her reflection in the mirror. There was something different about her face, but she couldn't quite put her finger on what it was. Shrugging off the question, she stepped under the shower and let the warm water and steam relax her sore muscles. As she lathered her body, she noticed a small mark just above her breast. She shook her head and laughed as she realized that Conner had marked her. Chuckling to herself, she tried to remember the last time she'd had a hickey. It had to have been when she was in college, maybe earlier that that. Normally she would have been furious, but for some reason, now she just thought it was cute.

When Alex got out of the shower, she noticed the time and knew she had to hurry if she was going to be on time for her 8:00 meeting with Jack Peterson. Her heart raced as she thought of the surprise she had in store for Conner, showing up to say hello.

As she drove into the city, Alex listened to an oldies rock station and soon found herself singing along with the music. She had decided to keep the top off the Jeep so that the morning air could finish waking her up. She pulled into the parking garage and had to drive up the ramp to the third level before she found any available spaces. She was running late, and the garage was deserted. As she headed toward an empty space she spotted Frank Bivins walking toward the stairs. He turned and looked in her direction, and Alex could tell by the way he stopped dead in his tracks that he had recognized her from Friday night. She took her time parking. Pulling her briefcase from the back, she turned and headed toward the stairwell.

Alex was about a half flight away from the ground level when she turned the corner and saw Bivins leaning against the wall. Slowing, she eyed him cautiously and continued on her way past him. She was almost by him when a hand grabbed her arm. Stopping, she slowly turned her head as she struggled to keep her temper under control.

"Is there something I can help you with, Officer Bivins?"

"I was just going to ask how your weekend was, Agent Montgomery."

Alex gave Bivins her best smirk. "My weekend was fine—well, except for a few sand fleas that crawled up on my beach Friday night." She gave Bivins a challenging smile. "However, I shooed them away, and hadn't really thought about it again until I saw you. Hmm, wonder why that is, you think?"

Bivins's face turned almost purple. He tightened his grip on her arm and pulling Alex roughly into his chest, he dipped his head beside her ear, breathed heavily, and growled, "You're new in town, Montgomery. You'll play nice if you know what's good for you. I finally got Harris to understand; maybe during your next romantic stroll on the beach she can fill you in on the details."

Alex took a deep breath and forced her body to relax, even though she was coiled and ready to strike. She tested the fingers on the hand pressed against his chest and slowly slid them up to his shoulders. Looking sheepishly up into his eyes, she whispered, "You're right, I-I'm sorry. Maybe we did get off on the wrong foot. I do want and need the help of the local police force, and I want us all to get along."

Bivins loosened his grip and grinned. "I knew you'd understand. We all have our *place* around here, right?"

"Yes."

Bivins was now boldly looking down the front of Alex's blouse. Licking his bottom lip, he tore his eyes away from her breasts and met her gaze. "Maybe sometime soon we can get together and I can show you around town, what do you say?"

"Well, I'm not sure that would be a good idea."

Bivins leaned in so close Alex could feel his breath on her face. "And why not? I'm sure I could show you a *real* good time, Agent."

Alex gave Bivins an embarrassed smile. "Well, you know, it's just that—" With lightening quick reflexes, she brought her knee up and drove it deep into Bivins's crotch. Stepping back, she grinned as she watched him grab himself and slide down the wall. As he lay on the floor groaning, Alex noted that his face had turned an unusual color of faded green. Chuckling, she knelt down, then took his chin in her hand and slammed his head back into the concrete wall, looking him dead in the eyes.

"Don't ever, and I mean ever, threaten me again. Is that clear?"

Bivins groaned and pulled away. Alex grabbed his hair and lifted his face up to meet hers. "You may think you're some big tough cowboy cop, but if you give me even the smallest reason, I'll smash you like the maggot you are."

She turned to walk the rest of the way down the stairs, but stopped and turned once more to see him still groaning on the floor. "Don't fuck with me, Bivins. I am way above your Little League games. I was nice to you the other night and let you save face in front of Officer Harris, but I don't give second chances." With that, she turned and walked the rest of the way down the stairs and out into the fresh air.

Taking a few deep breaths to settle herself, Alex moved through the door of the precinct. She fought her way through the mass of uniformed police heading out the door to their assignments. She finally managed to reach the main desk and was greeted by the jovial man Conner had fondly called Buet.

"Good morning, Agent, uh, Montgomery, right?"

"Yes, and good morning to you."

Buet had dropped his pen on the desk and was shuffling some papers as he asked what her could do for her.

"I have a meeting with Captain Peterson. I know I'm a little late, so if you could just point me in the right direction."

"Don't worry, they all just got in there themselves. First door on your left."

Alex yelled a "thanks" over her shoulder as she walked down the hall, frustrated that she hadn't gotten a chance to see Conner before her meeting. *That, of course, was thanks to Cowboy Cop in the garage. Well, I'll make time to stop by on the way out, and we can plan our lunch together.* She was still smiling when she opened the door, but it faded completely when she came face to face with her new lover.

Conner stood motionless, her mouth gaping open as Alex fought to regain some semblance of composure. Both women regrouped fairly quickly, and Conner stepped aside to let Alex enter the room.

"Shadow—Agent Montgomery. I was just telling my task force here how lucky we are to have you back. Come on in and have a seat; we're just getting started."

Alex moved to the other side of the table to an empty seat and put her briefcase down. Needing another minute to get herself together, she poured herself a cup of coffee.

Peterson hadn't seemed to notice the shocked recognition on the women's faces and was now boasting to everyone in the room about how the Shadow had solved one of the worst cases he had ever been involved in.

"The Shadow came in and royally pissed off every officer this side of the Georgia line with her arrogance. First time most of these good ol' boys had ever worked with a lady cop." Peterson knew this was the only place he could get away with teasing Alex, who would never do anything to slight him in the eyes of his officers. She stayed quiet, letting him have his fun, although she did give him one of her most dangerous stares. "Okay, okay, I'll save the bedtime stories for another day. We need to get onto why we're all here."

Alex had come back to the table and, much to her unease, sat down directly across from Conner. The two women locked eyes for a moment before Alex looked away. Conner could see the hurt and the anger in Alex's stare, and she knew she would have a lot of explaining to do once the meeting was over.

What really surprised her was finding out that Alex was the famous Shadow. Conner had heard stories about the dangerous FBI agent, but she would have never thought that Alex and the Shadow were one and the same.

The Shadow was rumored to be on more than one hit list among the criminal community. She had almost single-handedly taken out the Sarantos organized crime family, infiltrating the organization and spending months gathering information against Papa Paul while doing what she had to do to gain his trust.

The Shadow had set up a meeting between the Sarantos family and Malcolm Hernandez somewhere down near the river, and according to the stories, she had also set up a sting, intending to bring both groups down at the same time. Conner didn't know the details, but she did remember something about the Shadow getting caught in the crossfire. She was lost in thought until she felt a sharp kick her under the table.

"Harris, are you with us?"

"Huh? Oh right, Captain. Sorry, I was just thinking about the case."

"Must have had a late night, Harris. Hope I didn't wake you," Peterson scolded. "I was asking if you were ready to bring us all up to date on the Hernandez case. I got Agent Montgomery all the way over here to hear what you have to say, so why don't you fill us in?"

Conner could feel her face turn crimson as Peterson reproached her. Stealing a glance at Alex, she could see Alex's anger now that she realized that Conner was not only on the case, but one of the key players. Swallowing hard, Conner wasn't sure if her nervousness was from having to present her case to her new lover, who happened to be the lead FBI agent on the case, or if it was caused by the piercing eyes of the Shadow that seemed to be staring a hole though her.

"Well, the last time Hernandez was spotted, he was somewhere in the jungles of Colombia. Sources tell us that he has a safe house there, and that's where he runs when things get hot. From what I've been able to gather on the street, that's where he ran after, um, after Ms. Hughes was, ah, killed last year."

Alex's head shot up at the mention of Feryle's name, and Conner could see the raw pain in her eyes. She knew she had to continue her briefing, but all she wanted to do at the moment was reach out, take Alex in her arms, and help her through the pain.

"Continue on, Harris." Peterson noticed Conner's expression as she watched Alex. He knew Conner hated causing other people pain, and she was doing just that by refreshing the events of the last year for Alex.

They had a job to do here, and it had been Alex's decision to be a part it. He would honor that decision as long as she could handle the job. However, he also knew that he would ground her in a minute if the emotions and stress of the operation put her or any of his officers in any unnecessary danger. He watched her as Conner continued her briefing.

"Yeah, well, my sources tell me he's heading back this way."

Looking at Alex, she hesitated for a moment. Alex had shaken off the initial shock of their meeting and was nervously playing with a pencil. "His ETA is this Friday." Alex's head shot up once again. "Seems he has a major deal going down out in an old warehouse off of 295 on Kraft Road and wants to be here personally to see that everything goes according to plans."

"Where on Kraft Road is this warehouse?" Kevin Johnson, a tall lanky man with sandy brown hair, spoke for the first time.

"That's mostly what Seth's been working on for the last few weeks. He briefed me before he left on vacation, but I'll give you what I have. The warehouse sits about a hundred yards off Kraft Road, behind a 10-foot-high fence topped with razor wire. It backs up to an old, apparently abandoned, railroad track that once serviced Colorado Container. We've had some undercover guys watching the place for the last few weeks, and they're coming back telling us that there has been traffic along the tracks. Usually during the day, although nothing unusual during the night."

"So what's your take on all of this, Harris?" Peterson knew Conner had good gut instincts, and he wanted Alex to hear her viewpoint. As a rule the Shadow didn't trust anyone, and he knew if this case was going to be solved the two women had to develop a trust; otherwise, the lines of communication between his office and the FBI could be severely hampered.

"We figure they're somehow moving the drugs into different areas along the adjoining railway. That way they're seldom in the same place twice. Once they set up the meet, they transfer the goods onto those small maintenance tractors we've been seeing running up and down the tracks behind the warehouse and offload their stash through the back door."

"Come on, Harris, you want us to believe this jerk-off is running his drugs in railroad maintenance tractors?" Johnson sighed heavily and dropped his pen on the table.

Alex turned to look at Johnson, and for the first time since she sat down, spoke. "Hernandez is a ballsy guy. What better way to move his goods than in broad daylight, and he gets to laugh in our face at the same time. I happen to agree with Officer Harris. He doesn't like being in one spot too long—makes him a better target. This way he can spot-drop his shipments along the rail lines and truck them in under the guise of railway maintenance workers. How many times have you seen one of those little orange tractors rambling up the tracks?" Alex's cold flat eyes landed hard on Johnson's face. "Have you ever thought that they were carrying anything more than railroad spikes and toolboxes?"

Conner watched Alex as she spoke. The sparkle she had seen so often the last few days was gone, replaced by a flat, dull stare. For the first time since they had met, Conner saw fine lines around Alex's eyes and knew she was on the edge. *We have to talk this out and come to some understanding—we have to,* she thought. *I can't walk away from this case. I made a promise to Sam six months ago that I would find the man responsible for murdering her friend, and neither Alex nor the Shadow is going to keep me from delivering on that promise.*

She realized Captain Peterson and Alex were waiting for her to continue. "Anyway, that's about all I have. I'm going back out this afternoon to try and find out more about Hernandez's arrival time. Seth will be back tomorrow and then we can hit this thing hard. Maybe if you have some free time in the next day or two we can get together and compare files."

"Yeah, well, I have a lot of catching up to do at the office. I spent most of the weekend playing instead of focusing on my priorities, so now I have to pay the price."

Sensing the tension between the two women, Peterson cleared his throat, breaking the thick silence. "All right. If no one has any questions, we'll adjourn, and meet back here, say, Wednesday, same time." He stood and pulled out his cell phone, punching in a number as he walked toward the window. Johnson got up, threw his coffee cup in the wastebasket, and headed out the door, leaving Conner and Alex to sit in an uncomfortable silence across from each other.

Alex was chewing on her bottom lip as she glared at Conner, and she shook her head slightly. After what seemed like an eternity, she raked her hand through her hair and stood, reaching her hand across the table to shake Conner's.

Conner was a little taken aback by the sudden movement but rose and took the other woman's hand in her own.

Feeling a sudden shock at the contact of their skin, Alex closed her eyes for a moment before she spoke.

"It was...um...interesting meeting you, Officer Harris. Maybe I'll see you around sometime."

Alex's dull, flat eyes cut into Conner like a knife. Knowing there was no way she could explain everything to Alex where they were, she sighed an exasperated breath and squeezed Alex's hand, silently pleading with her eyes for Alex's understanding.

Alex pulled her hand from Conner's and picked up her briefcase. After one last hard, cold look, she was gone, leaving Conner standing alone.

Alex walked quickly out of the conference room and headed for the door. As she reached to push her way through, the door swung open and she was once again face to face with Bivins. Her cold flat stare sent a very clear message, and he stepped to the side, letting her pass. She entered the stairwell and took the steps two at a time, never slowing until she reached the Jeep. After tossing her briefcase in the back, she jumped in and roared the engine to life, then backed quickly out of the space. Her tires screamed as she shifted into drive. Taking the down ramp at an alarming rate of speed, she didn't slow until she was forced to stop for oncoming traffic.

As she waited for an opening, she glanced at the front door of the precinct and saw Conner standing there, hands in her pockets, watching. Seeing a small break in the traffic, Alex floored the accelerator and squealed into traffic, barely avoiding a collision and paying no attention to the blaring car horns.

After going about twenty blocks, she forced herself to slow down. "Damn it all," she screamed at herself as she slammed her fist into the steering wheel. "How could she do this to me?" Tears rolled down her face. She and Conner had spent two and a half days together, plenty of time for Conner to tell Alex she was involved in the Hernandez case.

"She was thinking too much about getting laid and knew talking about the case would put a real bummer on the mood." Alex raked her hand through her hair and angrily wiped the tears from her face. She drove for half an hour, trying hard to pull herself together. She had to face all of her co-workers soon and needed to look relaxed, well, and stable.

She let out a sarcastic laugh at that thought.

Stable.

"Yeah, I'm real stable. Blow back into town, and in less than a week, I've slept with a woman I don't even know and I've beat the shit out of one of the local cops. Real stable girl you are, Alex—real damn stable."

She finally pulled into the parking garage at 10:45. As she walked through the door, all of her old co-workers converged around her. After hugs, handshakes, and even a few tears, she finally made her way to her old office. The warm welcome had lifted her spirits. She had been worried about how everyone would feel about her return. Obviously her fears had been ungrounded, and as she closed the door to the noise outside and looked around her office, she was glad she'd decided to come back.

She sat at her desk and looked out the window, thinking about the meeting. "So you're coming home, Hernandez. Well, let's just see if I can make your homecoming as shitty as mine has been. I'll make you think all is well and good, then I'll pounce, just like Conner did, and watch you fall on your face once and for all."

A knock at her door brought Alex out of her thoughts. "Come," she called as she straightened and turned in her chair.

"Well, it's good to finally see someone better looking than Gonzolas sitting in that chair." The agent closed the door and took a seat in one of the chairs in front of Alex's desk.

Alex tried to laugh, but she managed only a lopsided smile. "Thanks, Donald."

"Not to spoil your warm welcome home, but I thought you might want to know José wasn't very happy that you were the one invited to the local powwow this morning." Rubbing his hand over his shiny bald head, Donald Fairfax sat back and sighed heavily.

"Oh, and why is that?"

"Seems like our humble Agent Gonzolas thinks he should have been the one to go since he's been sitting in that chair for the last few months." Donald rolled his eyes.

"Interesting."

"Yeah, a lot of people around here were worried that you wouldn't be able to make the comeback." Donald eyed Alex cautiously, seeing her eyes turn a dark blue. He knew what he had to say next would infuriate her, but he at least owed her some advance warning.

"Gonzolas has made it well known that he hoped you wouldn't be back. I got the feeling he kind of liked the feel of your chair."

Alex turned in her chair and stared out the window, taking several deep breaths before she continued. "Why are you telling me this, Donald?"

"Damn, Alex, you've saved my hide more than once. Do you really think I'd let you walk back in here and not tell you?" Donald couldn't sit still any longer, and he stood to slowly pace the floor. "That's not all there is, either."

"What, are you going to tell me he also took over my coffee mug in the break room?" Alex swung back around in the chair. *Damn, I don't need any more shit this morning.*

"Um, actually it's a little more serious than a stolen coffee mug." Donald moved closer to the desk and sat on the edge closest to Alex. "I know you have never trusted Gonzolas, and yes, I thought it was just your Shadow personality. Over the last few months, though, I've come to agree with your opinion of our colleague." Donald looked nervous.

"You know, Donald, we have a lot of catching up to do. What do you say you treat me to lunch, and we can kill two birds with one of Huey's hard-shell crabs?" Alex raised her eyebrows, silently telling Donald that she didn't want to continue the conversation in her office either.

"Sure. It's been a while since I've been down to Huey's. Let me go grab my coat, and I'll meet you in the lobby, okay?"

"Sure, see you in a few minutes."

Alex remained at her desk thinking about what Donald had said about José. She had always known he was at the very least a soiled, if not completely dirty agent, and she wondered if she had finally found the rogue agent who had blown her cover in the Hernandez/Sarantos case. She knew it had been someone from the inside. It had to be.

She had covered all of her bases carefully and had even sent Feryle out of the country for two months when things started to get hot. She herself had gone completely under, never going home, always staying near Papa Paul. There was just no way anyone in the organization could have linked her to the outside world. It had to have come from the inside.

Raking her hand through her hair, she got up and walked slowly out the door. She had only gone a few steps when she turned and walked back to the door she had just closed. She locked the door and made a mental note as she continued down the hallway to call and have the locks changed when she returned from lunch.

Donald was waiting for her when she reached the lobby, and he suggested they walk to Huey's. *This must be really serious if he wants to walk*, Alex thought. They strolled down Water Street, heading west toward the landing. The FBI field office was tucked in a cramped corner behind the courthouse, which meant that the people who worked there had to park several blocks away in one of the multilevel parking garages. Although the location was inconvenient, it did provide a view of the St. John's River to the south and close access to many good restaurants.

They walked several moments in comfortable silence before Alex spoke. "You remember the day I told you about Feryle?"

"Mm-hmm."

"Well, why is it that I have a feeling you're about to drop something as heavy right back on me today?"

They had reached the landing and Donald pointed to an empty bench in the open-air courtyard. Alex shrugged and sat down. Donald stood to her side, looking out at a solitary boat motoring up the river as he decided where to start.

Alex remained quiet, allowing Donald the space to gather his thoughts. He never spoke until he knew exactly what he wanted to say and how he wanted to say it. After a few moments he sat down beside her and leaned forward, placing his elbows on his knees. "As much as I hate to admit it, you were right about José."

"Okay, so Gonzolas is a jerk who hoped I couldn't get back up and who had the audacity to want my desk. Is that all this secrecy is about?"

"Only on a very superficial level, Alex. It goes much deeper than that, I'm afraid." Donald rubbed the back of his neck, trying to work out some of the tension that had settled there.

"I'm listening."

"Gonzolas wants a hell of a lot more than your job, Alex, he wants you out completely. Although I can't prove anything yet, I think he's the one who blew your cover on the Hernandez/Sarantos case."

Alex felt the adrenaline surge as she turned toward Donald. "Okay, you have my complete attention here. I'm listening. Now start from the beginning."

Standing, Donald held out his hand. "Come on. Let's go eat, and I'll tell you the whole ugly story."

They were waiting on the bill when Donald put his coffee down and looked across at Alex. He could tell she still had a long way to go before she was back to her old self, and he didn't want to add any extra weight to her problems. *Still,* he thought, *I at least owe her a warning.*

"A lot of things happened while you were gone, Alex. Not only did he take over your desk and your open case files, he decided he wanted to be the next Shadow."

Alex only raised her eyebrows.

"Anyway, he decided to go undercover in the Hernandez case. Everything was fine for the first few months. You know how things go— he hadn't made much progress until one day he got a call on his cellular and took off. No one saw him for four days, and when he got back he looked like he had been beaten to within an inch of his life."

Alex remained quiet, but Donald could see that she was going through different scenarios in her mind.

"So, he comes back, looking like shit and trying to act as if nothing happened. Of course, I called him in and drilled him, even threatened to suspend him for disappearing, but even that didn't break him down. You know as well as I do that when you're under, you have to do what is necessary to survive, but when you get back home, a total debriefing is in order. All he would say is that things were moving and he had finally made it inside."

Alex took drink of her coffee, sat back, and looked blankly at Donald. "How deep?"

"All I know—well, at least all he would tell me is that he had met Hernandez himself."

"I find that unlikely, unless—" Alex bit her bottom lip and looked out the window toward the river.

"Unless what?"

"Nothing, I was just thinking out loud. Has there been any movement in the Hernandez organization that you've been able to see since his infiltration?"

"Well rumor has it he's about to make a move, but we haven't been able to find out anything specific. Really, Alex, I don't have a clue. That's why I needed you back on the case. You've been able to do more than anyone else, and with Gonzolas acting so strange, well, let's just say I'm glad you're home."

Alex smiled and chewed on her fingernail. "Why don't you give me the night to work through some ideas, then we can meet back here tomorrow after work, okay?"

"Okay, what's up? Why are you suddenly so quiet?" Donald asked as they leaning against a railing, watching the boats motor up the river.

"How's Karen?" Donald could barely hear Alex as she whispered.

"All I can tell you, Alex, is that she's okay and as happy as she can be under the circumstances." Donald took in a ragged breath and looked down at the women he had admired for so long. He hated the lost look in her eyes and wanted to do something to make her feel better, but he knew he couldn't give her what she wanted—her sister.

"You know I can't tell you more than that. She's okay, and I know that one day soon you'll be able to see that for yourself." Putting a hand on Alex's shoulder and turning her to face him, he bent his head and gave her a fatherly smile. "With Hernandez hopefully on his way back here, we can lock this thing up, and you can finally be free of all of this guilt you choose to carry on your shoulders. We'll get him, Alex, I promise, and when we do I intend to see that you and Karen have a long vacation somewhere to heal."

Alex leaned into Donald's chest. He had always been there for her, and she knew he always would. She trusted him like a brother and prayed that he was right, that she would soon get Karen home where she belonged.

"Thank you, Donald."

"Don't thank me, you're going to be the one busting your ass to close this thing down. Now let's get back to work and let you earn your pay." Donald gave her one last squeeze.

As they headed back to the office, Alex was more certain than ever that she had made the right choice to come back. This was her time, she could feel it, and she had no intention of letting anyone get in her way.

Chapter Ten

Alex spent the rest of the day sorting through all the paperwork on her desk. Her cell phone and pager had gone off several times, but she steadfastly refused to answer, knowing it was Conner. She was back at her job, the only thing she could depend on to be a constant in her life.

Leaning back, Alex thought about the past weekend. Conner had not exactly lied, but she had conveniently failed to tell Alex about a very important part of her life. As she stood and walked to the window, Alex let out a tired sigh. *If truth were known*, she thought, *I wasn't exactly honest with her either*. She returned to her desk, deciding she had had enough of work her first day back. What she needed was a good long run on the beach.

She stopped by Donald's office to let him know she was heading out. He was on the phone when she entered, and she noticed the startled look on his face when she walked in. He quickly ended the call.

"You're going to have to come over sometime in the next week or two for dinner. I know Catherine wants to see you. You're are all she talked about last weekend when she was home." Donald rolled his eyes. "Soon, or she'll never forgive me, promise?"

Laughing, Alex agreed, promising to get with him during the week to make plans.

Traffic was light on I-95 as she headed home. She let the warm wind push the tension from her shoulders as she drove south. When she reached the house, she dropped her briefcase on the sofa and quickly changed into her running clothes. She quickly downed a PowerBar and a glass of juice and was soon running down the beach.

Alex blocked everything except the sea breeze out of her mind as she ran. The sun was setting over the horizon, but the heat of the day was still evident as sweat rolled down her face and between her breasts. She focused only on the cadence of her steps on the sand, and she stopped only when her legs screamed in pain. She stopped and bent, her hands on her knees, breathing hard. She did not know how long she had been running until she looked up and realized she was almost to JT Boulevard, at least five miles north of her house. *Great, Montgomery. A ten-miler is okay for the weekend, but damn! Not a Monday night.* She turned and started back in a slow jog.

About two miles from the house, she stopped and dropped to the ground, deciding to sit for a few minutes and let her legs recover. She watched as several couples walked by, holding hands and enjoying the romantic sunset. *Damn her, why did she have to go and ruin everything? She could have just been honest with me. Maybe I wouldn't have been so carefree and slept with her, but at least I wouldn't have gotten the slap in the face I got this morning.*

Slowly Alex stood up and began walking. *I really like her, damn it, but I can't get involved with her if she's this close to Hernandez. I've already lost someone I love to that murderer; I won't give him a chance at another.* She ran a hand through her wet hair, telling herself she would be bald by the time she was forty if she didn't control the bad habit.

"I can't," she said aloud, as she walked up the steps to her deck.

"You can't what?"

Alex jumped at the sound. She had not expected to have company when she returned, and certainly not the woman sitting on her deck in a lounge chair.

"What do you want, Conner?"

"I want to talk."

"I don't think we have anything to say to one another." Alex crossed her arms across her chest and gave Conner a dark stare.

"I think we have a lot to talk about, Alex." Conner leaned forward. "First, I think we need to talk about our meeting this morning, and why you got so mad that I was there."

Alex started to speak, but was interrupted by Conner's continued speech. "Secondly, I think I have a right to know why you stormed out and left me standing there." Conner's voice was now rising in pitch and volume, and Alex watched her face turn dark as her eyes glistened with tears.

"Thirdly, and most importantly I might add, I'd like to know why you stood me up for lunch today and wouldn't return my calls or pages." Conner threw her hands in the air. "After we figure all of that out, I'm sure we can find other things to chat about, but that will do for starters."

Alex could only stare at Conner, not knowing how to respond. Leaning against the railing, she took a deep breath. "Well, to answer your first question, I don't think there is anything to discuss. You didn't tell me this weekend of your involvement in the Hernandez case, and I can only assume that was a purposeful omission. You hadn't planned on my involvement and were obviously surprised when I appeared through the door. Secondly, I left because I didn't think we had anything else to say to one another. I have to deal with liars and cheats every day at work. I don't need them in my personal life." Alex walked to the door and slid the glass open.

"The answer to question number three is the same as for question number two." She moved through the door and as she was sliding the glass shut, she heard Conner speak.

"I didn't lie to you, and I would certainly never cheat on you, Alex." Conner turned and stood. "You don't know how many times I started to tell you this weekend, but I just couldn't." She wiped her tears away. "I knew one of two things would happen. Either you would turn your back on me and walk away, or you would want me off the case."

Raking her hand through her hair, she looked at Alex with pleading eyes. "I couldn't stand the thought of you walking away, and I can't take myself off the case. I made a promise to someone that I would break this thing, and I will, or I'll die trying."

She walked toward Alex and gently cupped her face in her hands. "Please Alex, don't turn away from me. I need you."

"No." Alex's eyes were hard, cold stones staring back at Conner.

"Yes. I don't want to go through this without you."

"Then quit."

"I can't."

"Why not?"

"I promised someone I would break it."

Alex's voice cracked as she yelled, "Well, why don't you just go back to that person? Maybe she'll be more understanding."

"I can't." Conner's eyes begged Alex to just accept it.

"I can't do this, Conner. I've already lost someone I cared about to this killer. I can't—no, I *won't* allow myself to care for you." Alex's voice was filled with emotion, and tears flowed freely down her cheeks. "I'm sorry, Conner, maybe at a different time and a different place, we might have been good, but I'm sorry, I just can't."

"Alex—"

"No, Conner. If you refuse to take yourself off this case, then no."

Conner's eyes and temper flared. "Would you have quit for Feryle, Alex? If she'd asked you?"

Alex felt like Conner had slapped her in the face. For a moment she was speechless as she processed Conner's question, then a blank mask fell across her face. "Leave, Conner, before we both say things we'll regret." She again moved to close the door, but Conner placed her foot on the track.

"Alex, God, I'm sorry, I didn't mean it the way it sounded. Please, it doesn't have to be like this."

Alex looked down at Conner's foot, and when she raised her head, Conner saw the face of the Shadow. Alex stared unblinking at Conner, radiating darkness and danger. For a long moment they stood, eyes boring into each other's, until Conner finally broke the stare, threw her head back and sighed heavily, then removed her foot. Alex quickly shut the door and as Conner dropped her head, she saw Alex turn and walk down the hallway, and a moment later, the house went dark.

Frustrated, Conner sat back down in the deck chair and stared out at the ocean. It was dark, but she could hear the waves crashing against the shore. She sat for a moment then moved down to the beach and sat on the sand.

She let all of the emotions of the last few months crash in unison with the waves. The tears she shed were for love lost on the brink of blossoming, for Alex and her pain and fear, for Sam and her loss of a good friend, and finally for herself and what could have been.

Conner cried for a long time, her sobs drowned out by the sounds of the ocean. When her weeping finally slowed to silent mourning, she rose and walked back toward the house. She stood just off the deck, looking at the door Alex had closed in her face, and wanted nothing more than to go inside and hold Alex until all of her fears were pushed away. Instead, she got in the Jag and slowly drove away from the woman who had, in a few short days, stolen her heart and her future.

Alex sat in her office staring at the swirling designs of the screensaver. She had turned off all of the lights in the house as she walked through, and she now sat thinking about her comment to Jack Peterson a few days earlier. She might not have intended to let the Shadow come home with her, but as she sat here in the darkness, she acknowledged that she and the Shadow were one and the same. They were a package deal, whether she liked it or not.

The Shadow had completely blanketed the house in darkness, not Alex. Alex knew Conner would not purposely do anything to harm her. The Shadow, however, never took any chances and knew the darkness provided an advantage, allowing her to watch the movements outside of the house while preventing anyone outside from seeing in.

The Shadow had stood at the kitchen window and watched as Conner sat on the deck, then moved out toward the beach. The Shadow interpreted the tears the other woman cried as a weakness to be exploited; Alex saw them as pain to be soothed. The contrast of surging emotions soon tore her from the window and to the comfortable, unemotional surroundings of her office. Alex needed to wrap Conner in her strong arms to protect her; the Shadow needed to push her away in order to protect her.

The argument in Alex's mind continued until her head was pounding. She stood and walked to the front window, pulled the blinds apart slightly, and looked out into the drive. Conner's car still sat there, empty. Alex moved back to the kitchen window and looked out at the beach. Conner sat in the same spot she had been in over an hour ago. With tears in her eyes, Alex turned and walked to her bedroom.

She lay in bed, listening for Conner's car. A part of her could not stand what she was doing to the other woman; another part of her knew it was the only thing she could do. She pounded the pillow, trying to beat a comfortable spot for her head, and rolled over on her side to face the front wall. She lay there for a long time until she heard a car door close. Rising quickly, she parted the blinds and saw Conner standing beside her car looking back at the house. Even in the darkness, Alex could tell she had been crying and felt a pain rip through her heart. Alex watched as Conner slowly turned, dropped into the Jag, and disappeared into the darkness.

Terror ran through Alex as she remembered another woman, in another time, driving away. She ran to the door and flung it open, running out into the yard.

"Conner, stop!"

Just as the words left her lips, the explosion ripped through the darkness. The force of the blast threw Alex off her feet, sending her backwards. The inferno from the exploding gas tank sent flames reaching for the sky. The teasing fingers of the fire licked the trees, and the hot wind blowing off the blaze forced Alex to retreat several feet away.

"No!" Alex screamed into the darkness.

A movement near the road caught her eye. Beside a black car stood Malcolm Hernandez, arms folded across his chest in proud defiance. When Alex made eye contact, he threw his head back and roared with laughter.

Alex shot up in the bed, sweat drenching her body and her chest heaving as she tore herself from the nightmare. She covered her face in her hands as the images of the explosion replayed in her mind, and she could almost feel the heat of the flames on her skin. Throwing back the covers, she sat on the side of the bed, waiting for the terror in her body to subside. On shaky legs, she walked to the bathroom and leaned over the sink, splashing cold water on her face.

Looking at her reflection in the mirror, she saw panic-stricken eyes stare back at her as tears welled up and streaked down her cheeks. The sobs came in a violent surge, and she dropped to the tile floor as her legs gave out beneath her. She leaned against the wall, succumbing to the heart-wrenching pain as she thought about Conner and the danger she was walking into. No one knew better than Alex what Malcolm

Hernandez was capable of. She had lived the nightmare before, only it had been Feryle sitting in the car.

Alex pulled down a towel and buried her face in it as she curled up in a fetal position on the cool tile. When her tears finally subsided, she fell into an exhausted sleep.

She was once again torn from her sleep, only this time it was her body screaming. The cold hard floor had caused her muscles to stiffen. Opening her eyes, Alex saw the soft morning light peeking in through the blinds and realized that she had spent several hours curled up on the floor. She reached for the sink and pulled her aching body erect. The dark circles under her eyes testified to the to the horrors of the night before.

Sighing heavily, Alex splashed cold water on her face, trying to wash away the redness. She knew she looked like hell and wanted nothing more than to crawl back into bed, but knowing she had a long day ahead of her, she trudged down the hall to the kitchen.

It was only 6 a.m. as she started the coffeemaker. She had three hours to pull herself together. She sat at the kitchen table thinking about what Conner had said the night before. She said she had promised someone that she would break the case, but who could it be?

Alex knew that Conner and Sam had been lovers, but she could not believe that Sam would have asked Conner to step into such a dangerous situation, especially since Conner herself had told Alex how Sam felt about her work. No, it could not be Sam.

The coffeepot beeped and Alex poured herself a cup, knowing that without it she would be completely useless. She stood looking out at the deck chair Conner had sat in the night before. Her eyes followed the trail down to the beach and she saw the indention in the sand where the other woman had sat for a long time crying. Running her hand through her tangled hair, Alex went back into her office. She logged on to the FBI database and typed in Conner's name.

She felt a tinge of shame for checking up on Conner, but she had to know more about her. Hernandez was a devious man, not above planting someone in Alex's life to keep an eye on her. *Damn, you're getting paranoid, Montgomery.* She read over the files covering Conner's career in the JPD. Her record was exemplary. Alex was impressed with the number of arrests and subsequent convictions attributed to Conner; there wasn't a district attorney alive that could convict anyone without tedious and accurate investigative work. Alex switched over to the personal information and saw that everything Conner had told her about her family was true. Conner's mother had died when Conner was 17, leaving her father to raise his only child alone.

As she read, Alex felt herself be drawn into Conner's world. Conner had been a little evasive about her finances, and Alex saw why: Conner's assets totaled a little more than $35 million. This had apparently thrown up a flag with the FBI, and she found several more pages concerning Conner's wealth. Seeing nothing suspicious, she switched back to the personal file. The FBI apparently had not picked up on Conner and Sam's relationship, marking Sam as only a roommate and completing only a cursory background check into her life.

When Alex pulled the front door open as she left for work, an envelope fell to her feet. After looking around the yard, she picked it up, turning it in her hand. She shut the door and walked over to the sofa, tearing open the flap as she sat. She pulled out a single sheet of yellow legal paper, and looking at the bottom of the note, she saw Conner's signature. Leaning back into the soft cushions, she read the brief letter.

Alex,

I don't know what you think of me at this moment. I really don't know what I think of myself either. I can't begin to tell you how sorry I am for my comment about Feryle. I was hurt and desperate to get you to see things from my perspective, and I didn't consider your feelings in the process. I can only hope that you will be able to forgive me one day.

I am sorry I can't end my involvement in this case. Just as you, I made a commitment to see this through, and even though I know my staying on the case means I will lose any chance I might have with you, I can't quit, Alex. I made a promise, and no matter what my personal feelings are I will see it through. I hope you understand.

I do want you to know that this past weekend was very special to me. Nothing I did or said this weekend was meant to deceive you. I know I should have told you, but I followed my heart for once, and it betrayed me. I will always hold this past weekend dear and remember the warmth we shared; I hope you will as well.

We have to work together on this case, and even though it is going to be difficult for both of us, I know we can both put our personal feelings aside and end this nightmare. I will not call or page you unless I have something to forward about the case. I don't intend to beg or make a fool of myself any more than I already have. However, always remember that I do care deeply for you, more than I ever have for anyone. Probably more than I should, but nonetheless, I do.

Take care, Alex, and know I will always be here if you ever need someone to talk to.

Love,

Conner

Alex sat for a long time and stared at the words Conner had written before folding and tucking the letter back into the envelope and placing it on the coffee table. Sighing heavily, she stood and once again opened the front door and made her way to work.

Walking through the front door at the field office, she felt a heavy weight settle in her soul. She knew the next few days were going to be tough ones as they prepared for Hernandez's arrival on Friday. Unlocking her office door, she stepped into the darkened room. The hair stood up on the back of her neck as she sensed rather than saw another presence. When she flipped the switch, light flooded the room, exposing the intruder sitting at her desk.

"Don't you know changing the locks can't keep me out of where I want to be?"

Alex smirked at the man sitting at her desk with his feet propped up on a stack of files. "What are you doing in my office, José?" With one swipe, she pushed his feet off her desk.

"I know you enjoyed keeping my chair warm while I was away, but I'm back now, so you can take yourself back down the hallway to your cubicle where you belong."

José glared at Alex. He took his time standing and intentionally bumped her shoulder with his as he moved to the door. "Welcome home, Alex. Sorry I missed your little party yesterday, but I was out working the case while you were all here eating cake and ice cream." He opened the door and moved to leave, then turned around again and shut the door.

"A lot of progress has been made on this case, Alex, in spite of your absence. You need me if you want to solve this thing before anyone else gets hurt. Remember that. I'll be around when you get ready to come down to the dungeon and chat with this little peon." He slammed the door shut as he left.

Alex massaged the back of her neck. "What next?" she grumbled, and reached for the top folder on the pile.

She spent a couple of hours reading the files on the Hernandez case. Donald had been correct in his assessment of José. He had provided only enough information to keep Donald in the loop but offered nothing concrete about Hernandez's movements or plans. Pulling her notes from the previous day's meeting, she read the details Conner had provided about the warehouse out on Kraft Road. Feeling restless, Alex grabbed her keys and decided to do a drive-by to see for herself the layout of the warehouse and adjacent tracks.

She followed Conner's map to Kraft Road, then drove as slowly as she could without bringing undue notice to herself. She cruised the road that wrapped around two sides of the property, searching for any weaknesses in the protective fencing that completely encircled the property. Noticing that the chain link and razor wire still shone in the sunlight, she concluded that it was not very old. She pulled off the road to study the tracks that ran directly behind the warehouse and continued onto the Colorado Container property. Anyone seeing railroad maintenance equipment on the tracks would assume that either the warehouse or Colorado Container was reconditioning the tracks.

Looking at her map, she saw that the water on the third side of the property was the Broward River. *So, you've got a sweet piece of real estate bounded on one side by a railway and on another by a river. Smart setup, Malcolm.* Alex backtracked the route she had followed in and looked closely at the warehouse as she drove by. The only access was a poorly maintained paved road intersecting Kraft Road. She made a mental note to access aerial photos of the area to get a better idea of the layout.

She was close to her exit when her cell phone rang.

"Are you standing me up?"

"What are you talking about, Donald? I would never stand you up. I'm on I-95, I'll be downtown in about fifteen minutes. Why don't I just meet you at Huey's?"

"Okay, sure. See you soon."

Donald waved for the waiter as Alex sat down. "I didn't know how long you would be so I didn't order you a drink. What are you having?"

"A glass of wine would be wonderful."

When the waiter left, Donald said, "Well, my day was fairly uneventful, but I heard your morning had a little excitement. You must have stomped on José's toes. Seems he stormed out of your door in a huff, grabbed his keys, and left the office. Want to talk about it?"

"Not much to talk about, really. I unlocked my door this morning and turned on the light to find José sitting at my desk with his feet propped up, waiting for me to come in." Alex ran a hand through her hair. "How he got in, I really don't know."

"Alex, I gave José a key to your office when he took over your duties."

"You don't understand, Donald. I had the locks changed yesterday, after our talk." Alex looked at Donald and saw the puzzled face. "You know I like to keep my current files in my office instead of the file vault—you even approved the purchase of the safe I had installed. Anyway, after our talk, I decided that if you had concerns about José's loyalties, then I wasn't taking any chances, so I had them changed."

Donald pursed his lips as he considered what Alex had just told him. "I didn't realize that. I'll call him in and put a reprimand in his file. That should make him think twice."

"Thanks, Donald, but I don't need big brother running to my rescue. I know you mean well, but I need to handle this myself." Alex gave Donald a warm smile letting him know she really did appreciate his concern.

"Oh, by the way, you'll probably want to order a new safe. We had to have someone come in and crack the one in your office after you...ah, you know, went away. I'll put in the requisition first thing tomorrow. Until then, you might want to lock everything up in the file vault."

"Sure, not a bad idea. On second thought, would you mind if I locked my things away in your office safe? Some of the files I have on the Hernandez case are rather sensitive, and I don't trust anyone around here right now but you, Donald."

"Sure, we'll run back to the office when we leave here and transfer them over, if you have time." Donald saw the concern in Alex's expression and wondered once again if she was ready to face the Hernandez case.

"I'll make time, Donald. Things are beginning to pick up, and I can't risk any of our surveillance information getting into the wrong hands."

"What kind of information are you talking about, Alex? From what we've been able to gather, Hernandez is in South America." Donald leaned in toward Alex and spoke in a low voice.

"Not here," Alex said, glancing around at the other people sitting near them. "I'll fill you in on the way back to the office."

"Fair enough." Donald said, smiling, and sat back in his chair. "Have you given any thought to our meeting yesterday?"

"Well, I may just be getting paranoid here, but I've always believed that there was someone on the inside who blew my cover in the Sarantos/Hernandez sting. I was thinking yesterday that maybe we had better be careful around José until we find out what he's up to."

"Maybe you're right, but I certainly hope not. If anyone, including me, finds out he was the one who blew your cover and almost got you killed..." Donald's voice faded off, but his point was made.

They finished their drinks and headed out the door for the short walk back to the office. On the way, Alex filled Donald in on the information she had learned at the meeting at the police department the previous day. He was surprised to hear that Conner had said that Hernandez was headed back to Florida.

"I wonder if José knows this, and just isn't telling?"

"I wouldn't venture a guess on that, but I don't think Conner's contacts are well imbedded in the organization. If José is on the inside like he's telling you, I can't believe that he doesn't know."

By the time they entered the back door of the office, it was after seven, and all of the other agents had left for the day. Donald flipped on the light switch and they walked together until the hallway spilt.

"I'll see you in a minute, I just want to grab those files from my safe." Alex turned left, pulled the keys from her pocket, and unlocked the double locks to her office. She flipped the light switch and surveyed the room. Sighing heavily as her frustration and paranoia surfaced, she walked over to the safe and had just begun to spin the dial when she heard the loud noises of a struggle down the hall.

Reaching into her jacket, she pulled her 9mm from the shoulder holster and ran to the door. Taking a quick look down the hallway, she saw that the path to Donald's office was clear and eased out of her office, keeping her back to the wall. When she was about halfway there, she heard a click followed by footsteps and knew that whoever had been hiding in the office was now fleeing. Her training told her to follow and apprehend the suspect, but her heart told her to check on Donald.

She ran down the hallway past the exit door and stopped just outside Donald's office. With her back against the wall, she leaned her head quickly around the doorjamb and peered through the opening. Seeing no one, she held her gun up in the ready position, bent low, and swung into the office, sweeping her gun around, alert for any movement.

With slow methodical steps, Alex continued to check the room, moving to the bathroom and closet. When she was convinced all was clear, she knelt next to Donald, who lay on the floor beside his desk. He moaned, but showed no signs of coming around.

Alex quickly surveyed his injuries, noting the gash in his head. She stripped off her jacket and placed it under his head as she reached for her cell phone and called 911. She held Donald's head in her lap while she waited for what seemed like a lifetime for the EMTs to arrive. The only time she left Donald's side was to open the door. Gun still in her hand, she was expecting the EMTs; instead, she saw a very pale and scared Conner Harris.

"What happened?" Conner asked as she moved past Alex into the hallway. She had been on I-95 heading north to the island when the officer down call came over the radio.

Alex headed back to Donald's office with Conner trailing behind. "I'm not sure. Donald and I had a couple of drinks at Huey's and walked back here so I could lock up some files. I went to my office, and he went to his. Next thing I knew there were shouts and sounds of a struggle. I came out into the hallway and heard someone run out the back door. When I got in here, I found Donald lying here, behind his desk."

Alex sat on the floor and cradled Donald's head in her lap. He still had not regained consciousness, and Alex was worried that his injuries were more serious than they looked. In the distance, she heard sirens, and a few moments later the office was in complete chaos as the EMTs saw to Donald and FBI agents began going through the office.

Conner gently took Alex's elbow and led her down the hallway, asking where her office was located. She gently pushed Alex through the door and closed it behind them. Before she knew what she had done, Conner had wrapped Alex in her arms.

"God, Alex, when I heard the call go out, I was so scared that it was you." She pulled Alex closer and inhaled the spicy scent she had come to love.

Alex was caught off guard by Conner's embrace, and for a moment stood there with her hands by her side, but when she felt the trembling of Conner's body against hers and heard the fear in her voice, she wrapped her arms around Conner and held her tight against her own trembling body. They stood for a long while, just holding and drawing strength and reassurance from each other, until they were shaken from their embrace by a soft knock on the door.

Alex moved quickly toward her desk as Conner opened the door. Jack Peterson stood on the other side with a concerned look on his face.

"I was on my way home when I heard the call. Alex, what the hell happened here?" Locking his eyes on Alex's bloodstained clothing, he felt a new surge of concern. "Alex, are you hurt?"

Alex followed Peterson's line of vision and looked down at her shirt. "Oh, no Jack, I'm fine. The blood is Donald's. He has a bad gash on his head, and..."

Her voice trailed off as she walked toward the door. "I really need to go see about him. Someone needs to contact his wife."

Alex reached the door to Donald's office just as the EMTs rolled the gurney out the door. Donald was still unconscious, but stable, and she told them that she would be along shortly to help with the paperwork.

She walked back to her office and stopped as she saw Conner standing alone at the window. Alex stood for a moment and watched as Conner wiped tears from her eyes, and her heart and her resolve broke at the sight of her pain. Stepping into the office, she closed and locked the door.

Conner turned, and Alex saw the pain and fear in those red, tear-stained eyes. Conner pushed her hands nervously into her pockets as

Alex moved across the room, stopping only inches away. She looked into Conner's eyes, and not saying a word cupped Conner's face in her hands as she gently brushed her lips against Conner's. Pulling back, Alex spoke in a quiet voice.

"Thank you for the note you left for me this morning." She breathed a deep, cleansing breath. "I have so many emotions running through my mind right now, but deep down I know you didn't purposely lie to me." She caressed Conner's face with the pad of her thumb. "I have a lot of things to sort out, and I can't make you any promises, but I know I don't want to do it alone."

She leaned her forehead against Conner's. "I have to go to the hospital to see about Donald and try to figure out what happened here tonight, but I want to see you later. Will you go to my house and stay there until I get home?"

Conner closed her eyes and knew Alex would not like what she was going to say next. "I can't, Alex. Please don't ask me to leave. This has to be tied in to the Sarantos/Hernandez case. I can help. You know I can."

Alex took a deep breath and massaged the tense muscles in her neck. "All right. Why don't you go and look in Donald's office for his wife's contact info—she's in Gainesville, going to law school—and I guess I'll see you at the hospital later." Alex moved away and dropped her tired body into her desk chair.

Conner was torn between fleeing and confronting Alex and her light-switch emotions. Having already had one confrontation with Alex, she was not looking forward to another, so she turned and moved toward the door.

Alex realized that Conner thought she had been dismissed and called out as she reached the door. "Conner?"

Conner turned and stuck her head back in the door, noticing for the first time the dark circles under Alex's eyes. "Yes?"

"I do want to see you later if you're not too tired. Would you come to the house tonight when you're finished at the hospital?" With an exhausted smile she added, "You can stay there tonight. It wouldn't be as long a drive for you and, um, maybe we could talk a little—that is, if you want to."

"I don't think I'll ever be too tired to see you," Conner whispered as she returned Alex's tired smile with one of her own. "I'll see you at the hospital and then at your house as soon as I can, okay?"

"'Kay."

Conner pulled back out of the room and hurried down the hallway toward Donald's office as Alex sat at her desk and wondered what the hell she had just done.

Chapter Eleven

Conner found Donald's rolodex and searched unsuccessfully for Catherine Fairfax's phone number in Gainesville. Catching Alex's attention, she motioned her over.

"What's up?"

Conner sighed in frustration. "Donald's rolodex doesn't have his wife's phone number in Gainesville. It could be in his desk, but it's locked."

Alex yelled over her shoulder at another agent, and after he told her that they were finished, he asked, "Um, are you planning to bust into your boss's desk, Alex?"

"I don't see as I have much choice. I can't seem to find the information anywhere else. My only other choice would be to go break into his house. Personally, I think the desk is the least intrusive avenue to take."

"Okay, but why don't you let me bust the lock? I can always say it fell under the umbrella of evidence collection. That way you're covered in case he gets pissed."

Alex thought about his suggestion and knew it made sense. She nodded.

The agent inserted a long, thin piece of steel between the desktop and the drawer and pulled up sharply, splintering wood as the lock broke free. Stepping back, he waved Alex forward. "There you go."

Alex searched through the drawer until she found a small address book. Just as she was pushing the drawer closed, she saw a folder all but buried beneath the other items, with her name on it. Pulling the folder out, she read it with a keen interest.

Conner had walked away as Alex searched through the desk, but as she glanced over, she caught the frown that formed on Alex's face. She strolled back toward Alex and stopped on the far side of the desk.

"You okay, Alex? You look like you've seen a ghost."

Alex could not believe what she was seeing, and simply passed the folder to Conner as she sat down heavily in her boss's chair.

Conner flipped through the pages in the file and let out a low whistle as she raised her head to look at Alex. "He's been having you followed for months, Alex...why?"

Alex was in shock and could only shake her head in confusion. "I don't have the slightest idea."

"Maybe he was making sure no one was watching you." Conner could not understand what Donald's reasoning could be, but was trying for Alex's sake to justify the file. "I mean, weren't you severely injured in some raid and had to take a leave for a while? Maybe he was just protecting you while you recovered."

Alex looked at Conner with a sad expression. "So you know about the raid?"

"Well, no, not any of the specifics, just what I've heard through the usual channels. It was kept pretty quiet, actually."

"Did you know who I was before we met at Mike's the other night?"

Conner looked around the room and saw that the FBI team had finished up and gone, leaving them alone in the office.

"No, I didn't, Alex." Conner's voice was a little harsher than she had intended, but she was tired of Alex being so suspicious of her. "All I had heard was that the infamous Shadow had almost been killed during a warehouse raid. It wasn't until Peterson went into his commentary the other morning that I put two and two together and realized that it was you he was talking about."

"So why didn't you ask me about it?"

Conner shook her head and glared at Alex. "Because I assumed that if you felt like telling me about it you would, Alex. I wasn't going to pry. If you want to talk to me fine, if you don't, fine. I don't put conditions on my relationships, Alex."

The jab shocked Alex out of her defensive mood. "Damn, Conner, I'm sorry. I'm just not sure of whom I can trust anymore, and now finding this, well..." Alex fell silent as José walked through the door.

"What the hell happened here, Alex?" José looked around the room, noticing the remnants of the fingerprint dusting powder. His dark, disapproving eye fell on Conner. "What are the locals doing here?"

Alex sighed heavily. "She's here on an unrelated matter."

"Is she cleared to be in here? We have a lot of sensitive files laying around here, and you never know who might decide to take one home for a little leisurely reading." José's eyes locked on Conner's.

Alex could see that Conner was having some difficulty holding her tongue. "José, until Donald is capable of resuming his duties here, I'm in charge, and I don't appreciate your questioning my judgment. Furthermore, I've already placed a call to the Orlando office, and they will have someone here first thing tomorrow morning to begin their investigation."

José turned back to Alex. "What do you mean, their investigation?"

"Look around you, José. There aren't any signs of forced entry, and as far as we can tell at the moment nothing was stolen. I think that calls for an outside investigation, don't you?"

"Well what about the desk? Somebody obviously forced that open."

Conner opened her mouth to speak, but was cut off by Alex. "That was me. Donald's wife is in school over in Gainesville, and since there wasn't a phone number for her in his rolodex, the logical place to look would be in his desk, don't you think?"

José looked between the two women.

"Anyway, I had another agent witness my entry into SAC Fairfax's desk, and the only thing I am leaving here with in my possession is his address book. Is that all right with you, Agent Gonzolas?"

"Whatever you say, Agent Montgomery."

José continued to eye Alex suspiciously and walked over toward the desk. Alex noticed the approach and slid the drawer closed before he had a chance to peer inside.

"Officer Harris, can you pass me a crime scene seal? I think I'd feel better if we secured the SAC's drawer so no one will be tempted to rummage through it before he returns."

Conner smirked and turned to Alex's bag. She slipped the folder containing the information on Alex into the side pocket, then reached in the main section, removed a seal, and handed it to Alex, who pulled the protective film off the back and placed the seal over the seam of the drawer.

"There, now we'll know if anyone tries to open the drawer." Alex took a marker from the cup on Donald's desk, then signed and dated the seal.

José glared at Alex. "Well, I'll be going. See you tomorrow." He turned and walked out the door. A few seconds later, they heard the sound of the back door closing.

"Is he a jerk or what?" Conner had taken about as much of José as she could handle, and her anger was apparent.

Alex placed her index finger in front of her lips as she walked to the window and peered out. She relaxed her shoulders as she saw José walk down the sidewalk. "Yeah, a big one. Look, I need to call Catherine. Why don't I meet you over at Baptist Medical in a little while?"

"No way, I'm not leaving you here alone. Make your call, I'll wait for you in the reception area."

Alex smiled and nodded her head in surrender as Conner left the room to give her some privacy. Catherine answered the call on the second ring. Her elation at hearing Alex's voice faded quickly when she heard the serious tone to her voice. Alex filled her in on the events of the evening and promised to call Catherine on her cell phone if she learned anything more before Catherine could get to the hospital. She quickly locked up and found Conner patiently waiting in the outer office, and they were soon walking back down the hall to the back door.

"Where are you parked, Alex?"

She had to think for a minute before she could remember. "I'm in the garage across from the landing."

"Let me give you a lift over there. I know you're in a hurry to get to the hospital."

Alex snorted as she spied Conner's car, half on the small patch of grass beside the building, half angled across two parking spaces. "Um, well, okay, but only if you promise to drive better than you park."

"Very funny. I was, um, sort of in a hurry when I got here, ya know."

Smiling at Conner's stammering, Alex lowered herself into the sports car.

The drive to the garage was short, and Conner waited as Alex got in and started the engine. Alex could not help but smile at Conner's protective behavior. *Well, she never has met the Shadow, and she obviously doesn't know I can take care of myself*, Alex mused to herself.

They arrived at the hospital only to find that Donald had been taken to surgery, which could take anywhere from one hour to several depending on what the doctors found. Frustrated, Alex ran her hand through her hair and decided that she might as well call it a night. She wanted to wait and talk to Catherine, but she knew it would be over an hour before she arrived, and she was dead on her feet. Glancing at her watch, she saw that it was well after midnight. She jotted a quick note to Catherine, leaving her pager number in case she needed her during the night, and said she would be by first thing the next morning.

Looking around, she spotted Conner talking with another officer. When Conner had finished her conversation, Alex said, "I'm going to head out now. There's nothing more I can do here tonight, and tomorrow is going to be hell what with this and our meeting. I have some more calls to make, but I'm going to do that from home, and if you, ah, want to come over, I'll be there." Alex looked everywhere but into Conner's eyes. She knew she had not been easy to deal with the last twenty-four hours, and she wouldn't have blamed Conner in the least if she told her to go to hell.

Conner gave Alex a tired smile and gently squeezed her arm. "I have some things I should check on myself, and then I'll be on my way. That is, if that's not too late to be coming over?"

"No, it's not. I'll leave the light on for you, okay?"

Conner gave Alex's arm one last squeeze before she dropped her hand. "Okay, I'll see you soon."

Alex walked out through the automatic doors and headed to her car. As she dropped into the seat of the Jeep, she felt the weariness in her body and could not wait to get home.

As soon as Alex got home, she called the evidence lab.

"Hey, Jan, this is Alex. Have you come up with anything yet on the prints your guys lifted from our office tonight?"

"Hello, Alex. I'm great, thank you, and how are you?" Janice Houghton was one of the best technicians in the local crime lab, and she had clearly stayed well past the shift change to work on the fingerprints.

"Sorry, Jan. I didn't mean to be so blunt, it's just this case is hot and I'm trying to get any kind of lead I can. How are you?"

Janice laughed. "I'm fine, Alex, but I know you didn't call to check up on my mental health. All I've been able to come up with so far is a lot of good prints that had no reason not to be there. Everything I've found so far matches personnel assigned to that office."

"Great, so in other words, I've got nothing to go on at the moment." Alex could feel the tension in her shoulders and shrugged them several times, trying to work out the stiffness.

"Well, we haven't even started on the fibers we picked up. Why don't you call it a night? Hopefully, we'll have something for you later this morning, okay?"

"Okay. Thanks, Jan. I know you're doing all you can. Talk to you later. Bye."

When Conner pulled into the drive, she noticed that Alex had left the light on for her. She rang the doorbell and stepped back to wait for Alex to open the door. After two more pushes on the button, she peered in the glass beside the door. Seeing no movement, she walked around to the back of the house, stopping short when she saw Alex asleep in the deck chair.

Conner did not want to frighten Alex by walking up on her, so she made a quiet coughing sound. After several tries, Conner decided she had no choice but to go onto the deck. She reached out to gently shake Alex's shoulder, but before she knew what was happening, Alex had brought her elbow up directly between Conner's eyes, sending her reeling backwards.

"Oh shit, Conner, are you all right?" Alex bolted out of the chair and knelt beside Conner, who lay flat on her back. Conner's only response was a soft moan, and Alex knew she had pinged her well. A large bump was forming between her eyes, and Alex felt terrible for being the cause of it. She gently caressed Conner's face as Conner worked her way through the fog and back to reality.

"Hey there." Alex gave Conner one of her best *I know I'm in trouble* smiles.

Reaching up to feel the still-rising lump on her forehead, Conner moaned. "Damn, what did you hit me with, a baseball bat?"

"Um, no, just my deadly elbow." Alex continued to stroke Conner's face.

"I hope you have a permit for those things—they're deadly."

"I guess I should have warned you about sneaking up on me. I have a tendency to react before I look."

Struggling to a sitting position, Conner growled, "Sneak up on you? I did not sneak up on you. I rang the front bell three times and then walked around here when you didn't answer." She rubbed the sore spot between her eyes. "After that I made stupid noises out in the yard trying to wake you up. Damn, I think I could have fired my gun by your head and you'd still be asleep, as long as I didn't touch you."

"Well, I *am* sorry. It's not something I have a lot of control over, so consider yourself warned. Come on, let's go put some ice on that lump, or you'll look like Muhammad Ali in the morning." Alex reached out her hand to help Conner to her feet, then wrapped her arm around Conner's waist and helped her through the door and to the sofa before heading back to the kitchen for some ice.

The man lay in the dunes and used his night vision binoculars to watch as the Shadow lay sleeping. She looked so frail, and he was a little disappointed to realize that she was no longer a worthy opponent. He continued to watch and was surprised when he saw another woman walk from around the house. She stood there for a few moments, watching the Shadow sleep, before stepping up on the deck.

To his amazement, he watched as the Shadow effectively took the other woman down in one quick movement. He had underestimated her, and he realized at that moment that she was not going to be as easy to stop as he had thought. He had to give her credit for her determination; he didn't know of anyone else who could have survived the injuries she'd had, much less have the drive to come back.

Tucking the binoculars into his backpack, he moved through the shadows until he was back at his car a mile down the road. He sat in the darkness, watching the smoke from his cigarette drift in the night air, thinking about the Shadow. She was a smart one, and he knew this time his intelligence and skills would be tested as never before. The dark man felt a surge of adrenaline run through his body at the thought.

Turning the key in the ignition and bringing the car to life, he decided that this time he could not allow the possibility of her return. This time he would stay behind long enough to make sure she was finished off, once and for all.

Alex brought Conner a bag of ice and a beer, then sat down beside her on the sofa. "I really am sorry for pinging you out there." She lifted Conner's chin, tilting her head back, and placed the cold bag on her forehead.

"No apology necessary. It was my fault. I shouldn't have startled you." Lifting the bag off her head, Conner gave Alex a mischievous grin. "Just be prepared, because next time I'm just going to stand out of the away and toss a bucket of water on you." She lay her head back and groaned as the weight of the bag pressed against her head.

"Well, I'll probably deserve that one."

Conner reached out blindly and captured Alex's hand in her own. They sat in the semidarkness, talking about the case while Conner held the bag on her face. Alex drew soft circles in the palm of Conner's hand as they talked, and she felt the tension drain away from the other woman. After a few minutes, Conner became quiet and Alex realized she had fallen asleep. She rose and went into the bedroom to pull the sheets down on the bed, then returned to wake Conner. Luckily for Alex, Conner did not have the same reaction upon being touched as Alex did and only groaned sleepily when Alex shook her shoulder.

Conner pulled the ice from her face and Alex returned it to the freezer. Taking Conner's hand, she pulled her up and led her down the hall to the bedroom. Conner came fully awake when she realized that Alex had led her into the master bedroom.

"Um, Alex, if you would rather I sleep in the guest room—"

Alex cut Conner's words off with a tender kiss. "No, I want you here beside me tonight." She led Conner to the bed and began pulling on the hard leather of Conner's belt. She gently dropped it to the floor. Starting at the top of Conner's shirt, she slowly undid the buttons and slid it off her shoulders, then undid the snap of her pants and pulled the zipper down. She tucked her thumbs into the sides of the pants and she pulled them over Conner's hips, pushing Conner backwards, so that she sat on the bed.

Conner was still a little dazed from the blow she had sustained earlier and could do nothing more than watch as Alex knelt in front of her and removed her shoes and socks before pulling her pants and underwear over her feet.

Alex stood once again and took hold of the bottom of Conner's t-shirt. "Raise your arms."

Conner did as she was told and Alex pulled the shirt over her head, taking great care not to make contact with the tender lump on Conner's head. Conner felt a chill run over her body as her bare skin was exposed to the cool air, but the chill was replaced with a searing heat as Alex leaned in and gently captured her lips in a tender kiss. Alex reached between Conner's breasts and unclasped her bra, sliding it off her shoulders. Conner was now completely naked, and she pulled on Alex's shoulders, trying to draw her nearer. When Alex knelt between her legs, she jumped as the cloth of Alex's pants made contact with the sensitive skin there.

They continued to explore each other's mouths, until Alex finally broke the kiss with a gasp. Taking a slow deep breath to gather herself, Alex pushed Conner back and pulled the covers over her.

Leaning in for one more kiss, she whispered, "I'll be right back. I'm going to lock up and turn out the lights." She straightened and gazed down at the woman lying in her bed before picking Conner's clothes up off the floor and quietly leaving the room.

Alex felt herself tremble as she walked down the hall to the kitchen. There had been no one in her life since Feryle, and it was strange seeing someone else lying in their bed. She walked through the house to the laundry room and put Conner's clothes in the washer, then retraced her steps through the house, turning out the lights and checking the doors before returning to the bedroom.

Alex eased into the bed beside Conner and felt her stir as she settled in. Conner turned and threw her arm across Alex's stomach.

"Cold."

"C'mere." Alex lifted her arm and Conner nuzzled her head into Alex's neck. Pulling her closer, Alex lay in the darkness and thought about how right it felt to hold Conner in her arms. It was not long before Alex heard Conner's rhythmic breathing. She planted a gentle kiss on the top of Conner's head, and laying her cheek against the silky hair, fell into a rare comfortable and dreamless sleep.

Chapter Twelve

A soft light was peeking through the clouds when the alarm sounded. Alex quickly hit the snooze button. Conner stirred behind her and pulled Alex closer, and Alex released a quiet moan as she enjoyed the warmth radiating from Conner's body.

"Morning."

"Mmph."

Chuckling, Alex remembered that Conner was not a morning person and turned to lie on her back. Conner groaned at the movement, but quickly snuggled back closer to Alex as she settled.

"As much as I hate to, we need to get up. We both have busy days today," Alex said.

"Sleepy," Conner whined as she buried her head beneath the pillow.

"I know you're sleepy, but you need to rise and shine." Smiling, Alex brushed her fingers across Conner's nipple.

Conner's eyes shot open, fully alert from the sensual caress. "No fair," she whined. "You can't do that unless you're going to finish what you start."

"You're such a baby in the morning," Alex teased, and placed a gentle kiss on the lump between Conner's eyes. "I'm really sorry for pinging you last night. How does it feel?"

"Not too bad." Conner reached up to feel the lump. "How does it look?"

Alex bit her bottom lip. "Looks like you've been pinged between the eyes. I *am* sorry." She gave Conner a quick peck on the lips before grinning and throwing back the covers.

"No, come on, ten more minutes."

"No way. If I stay here ten more minutes in this bed with you, naked, we'll be here for two hours. Come on, get moving. I'll go start the coffee." Alex slid from the bed and pulled on her robe. She got another robe from the closet, placed it on the bed for Conner, then headed down the hall.

She put Conner's clothes into the dryer, started the coffee, and went back to the bathroom to brush her teeth. Conner was beginning to stir, and Alex chuckled at how childlike the tough cop could be in the morning.

She had just set the coffee on the table when Conner padded in, rubbing her eyes with her fists. She walked over to Alex and gave her a sleepy hug.

"Morning." Conner tucked her face into Alex's neck and inhaled her spicy scent.

"Good morning, again, to you too. Did you sleep well?"

"Mm-hmm, what about you?"

"I slept okay, too." Alex drew Conner in for a proper good-morning kiss, their lips exploring and lingering as both women enjoyed the early-morning tenderness.

"This robe smells good." Conner nuzzled Alex's neck and nipped her ear.

"Thanks," Alex could only whisper, as she took in the scent of Feryle and of Conner at the same instant.

Conner picked up the unspoken words and went still in Alex's arms. "God Alex, I'm sorry. I'll go get dressed, and..."

"No, you don't have to do that. I'm the one who gave it to you to wear, remember? You're welcome to wear it—that is, if it doesn't bother you."

"No, it's just that I don't want it to upset you, Alex."

"It doesn't. Somehow, I think Feryle would approve." Alex gave Conner a gentle smile.

Conner's eyes widened in disbelief at Alex's declaration and before she could respond, Alex captured her lips for another kiss. The two women stood, holding each other for a long while and savoring their newfound emotions. Conner finally broke the silence and whined for coffee.

"God, you're impossible in the mornings. Maybe tonight, I will put you in the guest room," Alex teased.

"Well now, does that mean I'm invited back?" Conner asked, nipping Alex's ear as she slid by on her way to the coffeepot.

"Maybe," Alex smirked, walking over to the cabinet to take out a couple of cups. She pushed Conner toward the breakfast nook and prepared their coffee before sliding in beside her. They sat silently as they delighted in the first few sips.

"What are your plans for the morning?" Alex shook Conner out of her musings as she spoke, placing a soft hand on Conner's exposed thigh.

Conner cut her eyes toward Alex and reached down in a bold move to pull Alex's hand closer to her heat, stopping just short of the soft down between her legs.

"I know what I'd like to do, but I need to look up one of my informants and see if there's any new information on Hernandez's arrival plans." Conner gave Alex a sideways glance, trying to gauge the other woman's reaction as she spoke of their now-shared case.

"I also want to get another look at the warehouse, just to see if I can find any breaches in their security." She groaned. "Damn, and sometime this morning I have to go to the island and check on Magnum."

"Oh, Conner, I forgot about the poor little thing. He must be starving." Alex's hand tightened on Conner's thigh, sending a surge of heat up Conner's legs.

"Starving, hell. I'm worried about the house. He has plenty of dry food out, so I'm not worried that he's hungry." Conner waved her hand in the air dismissing Alex's concern. "I'm worried about what he's destroyed in the last twenty-four hours."

She let her face fall into her hands, remembering the destruction she had walked into a few nights before. "Anyway, I got a call from Seth yesterday. They decided to stay an extra night, but he'll be home sometime this evening, so I won't have to worry about the little shit any longer."

"Does that mean you'll have to go back to the island tonight to meet Seth?" Alex continued to gently stroke Conner's thigh as she looked into her flushed face.

"Well," Conner wiggled one eyebrow at Alex, "if that invitation comes through for tonight, I'll just bring him back to the station with me. Buet will spoil him rotten till Seth comes to pick him up."

Smiling, Alex saw the gleam in Conner's eyes and placed a tender kiss on her eager lips. "Consider the invitation delivered." Alex let her tongue slide over Conner's bottom lip. "Bring him back with you this afternoon. Okay?"

Conner groaned and wiggled her eyebrows in a bad Groucho Marx imitation. "Your wish is my command, Agent Montgomery."

Alex walked into the ICU waiting room and spotted Catherine asleep in a chair. She was quietly walking out when a weary voice called her back.

"Alex?"

Alex sat next to Catherine, then gently grasped her hand. "Any word?"

Sighing, Catherine looked at Alex with heavy eyes. "I talked to the surgeon at about 2 a.m. and she said the procedure went well. They put in a shunt to relieve the pressure, and they're optimistic that he will recover. They let me see him for a few minutes around five this morning, but he didn't wake up."

"I am so sorry, Catherine. I wish there was more I could do." Alex gently rubbed her thumb across the top of Catherine's hand, trying to provide at least some comfort.

"Just find the person who did this, Alex. That and getting Donald healthy again is all I want and need."

"I intend to, Catherine. You just concentrate on Donald and get some rest yourself. You're not going to be any good to him if you sit here 24/7 and wear yourself out, okay?"

"I will. I'm going to go home to take a nap and shower after they let me see him again."

Alex stood, still holding on to Catherine's hand. "Good. You have my pager number, right? You'll call me if anything changes?"

Catherine nodded and stood to embrace the woman who had become an adopted member of her family. They said their good-byes and Alex headed out of the hospital. She had a couple of stops to make before her meeting back at Precinct One.

When she arrived home, Conner called the precinct, and Buet told her Jack Peterson wanted to talk to her. She waited until the line clicked and she heard her captain's voice.

"Harris, I need you to get in touch with Agent Montgomery. I need to postpone our meeting until after lunch. Let's meet back here at one o'clock."

"Sure, Captain. I'll pass the word." Conner hung up, then dug in the dashboard console for Alex's pager number. Once she sent the voicemail message on its way, she decided to spend the morning tracking down her contacts to see what else she could come up with on the Hernandez case. She also wanted to check out the warehouse again and decided she would do that on her way to the island to pick up the cat from hell.

Conner headed down to Union Street. She was looking for Reggie Walker, a one-time Hernandez wannabe who couldn't even keep his own pushers in line. He had been a middleman somewhere in the Hernandez organization, but too many snorts of the white powder and far fewer breaks had landed him back on the streets peddling for the new middleman.

She spotted Reggie coming out of Buddy's Pool Cue and cut him off at the next alley. He looked up just as her tires screamed on the pavement, and the Jag came to swift halt. He turned and ran in the opposite direction, but Conner's youth and good health were too much for the worn-out junkie. She reached him in less than half a block and sent him sliding face first on the sidewalk as she tackled him from behind. Before he had time to recover, she grabbed the back of his smelly leather jacket and pulled him to his feet, shoving him against the wall.

"Where you running off to in such a hurry there, Reg?" Conner had twisted his arm behind his back and pulled up just enough to get his attention.

"Come on, man, I didn't do shit."

"Then why are you running?"

"Shit, every time I see you coming you hassle me. Whaddaya 'spect me ta do, send you an invitation?"

"Don't get smart with me, Reg. You know I'm not too happy in the mornings, and beating the crap out of a little shit like you might be just what I need to start my day off good." Conner twisted the junkie's arm higher, driving her point home.

"By the look of your face, somebody else's day started off good." Reggie knew the instant he made the comment that it was a mistake. He heard Conner growl, then felt a sharp pain in his face as she pushed him harder against the brick wall. "Okay, okay. Damn, whatcha want?"

"I want you to tell me who's been supplying you with the bad dope you've been selling on the street lately. I know you're a runner for them. I've hauled some of your customers to the hospital in the last few weeks. You tell me what I want to know and I'll let you alone—for a while. If you don't, then I'm taking you downtown to our friendly little bed and breakfast, and you know, Reg, I'll bet I could arrange it so you get to travel up to Starke and see Frankie. Maybe I could even work it so you two could be cellmates. What do you think of that?"

Conner's patience was wearing thin. She reached around and patted his pockets. Digging her hand inside the grimy jeans, she came up with three little squares of coke.

"Come on, man, you know Frankie'll kill me."

"Well, it's your call, Reg. Talk to me, or I'll make sure you get to share a cell with Frankie. Personally, after what you did to him last year, I think I'd talk." Conner pulled up on Reggie's arm again and heard the cartilage grind as the joint began to give under the strain.

"Okay, okay, just ease up on the arm."

Conner released the pressure just enough to satisfy Reggie, but kept him well within her control. "I'm waiting."

"All I know is there's something big happening this weekend."

"Tell me something I don't know, Reg. It's the middle of tourist season, something is always happening on the weekends." Conner was beginning to get pissed. She had a lot to do before her meeting and was tired of playing games with the junkie.

"Okay, have it your way." She pulled the handcuffs from the holder on her belt.

Hearing the familiar sound, Reggie gave in. "Whoa now, okay. I'll tell you everything I know."

"Five seconds, Reg, and you're going with me."

"Okay, word on the street is that the man is coming to town for a big deal."

"And?" This much Conner already knew. She needed something more concrete to take into the meeting that afternoon.

"Supposed to be at some warehouse out by the brewery." Reggie was sweating, and the smell coming off him was making Conner green.

"So, who's the big guy meeting with out there?"

"I-I don't know." Reggie hesitated just a fraction of a second too long, and Conner went in for the kill. She slammed his arm up behind his back, forcing his face into the brick wall.

"Don't fuck with me, asshole, I want names and I want them now."

Reggie howled as his nose hit the wall and he felt his shoulder begin to pull out of the socket. "Sarantos. It's Papa Paul and Hernandez. They've got a huge deal coming down, even better than the one that got messed up last year by that other lady cop. They ain't taking no chances this time. I hear the place is locked down tight. Can't get within a hundred yards of it without getting electrocuted, eaten up by a Rottie, or shot by a sniper."

Conner released Reggie's arm, more from the shock of what she had just heard than anything else. Reggie turned around and rubbed his shoulder, staring at her.

"Hey, I know my advice don't mean shit to you, but I'm giving it to you anyway. You want to live to see Monday, stay the hell away from there. Those dudes tote some serious weapons. Better than you'll ever touch."

Backing away and seeing his chance to flee, Reggie gave her one last warning. "They're expecting trouble, ya know? They know the Shadow's back in town."

Conner almost missed his last words as he turned and ran down the sidewalk. She stood there, staring him as she ran her hand through her hair. "Fuck, they're trying to set us up."

She walked back to the Jag and pulled out onto the road heading toward the interstate and the warehouse. She wanted another good look at the layout in the daylight to see how much, if anything, she could make out of their security.

She drove down the road at a normal speed, eyeing the fence and surrounding property as she passed. She pulled in at Colorado Container to turn around, and as she was backing out of the drive, she spotted a movement on top of the building. Not wanting to act too obvious, she glanced around, trying to appear lost, and saw another dark figure on the other end of the structure. She drove away from the building, speeding back to the interstate.

Why would a container manufacturer have armed guards on the rooftop? Unless... Conner pulled her cell phone from her backpack and dialed Buet at the precinct.

"Hey Buet, it's Conner. Listen, I need a huge favor, and fast."

"Sure, kid, what's up?"

"I need you to make a few discreet calls and see what you can find out about the Colorado Container Corporation. I need to know if they've had any changes in management, ownership, anything, for the last year. No, make that the last two years."

"Does this have something to do with the Hernandez thing?"

"Yeah, Buet, that's why I need it kept quiet. Do it yourself, all right? I don't want anyone else to know where I'm going with this right now."

"You got it. I'll see what I can come up with."

"I'll be back around one o'clock. I'll check in with you when I get there." Conner pulled the phone away from her ear and was about to end the call when she stopped herself, lifting the phone back to her ear.

"Hey, Buet? In case I haven't said it lately, um, thanks."

"Gee, Conner, you're getting me all misty eyed. Just go do what you gotta do and I'll see you later." Buet hung up before Conner could respond.

Conner was gathering up all of Magnum's toys when the phone rang.

"Hello."

She only heard silence in the background.

"Hello! Anyone there?" There was a long pause before she heard a deep, whispered voice speaking to her.

"Keep your distance, or you'll regret it."

"Who is this?"

"Just think of me as your guardian angel."

"Okay, Angel. We'll play it your way. Just what is it you think I'm doing?"

"You're out of your league, Harris. I'll only tell you once, stay away."

The connection went dead in Conner's hand and she stared at the receiver for a moment before replacing it in the cradle. She shook off the sense of dread as she finished gathering Magnum's things and went to pack an overnight bag for herself. Driving along the interstate, she was aware of other drivers around her. She could not spot a tail, but she knew that someone was out there lurking.

When she arrived at the precinct, she pulled Magnum and his luggage from the car and walked inside. Giving Buet a pleading smile, she asked him to watch the cat until Seth could come by and pick him up. Buet was not thrilled about cat-sitting, but given his fondness for Conner, gave in fairly easy.

"Thanks, Buet, I owe you one," Conner yelled over her shoulder. She stopped as she remembered the information she had asked Buet to check on earlier. Back at his desk, she leaned in close. "Did you find out anything about Colorado Container Company?"

Buet looked back and caught the eye of another desk jockey, calling him over to watch the main desk while he took a break. Motioning to Conner, he led her outside to the parking lot.

"Hmm, must be juicy to get me all the way out here."

"I think you'll be surprised to see this. It took a little digging to get through the dummy corporations until I found names, but here it is in black and white." Buet pulled several folded pages from his back pocket and handed them to Conner. She read over them quickly and looked up at Buet with shocked eyes.

"How can he afford this?"

Buet just shrugged his shoulders, offering no comments. Conner ran her fingers through her hair as she reread the information.

"I think the group will think this is very interesting. Although I don't know exactly what Agent Montgomery will say."

Conner planted a sloppy kiss on Buet's cheek. He turned a deep red and mumbled, "Um, welcome."

She just laughed at his embarrassment and turned to walk back inside. "I'll always love ya, Buet."

Once she reached her cubbyhole, Conner thumbed back through the papers Buet had given her. Before she knew it, it was almost one o'clock. She gathered her files and headed down the hall to the conference room.

Alex was sitting at the long conference table looking over her notes when Conner breezed in through the door. She snapped her head up at the sudden noise and broke out in a wide grin when she saw Conner. Their eyes locked as Conner returned the smile, and she could not help but recall the last time they had met in this room.

"I sure like this reception better than the last." Conner's voice was light and cheerful. As she walked by on her way to grab a cup of coffee, she stroked Alex's neck.

Clearing her throat and sitting up straighter in the chair, Alex fought to control the warm feeling Conner had elicited in her lower body with the gentle caress.

"How was your morning?" Alex asked in a throaty voice, still not having her emotions under complete control.

"Interesting, very interesting." Conner stirred her coffee as she thought about what she was going to say next. "Um, Alex, can I ask a favor of you?" She came around the table and sat directly across from the other woman.

"Sure, Conner. Is everything okay?" Alex set down the files she had been reading and looked up at Conner expectantly. She could see the fine lines of worry etched around the woman's eyes.

"I...well, if I act a little evasive in here today, don't push me for details, okay? A lot has happened this morning, and I've found that at least one member of our precinct has turned rogue. Well, maybe, anyway. I don't want to give up any more information than I have to until I find out if there are others."

Alex arched an eyebrow. "Are you going to fill me in or do I have to play the guessing game too?"

"Of course I'll tell you. Just not here, and not now." Conner's eyes blazed, and Alex instantly knew that her last question had hurt her. She opened her mouth to respond, but her words were cut short as Captain Peterson walked through the door.

"Good afternoon, Alex, Conner. I'm sorry we had to postpone the meeting. I hope it wasn't too much of an inconvenience." He dropped several files onto the table and sat down as he focused his attention onto Alex. "Is there any word from Fairfax?"

"The last I heard, Donald was waking up, but with all of the drugs, combined with the trauma he sustained, his recovery could take a while."

"If you don't mind my asking, have you heard anything from the lab?"

"Nothing yet. All of the prints that were lifted either matched FBI agents assigned to the office or the EMTs on the scene."

"Well, we'd be happy to give them as much help as we can. I know the feebs don't like our help—present company excluded—so they certainly won't ask for it." Peterson sighed heavily and leaned back in his chair. "Does anyone know where Johnson is?"

Both women shook their heads as Peterson rose and walked out to track him down. The two women's eyes locked and Alex leaned in to whisper, "Meet me at Huey's at three o'clock, okay?"

"Sure," Conner said as Peterson walked back in and sat down.

"I'm having Buet page him to get his ass in here. We're not waiting, though, so who wants to go first?"

Alex began. Peterson and Conner listened intently as she filled then in on what she had found out about Gonzolas and his personal covert operations.

"You know, something that struck me as odd last night at your office, Alex, is that not once while Gonzolas was talking to us did he ask about SAC Fairfax's condition." Conner tilted her head and shrugged. "I wondered about it then, but forgot to mention it to you after he left. Have you considered him a suspect in the assault?"

Alex leaned her head back and stretched the muscles in her neck. "Actually, he was the first person that came to mind. Without some evidence pointing in his direction, though, I don't think I have enough to even question him about it." She let out a slow sigh.

"Donald and I have had several conversations about José's actions since I returned, but as far as I know I'm the only one he's spoken to about his concerns."

"Um, Alex, I hope I'm not going to step on anyone's toes here, but has there been a complete background check on Gonzolas?"

"I'm sure one was done when he signed on with the bureau. Other than that, random checks are usually done monthly, so I can't say when the last one was done on him."

"Well, if you think it's appropriate, I can run a check from here. I know it wouldn't be as detailed as the FBI's, but it may give us something."

"That's a good idea, Jack." Alex sighed. "I know I can't run one in-house without drawing some attention to it, and if Gonzolas is involved he'll be watching every move I make." She bit her bottom lip as she mulled over the thought. "Do it, and if you get a hit on anything, then I'll follow up on it."

Alex looked at Conner, then at Peterson. She hesitated before she spoke, knowing what she was about to ask could be crossing the line. "Jack, I need you to run one more person through the system."

Conner knew what Alex was about to say, and when Alex glanced her way, she gave an almost indiscernible nod.

"I need you to run Donald through the system."

Peterson's face registered shock as Alex made the request. Releasing a heavy sigh, he studied her for a few seconds before responding.

"Alex, that's a big request. Do you want to tell me why you want a background check on your boss?"

Once again, Alex nervously glanced at Conner, silently asking for her support. "Last night, I was trying to find Donald's emergency contact information. He hadn't updated his rolodex since Catherine began law school in Gainesville, so I didn't know how to contact her. The only other place I knew to look was in his desk, but it was locked. I had another agent witness my breaking the lock to search for an address book or anything that would give me Catherine's number."

Peterson watched Alex, noticing the stress lines that had formed across her brow.

Taking a deep breath, she continued. "Anyway, while I was searching the desk, I found a folder with my name on it." Raising her hand to ward off any admonitions from Peterson, she said, "I looked through the file and saw that Donald has had me tailed since the warehouse incident."

Alex's eyes swept between Conner and Peterson. Her hands were in fists on top of the table and Peterson not only heard but could also see her turmoil. "Why do you think he had a file on you, Alex?"

"I'm not sure, Jack. Conner seems to think it may only be a protective tail, but I think—damn it, I don't know what to think. Donald and I have always been open and honest with each other. If it has been for my protection, I think he would have told me." Alex ran her hand through her hair. "All I know is I have to find out where everyone stands and who I can trust."

She gave Conner a torn look. "This thing is about to come to a head and I don't want anyone to be caught in the crossfire again."

Conner looked at Peterson, saw the uncertainty on his face, and knew she had to do something to tip the scale in Alex's favor.

"Captain, I ran down one of my informants this morning and I have information that is pointing not only to someone at the bureau, but also someone from our own house being involved in this."

At her captain's look of shock, she raised a hand to forestall his next comment. "I can't go into it until I've followed it up more this afternoon, but I think Alex is right, we need to know who we can trust."

Peterson leaned both elbows on the table and faced Conner. "Harris, if you have any information concerning one of my officers, I want it, and I want it now." His eyes bored into Conner's, and the tension in the air got noticeably thicker.

Taking a deep breath, Conner spoke the only words she could at the moment. "Sorry, Captain, I can't do that."

Peterson balked at the statement from his best detective. "Harris, I'm ord—"

Conner cut off his demand. "Captain, I can't. You know yourself what happens when an officer's loyalty comes under scrutiny. Even if it is later proven unfounded, there's always a mark. Always a hint of doubt. I will not let that happen. If this guy is innocent, then I'll drop it; if not, then you'll be the first to know."

Peterson sat back and ran a hand over his face. Blowing out an exasperated growl, he pointed a finger directly at her face, "Okay, Conner. I'll give you some leeway on this one. But it only goes so far."

Turning to face Alex, he shook his head in resignation. "Gonzolas—well, you can have everything I find on him. As for Donald, I'll run the check, but the information stays with me. If I feel there is anything relevant to the case, then I'll give it to you on a need-to-know basis. That's all I can give you on this one, Alex."

Alex released a pent-up breath. She knew what she was asking was tough for Peterson, but she had to know. As for Donald, if he was innocent in all of this, she hoped he would never find out about her reservations, and if he did, then all she could do was hope for the best and ask his forgiveness.

Peterson growled as he straightened the files on the table in front of him. "We'll meet back here tomorrow morning at ten o'clock; otherwise, you can page me if anything comes up." Peterson turned toward Conner, "Oh, and tell Johnson I want him in my office the minute he shows."

Peterson stood and walked to the door, then turned and looked back. "I don't know of two other officers I trust more than the two of you. Don't disappoint me on this one." He slammed the door behind him.

Alex and Conner sat at the table in silence for a few moments, both mentally exhausted. Finally, Alex spoke in a tired voice. "Well, we just opened the can, now let's see if any worms come crawling out."

Conner gave her a nervous smile and stood as she crammed her files into her satchel. "Let's get out of here and go somewhere we can talk."

The man watched as the two women walked out of the precinct. He hadn't gotten a good look at the woman on the Shadow's deck the night before, but he was almost certain that it was the same person. The dark man pulled a long drag from his cigarette, then tossed it in the gutter as he pushed off from the wall. Strolling toward his truck, trying to look inconspicuous, he kept a close watch on the two women now entering the parking garage. Once in the truck, he lit another cigarette and waited patiently until he saw the women exit the garage in the Shadow's Jeep. As he pulled into traffic, a safe distance behind them, a plan formed in his mind.

Alex pulled into the parking garage across from the Landing, shut off the engine, and turned to Conner. "You've been quiet since we left the office. What's on your mind?"

Conner stretched her neck, trying to work out the kinks as she put her thoughts into words. "I don't know. I just see how this is all getting to you. And I want to do something to help you through it, but I don't know what to do."

Alex saw the pain in Conner's eyes and reached out to take her hand. She looked out the window of the Jeep for a moment before turning back to her. "I don't need you to help me through this. I need you to help me finish it. Conner, I shut you out the other night. Well, I was wrong." Her voice broke. "I, ah, didn't respond very well, and well...I want to say I'm sorry."

Conner gripped the other woman's hand tighter as she gently stroked the soft skin beneath her thumb. "Alex, it's okay. I know."

"No, it isn't okay, Conner. I know you're good at what you do and I did not, and do not, have the right to tell you that you can't do it. It's just that—I've already lost someone I love to this madman, and it scares the hell out of me to think I might lose you too." Tears welled up in Alex's eyes as she looked at Conner. "I'm—I'm, well, I'm finding out every day that you're becoming more important to me. I don't want to lose you before I—"

"Stop it. You can't think that way. Don't you think I'm scared too, Alex? We have to work together on this—all of it, the case, the relationship, everything. I know there isn't a defined separation point for either, but I think we're both professional enough that we will do whatever we have to do to bring this to an end."

"Will you answer one question for me?"

"Sure, if I can."

"Tell me who you made your promise to?"

Conner held Alex's eyes with her own for several seconds before she turned and stared out the window. Both women sat for several silent moments before Conner spoke. "Alex, why is it so important to you?"

"I don't know. Something just tells me it should be."

"Can we talk about this later?" Conner began to pull away, but Alex pulled her hand back, forcing the other woman to face her.

"No, we can't."

Realizing she had no choice but to answer the question, Conner faced Alex as a single tear formed and ran down her cheek. "Feryle. I promised Feryle."

Alex's heart pounded in her chest as the words slammed into her brain, and she suddenly felt an overwhelming need to escape the confines of the car. She gripped the handle, shoved the door open, and practically fell out of the Jeep. She hesitated, not knowing where to go or how to escape the nightmare she now found herself living.

Seeing Alex's look of panic, Conner ran to the other side of the vehicle. She touched Alex's shoulder, but found her hand shrugged away.

Alex struggled for words but found herself utterly speechless. She walked to the railing of the garage, four levels above the street, and leaned on her elbows as tears formed in her eyes, blurring her vision. She tried to get her emotions under control and tensed as Conner walked over and leaned next to her.

Conner didn't say anything as she allowed Alex time to gather herself. She almost didn't hear Alex when she finally spoke a few moments later.

"Did...did you know her?"

"No, I never met her."

"Then how?"

Conner took a deep breath. "Can we go somewhere a little more private?"

"No! You tell me now! Here! If this involves Feryle, then I have a right to know." Alex glared at Conner through red eyes.

Conner could see Alex's hands trembling as she played with her keys. "Well, you know Sam and I used to be together. Right?" She did not wait for a reply. "Anyway, it took a while, but after we broke up we managed to salvage our friendship. When she and Kelly first got together, we hadn't worked our friendship out yet. That's when they ran into you and Feryle at Antonio's, and your friendship began."

"Why didn't we ever meet?" Alex voice was a whisper as she pulled herself from the memory.

"I don't know. It took a while after Sam and I called a truce for Kelly to warm up to the idea that we wanted to stay friends. Sam and I would usually get together for drinks after work, and we kept in touch that way. Kelly didn't exactly like it, but after a while she realized that I was no threat to their relationship, and she began to drop by as well. It was usually just the three of us when we did get together. I don't know, but I think Kelly thought it was strange that we were all friends and thought everyone else would as well, so I never pushed the issue. I love Kelly like a sister and I know she makes Sam happy. A lot happier than I ever could have."

Conner took a deep breath to clear her head. "I...ah...was going through a rough time, um, basically taking all my frustrations out on a bottle and releasing my stress with whoever was willing. I got pretty wild there for a while and I don't think I would have really fit in with Sam's weekend barbecue crowd, even if Kelly had been comfortable with the idea."

Conner saw Alex smirk and decided that her honesty, at least for the moment, was working to ease the tension. "Anyway, last year after the, um, accident, Sam was pretty torn up about it all. The four of you had become great friends and—well, she was in a lot of pain. She didn't feel like she could talk to Kelly about it and so she talked to me. I've never before, or since, seen Sam in so much pain."

Alex lifted her head to look out at the river, and Conner could see the tears streaming down her cheeks. She gently took Alex's hand in hers. Alex didn't pull away, and Conner intertwined her fingers with Alex's. "Sam's pain was so raw, and during our conversations about the two of you I felt like I got to know you both as well. It wasn't but a few weeks after Feryle's death that you were almost killed. That sent Sam over the edge, and Kelly and I were afraid that we'd never get her back."

"I never knew," Alex whispered. She had been so caught up in her own torment and anger that she hadn't realized that other people had also been devastated by Feryle's death.

"Sam is like that. Always the happy friend, ready to lend a helping hand, but never letting anyone else know when she's in pain or needs someone else. It was only because she was so overwhelmed that she reached out to me."

"I'm sorry, finish your story." Alex wiped the tears from her face and glanced at Conner. She saw the stress etched on her face and knew this was agonizing for her. Unconsciously, Alex tightened her grip on Conner's hand.

"After you were taken away, Sam almost went crazy. All anyone would tell her was that you were alive—nothing more. I sat up with her all night one time when Kelly was out of town on business and the look I saw on her face that night scared me, Alex." Conner ran a hand over her face as she remembered her friend's pain. "She was so...so lost. She didn't think they would let you come back until the murderer was found, and she kept asking me about the progress in the investigation."

"We had both been drinking that night. She finally passed out and I got her to bed sometime early that morning. I had been up for almost two days working a case and desperately needed a shower and a change of clothes. I left to go home for a while and as I was driving, I rode by Pinecrest Cemetery. I remembered Sam saying that was where you had buried Feryle. I don't know what made me stop, but I did, and I spent over an hour searching before I found her grave. Before I left the cemetery that morning, I promised Feryle I would put an end to this."

Conner turned Alex's face toward hers. With a gentle thumb, she wiped a tear away and took a ragged breath as she fought to keep her emotions under control. "I knew Kelly and I needed Sam back—and we both knew Sam needed you."

Conner ran a trembling hand through her hair and released a frustrated sigh. "The case I was working on involved some bad drugs. Junkies were dying left and right. It wasn't happening in one isolated area, it was all over central Florida. I knew it had to be a well-organized ring, and I finally followed the trail back to one of Hernandez's groups. I went to the captain, told him about the link, and asked to be let in on the case. Since then, that's been my main priority."

The women stood quietly for a while, looking out over the street below and gathering their thoughts. Conner could tell there were still questions in Alex's mind, but she felt better now that the truth was out in the open.

"So you knew who I was that morning when we first met at the precinct."

"No, I didn't. I didn't realize it until later that night when you told me about Feryle's death. In fact, when Sam introduced you, I didn't even know. Sam always called you feebie." Conner gave a sad snicker. "I always thought she was calling her friend Phoebe, you know, P-h-o-e-b-e.

"Anyway, even after I made the connection, I still couldn't say anything. I knew you were going back to work, but I had no idea they would let you back on the case. Information was being passed out on a need-to-know basis, and everyone was under a gag order. We didn't even talk about it amongst ourselves, unless we had a team meeting. Everyone reported directly to the captain. I couldn't say anything about it to you, Alex, I just couldn't." Conner turned to face Alex.

"I would have told you if I could. I know I shouldn't have let things progress as far as they did last weekend, but we were having such a good time. I was and am attracted to you, Alex, and I could feel the same thing from you."

Conner looked Alex in the eyes, silently challenging her to deny that one truth. "I know in the end it was a selfish thing to do, but I've never met anyone like you, Alex. Never had the feelings that I find myself having for you. I know you don't understand—"

Alex cut her off. "I won't pretend to understand everything that's happened during the last week, and I'll be honest with you and say that I'm still...hurt and confused that you could make love to me knowing all of this and not tell me."

Alex turned again to face the river, taking a ragged breath, remembering all the times she'd wanted and needed to talk to Feryle about her cases and couldn't. "But I also understand the job, and I know it's not easy to maintain security while preserving the honesty we need to have with the people we care about."

Alex bit her bottom lip, shook her head, and looked at Conner as she continued. "I also can't deny the attraction I feel for you, Conner. I can't, and won't, make any promises to you. It's going to take some time before I truly trust you on a personal level."

Conner felt her heart constrict as Alex said, "Even if you couldn't tell me about the case, you could have, at the least, told me you knew who I was."

Conner looked down at her feet. She felt a warm hand touch her chin and lift her face until she was once again looking into dark blue eyes.

"Honesty is one of the most important factors in a relationship. We don't stand a chance without it." Alex felt a pang of guilt as she spoke the words, knowing she herself had not been completely honest with Conner over the past week. "I want that chance. Are you willing to be totally honest with me about everything in the future, Conner?"

"Yes."

It was one simple word, but Alex felt the emotion and commitment behind it. "Thank you for telling me. I know it wasn't easy, and I do appreciate it."

Conner's mouth curled up in a slight smile. "I'll do whatever it takes to make it up to you, Alex. I don't want to lose this chance with you."

Alex could see the regret in Conner's eyes. In an attempt to break the awkward silence that had fallen between them, and to release some of her pent-up frustrations, she slugged Conner hard in the shoulder. She turned and shouted back over her shoulder as she walked toward the stairwell, shaking her throbbing hand, "Come on, then. Your first penance is buying me lunch."

Alex missed Conner's gleaming grin as she rubbed her stinging shoulder and trotted to catch up.

After placing their order, Conner said, "I was hoping we could go sailing Sunday afternoon. Hopefully this mess will be over by then, and we can get a chance to relax for a while."

"Sounds nice," Alex purred. "Hey! I thought the boat was broken."

Conner laughed at Alex's terminology and shook her head. "It's not broken, Alex, just, well, a little sick. Anyway, I asked Benny to get her seaworthy by this weekend. I was hoping we could cruise with the group. I know that's not going to be possible, but maybe a day cruise would be doable."

"I hope so. I loved Cumberland Island."

"Cumberland is one of my favorites too. I also want you to see Blackbeard Island. It's a barrier island off the coast of Shellman's Bluff, Georgia. It's a lot like Cumberland, but there are a lot more people milling around."

The waiter brought their lunch as Conner told Alex about the surrounding islands and other places she wanted to share with her. After finishing their meal, the women ordered coffee and decided to share a slice of cheesecake.

"God, I'm going to weigh a ton if you keep feeding me like this," Alex complained.

"You need some meat on those bones. I'll not have you falling overboard. I intend to set the sails the next time we're out, and you're going to need your muscles for that. Gotta keep you healthy."

When the waiter placed the check on the table, Alex passed it to Conner with a stunning grin. Conner paid the check, and as they were standing to leave, she felt a hand on her arm.

"Excuse me."

Conner turned to look at the man sitting at the next table. "Yes, can I help you?"

Looking slightly embarrassed, the man stood and offered his hand to Conner. "My name is Peter Jones, and—well, I couldn't help but overhear your conversation about the sailing in the area."

He shook Conner's hand, then Alex's. "I really didn't mean to eavesdrop, but I'm new to the area, just moved here from New Orleans, and I'm an avid sailor too."

Conner eyed Alex, then turned back to the man. "Well, what can I help you with, Mr. Stone, was it?"

"Jones. Peter Jones. Well, I'm having my boat brought around in a couple of weeks and I was wondering if you could give me the names of some marinas in the area."

"Sure, Mr. Jones. What area of Jacksonville do you live in?" Conner was always happy to help fellow sailors. Several of the sailing club members had taken her under their wings when she bought the *Shady Lady,* and she liked to help others out in return.

"I'm currently staying with some friends here in Jacksonville until I get settled. Frankly, I've had my fill of the city and would like to get a place somewhere in the surrounding area. I've been looking at a few places north of here, since I travel to Georgia often on business." The man looked between Conner and Alex as he spoke.

"Hmm, well there are quite a few marinas in the area. On the intercoastal, there's Clapboard Creek and Dunn's Creek Marinas, or if you're looking to get farther away there's always St. Mary's or Amelia Island."

"I've heard of Amelia Island. Isn't that north of here?"

"Yes, actually that's where I have my boat, at the Amelia Yacht Basin. It's the smallest of the three marinas on the island, but the slips are well protected and the channel is well kept."

"Do you have the dock master's number, by chance? I think I would like to give him a call and maybe pay them a visit."

"Um, sure. I think I have it here somewhere." Conner out her address book and searched through it for the number. When she found it, she wrote Benny's name on a slip of paper along with the number and handed it to the man. "Here you go, just ask for Benny and tell him Conner sent you."

"Well thanks for the information, ladies. I'm sorry to have kept you. You have a good day." The man shook Conner and Alex's hands and, smiling to himself, dropped two twenties on the table and strolled away from the restaurant.

Alex and Conner walked in silence for a few moments before Conner spoke. "Why are you so quiet, Alex?"

Shaking her head, Alex bit the inside of her lip. "I don't know. There was something strange about that man in the restaurant. He seemed so familiar to me, but I couldn't place where I've seen him before."

"Come on, Alex. Aren't you getting a little paranoid? He just moved here from New Orleans. Hell, he even had that low country drawl." Conner eyed Alex. "He just wanted some information about marinas. What's so spooky about that?"

Alex tried to shake off her sense of foreboding. "Yeah, you're right. Maybe I am getting a little too paranoid for my own good."

The women walked to Alex's Jeep, then headed back to Conner's office. "Why don't you come on over when you get off work, Conner? I'll make some dinner for us, then we can go over everything we have so far. And you can tell me all about this new information you got this morning."

"Okay. It's three o'clock now. I need to check in with the office and make a few calls. How does five-ish sound?"

"Sounds like a plan. I'm going to swing by the hospital and the office, and then I'll be home. There's a key to the back door in the motor housing of the Jacuzzi. If I'm not home when you get there, go on in and make yourself comfortable."

Conner gave Alex a shocked look, then smiled as she realized Alex was extending her a new chance for trust. "Okay, thanks. I'll pick up some beer. What do you need for dinner?"

"Nothing. I have everything I need at the house, but you can pick up a bottle of wine." Alex sighed and smiled to herself as she thought about how domestic the conversation sounded.

Alex dropped Conner off at the precinct and headed for the hospital. She was so lost in her thoughts over the pleasant lunch they had shared after the uncomfortable confrontation in the garage that she did not see the truck tailing her a few cars behind.

Chapter Thirteen

Not seeing Catherine in the ICU waiting room when she arrived at the hospital, Alex inquired at the nurse's desk as to Donald's condition. To her surprise, he had improved and had been moved into a private room on the fourth floor. As she waited for the elevator, she turned to see Gonzolas exit the stairwell.

"Well, José, I'm surprised to see you here."

"Why is that, Alex? Donald's not only my boss, but a friend as well."

Alex snorted and rolled her eyes. "I guess that's why you were so concerned about Donald last night that you didn't even bother to ask about his condition." She turned back to face the elevator.

"You know, Alex, I don't understand the problem you have with me. I worked my ass off after you left for your vacation, and I closed most of your outstanding case files. You should appreciate me more. I could help you, you know, but that condescending attitude will have to go."

The two agents stared at one another for a long moment before Alex smirked and shook her head.

"José, I don't trust you to help me with anything. Trust is something you have to earn, and you've never shown me one reason why I should." There it was, finally out in the open. She had just drawn the line in the sand; now it was time to see where it took her.

"And what does one need to do in order to gain the trust of the high and mighty Agent Montgomery?" José was too caught up in his own hostility to realize he had just opened himself up to Alex's attack.

"You want to gain my trust, José, fine. I'll be back at the office in an hour or so. Have all of your notes and files concerning the Hernandez case on my desk when I get there." *Gotcha, you little slimeball,* Alex thought. *You might be able to fool Donald, but not me.*

José glared at Alex for a moment before he turned back toward the stairwell. He was halfway through the door when he heard Alex call out.

"Oh, José! Remember, I want everything you have. I've been inside the organization. I know how it works and who's who. Don't think you can pull anything over on me like you did Donald." Alex's eyes revealed the dangerous dark side of her persona. "You try to lead me down the wrong path, and I promise you, you'll regret it dearly." The elevator doors opened as Alex voiced her warning. Stepping into the car, she pressed the button for the fourth floor.

Only when the doors closed did she release a pent-up breath. She rubbed her head as a headache started to form behind her eyes. Her cell phone rang just as the elevator reached her floor, and her stomach lurch at the shrill sound.

"Montgomery." Alex held the phone to her ear as she made her way down the hall to Donald's room.

"Hey. What ya doing?"

Alex smiled when she heard Sam's highly energized voice on the other end of the phone, and she stopped to lean against the wall as she continued her conversation.

"Well, at the moment, I'm walking down a hospital corridor. What are you up to?"

"God, Alex, are you okay?"

"Calm down, I'm fine."

"What are you doing in a hospital, Alex? Oh no, it's not Conner, is it?"

"Sam! Will you please calm down? Conner's fine, I just left her a few minutes ago. I'm here checking on my boss. He got bumped on the head last night, and they wanted to keep him for observation."

"Oh."

"So, Sam, did you just call to say hello? Better make it fast—I don't think I'm supposed to use my phone in here."

"Uh, no. I was calling to see if you were going to make it over this weekend. Kelly really wants to see you, you know."

"Yes, I'll be there. What do I need to bring?"

"Nothing, everything is taken care of. Just your presence is required."

"Well at least let me bring the beer. How many people are going to be there, so I'll know how much to buy?" Alex bit her lip to stifle her laugh. Sam obviously had no clue that Alex and Conner were each aware of the other's invitation.

"Um, it's just a small get-together. Just grab a couple of twelve-packs. That should be plenty. Well, I've got another call holding. See you Sunday, Alex."

"Okay, Sam. I'll talk to you soon. Bye." Alex flipped the phone closed and smiled as she continued down the corridor. *You think you're so sneaky, my friend. Just wait until you really see what I've been up to lately.*

Her smile was cut short as she thought about her two best friends. *I hope they're happy for us. If not, well, we'll cross that bridge when we get to it. Just because Sam and Conner were once lovers doesn't mean we can't see each other.* Alex pulled herself from her inner deliberation as she reached Donald's room. She took a deep breath and quietly tapped on the door.

The door opened slightly until Catherine saw Alex. With a grin, she swept the door open wide and pulled Alex into the room.

"Donald, look who's here." Catherine's excitement over Donald's improvement was apparent in her voice and body language, a complete change from the woman Alex had seen earlier in the day.

Donald opened one eye at Catherine's excited squeal. He tried to sit up, but fell back as pain tore through his injured head. He scowled at Alex. "What the hell are you doing here, Montgomery? Why aren't you in the field tracking the son of a bitch that did this to me?"

"Donald! You behave yourself. Alex has been—"

Alex held up a hand to stop Catherine's admonition and laughed. "Oh, Catherine, he's fine. He acts like this all the time at the office." She raised an eyebrow. "Obviously, you've been able to train him better than we have; you must tell me your secret."

She moved to the side of the bed. "Nice to see you too, Chief. How are you feeling?"

"Sorry, Alex. I'm just not a very good patient." He pulled the sheet higher on his chest, embarrassed and feeling exposed in the thin hospital-supplied gown.

"Humph. Most overbearing control freaks aren't, Donald, and you could be the national poster boy." Catherine was determined to get her reprimand in to her husband. Alex meant a lot to them, and she wouldn't stand for Donald's verbal abuse, even if he was hospitalized.

"Get me out of here, Alex." He glanced at his wife, then back to Alex. "Please."

"Hell no! First you yell at me for being here, then you want me to rescue you from your wife, who, by the way, is absolutely right." Alex's eyes sparkled. "Absolutely not. Suffer, my friend."

Catherine laughed, picked up her purse, and headed for the door. "Well, now that I see neither of you are going to draw blood, I'm going to take a break and get a little peace and quiet." Giving her husband a stern look, she shook her head. "You be good, and behave yourself. I'll be back in a few minutes."

Alex walked Catherine to the door and mouthed a silent *thank you*, knowing Catherine was giving them some privacy. There were things the two agents needed to discuss, and though Alex trusted Catherine implicitly, there were some things spouses and significant others were not privy to. For a moment, Alex was taken back to the confrontation she and Conner had in the garage earlier. Sighing, she closed the door and turned back to her boss.

"Well, now that we're all alone, how are you really?" Alex sat on the side of the bed and took her friend's hand.

"I'm good. A hell of a lot better than last night, from what I'm told." Donald shook his head. "I can't believe I let myself be waylaid in my own office."

"Well, Donald, your office isn't exactly a dangerous place to be—usually."

"Do you have any leads?" Donald absently rubbed the lump on his head. "Catherine wouldn't tell me anything and hasn't allowed anyone near me all day, so I'm a little out of the loop."

"We're following up on some leads, but right now, nothing looks promising."

"Do you think it has anything to do with this Hernandez case?"

"I can't say at the moment. Maybe. I just don't know." Alex sighed in frustration. "Donald, I need to ask you some questions."

"Okay, shoot. Whatever I can do to help, Alex."

"Well, I—um, I couldn't find Catherine's number in your rolodex, so I sort of had to break into your desk."

"Well, that's understandable, Alex. I'm not going to blame you for doing what you had to do in order to reach Catherine." Donald could see Alex's hand trembling. "This isn't about me being mad because you broke into my desk, is it?"

Alex took a long sigh and looked past Donald and out the window. "No, Donald, it's not." Turning back to face her boss and friend, she asked the question that had been tormenting her. "When I was searching for Catherine's number in Gainesville, I also found a folder with my name on it." She walked to the window, her back to Donald. "Donald, you've been having me followed for months. Why?"

Donald's head fell back on the pillow and he let out a ragged breath. "It's not what you think, Alex."

She turned around. "Then why don't you tell me exactly what it means?"

Donald's hand swept over his face as he tried to gather his thoughts. "Alex, after you were injured in the warehouse incident, we ran out of leads. You were on the inside of the organization and knew more than anyone else what was going on. With you out of the picture...well, we didn't know where to go with the case."

Alex shook her head in frustration. "Donald, that still doesn't tell me why."

"I'm getting to that." Donald watched Alex pacing. "Will you please sit down? You're making me dizzy."

Alex sat in a chair at the end of the bed. Her move to place some distance between them did not go unnoticed by Donald. "This wasn't an easy decision to make, Alex. I was getting a lot of heat from higher up. We needed to close the case. The decision was made to leak your location to people we thought were in the Hernandez organization and see where it led. We put the tail on you in hopes of picking up anyone who came after you."

Alex stared at Donald in disbelief. "Damn you, Donald! I was unconscious for a week after the accident and flat on my back for almost a month after that. You're telling me you sent Hernandez's goons after me when I couldn't even defend myself?"

"Alex, we had someone on you the entire time. We were protecting you."

Alex turned and glared at Donald with the dark, blank stare he had come to associate with the Shadow. "No, Donald, you were protecting yourself. How dare you set me up?"

"Alex, please, hear me out." Donald was trying to sit up, but the pounding pain in his head kept him prone.

"No, Donald! You hear me. I have given everything to this case. I've lost Feryle and Karen. Hell, Donald, I may have even lost my soul to this case." She glared down at him. "I will not stand here and let you sacrifice me for your precious cause, Donald."

Tears stung Alex's eyes as she whispered, "Don't you think I've sacrificed enough?" She saw his regret and pain, but it did little to alleviate the betrayal she felt.

"Alex, please, you have—" Donald words were cut short as Catherine entered the room. The tension was almost palpable as she observed the staredown between the two agents.

"Um, I didn't mean to interrupt. I'll come back later." Catherine turned and headed back toward the door.

Alex broke the stare picked up her purse. "No, Catherine, I was just leaving." She hugged Catherine. "It was good to see you again. Let me know if there's anything I can do for you."

Feel the tension in Alex's body, Catherine whispered, "You okay?"

Alex nodded as she pulled away. She gave Catherine a sad smile, and then with a hard glance at Donald walked out the door.

Catherine stood in the doorway until Alex was out of sight, then closed the door and faced her husband. "Okay, Donald. What the hell have you done now?"

Donald turned away from his wife of twenty years, lost in his thoughts...pondering his regrets.

Alex decided halfway home that she didn't want to spend all night in the kitchen, so she stopped by the grocery store and picked up a couple of steaks for dinner. Pulling into the drive, she saw Conner's Jag, and a smile crept onto Alex's face as she remembered she wouldn't have to suffer through the evening alone.

She walked into the house, called out to Conner as she dropped the groceries on the counter, and made a beeline for the bar in the den. She poured herself a healthy shot of scotch and finished off half of it in one swallow as she headed back toward the kitchen. She was standing at the sliding glass door when she felt arms wrap around her waist from behind, followed by a soft warm kiss to the back of her neck.

Conner could feel the tension in Alex's shoulders release as she leaned back into the embrace. She raised an eyebrow when she saw the drink in Alex's hand.

"Hmm, looks like your afternoon didn't go so well."

Alex smirked and pulled Conner closer. "Yes, a very bad afternoon."

"Wanna talk about it?"

"Yes, but after dinner, okay?" As Alex turned around, she tried to wipe the events of the afternoon from her mind. What she needed, at the moment, was to escape the day. She wrapped her arms around Conner's neck and pulled her into a warm slow kiss.

"Hmm, you smell good...almost as good as you taste."

"I hope you don't mind. I felt grimy when I came in and wanted to shower and change."

Nuzzling Conner's neck, Alex mumbled through wet hair, "Not at all. I'm just sorry I wasn't here to share it with you."

Conner felt a tantalizing warmth spread through her body. "I can always go back for another," she whispered in the low sultry voice she knew Alex loved.

After nipping Conner on the neck, Alex pulled back and placed a quick peck on Conner's lips. "Now that sounds tempting, but I don't think we'd ever get around to eating if that happened."

Conner grinned. "Well, I think I could find something to nibble on."

Alex rolled her eyes and swatted Conner on the shoulder. "You're bad—very, very bad." She moved away, heading for the hallway. "I'm going to take a shower...alone. You think you can light the grill and put the potatoes in the oven?"

Conner laughed at the emphasis Alex had put on *alone* as she watched her walk away. "Sure, but please let me know if you need any help in there."

Alex chuckled. It had been a long time since she had smiled as much as she had the last week. She was falling hard for the tough cop, and she knew that there was no way she could turn her back on what they had shared the past weekend.

Hearing banging noises from the kitchen, she flashed back to the Sunday brunch Conner had prepared for her, and she almost returned to the kitchen to protect her precious cooking utensils. She decided the kitchen would survive, turned on the water in the shower, and pulled her clothes.

Alex leaned against the shower wall and let the warm water wash away the grit and frustrations. She closed her eyes and visualized the stresses of the day going down the drain. After a few minutes, she felt re-energized. She turned off the water, and cracking the shower door, reached out for the towel. Not finding it, she realized that Conner must have used it for her shower. Pushing the door open in frustration, she stepped out to see Conner leaning against the doorframe with a cheesy grin on her face.

"Looking for something?" she asked, holding the towel just out of Alex's reach.

Dripping on the floor, Alex tried unsuccessfully to snarl. "Harris, give me my towel, now!"

"Ooh, I can see we're still a little grumpy." Conner walked slowly toward Alex. "Let me see if I can do something about that nasty mood you're in, Agent Montgomery." She slowly wrapped the warm towel around Alex's body.

"It's so warm." Alex realized Conner had heated the towel in the dryer as she showered. The tenderness the tough, hard cop displayed when they were alone amazed Alex.

"Just for you." Conner pulled another towel from the counter, knelt, and dried Alex's legs in slow, soft strokes.

Alex could feel the tension in her body rise, but it was a completely different tension from the one she had just washed away. Her breathing became rapid as Conner moved up her legs. Alex swallowed hard when Conner's hands touched her thighs, and she had to reach out to the wall to steady herself.

Conner removed the now-damp towel from around Alex's body and continued to dry her off. Alex was aware of every movement, closing her eyes as Conner's hand brushed her chest. She was lost in the moment, enjoying the warm rush surging through her, and groaned when she felt Conner move away. Alex opened her eyes only to find Conner looking intently at her.

Conner leaned in and captured Alex's lips in a soft tender kiss before taking her by the shoulders and turning her around. She lifted the robe from the hook on the door, holding it for Alex. She slid the robe onto her arms, then turned her until they were once again facing. She tied the belt loosely around Alex's waist, then knelt and slipped her feet into the slippers that had been sitting by the chair.

Neither woman had spoken since Conner had begun her slow ministrations. As they faced each other, both knew words were not necessary. Alex took Conner's face between her hands and bent to capture the soft lips that were open and ready for her. They relished the warmth and comfort of each other for a long moment. The emotions racing through each of their minds had nothing to do with sex or lust. What they were feeling, standing in each other's arms, had everything to do with comfort, promise, and hope. It was then, at that moment, that Alex realized she had returned to life; she had come home.

The women were torn from the tender moment as the buzzer in the kitchen announced the potatoes were ready to be turned. Alex broke the kiss and pulled back to look deeply into her lover's eyes. "Do you have any idea how you make me feel?"

Conner smiled and stole another kiss. "No. Why don't you tell me?"

Alex drew in a ragged breath when Conner bent to nip her neck. "I will, as soon as I rip the damn timer out of the oven." She bent and placed a quick kiss on Conner's lips, untangled herself from her strong arms, and headed to the door. Halfway through, she turned and looked back.

"You know, I could get used to coming home to you." She turned and continued making her way to the kitchen...to kill the timer.

The grin that broke across Conner's face at Alex's words was indescribable. She shot her fist in the air, and screamed a silent *yes*, then floated out of the bathroom, back to the kitchen.

"So, you want to tell me why you were so upset when you came in this afternoon?"

Alex felt the tension return to her shoulders as she remembered the confrontation with Donald at the hospital. She felt an overwhelming need to flee, and she stood up. Conner reached out with strong but gentle hands.

"Don't! Come here, I want to hold you."

Alex took a deep cleansing breath and sat on the chaise lounge. Conner dropped a leg on each side of the chair and pulled Alex back against her stomach. Alex allowed Conner's arms to wrap around her, and they sat for a few moments before she spoke.

"I found out this afternoon why Donald had me tailed." Alex was trembling, and she felt Conner pull her closer. "He set me up." Her voice broke, and she struggled to keep her composure.

"What do you mean, set you up?"

Alex sniffed and wiped the tears from her face. "After the accident. He leaked my location to the Hernandez organization in hopes of luring someone out to kill me. Supposedly, the tail was for my protection, but I honestly think it was there to nab the perp and not to protect me."

Conner could feel the anger surge through her and fought the urge to react. "So, I take it you talked to Donald this afternoon?"

"Screamed is more like it. Damn, Conner. He was lying there in that bed and could hardly move, and I attacked him like some suspect." Even through her anger, Alex felt guilty for confronting Donald about the folder while he was incapacitated.

"Humph. Sounds to me like he didn't really care about your feelings or condition when he sent the goons after you." Conner softly stroked Alex's arm.

"Yeah, and that makes me no better than him." Alex sniffed and wiped a few more tears from her face.

"So did Donald say what information they got from his little stunt?"

"Actually, I never got a chance to ask him. Catherine came back in the middle of the conversation, and I left."

At the sound of a sudden loud boom, both women flew out of the chair and dove onto the deck, taking cover. They stayed still for a few moments until another blast ripped through the night. The women looked at each other as they heard laughter out on the beach beyond the house. Conner peeked over the railing to see several people running down the beach. As she watched from her covered position, she stared in disbelief as one of them set off another firecracker.

"Fuck!" Conner stood up and took a shaky breath. "Damn kids! Are you okay?"

She looked down to see Alex doubled over in spasms, and ran to her side. "Damn it, Alex, talk to me. Are you okay?"

Alex looked up into Conner's face but could only shake her head. "You...should have...seen...your face." She had to take gasps of air between her words, she was laughing so hard, the tears of sadness now replaced by tears of laughter.

Conner wanted to be mad but was soon sitting beside Alex on the deck laughing with her. They sat, leaning against the Jacuzzi holding hands, and listened to the laughter on the beach.

"I think we're strung a little too tight tonight. What do you think?"

"Hmm, yeah. Me too. Although I know I could think of some productive way to work off all that tightness." Conner captured Alex's lips with her own. They sat in the darkness, exploring, searching, and savoring each other until they heard a scream from beyond the dunes.

"I think we need to take our little party inside before we get caught necking on the beach." Alex rose and pulled Conner up beside her. They could see three kids out on the beach huddled near one of the dunes.

"You think they're okay? They seemed to be looking down at something in the sand."

"One of them probably just stepped on a hot leftover firecracker. They don't look too injured to me. Come on, let's go inside." Alex pulled on Conner's arm and led her into the house.

She refilled their wine glasses while Conner went into the den and looked through Alex's CD collection. Conner selected a few soothing disks, placed them in the player, and then sat beside Alex on the sofa.

"I don't know about you, but I had my fill of excitement for one day." Conner leaned her head back against the cushion and turned her head to look at Alex.

"That's right, you had a full day too. I'm sorry, Conner," Alex stroked her hand across Conner's cheek. "I was so caught up in my conversation with Donald, I forgot to even ask you about your day. Tell me about this new information you have."

"I looked up one of my old contacts this morning and got an earful. According to my source, the meeting scheduled for Friday is between Hernandez and Sarantos."

Conner looked at Alex and noticed her face had paled. "Um, they know you're back in town, Alex."

Alex felt her heart rate quicken at the news. The last time she had been in the presence of Hernandez and Sarantos at the same time she had almost been killed. She whispered, "How do they know I'm back?"

"That I don't know. Could be from the leak Donald put out a few months ago. They may have been keeping an eye on you and just not moving to do anything." Conner squeezed Alex's hand firmly within hers. "All I know is Reggie, my contact, said they knew the Shadow was back in town."

Conner turned Alex until she was nestled in the crook of her arm. "I know I'm being followed." She could feel Alex stiffen. "I went back out to the warehouse to look around this morning and I noticed some men on top of the Colorado Container building, next door. I think they're setting us up, Alex. I don't think the meeting is going to be in the warehouse. I think it's going to be in the Colorado Container building."

"Why do you think that?" Alex's mind was turning, trying to make sense of the information.

"After I spotted the men on the building, I called Buet and had him do some checking on the ownership of Colorado Container. It seems our friend Bivins is part owner of the building."

Alex pulled away and sat up to face Conner. "You mean that cowboy cop from the beach the other night? Come on, Conner. You can't be serious?" She pulled a hand through her hair, then sat with her elbows on her knees staring at the floor. "This makes no sense at all. A two-bit cop, part owner in a multimillion-dollar corporation that just happens to have snipers on the roof?"

"Actually, Bivins doesn't own any of the corporation, just the building. It was sold six months ago to H&S Imports, and Bivins is listed as the chief financial officer."

Alex stood up and walked to the other side of the room. She looked out the window into the darkness for a minute, then started pacing across the room. "Okay, let me see if I have this right. There is a meeting between Hernandez and Sarantos on Friday night. They know I'm back in town and want us to believe it's going to be held in the warehouse, but it's really going to be in the Container building. Am I right so far?"

Conner nodded as Alex continued to pace. If she hadn't seen it for herself she would never have believed the transformation from the soft sensual woman she was falling in love with to the Shadow, a cold, dark, and dangerous panther pacing the floor. In the light Conner couldn't be sure, but she was almost positive Alex's eyes had changed from dark blue to almost black.

"You said earlier you were being followed. Why do you think that?"

"After I left the Container building, I drove home to pick up Magnum and some clothes. I was at the condo maybe ten minutes total. About five minutes after I walked in, the phone rang. It was a man warning me away from the case."

"Exactly what did he say?" Alex continued to pace like a caged animal. Her face was expressionless, but her body was tense and ready to spring.

"Not much. Just told me to keep my distance. He said something about being my guardian angel, told me I was out of my league and to stay away from the case."

"That message had to be from someone in the Sarantos organization." Alex stopped and looked at the ceiling, deep in thought.

"Why Sarantos?"

"Sarantos is into all this mystical shit. He talked about guardian angels all the time. Had most people in the organization believing he was theirs. Did you spot a tail on the way back to town?"

"No, I went back to the station for our meeting, then had lunch with you, ran some errands, drove around in circle for a while trying to spot someone, then came here." Conner couldn't sit any longer and got up to join Alex in pacing the floor.

Conner's cell phone interrupted their thoughts, and both women jumped at the shrill sound.

"Harris," Conner barked into the phone, then walked over and sat on the sofa.

Alex watched Conner as she talked and saw the color drain from her face. After talking for a few more minutes, Conner told the person on the other end of the phone that she was on her way. She closed the flip phone and looked up at Alex with dazed eyes.

"What's wrong?"

"That was Peterson. They just found Kevin Johnson." Conner stood and walked to the window. "At home, in his bathtub, with his throat slashed." Conner could hear Alex's intake of breath, and she turned to face her. She could see Alex's eyes clearly now, and they were almost black.

Alex walked to the closet and pulled her holster. Both women were silent as she slipped it over her shoulders. Conner picked up her keys from the counter in the kitchen, and they walked out the back door. When Alex turned to lock the door, Conner wrapped her arms around her from behind and held her for a moment. Alex leaned back into the embrace as both women came to the realization that the war had begun.

Alex took a deep breath as she thought about the woman holding her close. In the next few days, people were going to die. She silently vowed that Conner would not be one of them, and she prayed that she too would be lucky enough to survive this next step into hell.

Conner heard Captain Peterson before she spotted him talking to the medical examiner in the far corner of the living room. Alex stood off to the side as the paramedics rolled the gurney that held Johnson's body out the door. Some of the officers on the scene knew who Alex was, and she was well aware of the animosity between the local police and the FBI. Johnson's death had not officially been linked to the Hernandez case—yet—but Alex knew that by morning she would officially be part of the new case. Until then, she would stand down and unofficially observe the scene.

When Captain Peterson finished talking to the ME, he motioned Conner and Alex over. Conner noticed the stress on his face and couldn't help worrying about her commanding officer. This was the third officer he had lost in this case. The first two had died at the warehouse the night Alex was almost killed. He took a deep, ragged breath as he looked at the two women.

"I'm sure you have already figured out this is linked to the Hernandez case."

Conner nodded. "Who found him?"

"Rodgers. Buet called him looking for Johnson after our meeting. Apparently, Johnson told him he had a doctor's appointment after lunch, and they split up about noon. Rodgers went back to the precinct to finish some paperwork, then went home about five o'clock." Peterson stopped to answer a question from another detective, then turned back toward the women.

"Anyway, when I left around six, I still hadn't heard from Johnson. I told the desk sergeant to page him, and when Johnson didn't answer the page, the sergeant called Rodgers." Peterson sighed. "Rodgers eventually came by here when he couldn't reach Johnson, and he found the back door open. He knew Johnson had gone to the doctor earlier in the day and thought he might be sick, so he entered the house. The shower was running, but when he called out, Johnson didn't answer, so he went in the bathroom and found him in the tub."

Conner saw his Adam's apple jump. Not knowing what to do, she took his arm and inconspicuously pushed him toward the door. "Captain, I need some air. Let's walk outside for a minute."

When they were outside in the front yard, Peterson turned to Alex. "I want to make this official, Alex. I want you and your office in on this case. We will lead the investigation, but I would appreciate your help. I know this is tied into the Hernandez case, although I can't prove it yet."

Alex moved a little closer to the captain. "I agree that it probably is tied to the other case, but what other cases was he working?" She stopped talking until one of the detectives passed by them. "Anything that could even be remotely linked to this?"

"Not that I'm aware. My opinion is, Hernandez wanted to send you a message and knew Johnson was the easiest target. He was young, inexperienced, and well, you heard him on Monday—he wasn't convinced Hernandez was capable of this. Unfortunately, this is another case of blind inexperience."

As he turned back to Conner, his eyes grew cold. "I'm sorry, Conner, but all agreements are off. I want to know everything you have on whoever you were talking about in the meeting this morning, and I want to know now."

For a moment, a tidal wave of guilt poured over Conner as she realized that if she had filled the captain in earlier in the day, Johnson might still be alive.

Alex read all of the familiar emotions, then touched Conner's shoulder and glared at Peterson. "Conner, from what you've told me tonight, there is nothing that could have been done to prevent this. No one," she said, looking back at Peterson to emphasize her words, "no one could have known this would happen, so don't even go there with the guilt. We need to stay focused if we're going to solve this thing, okay?"

Alex glared at Donald, silently warning him to back off. "I suggest that we get out of here and go somewhere private, where we can talk. Conner's made a lot of progress on this case today, Jack, and I think you want to hear it."

Peterson agreed and went back inside to finish handing out orders. When he was out of hearing range, Conner turned to Alex. "You didn't have to do—"

Alex cut Conner's words off. "No, I didn't have to, but he was out of line, Conner. No one could have prevented this, based on the evidence we have right now, and you know it."

Not caring what anyone around them thought, she took Conner by the shoulders and turned her until they were facing. "You're a damn good cop, Conner. I'm glad that you're on this case with me. Together, we're going to bring these bastards down. I need you focused on the next few days, not on the past, and certainly not on what happened here tonight. If we're going to get through this, alive and well, I need you at a hundred percent. Can you give me that?"

Conner leaned her head back and drew in a long, deep breath. "Yeah. Yes, you've got me."

After a long, intense conversation with Peterson at an all-night diner, the women arrived back at Alex's at two in the morning.

Conner lay in the bed with her back to Alex and tried unsuccessfully to silence her sobs. Alex turned and gently pulled on Conner's shoulder until she was snugly cradled in her arms. The tender gesture broke down what was left of Conner's resolve, and she lay in Alex's arms as Alex whispered soothing words and gently rocked her until the exhausting sobs stopped and she finally fell asleep.

Alex held Conner as she slept, thinking over the events of the last few days and contemplating what was to come in the next few.

Out in the darkness, smoke curled in the night air as the man sat in his truck and watched the lights go out, one by one, in the house down the street. He sat there for over an hour and simply watched and made his plans.

"So, the Shadow now has a shadow," he said to no one. "This is going to be easier than I thought." He man started the truck, then drove slowly down the street and away from the house, a little disappointed that the mission was not going to be as thrilling as he had once hoped.

Chapter Fourteen

"Good morning, Donald. How are you feeling?" Alex's question was polite but flat, and her voice did not hold any of its usual warmth.

"I'm feeling better, Alex, and yourself?"

"Well, so far I've had a great morning, and I'm looking forward to an uneventful day. Hopefully, it will be better than others I've had lately," Alex said matter-of-factly, letting Donald know that she had not discarded, nor accepted, his reasoning for the tail.

Before he had a chance to say anything more, she turned to Conner. "Donald, I'd like you to meet Conner Harris. She has been working this case for a few months now with the JPD and has made a lot of progress. I think you'll be pleased to hear what she's been able to come up with in the short time she's been on board."

Conner walked over to the bed and shook Donald's hand. He looked closely at her face. "Haven't we met before?"

"Actually we have, about four months ago, after we raided Frankie Roberts's hideout." The police department, as well as the FBI, had been trying to pin something on Frankie for months, but to no avail. It had been a huge feather in Conner's cap to be the one to make the collar.

Donald looked at her with a newfound admiration. "Well, welcome aboard. Anyone who can take down Frankie Roberts is welcome on any case of mine."

Alex let Donald's comment pass uncontested. This was her case and everyone knew it, but she wasn't going to get into a power struggle with Donald. She had better things to do with her time.

The room fell into an uncomfortable silence until Catherine came in. "Alex. Good morning, dear, how are you?" She pulled Alex into a warm embrace. "Donald hasn't been an ass again to you this morning, has he?"

Alex's eyes widened. She knew Catherine to be a strong-willed woman, but this was a side of her she had never seen. Trying to ease the tension that had suddenly filled the room, she smiled. "Catherine, Donald is always on my ass about something. Why should this morning be any different?"

Catherine glared at her husband and put his coffee on the rollaway tray.

Donald noticed the look, but did not acknowledge it in front of Alex and Conner. He knew it would be a long time before he would be able to redeem himself.

Alex introduced Conner to Catherine and they all sat and chatted until a knock on the door announced the arrival of the others. Catherine rose. "Alex, if he needs anything while I'm gone, just call my cell phone, all right?"

"Sure, Catherine." Alex glanced over at Donald, who was greeting Peterson and José. Once everyone had settled in, Donald asked Alex to run the meeting. She summarized the details of the case, and when she was through, she opened the floor for suggestions and comments.

José had positioned himself in the corner of the room and seemed to be listening intently. *He's more interested in gathering information than sharing*, Alex thought. *Well, I'll just put him on the spot here, in front of everyone.*

"José, Donald tells me you were running undercover while I was out. What, if anything, did you come up with?"

No one missed the challenge in Alex's voice. José glared at her until he realized everyone was looking at him, waiting for his answer. "Actually, I wasn't as lucky as you were in getting inside the organization. You know that takes months of undercover work, and I didn't have that much time to invest in it." José noticed Peterson raise an eyebrow at his comment.

"I'm not saying it wasn't important, just that I couldn't go completely under." José looked at Peterson. "I did have a chat with your friend Frankie Roberts, up in Starke. He did tell me that Hernandez and Sarantos both had contracts out on you. You pissed them off good on that last case, setting them both up for a double sting. I guess they decided to team up and work together after that." José looked at Donald. "You probably know by now that we had a tail put on you after we found out that news, but so far we haven't been able to pick up anything on that end."

Alex glanced at Donald, then back at José. "Really, José. The story I heard was that my own agency leaked my whereabouts to the Hernandez organization. So tell me, José, which is the truth? Was it Hernandez or the FBI that put a contract out on me?"

José's face paled as Alex's eyes grew dark and her voice went flat. He had seen the Shadow enough times to know that he never wanted to be on the receiving end of her wrath. He looked at Donald, then back at Alex, and stammered, "I—I'm not sure what you mean, Alex."

Alex leaned against the wall and glared at José. The room was eerily quiet as the two agents' eyes remained locked. Alex finally broke the stare, turning to Donald. "I guess that's not the important issue at this point, is it? However, when this case is put to bed, I *will* find out, and I'll with it accordingly."

Conner felt a chill settle in the air and was glad she hadn't seen more of the darker side of Alex. *Damn, I hope I never really piss her off, or there'll be hell to pay at home,* she thought.

"Okay, so the only information we have so far is what Officer Harris has been able to come up with. Anyone have any thoughts on what Hernandez and Sarantos's plans might be for tomorrow night?"

They bounced around several scenarios, knocked each one down for one reason or another. Everyone was frustrated by noon, and Alex suggested they break for lunch when she saw that Donald was getting tired. "Okay, we'll meet back here at two-thirty for round two. I want to get another look at the warehouse area, but I don't want to run the risk of another drive-by." Alex glanced at Conner. "You up for a helicopter ride during lunch?"

"Sure." Conner hated flying, but was not about to let everyone in the room know about it. *God, I hope I don't make a fool of myself and throw up all over the helicopter in front of Alex,* Conner thought, as she returned a confident smile.

"José, why don't you go visit Frankie one more time and see if he can give you any other information. Deal with him if you need to; I want Hernandez a lot worse than I want to keep that slime in the pen."

"Sure, but I'll need to go back to get my car. I went by the precinct before coming here and I just rode with Jack. Probably can't make it back by two-thirty."

Alex pulled out her keys. "Here, I'm in a bureau car today. Go ahead and take it, and let's make it four-thirty. That should give you time to talk to Frankie and get back here. Jack, you're going to work some more on the Bivins angle, right?" Alex didn't want it to seem like she was giving him orders, but she wanted more information on Bivins and his role in the Colorado Container Corporation.

"Yeah, I got it. I'm also working on some other things, and I should have more information back on those this afternoon as well," Peterson said.

Alex looked toward Donald. "Anything else you want us to check out this afternoon?"

"No. I guess that about covers it. I just wish I could be out there with you."

Alex saw the sincerity in his eyes and felt a momentary surge of guilt. *Stop it. That's how you get killed in this business. Trust no one, and always suspect everyone.*

"Okay, gang, let's go." Alex held the door for Conner. They were waiting for the elevator when José walked up beside them. He looked at Conner, obviously uncomfortable with her presence, but decided what he needed to say was more important.

"Alex, look, I just want you to know I wasn't aware of the leak. If I had been, I would have come to you and told you about it." He gave Alex an uncomfortable look, then continued, "As much as we disagree about almost everything, the one thing I won't stand for is putting an agent's life on the line unnecessarily in order to catch a perp. I just want you to know that."

Alex didn't know how to respond. They had shared many things over the years, but honesty and concern for each other was foreign terrain for both agents. "Um, thanks, José." Before she could say anything further, the elevator opened. They filed in and waited quietly until they reached the garage level.

They walked out into the garage where Alex pointed out her car to José. Just then his cell phone rang, and he leaned against the bureau car to answer. Alex dropped into the Jag with Conner. As they were about to drive off, they spotted Peterson coming out of the stairwell and stopped at the end of the row. He leaned down and was about to speak when a blast tore through the garage.

"Fuck!" Peterson yelled as he fell to the concrete floor, covering his head against the debris that flew through the air. He pulled out his cell phone to first call 911, then the precinct.

Conner and Alex ran back to where Peterson lay, stopping short as they saw the blaze before them. All three were stunned speechless as they realized that the inferno was actually Alex's bureau car.

"Oh my God, Alex." Conner turned to face the silent woman beside her. "That was meant for you."

As the heat inside her soul rose to match the heat coming off the flames, Alex didn't say a word. Her eyes had turned a deep blue, almost black, and her fists were tight beside her hips. Her jaw flexed as she clenched her teeth.

Conner and Peterson could see that Alex had just allowed the Shadow to come back full force. What scared them both the most was the look of pure hate in her eyes as she watched the car burn.

At Conner's touch, Alex came out of her trance. She closed her eyes for a moment to compose herself and then slowly turned her head to face the only two people she could trust. "I want this entire garage cordoned off. I'm going to get our explosives experts over here. I want to know what it was, and where they put it."

Alex continued to bark orders as Peterson and Conner reached for their cell phones. She pulled out her own cell phone, then walked a discreet distance away and dialed the number to Donald's room.

"Hello." Donald's voice told Alex he had been asleep.

"Donald, this is Alex. I don't have time to explain everything; I just need you to get this done. My car was just blown up in the garage. José was leaning against it when we drove off, so I can only assume he's dead."

"Whoa, Alex, slow down." Donald now sounded fully awake.

"I don't have time to slow down, damn it. That bomb was intended for me. First and foremost, I need you to have Karen moved from wherever you have her and put somewhere safe. Have her moved to the basement." Alex took a ragged breath. "Then I want you to call Ned Owens at Quantico and tell him I need twenty of the best special ops men he has, and I need them now. I want them here tonight."

"Okay, Alex, take a breath. I'll make sure Karen is safe and I'll get you the men you need, whatever it takes, but you need to level out. I'm getting out of here, Alex. I'll call you as soon as I have all the arrangements made."

Alex flipped the cell phone shut and turned back to Peterson and Conner. She heard the sirens echoing off the walls of the garage and saw Conner head toward the Jag to move it out of the way. "No, don't get in there," Alex yelled as Conner was about to drop into the car. "I don't want to take any chances. There may be a time-delayed mechanism on the car. Leave it and let the bomb squad take care of it."

Conner's face turned ashen and Alex could see the shock there. As Conner walked slowly back toward Peterson and Alex, she let out a ragged breath. "Damn, I hadn't even though of that."

"Well, we can't be too careful. They must know we're getting close, or they wouldn't be trying this hard to stop us." Alex looked over at Peterson. "Okay, as much as I would like to stay here and help, I think we need to stay focused. This little stunt was meant to stop me, but it failed. Someone from the bureau will be here soon. Come on, Conner, we have a helicopter ride to take."

Once they were outside in the fresh air, Alex phoned for a taxi., They sat down on a nearby bench. Seeing Conner shaking as she sat with her face in her hands, Alex said, "Hey, Conner, it's okay. We're both fine." She placed a warm hand on Conner's shoulder and gently kneaded the tense muscles.

"God, Alex, that was meant for you. If José hadn't..." Conner's voice faded.

"Unfortunately for José, fate once again saved me." Alex sat back. "One thing's for sure. If José *had* infiltrated the organization, he wasn't aware that they had planted a bomb in my car."

"Maybe after we do the fly-by, we should go to José's house and take a look around. If he was involved, he wouldn't have kept any files at your office." Conner ran one hand through her hair. "Did he ever bring his files to you?"

Alex smirked. "Yeah, he brought me a tall stack of nothing. Everything that was in his files were things I knew a long time ago." She cocked her head to the side and pursed her lips. "You're right. After the fly-by, we'll go to José's and see what's there."

Conner thought about their next steps as Alex called Peterson, who was still in the garage. "Hey, Jack? I need someone to go over to José's and keep the place locked up until I get there. No one goes in, understood? Yeah, I understand that...If anyone gives you problems, tell them to call me...Yeah, I will...Okay, bye." Alex flipped the phone shut and stood as she saw the taxi pull to the curb.

The women slid into the back seat of the taxi, and Alex gave the driver instructions to take them to the charter office at the airport.

"Jack's in a tough spot, but I think he can handle it. Until Donald is released, I'm in charge of the office, and I say no one goes inside José's until I get there." Alex looked out the window and noticed that the clouds were getting thicker and darker. *Great, just what we need, a storm to make things worse*, she thought.

The taxi came to a stop just outside the charter office. Once inside, Alex pulled out her identification and asked to see the manager. A few minutes later a tall, dark woman in navy blue coveralls strolled over to them.

"Good afternoon, I'm Olivia Morgan, the manager. What can I do for you?" She stood with her hands in her pockets, not showing any signs of being uncomfortable with the unexpected visit from the FBI.

"We would like to speak with you privately for a moment, if that's possible, Ms. Morgan?" Alex looked around the outer office and noticed that they had attracted several onlookers.

"Sure, no problem, follow me." The dark woman turned and led them to an inner office. She unlocked the door and pushed it open, gesturing for Alex and Conner to go ahead. Before she closed the door she told her assistant not to disturb them, then walked to sit behind her desk.

"Well, Agent Montgomery, how can I be of service?" The woman gave Alex a small smile, then turned and looked at Conner. "Oh, where are my manners?"

She moved over to a credenza on the far wall. "What would you like? Coffee, tea, or me perhaps?"

Alex had to bite her bottom lip to keep from laughing at Conner's shocked expression. Olivia Morgan, on the other hand, threw her head back and whooped out a loud laugh before remembering the interested parties outside the door. After pouring three cups of coffee, she came to the desk and sat down.

"So, how ya been, Monty?" She sat with her hands behind her head, rocking back in her chair as she observed her old friend. "It's been, like, for-fucking-ever since I've seen you around."

Conner still sat with a combined look of shock and confusion on her face. Alex chuckled and decided to take a moment to get her back on track. "Hold up a second, Morgan, I think my partner here is going into shock."

Turning to Conner, she snorted, "Sorry, but I didn't want to mention Morgan around the others or in the taxi."

Conner swiveled her head from one woman to the other. "Um, I take it you two know each other?"

Alex looked at Olivia Morgan, a sad smile crossing her face. "Yeah, Morgan used to be one of us, an FBI agent that is, when we were in Chicago."

A look of understanding finally crossed Conner's face. "Oh, okay." Conner gave Alex a sidelong glance, letting her know she hadn't heard the last about the subject.

Olivia settled back in her chair. "So, what brings you out to visit, Alex? Looks like something official to me."

"Actually, Morgan, I need a favor." Alex could see the look of trepidation on the other woman's face and held up her hand to stop the refusal she saw coming. "I just need to borrow your chopper for a couple of hours, that's all."

"That's all, huh?" Olivia dropped her chin in her hand and watched Alex closely. "May I ask why you need my brand-new chopper, and is it likely to get any stray bullet holes in it during the trip?"

Alex looked at Conner and saw a single eyebrow rise in deference to Alex's judgment. Although Olivia had been officially out of the FBI for several years, she had been retained on several occasions for special ops jobs when her expertise was needed. She was not only an expert pilot of planes, but helicopters as well. Her specialty in the bureau had been in communications and surveillance. There were very few things Olivia couldn't bug or video. As far as Alex was concerned, Olivia could be trusted, and so, taking a deep breath, she told her of their new case.

Olivia listened intently, appearing to share Alex's pain as she heard the story of Feryle's death and watched the tears form in her friend's eyes. Hands steepled in front of her face, she watched Alex and Conner closely, suspecting that there was more than a professional relationship between the two women.

Conner was also silent as she absorbed the story. Alex had told her a lot of what happened the night at the warehouse, but she had never gone into detail when she spoke of the moments just before the blast, or the ensuing gunfire. Conner now understood the danger before them and was a little overwhelmed by the task they faced.

Olivia took Alex's coffee mug, walked over to get a refill, and took a moment to take everything in. She reminded herself that she was no longer a part of that world and had to remain removed. *Sure, you love Alex, but this isn't about Alex. It's a case, only a case,* she told herself over and over again as she stirred the coffee. Placing the steaming mug in front of Alex, Olivia sat down and glared at her old friend.

"Damn you, Monty." She pulled her hands through her hair. "How many people do we have on this thing? Do we have a tap on their phones? If they're on the rooftop, have you shot in any darts yet?"

Olivia only stopped when Alex threw up her hand. "Olivia. I was serious. All I need is a chopper ride. I'm not asking you to get involved with this."

Olivia rolled her eyes and shook her head. "If you think for a minute I'm going to let you walk into this alone, you're out of your mind. The Keystone Kops and agents we have in this town—" She stopped and looked at Conner. "Obviously you're not included in that category, or you wouldn't be sitting here with the Shadow...you heard any of those stories yet?"

Rolling her eyes, she then turned back to Alex, "Are a joke. You need me on this, and I'm in whether you like it or not." She pushed herself out of the chair and headed for the door. "Let's go take that chopper ride now."

Alex glanced at Conner, who was still trying to absorb the whole conversation. She gave her a quick smile, then they rose and turned toward the door.

Just before Olivia swung it open, she turned back to Alex, their noses almost touching. "If I so much as break a nail on this job, Monty, I'm gonna kick your ass."

Alex smirked and under her breath mumbled, "Yeah, right, like you could."

"I heard that." Olivia told her assistant that she was taking the agents sightseeing, and they walked out into the overcast day.

Conner snorted at Olivia's remark. The woman was obviously not intimidated by Alex's reputation as being the dark and dangerous Shadow, and Conner suddenly felt some relief wash over her.

Alex bit her bottom lip, smiled, and shrugged at Conner as they made their way through the office. She had never even thought of asking Olivia to come in on the case. She had always respected the other woman's decision to leave the bureau, but she was glad she had the woman on the team—although, in Olivia's usual headstrong manner, she hadn't given them much of a choice in the matter.

Olivia stopped beside a small Bell 206B helicopter. She walked slowly around the machine and completed her pre-flight check, then opened the side door to allow the women inside.

Alex climbed onboard then turned back to Olivia. "What, we're not taking the new bird?"

"Hell no, we're not taking the new bird. That's a two-million-dollar helicopter, and she doesn't have a scratch on her." Olivia growled, then swung her lanky form up into the cockpit. "I left the side door open so you could get a better view from back there. Hope you're not scared of heights, Harris." Olivia had seen Conner's surprised look when she threw the lock, securing the sliding door in the open position, and seen that Conner was unfortunate enough to climb in last, which meant she was closest to the door. *Damn, I just hope she doesn't throw up in my bird.*

Alex glanced at Conner and noticed her left hand was gripping the edge of the seat closest the door so hard that her knuckles were white. She handed Conner a headset and put one on herself, then flipped a switch on the control panel activating the cockpit intercom. "Okay, Olivia, it's been a while since I've been in one of these birds, so no fancy stuff today."

Olivia smiled and rolled her eyes, "You're no fun anymore, Monty." Shaking her head, she powered up the chopper, *Hmm, Monty must be sweet on her partner, she's always loved the tricks and stunts.*

"Here we go, kids, hang on."

As the chopper lifted higher and higher, Conner's knuckles got whiter and whiter. Alex smiled. *Hmm, I'll have to remember that tough girl here is afraid of flying.*

Conner stared straight ahead at the panel separating the cockpit from the passenger compartment. She let out a yelp as the chopper banked sharp to the left, and she unconsciously grabbed Alex's thigh in a vise-grip hold.

Alex pried Conner's hand from her thigh, lifting it to her lips. She took one of Conner's fingers into her mouth and gently ran her tongue over the tip. The distraction worked wonders for Conner's anxiety level, and Alex held Conner's hand as they flew over the northern section of Duval County.

In the cockpit, Olivia looked in the overhead mirror that gave her an unobstructed view of the passenger area and when her eyes locked with

Alex's, she gave her friend a thumbs-up sign and a wink. *Ha, I knew it.* Smiling, she turned her attention back to her flying.

Alex bit her bottom lip to keep from grinning. *Never could hide anything from you.* She sighed and leaned over to look out the chopper door as Olivia's voice came over the intercom, telling them they had arrived at their destination.

"We're only going to get one shot at this. I'm going to set her down and make it look like I'm checking out the rotors. There's a clear landing spot on each side. Which one do you want me to take?"

Alex looked down on the landscape. "Take the west side, near the river. We haven't been able to get a look at that side from the roads."

"Roger. Okay, guys, nothings wrong here, I'm just trying to make us look realistic to the eyes below." Olivia smiled to herself. *Here's another chance, Monty, make it count.*

Conner looked at Alex as Olivia spoke. Just as she was about to ask what Olivia meant, the chopper started to stutter, and the back end began to swing to the left, then to the right. "Fuck, what the hell is going on?" Had Conner not been strapped into her seat, she would have jumped into Alex's lap.

"It's okay, Conner. That's just Olivia giving us a good reason to land. Nothing's wrong. We're fine."

Conner swallowed hard and looked at Alex, trying to read her face. Alex wasn't even breathing hard and was showing no signs of discomfort. Conner forced herself to relax as Olivia lowered the chopper to the ground. It was only when they landed with barely a bump that she released Alex's hand.

Conner unbuckled her seat belt and climbed out of the chopper. Alex followed close behind, and they both walked a short distance away from the craft. To anyone looking on, it would appear they were having mechanical difficulties, as Olivia climbed on top of the chopper and pretended to check the rotor.

"It's the warehouse directly ahead of you. The Container building is just to the right of the warehouse." Alex pointed out the building to Olivia while she sat on top of the chopper. Her head was bent down, but her eyes scanned the structures in front of her. She noticed a small dock that stretched out about ten yards into the river. A fence ran alongside it, out into the water.

"Well, what can you see from up there?" Alex yelled from the ground.

"Come on up and look for yourself. Just make it look like you're helping me with the rotor. Conner, go back in the chopper, there's a camera in the storage hatch behind where you were sitting. Put the telephoto lens on it and get us some pictures of the building from the rifle hole in the other side."

Alex climbed on top of the chopper. Keeping her head down, she saw the dock Olivia was talking about and agreed that it was the only shortcoming in their security. They didn't see any signs of life in either of the buildings, but that didn't mean no one was watching. The snipers that had been on the roof of the Container building the day before were also absent. *Well, they probably think that I'm dead, and they have nothing else to worry about*, Alex thought.

After a few minutes, they jumped back to the ground and climbed back into the back of the chopper. Taking the camera from Conner, Olivia handed it to Alex, who was now to her amusement sitting by the door. "When we lift off, I'm going to make a wide sweep of the area. I want you to get some photos of the dock area, as well as the rooftops of both buildings. Take the entire roll and get as much as you can. It's set on automatic, so just point it and shoot, but don't be too obvious about it."

Olivia moved to the cockpit and readied the chopper. Conner held the camera while Alex crawled to the floor and lay on her stomach. "What the hell do you think you're doing?"

"Take the seat belt and loop it through my belt. I'll be less likely to be spotted here on the floor." Alex looked back at Conner and saw the apprehension in her eyes. "It's okay, come on, we're about to lift off."

Conner did what Alex asked, but loosened her own seat belt so she could hold on to the waistband of Alex's slacks. "I have an idea about the river, so make sure you get some good shots from that angle."

"What's your idea?"

"I'll tell you about it when we get back, just pay attention to what you're doing."

The chopper jerked as it rose slowly into the cloudy sky. Olivia continued to make the chopper behave oddly so anyone watching would think they were having some minor rotor problems. It also gave her an excuse to fly at a low altitude, thus allowing Alex the chance to get better photographs. Alex shot frame after frame, trying to get good overall coverage of both buildings. She asked Olivia to follow the river back to the Atlantic Ocean.

Conner had become so interested in the river and her new idea that she was leaning over to look out of the open door. To Conner's embarrassment, Alex looked up and gave her a wink, and to Alex's shock, Conner pinched Alex's butt, then lightly stroked the vee between her legs, sending shock waves through Alex's body.

"Okay, you guys, you're having a little too much fun back there. No fair."

Conner's face turned dark red when she realized they had been seen. Alex's body shook as she dropped her face onto her arms and laughed at Olivia's remark.

"Never could get away with anything from you, could I, Morgan?"

Olivia smiled. "Nope, so don't make a mistake and think I'm getting soft in my retirement."

"You soft, Morgan? Not a chance." Alex took Conner's hand, squeezing it firmly, letting her know that everything was okay.

The rest of the trip back to the charter office was uneventful. Olivia set the chopper down, and the women went back into Olivia's office. "Okay, looks like we have a lot of work to do here. I need to get this film developed before we do anything. Let's meet later this afternoon. Where would be a good place for you two?"

"We have to go to José's now. How long that will take depends on what we find. Let me give you directions to my house. We can meet there, let's say around seven, and I'll throw something together for dinner." Alex drew out a rough map to her house and handed it to Olivia. "One more thing. Could you bring your sweeper? Maybe I'm getting paranoid, but I want to make sure the house is clean."

"No problem. See you about seven."

Alex asked Olivia to call them a taxi, and as she and Conner walked to the door, Olivia shouted "Heads up!" Alex spun around to see keys flying toward her face. Before she could react, they were plucked out of the air by Conner.

"Nice hands," Olivia said, "but we've already established that fact now, haven't we?" She winked at Alex as a red wave washed up Conner's face. "Take my car, I'll get it from you later."

Conner tugged on Alex's sleeve. "Come on, let's get out of here before your friend here makes me die of embarrassment."

All three women laughed as they walked out into the parking lot, "Really, Morgan, I'm not sure it's a good idea for us to take your car. Remember, mine was blown up earlier in the day." Alex's comment brought them back to the seriousness of the situation.

"Let 'em blow it up, I want a new one anyway." Olivia gave Alex a hard look. "Just make damn sure neither of you are in it."

Alex smiled and shook her head, "You're crazy, you know that, don't you?"

"Of course. That's what made me the best." Olivia scowled and poked Alex in the shoulder.

"Second best, and don't forget it," Alex shot back with a grin. The bantering went on for a few more minutes until Alex's face took on a more serious expression. "You do know what you're getting yourself into here, don't you?"

"Yep. Just one more picnic where I get to ride in and save your ass." Olivia winked at Conner.

"God, you're insufferable." Alex shook her head and climbed into Olivia's Explorer. "Come on, Conner, let's get out of here before I get nauseous."

Olivia waited until they were out of sight, then walked back to her office. After closing and locking the door behind her, she walked over the credenza, lifted the bottom edge of the front panel until it was level with the top and slid it into the recessed slot. She knelt down and spun the combination lock, entering the number she had burned into memory long ago. After turning the lever and hearing the familiar click, she opened the safe.

Olivia sat for a moment, looking at the contents. She let out a ragged breath, removed the Sig Sauer from the holster, and let her fingertips run over the smooth dark surface of the weapon. This was a part of her life she had hoped never to revisit, but she had always kept the equipment in prime condition, just in case something to make her go back. After an experience similar to Alex's, she had left the FBI. She moved to her desk, laid the Sig on the desk pad in front of her and sat back in the chair, remembering the case.

Jennifer had been her life, a part of her very soul. They had been together for three wonderful years and had settled down to a life of happy contentment. Before meeting Jennifer, Olivia had always lived from day to day, knowing that each morning she walked out the door might be her last.

Olivia's eyes filled with tears as she remembered the day Jennifer had died. The case had been unusually long, involving an organized crime family in New York, taking Olivia away from home for weeks at a time. When the case stalled, Olivia had gotten lucky and was able to fly home to Jennifer for the weekend. They had spent two wonderful days taking long walks, making love, and enjoying their time together.

They had decided to go out to dinner before Olivia's flight back to New York. As they were walking toward the restaurant, a car sped down the street beside them. Olivia was turning her head to see what the commotion was about when she heard the shots and saw the blood spread across Jennifer's chest as her lover fell back into her arms. Jennifer had died instantly from the shot to her heart.

With Alex's help, Olivia had survived that first terrible night, and the next one, and the next. Alex had asked to be reassigned to the case, and Jennifer's murderer was now on death row.

Olivia picked up the gun again and ran her fingers along the surface. She sighed heavily and placed the gun back down on her desk as she picked up the phone. After punching in the numbers, she waited for the call to be answered on the other end.

"Is he in?...Yeah, it's me. I got some information you might be interested in...Well, I think you'll be interested in this. Yeah, meet me at the dock, one a.m.," Olivia growled into the phone, leaving no room for debate. "Oh, and Malcolm, come alone. I don't like your cronies."

She slammed down the phone and sat for a long moment before walking back to the locker. She strapped the Sig on her shoulder, removed an attaché case, relocked the locker, replaced the false front panel, and walked out the door to her other car.

Once behind the wheel, she placed the attaché case onto the passenger seat and opened it. She flipped on the power switch and adjusted the knobs until a satellite map of Jacksonville appeared on the screen. She punched a code into the keyboard, and a small dot blinked on the screen. Olivia followed the dot as it slowly moved across the screen until she could determine which direction the Explorer was moving in. She started the engine of her black Spyder and pulled out of the parking lot. She smiled sadly a few minutes later as she sped down the road. *The Black Widow in her black Spyder in pursuit of the Shadow,* she thought to herself sardonically, as she glanced again at the flashing dot on the screen.

Conner watched as Alex maneuvered the Explorer through the afternoon traffic. "So, you going to tell me about this secret friend of yours?"

Alex laughed. "You should have seen your face, it was priceless."

Punching her in the shoulder, Conner said, "Don't change the subject. Spill it."

Alex rubbed the sore spot on her shoulder. "Okay, okay, you don't have to get mean. It's really a long story, so for now I'll give you a summarized version."

Conner's stomach tightened into a knot when Alex told her about Jennifer's murder, and she understood why Alex and Olivia seemed so close and comfortable with each other. Conner was having trouble wrapping her head around something, though, but couldn't put her finger on what it was. She shook her head to clear the thoughts.

The ringing of Alex's cell phone startled both women, and they laughed nervously. Alex answered the call to hear Donald's voice. "Donald, why are you out of the hospital?"

Conner could only hear Alex's side of the conversation, but knew Donald was back at the office and hard at work.

"No, Donald, with José dead, plans have changed. What time is the special ops team getting in tonight?...Okay. Meet me at my house around eight tonight. I've enlisted an old friend's help on the case, and I want you to meet her...Yeah, I will, and Donald, take it easy, okay?"

Alex flipped the phone shut and turned back to Conner. "He checked himself out of the hospital and is back at the office. Damn, he's a stubborn man."

Conner smiled, but kept her thoughts to herself. *Yep, Alex, and he taught you well.*

Chapter Fifteen

They arrived at José's a little after four o'clock. Peterson had posted two police officers at each exterior door, and as Alex walked toward the house, she heard Donald's voice.

"I don't give a fuck what your orders were! This is a federal case and I am ordering you to move your ass, now." Donald's nose was in the officer's face as he screamed the orders.

The unaffected officer simply wiped the spittle off his face. "Sorry, sir, I have my orders."

"And just who the hell gave you the order, Officer?"

Alex decided to end it and save the poor officer from any more of Donald's wrath. "I did."

"Alex? Why do you have the local police guarding José's house?" Donald turned away from the officer and walked down the steps toward Alex.

"Let's just say that I don't know who I can trust anymore, Donald. I wasn't going to take the chance, so I had Jack place guards by the doors with orders not to let anyone in or out." Alex walked up the steps to the house. "If that's a problem for you, Donald, I'm sorry, but I gave the order while you were still in the hospital."

She showed her identification to the guard. who immediately stepped aside to let her enter the house. Looking over her shoulder, she saw Donald and Conner still standing on the front lawn. "Well, are you two coming in, or am I going to have to search this place by myself?"

Donald walked up the steps and into the house, followed by Conner. Alex knew she had been harsh with Donald. *Damn it all, the stakes are getting too high. I'm not letting friendship come in the way of doing my job.*

Alex asked Conner to start with the bedroom and work her way back to the living room. As Conner made her way down the hall, Alex was left alone with Donald. "Look, I'm sorry for being rough out there. Tomorrow night is coming fast, and we need a break in this case. The only thing I'm halfway sure of is that the four of us—you, me, Jack, and Conner—are on the same side. I don't trust anyone else in either the police force or the bureau. I'm not taking any chances here, Donald. Too many people have already died because of this man, and I'm going to put a stop to it once and for all tomorrow night."

Donald took a long hard look at Alex. He could see the evidence of the toll this case had taken on her. She no longer had that glow of life about her, and her eyes were flat, holding no emotion whatsoever.

Neither agent spoke, but they held each other's examining looks until Alex finally broke the stare and moved away. She walked into José's office and began searching through his desk. Donald followed and began scanning through the file cabinet on the other side of the room. For over an hour, the house was quiet as Alex and Donald pored over the files and papers in the office and Conner searched the bedrooms.

Alex jumped when she heard Conner call out. She walked down the hall, but could not find her anywhere. "Where are you?"

"In here. Push the clothes apart, there's an access door near the floor."

Alex looked toward the closet as Donald walked in the room. They walked into the cramped space, following Conner's instructions, and crawled through the small door. When Alex stood up, she was frozen in place as her brain tried to take in what she saw before her.

"Holymotherofgod," was all Donald said when he rose.

Conner looked around the small closet-like space, "Looks like a war room," she said, then handed Alex a sealed envelope. "I found this pinned to the wall here," she added, pointing to the spot.

Alex turned the envelope in her hand as Donald came up beside her. "Careful, Alex, it could be booby-trapped. Let's have the bomb guys take a look at that envelope before you open it."

While Donald called for the bomb squad, Alex slowly walked around the room, which was approximately five feet by five feet with walls of unfinished plywood that looked new. She walked to the makeshift desk and looked down into the half-empty coffee cup, then turned to the walls to look at the maps and drawings. On the north wall was an aerial map of the warehouse. Next to it was a detailed floor plan of the interior, showing all windows, doors, and a suite of offices.

Alex followed the wall around to the east wall above the desk. Pinned to the center, at eye level, was a photograph of Hernandez with a black X drawn across his face. This was the first indication to Alex that José had been on her side. She glanced at the papers on the desk, careful not to disturb anything until the FBI team arrived, then moved to face the south wall. There she found a detailed list of the people involved in the Hernandez organization. She recognized many of the names and was impressed that José had not only discovered their names, but also their ranks.

The west wall was the most interesting to Alex. José had managed to compile a detailed list of the Sarantos family as well that listed the rank and status of its members. Many of the names on the list were new, and Alex smiled, acknowledging that at least one good thing that had come from the raid: many of the high-ranking members of the family had been arrested. Some of the cases were still being tried, but most of the suspects had been convicted and sent off to serve their sentences in federal prisons.

Alex scanned further down the wall finding, to her surprise, a resume of sorts for each of the new Sarantos members. *Way to go, José,* Alex thought as a pang of guilt settled in her gut. *I guess you weren't the bad guy after all.*

"The bomb squad said it's okay," Donald said, dusting off his pants.

"Thanks, Donald."

"Um, I'll give you a few minutes here. Let me know when you're ready for the evidence team, okay?" Donald looked at Alex and saw the guilt and regret written on her face. "Alex, just so you know, I thought the same thing; so did some others in the bureau. Why he didn't share all of this information with the rest of us we'll never know, but one thing's for sure, it's no one's fault he's dead. He was in the wrong place—"

Alex raised one hand. "I know, Donald. It still doesn't make it any easier to swallow. That was supposed to be me today in that car. No matter what anyone says, I will always carry that with me."

"Well, like I said, just call when you're ready for the team." Donald crawled back through the opening.

Alex could hear voices beyond the wall, but they faded away as she opened the envelope and began reading the letter José had written in his own hand for her.

Dear Alex,

It is Tuesday morning, three days before the expected meeting between Hernandez and Sarantos. I know someone has been following both of us for a while, but I haven't been able to figure out who it is. I hope one of us lives long enough to put this case to bed, once and for all.

If you are reading this, then you must have found my little room. It also must mean that I am either dead or probably wish I were. If you've had time to look around, I'm sure you have seen that I have been busy the last few months while you were away. Everything should be self-explanatory.

You were right, you know. I did want your job. Not because I thought you were bad at it, but because I thought I could do it better. You allowed your emotions to get between your brain and the case. You were more interested in protecting your family and friends than in finding Hernandez. I guess I was lucky in that respect. I have no family, and I don't waste my time on friends.

I guess now this all falls back into your lap. Use the information before you, and make it work this time, Alex. Whoever has to die will die. Just get the bastard, you probably won't get another chance.

Take care, Alex, and good luck. I hope that I won't see you on this side of Hell anytime soon.

José

Alex stood motionless as she read the letter again. *Was José right? Of course he was. Too many people have died because of me.* Alex looked around the room one last time before bending and crawling back through the small door. Faces turned and eyes stared as she stood. She didn't speak to anyone, simply handed the letter to Donald and walked out the door.

Conner watched Alex leave and as she was turning to follow her, she felt a hand on her arm.

"Give her a minute, okay?" Donald led Conner to the corner of the room and held the letter so that they could both read it.

"Son of a bitch," Conner growled when she finished reading. "How could he say things like that to her? Of course she would protect her family and friends; who wouldn't?"

Donald just shook his head. "Conner, you had to know José to understand him. He was really a good guy deep down. He knew attacking Alex's integrity like this would give her the determination to do what had to be done to bring this to an end." Donald placed a hand on Conner's shoulder. "My wife tells me I'm not very observant when it comes to, um, personal issues. Go to Alex and get her out of here. As soon as the evidence team is finished, I'll load all this up and see you at the house around eight, okay?"

Conner stood, dumbfounded. "Sure, okay. Um, well, I guess I'll see you at the house then."

Donald watched Conner leave and silently prayed that this time, Alex would get lucky and not only get her man, but keep her lady in the process.

Alex was staring out the window and didn't seem to notice as Conner climbed into the Explorer. Conner didn't know what to say, but felt the silence was deafening. "Alex, I read the note. You're a good agent. Don't let that letter get to you."

Alex turned toward Conner, tears streaming down her face. "He's right. I was too busy with my own emotions to do my job well, and look at how many people are dead. I should have just killed them myself."

Conner grabbed Alex's arm, probably harder than she should have, but she wanted to make sure Alex got her point. "You didn't kill those people, Alex! Hernandez or Sarantos killed them."

Conner's voice grew louder and more passionate as she continued, "As far as protecting your family and friends, well, if you hadn't, then you obviously wouldn't be the person I've...fallen in love with." She finished her sentence in a whisper. The words shocked her as much as they did Alex, and they sat quietly in the car as they both absorbed her statement.

Conner reached for the door handle. "Ah, slide over here and let me drive."

Alex slid to the other side of the truck as Conner moved around to take her place in the driver's seat. She started the engine and moved slowly through the neighborhood. She was grateful for the distraction when Alex's cell phone rang, but as Alex made no move to answer, she picked it up for her.

"Harris."

"Yeah...Okay...Sure. No, we didn't think that was a good idea. Okay, I'll call my captain and let him know...Bye." Conner dropped the phone on the seat. "That was Donald. They have the preliminary report back on your car. He said he'd fill us all in on everything at your house."

Still staring out the window, Alex only nodded. They drove the rest of the way to Alex's, both lost in their own thoughts. Conner pulled into the drive, swinging Olivia's Explorer around to the back side of the house to park near the garage. She turned off the engine and was reaching for the door handle when she felt Alex's hand on her arm.

"Did you mean what you said back there?" Alex's head was still turned toward the window, her eyes staring out at nothing in particular.

"Of course I did, Alex. There is no way you're responsible for Feryle's death or José's. You're the best agent they have here! Don't let José and his jealous words make you believe otherwise."

Alex remained silent, and Conner wanted to shake her to get through to her. "Do you remember what you said to me just last night about staying focused on the next few days and not on the past?"

Alex continued to look the other way. "Well, I do, and you need to take your own advice. There was no way you could have predicted Feryle's or José's murders."

Conner looked at Alex again and still saw no emotion. Feeling her own anger boil to the surface, she grabbed Alex's shoulder and forcefully turned her until they were facing. "I can tell you one thing though, Alex—if you keep worrying about what could have been, you'll be no use to any of us on this case. You might as well go in the house, crawl in the bed, and feel sorry for yourself. I'm sorry, but I don't have the time to do that with you. I've got a murderer to catch tomorrow night, with or without your help."

She slammed the door as she stormed from the truck and headed for the beach. She didn't slow down until she was on the ocean side of the dunes. As the tears surfaced and overflowed onto her cheeks, she dropped her face to her hands.

Damn you, José. The last fucking thing you do in life is hand Alex a double-edged sword. Give her the answers we've been searching for and then rip her apart until she doesn't have the strength or confidence to use the information. Well, fuck you, José, you can burn in your hell.

Conner didn't know how long she had sat in the sand. Her first thought of the world outside of her mind was a light touch on her shoulder. She placed her hand on top of Alex's.

"I'm sorry. I didn't mean to—"

"No, Conner, you were right. I have no business looking back at things that can't be changed. I need—no, we need to stay focused. I'm sorry I wasted so much time this afternoon feeling sorry for myself."

Alex sat down behind Conner and pulled her into her arms. "You scared me when you left the truck. I thought you were leaving. Please don't leave me, not now."

"I'm not leaving you, Alex Montgomery." Conner's voice was strong and reassuring. She turned to steal a kiss and added, "Even if I wanted to, I don't have a car."

Alex snorted and pinched Conner's arm. "You are so damn bad, Conner Harris. Remind me to ask the bomb squad to keep your car locked down for the next few weeks until I can get you back in line."

Conner turned in Alex's arms and pushed her back into the sand. "Get me back in line? If I remember correctly, I'm the one who just snatched your ass back in line, Agent Montgomery."

While Conner had Alex pinned in the sand she decided to take advantage of the situation. *To hell with the tourists*, she thought, and bent to capture her lover's lips with her own.

After a few moments of heated bliss, she sat back and reached out her hand to Alex. "Come on. Let's go get ready for the powwow."

Alex grabbed a beer after she sent Conner off to shower and change. She sat on the back deck, listening to the music flowing through the sound system, and reflected on Conner's words to her outside of José's house. *I wonder if she even realized that she said she had fallen in love with me*, she thought. Taking a long pull from her beer, she lay her head back on the cushion of the lounger and closed her eyes. She felt Conner's presence only an instant before she felt her lips softly brush against her own.

"Mmm, you taste like beer. Got another one?"

Alex pulled another cold bottle from the bucket beside her chair and handed it to Conner, "Yep, here you go. Just what the doc ordered after the day we've had."

"It has been a hell of a day. What time is it?"

"Almost seven. Olivia should be here soon." Alex jumped as Conner shot out of her chair.

"Jesus, Alex I forgot to fax the directions to your house to Captain Peterson."

"Conner, I—"

"Damn, where's a pen? God, he's gonna be pissed." Conner ran back into the house and started pulling drawers open.

"Conner, I—" Alex leaned against the sliding door watching her lover panic.

"Damn, how could I be so stupid?" Conner frantically drew lines and scribbled road names on the paper. After a few moments, she looked up at Alex with a wild look in her eyes. "Where's your fax machine?"

It started as a chuckle, then grew to a full blown snorting laugh as Alex held her stomach. "You should see your face, Conner. It's priceless."

"Damn, Alex, the fax machine. Where the hell is it?" Conner threw up her arms in disgust.

"It's...in the...office." Alex tried to catch her breath as Conner almost flew out of the kitchen and down the hall.

Alex followed along behind and entered the office just as Conner was about to push the send button. "He already has the directions, dear."

Conner's head flew up, the question clearly in her eyes.

"While you were in the shower," Alex said, laughing again, "I faxed it myself." She backed away when she saw the look in her lover's eyes.

Conner caught up with Alex in a few steps and pushed her playfully against the wall.

"You mean to tell me," Conner bit Alex's neck, "that you stood there and let me panic," she bit the other side of Alex's neck, "when you knew the entire time," she bit Alex's chin, "that he already had the directions?"

"Um...yeah...yep, and uh-huh. That would be correct." Alex gave Conner a sheepish smile, wrapped her arms around her neck, then kissed her quickly on the lips.

Conner gently took hold of Alex's arms and in one quick move pinned them to the wall above her head while sliding her leg firmly between Alex's.

"You will pay dearly for that one, lover." Conner took Alex's bottom lip between her own. She bit gently and pried Alex's lips apart with her insistent tongue. Both women's passion surged out of control as Alex's hips rocked against Conner's thigh. Conner released Alex's hands, reaching for and pulling the shirt from the waistband of her pants. After tugging the shirt over her head, Conner quickly unhooked Alex's bra and bent to capture a hard nipple between her teeth.

"Oh my God, Conner." Alex grabbed the back of Conner's head and pulled her closer. With her free hand, she found Conner's breast and the hard nipple that begged to be touched. She heard the quick intake of breath and felt Conner's wet lips suck harder on her nipple. She could feel Conner lowering the zipper of her pants, shivering as she heard the sound, followed by and a surge of heat as Conner's hands pushed the pants off her hips.

Conner stood and captured Alex's mouth in a possessive kiss, and she reached into the wetness between Alex's legs, searching, until she found the hard shaft, already pulsing with desire.

"Ohh, God yes." Alex threw her head back as Conner stroked her and trailed long wet kisses down her neck, once again finding the hard dark nipple. Alex thrust her hips to meet Conner's eager hand and felt her legs begin to shake as all of her body's energy converged inside the small hard shaft beneath Conner's fingers.

Ding Dong.

"Let her wait," Conner growled as she continued to stroke Alex.

"Oh God, Conner." Alex hips were bucking, trying to force her over the edge.

Ding Dong, Ding Dong

Alex pulled Conner's hand away. Breathing heavily, she looked into her eyes, "Fuck, I can't, baby."

Both women were breathing hard, and they were both bathed in a sheen of sweat. Conner put her forehead against Alex's and nodded, "Okay, okay." Taking a few more deep breaths, she stood and tucked her shirt back in her pants, "I'll, uh, just go get the door."

Alex smiled and leaned her head back against the wall, trying to catch her breath, as Conner walked down the hall to the front foyer.

Ding Dong, Ding Dong, Ding Dong.

"I'm coming, I'm coming," Conner shouted as she headed toward the door.

Alex couldn't help but snicker as she slipped down the hall and into the bedroom. *You wish you were, Conner Harris. Hell, I know I wish I had,* she thought as she stepped into the cold shower.

Conner pulled the door open to greet Olivia. "Sorry. Come in."

"Damn, I was about to break the door down. What took you so long?" Olivia took in Conner's damp, flushed face. She raised her hands and laughed, "Oh Jesus, never mind. I should have known." To her amusement, Conner blushed a deep red. Olivia shook her head as she walked into the house and sat down on the sofa.

"I need a cold beer." Looking up at Conner, she snickered, "And by the looks of you, I think you need something cold too, huh?"

Conner swallowed hard and headed to the kitchen. "Um, yeah. I'll be right back."

Olivia smiled. *Damn, and she's a cute one too.*

Conner returned with their beers and sat in the chair across from Olivia. "Alex will be right out, she's taking a quick shower."

Olivia took a long pull from her beer, her only reply being a single raised eyebrow.

They sat in silence for a few moments before Olivia asked, "So, how long have you known Alex?"

"Not long."

"Did you know Feryle?" Olivia had already found out most of the answers in the few hours since the pair had left her office, but she wanted to see how much Conner was willing to share.

"No, actually, I didn't, but through Alex and a few mutual friends, I feel like I have a pretty good idea who she was."

Olivia was impressed with the answer Conner gave. Honest, yet not too revealing. She walked over to the fireplace and looked at every picture on the mantle. Not seeing any photos of the woman sitting before her, she asked, "Do you live here with Alex?"

Conner smiled. "No. I have my own place."

Olivia walked back toward the sofa, looking down the hall as she crossed the room, and sat down on the sofa, "So, how is Alex really doing? Is she ready for tomorrow night?"

Conner was about to let Olivia know she had had enough of the inquisition when Alex walked into the room. "I'm doing fine, Olivia, and yes, thanks to Conner, I'm more than ready for tomorrow night."

Olivia looked a little shocked to hear Alex's voice behind her. "Well, you haven't lost your touch at sneaking up on people, I see."

"There's a lot of things I'm finding out I haven't lost my touch at," Alex said as she quickly glanced at Conner.

Conner turned a shade of red Alex hadn't yet seen. "I...um, think I'll go check on dinner. You two need anything?"

"I'm fine," Olivia smirked, "but it looks like you could use some cold water."

Alex snorted and swatted Olivia on the arm. Conner gave Alex an evil look and headed off to the kitchen for some peace.

She was stirring the spaghetti sauce when she felt a pair of warm arms circle her waist, then warm wet lips nipped her earlobe. "Humph, don't come in here playing nice now. I see whose side you're on."

"Come on, baby, I'll make it up to you later," Alex purred in her ear.

Conner gasped as she felt Alex pinch her nipple. "Oh, I already have plans for you tonight, my dear."

"Where did you leave the twenty questions lady?"

"Play nice. She's doing the sweep of the house. With everything that's been happening, I want to make sure no one's come in and bugged the place."

The doorbell rang again and Alex pulled away, but not before she gave Conner's nipple one last pinch. Conner tried to regain her composure when Peterson strolled in the room.

"Harris, you're looking all domestic tonight. Trying to learn more tricks for your undercover persona?"

"Not you too. Geez, is this beat up on Conner night at the Montgomery house?" Conner smiled and shook her head. "You want a beer or something? I think Alex has some scotch if you'd prefer that." She leaned in the refrigerator and pulled out a beer for herself.

Sitting down at the kitchen table, Peterson leaned back and blew out a long breath. "Yeah, a scotch, neat, would be good."

Peterson didn't miss the fact that Conner was familiar with the layout of Alex's kitchen as she opened the overhead cabinet and pulled out the bottle of scotch. "So, how are you and Alex getting along?"

Conner's hand paused for just an instant over the glass. "Fine, sir. I like working with her. She's teaching me a lot."

Peterson walked to stand beside Conner. She handed him the scotch and then turned back to drop the spaghetti noodles into the boiling water as he followed her over and leaned against the wall.

"You know, Conner, the parts of this job I hate the worst are things like tomorrow night. Seeing friends and colleagues walk into a dangerous situation can sometimes make an officer second-guess their actions."

Peterson noticed Conner hesitate as she stirred the sauce. "One thing I've always had to do to keep from losing it during those times is to remember that everyone there knows what they are walking into. Everyone knows the danger. A good officer has to keep their emotions intact and not let it get in the way of the mission."

Peterson stopped Conner's hand, "Can you handle that, Conner?"

Conner's head shot up. "I-I don't know what you mean, Captain. Of—of course I can."

"Conner, don't bullshit me with the Captain stuff right now, okay? I'm talking to you as a friend right now." Glancing at the door he continued, "I've seen the way you two look at each other. I may be old, Harris, but I'm definitely not blind. Okay?"

Conner smiled and looked down into simmering the pot. "Is it that obvious?"

"Probably only to those of us who know both of you well."

"Yeah, Donald said something earlier today, too." Conner took the pasta off the stove and walked over to the sink to drain the noodles. Setting the pot in the sink, she turned back to Peterson. "This is Officer Harris asking Captain Peterson. Do you have any doubts that I can handle this?"

Peterson placed his hand on Conner's shoulder. "Captain Peterson doesn't doubt you at all. I just want to make sure Officer Harris doesn't doubt herself."

"Geez. If you weren't such a big lug, I'd hug you."

"Well, this big lug just happens to like getting hugs from his favorite friends." Peterson smiled at Conner, then enfolded her in a bear hug.

"Hey, no hugging in my kitchen unless I get one too." Alex smiled at the intimate moment between Conner and Peterson.

Peterson pulled back, then lifted Conner's chin. "Remember what I said, okay?"

Turning and walking by Alex, he patted her on top of the head. "As for you—you'll get yours tomorrow night when we go out celebrating," and then he left them alone in the kitchen.

"Well, that looked like it was an intense conversation," Alex said as she moved to the sink to finish the noodles.

"Yeah, it was. Remind me and I'll tell you about it later."

"I will." Alex poured the sauce and asked Conner to get out the plates and glasses. Soon everyone was gathered around the table, eating and discussing the plans for the next night. The special ops team was expected later that night, and Donald had arranged for them to stay in several different hotels around the city.

"I'm impressed, Donald. You've put together a good team, and with Olivia, Conner and I leading the pack, I'd say we have the best chance we've ever had to bring these guys in."

"Well, they're all yours, Alex. I've set up a meeting place for tomorrow morning at eleven. I'll give each of you a call around nine to tell you where to go." Donald held up his hands to fend off any objections. "I think we can all appreciate the need for secrecy here. Too many people have found out too many things in the past and it's just a precaution."

Everyone became quiet as Donald's words registered. This was the countdown they had all been waiting and hoping for. Now that it was here, everyone hoped they were ready.

Conner and Alex quickly cleared the table while Donald, Peterson, and Olivia went into the den to get acquainted. Whenever Donald laughed and yelled something indecipherable to Alex, she just shook her head. "Olivia is probably in there telling them about all my worst moments with the bureau."

Conner dropped the towel as she headed to the door. "This I gotta hear."

Alex grabbed her arm. "Not a chance! You want to know something, ask me. I'll tell you the true version, not Olivia's."

"You really trust her, don't you?" Conner picked up the towel and began wiping off the counter.

"With my life. We've pulled each other out of quite a few tight spots along the way." Alex smiled sadly as she put the last glass in the cabinet. "Why? Don't you trust her?"

Conner looked uncomfortable. "No, it's not that." She shrugged. "I don't know, she just seemed very inquisitive in there tonight, while you were taking a shower."

"Yeah, I know. I heard it all." Alex smiled and kissed Conner on the cheek. "They don't call me the Shadow for nothing, you know."

She crossed her arms over her stomach and leaned back against the counter. "Seriously, though, I think she was just being protective. Except for when Feryle died, she's seen me at my darkest times and has always taken on the mom role in our friendship. She's a good person, Conner. You can trust her, I promise."

They joined the rest of the group in the living room. Donald had already pulled out the maps the evidence team had removed from José's war room and spread them on the coffee table. He then passed each of them a folder containing copies of the lists and other notes taken off the wall. To Alex's surprise, he had also included a copy of the note José had written to her.

Alex had just opened her folder when Olivia said, "You mean to tell me this guy was an agent? He sounds like he should be in fourth grade. What an asshole."

Conner smiled. *Maybe she's not half bad after all,* she thought.

"Come on, Olivia. He had a right to his opinion, and he did do a hell of a lot better than I ever did compiling information on this group." Alex spread her hands out over the pile of folders and maps. She noticed that everyone in the group had stopped to stare at her. "However, no one, and I mean no one, is better than the Shadow, and tonight, thanks to Conner, the Shadow came home."

Everyone sat speechless. Seeing the uncomfortable looks on all of their face, she rubbed her hands together and smiled. "Come on, guys, let's get to work here."

They spent the next two hours looking over the maps and planning their approach. Conner suggested they move the *Shady Lady* into the river and use her to get close to the dock and as a method of escape if things went wrong. Everyone agreed the idea was a good one, with only one comment from Peterson not to expect any rental fees for her use, which got a round of laughter from the group.

Conner got up to call and ask Benny to motor the boat to a nearby marina the next morning. As she walked into the kitchen, she saw movement outside the sliding door. She eased over to the phone, opened the phone book as a ruse, and pretended to look up a number while punching the buttons on the handset. She heard Alex's cell phone ring in the other room and was glad she had guessed correctly.

"Montgomery."

Conner could hear Alex through the handset as well as through the doorway. "It's me. Don't talk, just listen. I'm in the kitchen and there's someone out back. Take Olivia with you and go out the front door, split up, and come around. Tell Jack to give you ten seconds and then give me the go-ahead to go out the back door." Conner was smiling so that to whoever was outside, it would appear that she was having a nice chat with a friend.

"Got it. We're on our way." Alex flipped her phone shut and quickly filled the others in as she moved to the door. She grabbed her Sig from the front closet and was about to hand it to Olivia when she saw Olivia pull her own weapon from her shoulder holster. She raised an eyebrow.

Olivia shrugged. "I always go prepared, Alex. You know that."

The women quietly slipped out the front door, Olivia taking the right, Alex the left, as Peterson and Donald sat helpless in the living room, their egos bruised but their brains acknowledging they were too damn old for the run-and-gun games anymore. Peterson waited the prescribed ten seconds, then gave Conner her go-ahead.

Alex moved against the side of the house, staying in the shadows. She peeped around the corner as she reached the back and saw movement off the far end of the deck. She knelt down, using the shadows to her advantage as she crawled closer. She was about fifteen feet from the deck when she rose up and had the intruder in her sights when Conner came through the sliding glass door and took a dive off the other end. Alex heard a thud, followed by a deep groan, as she shot to her feet and began running.

Just as she reached the far corner, Alex heard another thud, followed by a weak moan and footsteps running away from the house. When she rounded the corner, she saw Conner lying on the ground, and her heart lurched. Olivia came running from the other end of the house and Alex pointed her after the fleeing intruder as she bent to tend to Conner.

Blood had already saturated the sleeve of Conner's shirt. Alex quickly stripped away the cloth, made a makeshift bandage, then tied it above the open wound. She helped Conner to her feet and led her to a deck chair.

"Are you okay?" Alex's eyes ran over Conner's body looking for more injuries, but found none.

"Yeah, I'm okay. I almost had him, damn it. He had a knife and got me before I knew it. I'm sorry, Alex, I blew this one."

Donald and Peterson, hearing the commotion, ran out onto the deck. Seeing that Conner was fine, Donald asked about Olivia.

"She took off after the perp. He headed out into the dunes, but I don't think she'll get lucky enough to find him out there."

Alex turned back to Conner. "Come on. Let's get this wound seen to."

Olivia lay in the shadows of the dunes, watching as the four went inside and closed the door. She pulled out her cell phone, punched in the numbers from memory, and waited until the call was picked up on the other end.

"Yeah, let me talk to him," she barked into the phone. "I don't give a flying fuck what he's doing, put him on! Now!" She waited until she heard the familiar voice. "Just what the fuck do you think you're doing, Malcolm?...I don't give a rat's ass about your concerns! You want me, then you have to trust me. Otherwise, you can go fuck yourself." She listened to Hernandez's response. "Just call your cowboys off, or I'm out of here, got it?...Good."

She slammed the phone shut, shoving it back into her pocket before taking off down the beach in a hard run. When she had gone about half a mile, she turned back and continued her all-out sprint back to the house. When Olivia walked back into the house, sweat sliding off her brow and breathing hard, Alex knew Olivia had not been lucky. Disappointed, she turned her attentions back to Conner's arm.

The gash wasn't very large, but it was deep. Alex cleaned the wound with peroxide, applied two Steri-Strips, then covered it with a bandage. The others had moved back into the living room and were discussing the incident when Alex and Conner returned a few minutes later.

"Don't know, I didn't get a good look at him. He was too far ahead of me by the time I hit the beach. He ran off into the dunes before I could catch up."

"Male Caucasian, mid-thirties, dark brown hair, medium build, but muscular, scar on the right side of his neck, and smelled like cigarettes."

"Very good, Officer Harris," Olivia didn't turn around. "And you saw all of this in the dark?"

"Ah, no." Conner gave Alex a sideways glance. "I flipped the light switch as I went out the door, so I got a pretty good look."

Alex sat down on the fireplace hearth. "Which direction did he go, Olivia?"

"He went north, up the beach, probably back in the city by now."

Both men felt the tension building between Conner and Olivia, but remained quiet for the time being. Donald decided he would discuss the situation with Alex privately and hope she would come to the same conclusion that he had: the two women definitely needed to be separated the next night. They didn't need a power struggle interfering with the mission.

Peterson looked at his watch and saw that it was past midnight. "I say we call it a night, people. It's late and we all need to get some rest before tomorrow."

Everyone agreed. As Donald pulled his jacket on, he reminded them that he would be calling around nine to give them the meeting details. He had Olivia write her number down and then looked at Conner, expecting the same.

"Conner, why don't you stay here tonight? I have a spare room, and it's a long drive for you." Looking at Conner, Alex missed Olivia's smirk and the smiles that formed on the faces of the two men.

"Okay, thanks." Conner nervously rubbed her chin, trying to hide her amusement as she glared over Alex's shoulder.

When she saw Conner's expression, Alex turned around bewildered and looked into the sober faces of her guests. "Okay, I guess that's settled, then. You guys drive carefully going home, okay?"

The three left, and as the two women walked back into the house, Alex noticed the smile on Conner's face. " And just what is so amusing to you?"

Conner let out a snort. "Well, it's just that everyone thought your subtle invitation to me was, well, cute."

"Huh?"

"Yeah, cute. Olivia obviously knows, after catching us in the chopper today," Conner wrapped her arms around Alex, "and Donald mentioned it to me this afternoon at José's."

Conner saw the shock register in Alex's eyes. "And that's what the captain and I were discussing when you walked into the kitchen tonight."

Alex groaned and dropped her head to Conner's chest. "So I, um, just made a royal fool of myself here, didn't I?"

Conner tightened her embrace. "No, you didn't. I told you, they thought it was cute."

Alex lifted her head and gave Conner a serious look. "So what did Donald and Jack say to you?"

"Donald is okay with it. He told me to get you out of there today and bring you home. He was concerned about you, and a little embarrassed because of his lack of observation skills." Alex raised an eyebrow. "It seems his wife had to clue him in on our, um...situation."

Alex nodded. "Yeah, Catherine would have to do that. I can't say that Donald is the most observant person when it comes to interpersonal relationships."

Her expression changed from amused to concerned. "What about Jack? It looked like a very serious moment in there."

Conner pulled Alex over to the sofa and sat down beside her, "Yeah, it did get intense. Jack is concerned that I won't be able to stay focused tomorrow night, especially where you're concerned. He thinks our involvement may lead us to make mistakes."

Alex pulled Conner's hand onto her lap. "What do you think, Conner? That's the important question."

Conner leaned her head back and looked at the ceiling, searching for the answer. Alex remained quiet and gave Conner a minute to gather her thoughts. When Conner finally spoke, her voice was confident yet subdued.

"I know we both have a job to do out there tomorrow night. I also know we'll do whatever it takes to bring these guys in, Alex." Conner lifted her head and her eyes met Alex's. "Don't think for an instant, though, that I'm not going to keep an eye on your back out there. It's taken me too damn long to find you, and I have no intention of losing you."

Alex smiled and kissed Conner on the forehead, assured that her lover would carry out her duties the next night without hesitation. Lowering her lips to Conner's for a tender kiss, she sighed, "Let's go to bed. I need to make love to you."

Conner rose. "I think I need a quick shower first. Why don't I meet you there, okay?"

"Okay, I'll lock up." Alex ran a finger down Conner's chest and made small circles around her already hard nipple. Conner gasped, and Alex raised an eyebrow as she looked into her eyes. "Don't take too long. I'd hate to have to start without you," she said, then smiled and bit Conner's bottom lip.

Conner released a long moan. "Start without me, and you'll regret it, I promise." She turned and jogged down the hall.

Chapter Sixteen

Out in the dark shadows of the dunes, Olivia set a receiver down in the sand. Planting the small listening devices throughout the house had been easier than she had anticipated. In Alex's haste to check on her lover, she had left Olivia alone to do her search. The bugs she'd planted were the size of small thumbtacks, and Olivia was sure Alex would not search for the little dots after the meticulous sweep she had just completed.

She had placed the tiny devices in the master bedroom, office, and kitchen—the three locations she felt sure most of their conversations would take place. She raised the antenna of the receiver, settled the headset over her long hair, then leaned back into the cool sand.

Olivia smiled as she waited for sound to come from the bedroom. After seeing Conner's flushed face when she had answered the door earlier that evening, she'd known that she'd interrupted them in the heat of passion. She was almost certain that she'd soon be privy to a continuation of that hot action.

She listened as footsteps traveled back and forth across the floor and then stopped. She heard several identical scratching sounds she couldn't quite make out followed by the sound of covers being pulled back on the bed, and she wondered if the person she heard was Alex or Conner.

A few moments later, she heard another set of footsteps abruptly stop, followed by a deep growling moan, and then resume. The footsteps got louder as they approached the bed, then stopped again. She heard the sound of covers being pulled away, followed by a moment of silence.

Shivers ran down Olivia's spine as she heard Conner's voice through her headset. *God, you are so beautiful,* the voice said. Olivia felt a warm wetness spread between her legs as she interlocked her fingers behind her head, closed her eyes, and listened.

Conner let her eyes wander down Alex's body, delighting in the smoothness of her skin, her fingertips following her eyes, and she smiled when she saw Alex shiver under the gentle touch. She placed a soft kiss in the middle of Alex's stomach, watching as the muscles beneath rippled. The tender kisses continued as she moved up Alex's body, pausing only for a moment to place one single kiss on the swell of each breast before continuing on her journey.

Using her strong legs and muscular arms to hold herself up, Conner moved until her body was only inches above Alex's, close enough that she could feel the heat radiating from her body. She softly took Alex's parted lips in her own.

Alex placed her hands on Conner's hips as she parted her legs in anticipation. "Please, baby," she pressed her hands harder against the firm muscular hips. "Please, Conner, I need to feel you next to me."

Conner's arms were shaking, not from the injury she'd sustained earlier or from any muscular fatigue, but from the powerful surge of energy she felt pulse through her body. She lowered herself slowly, breast meeting breast, torso meeting torso, until finally their bodies melted together in an explosion of sensual passion.

"God, you feel so good next to me." Alex could barely speak as the overwhelming sensation forced the air from her lungs. She wrapped her arms around Conner, pulling her even closer as their mouths met with a consuming need. Tongues met, probed deeper, dueled for control, and sought release, until Alex broke the kiss with a gasp for air.

Planting one heel on the bed, Alex flipped Conner over so that she was on top of her. Conner reached for Alex, but her hands were quickly snared and pinned above her head. Looking down into dark green eyes, Alex felt her heart skip a beat as she took in the intense beauty of her lover, then bent to once again capture Conner's swollen, ready lips between her own. She let her body relax onto Conner's as the embrace took their passion to a higher level. She tore her lips from Conner's only to move lower and taste the sweet flavor of her neck.

"You taste good," Alex moved lower, "and feel good," she slid lower still, "and smell good." She traced circles around Conner's navel with her tongue. Looking up, she saw that Conner was following the path of her tongue with dark needy eyes, and she smiled as she bent to nip the soft flesh of her muscular stomach. A hand touched her shoulder.

"Come here. I want to feel you next to me again."

Alex grinned and took one last nip of the soft flesh between her teeth, then raised herself onto her hands and knees, crawling like a stalking panther up Conner's body. When she came level with the dark green eyes, she relaxed and leaned in to kiss Conner's warm lips. Before she realized what was happening, she was catapulted across the bed and Conner slid on top of her. Conner used Alex's own tactics and pinned her hands above her head before she had a chance to react.

"I intend to finish what I've already started *twice* tonight." Using her legs, Conner opened Alex's, then took a hard nipple in her mouth. She sucked it gently and flicked the tip with her tongue as she brought her other hand down to caress the other.

"Oh, Conner, yes." Alex thrust her hips, trying to bring her sensitive clitoris in contact with Conner's taut stomach.

Conner pulled one of Alex's legs up as she moved lower, nipping and licking the taut flesh on her way down. When Conner reached the apex of Alex's legs, she rubbed her cheeks against the soft skin. Pulling Alex's other leg up, Conner settled Alex's feet on her shoulders. She pushed gently on each of Alex's thighs, opening her and exposing the hard nub nestled between the swollen folds.

Alex pushed against Conner's shoulders with her feet, bringing her hard, aching clitoris closer to her lover's lips. "Taste me, Conner, please."

Conner let a ragged breath escape her lungs, and the warm rush of air across Alex's clitoris made her hips spasm in Conner's hands. Conner continued to rub her cheeks against the sensitive skin of Alex's thighs, and in long slow strokes, she licked the swollen lips that held the hard nub Alex begged her to touch.

Conner felt Alex's hand on the back of her head, urging her closer to her heat. In response, Conner took the wet swollen folds between her teeth and gently bit down, causing Alex to again thrust her hips up, pleading to be touched.

She looked up and saw the raw need in Alex's dark eyes. "Behave yourself. Do you want me to stop?" She flicked her tongue, just barely touching the hard clitoris.

"Conner, you're killing me...please." Alex pulled on Conner's head.

"Do you want me to taste you, Alex?"

"Yes, damn it, Conner, yes...please."

Conner could feel the involuntary spasms in Alex's hips as she lifted the hot, wet center closer to her lips.

"Then tell me, Alex." A soft nip to the thigh. "Talk to me." A warm breath against the hard shaft. "Tell me what you want me to do to you." A long slow stroke of her tongue against the hard, wet shaft. "Is this what you want?"

"Ah, God, Conner. Yes, lick me."

The endless teasing was as much torture to Conner as it was for Alex. When she heard her lover scream her name, she could no longer take the sensual pain and enveloped the hard nub in her lips.

Alex's hips bucked against Conner's face, and she threw her head back in sheer ecstasy as she felt Conner's tongue slide up and down her hard shaft. She gripped the sheets in her hands as Conner took her higher and higher. She was floating on a plateau of bliss when she felt Conner gently slide three fingers inside her. "Oh, yes, that's it, baby. Deeper, please...come on, baby, deeper."

Conner pulled back and bit Alex's thigh. "Oh, I'm going to take you there, Alex, but I'm going to take you slow." She resumed the slow rhythm of her fingers in and out of Alex's hot core. Using her free hand, she separated the swollen folds of Alex's outer lips, forcing the tip of her hard clitoris out of its protective sheath. She bent and blew softly, feeling the engorged muscles contract around her fingers.

"Conner, yes, that's it, baby...take it, Conner, please."

As if in slow motion, Conner gently captured the aching nub between her lips and lightly sucked as she slid her tongue softly across the sensitive nerves.

Alex arched her back, pushing herself closer to Conner's mouth. "Oh my God, Conner. What are you doing to me?" She seized Conner's head, weaving her fingers in the soft silky blonde hair. "That's what I want, baby, just like that. Oh God yes, deeper."

Conner's own senses were reeling as she focused on the feel and flavor of her lover beneath her tongue. She had always enjoyed the sweet taste of Alex, but on that night, at that moment, the juices of her lover flowed sweeter and freer than she had ever experienced. Conner felt herself losing control as Alex bucked beneath her. Alex's hands guided her, pushed her, pleaded with her to grant the release she so desperately needed.

Conner relinquished control of her body to the energy consuming her as she pushed deeper, harder, and faster into her lover.

"Ah yes, that's it. Yes...yes...take it, baby...take it."

Conner could feel the wetness between her legs, and she pressed her hips against the mattress struggling to find some relief of her own. She growled with a primal need when Alex grasped her own legs under the knees and pulled them higher and wider, opening herself up completely. Conner's response was hot and swift as she felt herself suspended on the precipice of orgasm.

She felt the first spasms of Alex's orgasm as the slick muscles began to squeeze her fingers. Pulling back slowly, almost completely, out of the warm, wet cocoon, she hesitated for only a moment before burying her fingers deep inside her, again and again.

"Yes...yes...oh Conner...I'm com—Ahh." Alex felt the orgasm overtake her body. Every nerve ending screamed as Conner continued to take her higher and higher. She seemed to stay on the apex forever, until Conner pulled back, and with one long stroke of her tongue sent Alex over the edge, falling into the abyss.

Conner lost all sense of time as she let Alex's orgasm consume her. The muscles seized her fingers, and the nub beneath her tongue pulsed as she continued the long, gentle strokes. She screamed out as her own unexpected orgasm surged through her body. "God, Alex, yes."

Alex felt another surge course through her body when Conner cried out her name, knowing Conner had experienced her own orgasm from merely touching and tasting her. As Alex floated back to reality, she looked down at her lover licking the remaining juices of her orgasm from her. Further down, she saw Conner's hips still thrusting into the mattress, and she knew her lover still ached for relief.

Alex grasped Conner's arm, urging her up. "Come to me."

Conner slid up Alex's glistening body before joining her in an all-consuming kiss. Alex could feel Conner's body trembling and gently slid from beneath her. Conner relaxed and let her body fall onto the warm sheets. She moaned as Alex rose to her knees, straddled her hips, and nipped the back of her neck.

With a feather-light touch, Alex ran her fingers down Conner's spine, and she gasped when Conner's hips thrust up and made contact with her still-sensitive clitoris.

"Don't tease me, please," Conner groaned. "I need you, now."

Alex bent and slowly licked Conner's earlobe, then took it between her lips and gently sucked. "I'll bet that's what you want me to do to you, isn't it?"

"Baby, please," Conner pleaded, clutching Alex's leg.

"Now, now," Alex whispered, "play nice, or I'll just make you wait longer."

"No, now...please."

Alex slid down Conner's body, nipping, licking, and teasing until she reached the firm, taut muscles of her hips. Spreading Conner's legs with her own, Alex sat back on her knees, softly massaging Conner's thighs. She smiled as her lover lifted her hips in a wordless invitation. Gripping her hips, she pulled Conner up until she was settled on her lap, and Conner moaned when Alex pulled her back to rest against her breasts. Wrapping her arms around Conner's waist, she kissed a sensitive spot on her neck. She captured Conner's hard nipple between her fingers, lowering her other hand until her fingers brushed the trimmed blonde hair between her legs.

"You feel so good, Alex." Every nerve in Conner's body shouted for relief when she felt Alex's hard nipples press into her back. "Please touch me."

Alex softly ran her fingers across Conner's swollen folds, her middle finger teasing the hard nub pushing out through the wet slit. "Do you want me inside you?"

Conner thrust her hips out. "Yes...oh God, yes."

"Well, tell me, then." Alex dipped her finger between the folds and slowly circled the hard nub. "Tell me what you want, and it's all yours."

Conner grabbed Alex's hand and pressed her deeper, until both their fingers were buried in the hot, wet opening of her core. "Ah, Alex, please. I want you inside me...Godplease, Alex."

Alex gently pushed Conner down onto her back. She sat there for a moment, taking in the beauty of the woman lying in her bed. Sliding her body on top of Conner's, she gently kissed her ready lips. "Conner, you've made me feel so many things this last week. I can only hope I've made you feel the same."

Conner placed her hand against Alex's cheek. "You have...you do."

Alex's hand trailed down Conner's body, and she felt the rippling muscles under her fingers. She followed their path, placing soft kisses along the way until she had settled snugly between Conner's legs. She ran her chin through the soft triangle of blonde hair and heard Conner's soft moans as she kissed the wet folds guarding the hard, waiting clitoris beneath. Alex spread Conner's legs wider, parted the swollen folds, and with the gentlest touch, ran her tongue the length of the bulging shaft.

"Oh God, Alex...yes."

Alex licked and teased the small nub until it was swollen and hard, pulsing with every touch. She slowly pushed two fingers into the wet opening and felt the muscles instantly tighten around her. Alex knew Conner was close, but wanted to prolong the sweet torture as long as possible. She continued her slow ministrations, keeping Conner teetering on the edge.

"Alex, come here...kiss me." As Alex moved up, Conner wrapped her arms tightly around her neck. "I want to feel you next to me." She held on tighter as Alex probed deeper and harder into her core, and she drew her into a passionate kiss. Their tongues met and danced, as Alex took her higher and higher. Conner broke the kiss, gasping for air, and threw her head back as she felt the first spasms of the orgasm overtake her body. She rode the wave as Alex plunged harder and deeper.

Conner opened her eyes to see dark blue staring down at her as she felt herself falling. "Alex, I...oh God...I...I lo—ah—"

Alex kissed her softly. "I know, baby. I love you too, Conner."

Conner felt the spasms rip through her body at Alex's declaration. She opened her eyes to see Alex smile down at her. Alex whispered softly as Conner fell into the orgasm, "Let it go, baby. That's it. I've got you."

She pulled out of Conner and slowly and tenderly stroked the pulsing shaft beneath her fingers until Conner collapsed, exhausted from the powerful release. She continued to plant light kisses on Conner's forehead, cheeks, chin, and lips, allowing her to savor the aftershocks of their lovemaking.

After a few minutes, Conner opened her eyes once again. "God, Alex, I love you." She kissed Alex deeply, passionately, and completely as they shared their first few moments as committed lovers, then drifted off to sleep in each other's arms.

Much too soon for Olivia, the headset went silent, and she groaned aloud as the burning need between her legs was left unfulfilled. She removed her hand and leaned back heavily in the sand.

If you only knew how much I've wanted you Alex. Soon, my dear Alex...soon.

When she had first laid eyes on Conner Harris earlier in the afternoon, her primal instincts had taken over, and she'd vowed to see what she looked and felt like beneath those clothes. She had only been slightly disappointed when she saw Conner slide her hand between Alex's legs during their flight. W*ell,* she thought, *I'll have to get creative, but with Monica's help I'm sure I can manage something to get that little detective out of my way.*

Knowing she would not rest until her burning desire was satisfied, Olivia pulled the small cell phone from her pocket and punched in a familiar number. "Hey, gorgeous. You wearing anything right now?"

A deep throaty laugh filled the quiet night. "In that case, I'll be over in a little while. I have a quick errand to run first." She quickly gathered her equipment and headed down the beach toward her car.

She arrived at the dock a few minutes before 1 a.m. and was leaning on a tie post when she heard footsteps behind her. She didn't bother to turn around—she recognized the limping gait—and she smiled in the darkness. "Right on time."

Hernandez sighed heavily. "You didn't leave me much of a choice, did you, Liv?"

"Guess not."

Lighting a small cigar, Hernandez turned to face her. "So, what is it that's so important that you have to get me out here in the middle of the night?"

"Well, I thought you might like to know I had visitors this afternoon. A feebie and her sidekick wanting a chopper ride out here to see your little warehouse."

Hernandez sighed, "That's old news, Liv, I heard about that ten minutes after you landed in the adjacent field. Tell me something I don't know."

Olivia smirked. "Okay. They're going to hit the Container building. Seems the sidekick saw some of your men on the roof. That was a mistake, Malcolm my friend. I tried to tell you. One slip-up by those goons you call guards, that was all it took. I suggest you try to contact Sarantos and move it back to the warehouse, or even better, somewhere else entirely."

Hernandez's voice carried over the water as he laughed. "You have to be kidding me. It took months to set this meeting up, and now you want me to just move it down the street. I don't think so. Anyway, I've waited almost a year to put an end to the Shadow for what she did to my leg, not to mention what she's done to my business. I'm not going to miss this opportunity. The meeting stays where it is, and it's your job to make sure it's safe."

Olivia walked to the end of the dock and hopped down into the small boat. "It's your ass, Malcolm. Don't say I didn't warn you."

He followed her to the end of the dock, leaned down, and whispered, "No, my friend. If anything goes wrong, it's your pretty little ass, so I suggest you make absolutely sure our security isn't breached."

She pressed the ignition button and the small engine sputtered to life. Without a word she disappeared into the darkness.

When Olivia arrived back at the car, she reached into her shirt and pulled off the tiny microphone she had taped between her breasts. She removed the recorder from the floor of the car and pressed the rewind button. When the machine stopped, she pressed play and listened to her conversation with Malcolm Hernandez.

She took a shuddering breath as she listened to one of Hernandez's main goals for the meeting the next night. *Anyway, I've waited almost a year to put an end to the Shadow for what she did to my leg, not to mention what she did to my business. I'm not going to miss this opportunity.* Olivia punched the stop button, pulled the tape from the machine, and tossed it in her briefcase.

As she sat there, she thought of Alex and all they had been through together, all the pain they had shared. She felt a gripping band of guilt constrict in her stomach for the things she had been forced to do the last year as she thought of the woman she had admired—no, loved, for years possibly dying the next night.

I couldn't stop it, couldn't even warn her. Gonzolas is dead; I'm no longer your little pawn, Malcolm, and you're a dead man.

Olivia leaned her head back and let the cool night air clear her senses. She thought back over the events of the day and found her mind wandering back to the sensual sounds she had heard coming from Alex's bedroom as she and Conner made love. She felt the heat creep down her body and settle between her legs, and she started the engine and drove the two short miles to Monica's apartment.

Oh well, if I can't have what I want right now, I'll take what I can get. Her speed quickened as images of Alex flashed through her mind, and she soon pulled into the parking lot and bounded up the short flight of stairs to her temporary distraction.

Chapter Seventeen

Olivia woke with a warm body pressed against her back. She had arrived at the apartment a little after 2 a.m. to a very naked and ready Monica, who had pulled her through the door and immediately backed her against the wall, ravishing Olivia's mouth with hot, wet kisses. Eager hands tore at the buttons on Olivia's shirt after the shoulder holster dropped to the floor with a thud. The rest of Olivia's clothes were scattered haphazardly down the length of the hallway, having been quickly discarded as Monica pulled them from her body in her haste to get to the bedroom.

Olivia turned over and felt her spine crack as she stretched her aching muscles. Monica was always good for a nice round of sexual distraction, and she usually had the power and stamina to quell her surging libido. However, this morning, Olivia still felt a hot need between her legs. According to the digital clock on the nightstand, it was only five o'clock.

Smiling, Olivia rolled Monica onto her back, immediately capturing a dark brown nipple in her mouth and sucking it hard and deep while flicking her tongue over the sensitive tip. Monica opened her eyes as Olivia threw back the covers, pushed her legs apart roughly, and plunged two fingers deep inside her.

"Slow down, Liv, what's your hurry?" Monica growled as Olivia's hands and mouth assaulted her body. She moved to touch Olivia's shoulder but quickly found her hands pinned above her head. "What's the matter with you, baby? Slow down."

Olivia heard Monica's pleas to ease up but ignored them. Nothing, not even Monica herself, could keep her from having what she wanted, the way she wanted it. She tore her mouth away from the hard nipple only long enough to breathe out, "Stop talking! I have to go soon and I want you again, now." She recaptured the hard nipple between her lips and closed her eyes, trying to conjure up the images that had been so easy to see in the darkness last night.

Images of Alex screaming *her* name instead of Conner's, begging *her* to go deeper and harder. She resumed the relentless pumping. Olivia knew Monica liked her sex rough and she smiled, interpreting her cries as encouragement as she pumped faster and harder.

In the fogginess of waking, Monica didn't really comprehend all that was happening to her body until Olivia began the unrelenting, painful pounding. She had always known Olivia was good for some fast hard sex, but never like this. Olivia seemed possessed, using her mouth and hands to drive the demons from her soul. Monica knew that trying to slow Olivia down was useless and would only prolong the painful experience. Closing her eyes in defeat, trying to shut out the pain, she arched her back, moaning loudly as she feigned an orgasm, hoping Olivia would relent.

She fell back into the pillows, breathing hard, and focused on blocking out the burning pain between her legs. Olivia soon rolled over on her back, pulling Monica on top of her. Grabbing Monica's hand, she thrust it between her legs, pressing her fingers into the slick wetness, and moaned as she thrust her hips higher.

It had been a long time since Monica had felt Olivia this wet, and she silently wondered what had driven her to this frantic need. Monica knew when the woman beneath her needed hard, raw sex, and this was one of those times. She knelt between Olivia's legs, pushing them wide apart, and added another finger as she plunged deep into the hot wetness. Olivia's hips thrust up violently as she tried to take Monica deeper.

"I want all of you in me, *now*." Olivia stared at Monica with glazed eyes as she grasped her hand, pushing her deeper.

"Hold on, baby, you're not ready. I'll hurt you." Monica had never seen Olivia so fiercely aroused.

"Push harder...I need you in me...all the way." Olivia's head was pressed back into the pillow, hips thrust upwards, open to the fierce assault she so desperately needed.

Monica continued to pump her fingers into Olivia while tucking her thumb into her palm. She pinched one of Olivia's hard nipples between her fingers, then clamped down hard. When she heard Olivia's cries, she slowly eased her hand into her and slowed her pumping to the barest movement, knowing from experience that just the filling presence would send her over the edge.

Olivia was lost in her fantasy. Images of Alex flew through her mind, and she lost all sense of control as she felt the small hand completely fill her core.

"Ah, yes baby, that's it...fuck me, Alex...fuck me."

Monica raised an eyebrow, wondering if this mysterious Alex was responsible for Olivia's insatiable need. *Oh well, who cares who got her here. She came to me, and that's all that matters right now*, she thought, as she waited for Olivia's thrashing to slow.

The orgasm was longer and stronger than any Olivia had ever experienced. She felt the muscular walls of her core squeeze Monica's hand tightly and the blood pulsed through her veins as Monica slowly pumped her hand inside. After what seemed like an eternity, Olivia's body relaxed and slumped back against the mattress. Her chest heaved as her lungs attempted to supply the oxygen her body so desperately needed, and the arteries in her neck pulsed as they rushed oxygen-rich blood to her brain.

Monica felt the aftershock spasms as she pulled her hand slowly out of Olivia. She knew Olivia loved hard rough sex, but she was somewhat frightened by what had just happened. Olivia opened her eyes and looked up at her with a blank stare, then rolled over and crawled out of bed, already in search of her clothes.

"Do you have to go already?" Monica leaned back on the headboard and pulled the covers up around her hips. Olivia had never stayed around long after sex, but for some reason, this morning's tryst had made her feel cheap, used, and Olivia's swift retreat only magnified the feelings.

Olivia retrieved her sports bra from in front of the dresser, pulled it over her head, and walked to the door to search for the rest of her clothes. "Yeah, I gotta go. I have a meeting this morning."

"Wouldn't be with someone named Alex, now, would it?" Monica asked in her usual sarcastic tone.

Olivia stopped dead in her tracks and turned dark, dangerous eyes back to Monica. "And what if it is? That's never stopped you from fucking me before," she growled.

"No, it hasn't. But then again, you've never been quite like you were with me this morning, either."

"Give it a rest, Monica, and don't pretend you didn't like it. I have to go. I'll see you in the office later." Olivia continued down the hallway, pulling on her clothes as she went. "Oh, and don't think that just because I kept you up a little late last night, you can be late for work. I have a charter group coming in at eleven. Tell Bobby he'll have to handle it. I'm going to be busy this morning."

"Yes, boss," Monica yelled down the hallway as she headed for the bathroom to shower. A few minutes later she heard the door slam and knew she was once again alone in the apartment. She stepped into the shower, letting the warm water wash away all evidence of the strange sexual encounter. She reached for the soap and saw the bruises that were beginning to form on her arms and hips. *Jesus, Olivia, what the hell has gotten into you?*

A little after six, Olivia pulled her sports car into a beach access road about 100 yards south of Alex's house. She turned her car, parking to face the road so that she could easily see anyone driving in. Scanning the area to make sure she was alone, Olivia pulled the antenna up on the receiver, placed the headset over her ears, and listened for any sounds indicating the women were awake.

Her eyes flew open when she heard rustling sounds through the headset, and glancing at her watch realized she must have fallen asleep. Olivia smiled, pleased with her decision to place the bug behind one of the slats of the headboard. The reception was so clear that she could hear the faintest noise. What she was hearing now told her that someone was waking up and moving around in the bed. She leaned her head back and listened as the sun began to rise over the horizon behind her.

Alex woke a little after six-thirty as the morning light was just breaking over the horizon. She propped her head in her hand as she watched Conner sleeping soundly beside her. She gently caressed her lover's face and soon felt a warm stirring between her legs. She touched a soft dark nipple and smiled as it soon grew hard between her fingertips. Conner stirred beneath the gentle touch but didn't wake.

Alex continued with the caresses, letting her fingers flow across the lean muscles of Conner's stomach, eliciting a soft moan as she traveled lower. Alex stopped, waiting to hear the rhythmic breathing resume, indicating that Conner was once again asleep, then continued until her fingers reached the soft triangle below. Even while asleep, Conner parted her legs and tilted her hips up, seeking Alex's touch. Slowly Alex slid her hand between her lover's legs and pressed a single finger between the already wet lips. Conner moaned again, this time louder, and Alex stopped until Conner had once again settled.

She leaned in and placed a warm kiss on Conner's cheek as she began massaging the sensitive clitoris beneath her finger. She smiled as it hardened and Conner's breathing quickened. Conner moaned and arched her back as Alex brought her slowly into the waking world.

"Um, baby," Conner mumbled in her sleep.

Alex chuckled as she remembered what a sound sleeper Conner was and pressed harder. Her slow deliberate nurturing was soon rewarded as Conner moaned louder, opened her eyes, and realized what her body was responding to so early in the morning.

"Oh my God, Alex...oh...yes." Conner's eyes were wide with amazement.

Alex kissed Conner lightly on the lips. "Good morning," she said, then slowly slipped two fingers deep into her lover. She continued to place soft, warm kisses on Conner's lips as she watched and felt the orgasm consume her.

Conner's head fell back into the pillow and she arched her back, the orgasm surging through body. Alex slid her arm under Conner's shoulders and pulled her close as throbbing muscles seized her fingers in a tight grip.

"Alex...yes."

"That's it, baby, give it to me. Mmm yes, let it go," Alex whispered. When Conner fell limply back onto the pillow, Alex pulled her over until she rested in the crook of her arm.

Conner draped her arm across Alex's stomach. "I love you, Alex."

Alex smiled. "And I love you too, Conner Harris. I love you too." She pulled Conner closer and they once again fell into a peaceful slumber.

Olivia sat in the small sports car and let her breathing and heart rate return to normal. Hearing nothing more from the house down the street, she pulled the headset off, threw it on the seat beside her, and turned off the power. She started the engine and pulled out onto the highway. Glancing at her watch, she calculated that she would have just enough time to get home and shower before Alex called to tell her where the morning's meeting would be held.

When Conner woke for the second time that morning, all she felt was cool sheets beneath her fingers. She sat up, looked around the bedroom, and noticed that Alex's robe was not on the end of the bed, at the same time catching an enticing whiff of coffee. She pulled herself out of bed and after brushing her teeth and combing her short blonde hair, she padded into the kitchen. Alex was sitting at the small kitchen table with her back to the door, reading the morning newspaper and sipping a cup of the delicious-smelling coffee.

Conner crept up behind Alex and just before she was about to nip her on the back of the neck, Alex let out a deep throaty laugh. "Don't you know you can't sneak up on a shadow?"

"Damn!" Conner gave Alex a slow good-morning kiss. "I can never sneak up on you. You're no fun."

"Humph, you weren't complaining about that earlier this morning." Discarding the paper, Alex pulled the sulking woman down to straddle her lap.

"Well, if I remember correctly, you were the one who snuck up on me."

Alex slid her hand in the front of Conner's robe and grasped a nipple. "And I enjoyed every minute of it, too."

Conner pulled Alex closer, easily slipping her tongue between her lover's eager, waiting lips. Conner could feel Alex's hips rise up to press against her as she slowly searched and probed. Their breaths quickened and Alex pushed the robe off Conner's shoulders, letting it fall to the floor.

Conner pulled back and gave Alex a deep sultry look. "I think it's my turn, don't you? Let's go take a shower."

"Hmm." Alex sucked an alert nipple between her lips, sliding her tongue back and forth across the hard tip, then brought her head back up and stole a quick kiss. "I would love to, but Donald is going to call soon. If we start anything, I might not be in any condition to answer the phone."

"You're a hard woman, Alex Montgomery." Conner slid off Alex's lap, retied her robe and headed to the coffee maker. After pouring herself a cup, she sat down across from Alex. "How do you feel about tonight?"

Alex sighed heavily. "I feel a lot better now that we have some reinforcements coming in. Donald really came through on that, and Olivia, with her experience, will be a big help as well."

"Olivia has it bad for you, you know." Conner eyed Alex over the rim of her cup.

Alex rolled her eyes. "Olivia isn't my type, dear. She's always liked to play too much; never stays with one person very long." She bit her bottom lip and slid off her chair to kneel down between Conner's legs.

"Anyway, I've found the woman I want to spend my days and nights with. So even if she does," Alex softly nipped Conner's neck, "she's out of luck, I'm taken." She pulled Conner into a tight hug.

Conner opened her lips to accept Alex's probing tongue and soon their breathing quickened once again. Conner dropped her hand from Alex's waist and moved it lower until her fingers mingled with soft curls. A low moan came from deep in Alex's throat as she pushed her hips forward into the touch.

Conner, aware of the warmth spreading through her own body, slid her fingers into Alex's hot wetness and felt slick muscles embrace her fingers as she slowly probed deeper. "Do you know how much I love you, Alex?"

"Mmm, yes, you're showing me right now." Alex tore the sash open on Conner's robe and pressed their bodies closer. "You make me feel so good."

Conner slid her fingers in and out of the hot wetness and with each stroke felt Alex climb toward the apex. Her breath caught in her throat when Alex reached down and plunged into her deeply, curling her fingers up and pressing Conner's most sensitive spot. "Oh my God, Alex."

Alex moaned when she felt how wet Conner had become. Their tongues and hands probed and searched as the women took each other to the edge. Alex, feeling herself on the verge of climax, tore her mouth away from Conner's and whispered, "Slow down, I don't want to come yet. I want us to go together."

Conner slowed her stroking as Alex increased hers. "You feel so good, Conner. I love being inside of you, feeling you squeeze my fingers." She pulled Alex up. "Come here, sit on my lap. I need you closer."

Alex rose and straddled Conner's legs. Hands and arms brushed against each other as they began to probe deeper and harder. Conner rubbed her thumb over Alex's hard nipple, smiling when a deep moan escaped Alex's throat her hips thrust forward, pulling Conner in deeper. Both women's senses focused, blocking out everything except each other, as they moved together in complete harmony. Conner felt the first small contractions within Alex and knew she couldn't hold back much longer.

"No," Alex cried out as the phone on the wall behind Conner's head began to ring.

Conner grasped Alex's hips, pulling her forward, as she increased the depths of her strokes. "No! Let it ring, he'll call back. Please don't stop Alex...please."

Alex was reaching for the phone, but she dropped her free hand back to Conner's face when she heard her pleas. Lifting her chin, Alex seized Conner's lips and plunged her tongue deep. Conner's hips bucked hard and she let out a ragged breath, throwing her head back and crying out, "Now, baby...come with me, Alex...yes...oh God, Alex."

Alex completely lost control as she heard Conner's cries and matched them with her own. She bent her head to the crook of Conner's neck and bit down on the soft sweet skin. "Yes, baby, I'm there...God, you're so tight...oh...oh...yes."

They continued to move in sync with one another as the orgasms swept through them, drowning out everything but the sensations surging through their bodies.

When the spasms slowed to gentle pulses, Conner pulled Alex to her and gently kissed her. She felt a tear fall from Alex's face onto hers. "What's wrong, baby? Did I hurt you?"

Alex smiled and shifted her hips forward, wanting Conner to stay deep within her still-pulsing core, "No, God no."

"Then why are you crying?" Conner kissed away a salty tear as it slipped down Alex's cheek.

Alex leaned her forehead against Conner's and softly kissed her. "Because you make me so happy." She brought her hand up to cup Conner's cheek. "I never thought I would feel this way again."

Conner captured Alex's lips with hers and they savored the sweet taste of each other until once again the phone started ringing on the wall behind Conner's head.

Nipping the swell of Alex's breast as she reached for the phone, Conner laughed, "Tell Donald his timing sucks." Alex swatted Conner's shoulder before picking up the handset.

Conner, still buried deep inside Alex, rubbed her thumb against the ultrasensitive clitoris. She felt the slick muscles squeeze her fingers as Alex gasped, trying to speak into the phone. "Ah Jesus...hello."

She glared at Conner. "No, Donald, I'm, ah...fine. Just got out of the shower and I almost slipped, that's all." Alex grabbed Conner's hand, silently mouthing *stop it* to her grinning lover, but found herself pressing the insistent fingers deeper.

Alex's hips moved of their own volition as Conner gently stroked in and out of the tight wetness. Alex was quickly losing control and she tried to pull away, but Conner wrapped her arm around Alex's waist and pulled her closer.

"Yes, um, okay...we'll be there at eleven. Okay, Donald, see you....um...soon. Bye." Alex replaced the phone in the cradle and looked down at Conner, who was smiling sheepishly back at her. "You will pay dearly for that."

Conner looked back at Alex innocently and shrugged. "I couldn't help it. I got a cramp in my hand." Conner continued to slowly probe the slick folds, and soon Alex was racing toward another powerful release. Conner lifted Alex, sitting her on the edge of the table, then knelt on the floor.

Alex could feel Conner's breath on her thighs as she drew closer, and she guided her lover's face into the warm wetness that longed to feel her tongue.

Conner hesitated for only a moment before placing a soft kiss on Alex's thigh, then she parted the swollen folds, exposing the hard clitoris nestled below. Locking eyes with Alex, Conner drew her tongue slowly along the length of the pulsating shaft, stopping to suck gently on the tip.

"Conner, my God...yes." Alex pressed her hand against Conner's head, pulling her lover closer.

Conner pulled Alex's legs over her shoulder and rose up, forcing Alex to lean back on her hands. Using her foot, Conner slid the chair behind her and sat, giving Alex a teasing smile before once again dipping her tongue into her warm juices.

Alex's body trembled as Conner's tongue slid inside, probing deeper with every thrust. She thrust her hips to match Conner's rhythm and soon found herself on the verge of another powerful orgasm.

"Conner...yes, baby...go inside me, please." Her arms trembled her and she struggled to remain in the half-sitting position as she watched Conner make love to her. "Baby, please...I need you inside me."

Conner's eyes remained locked with Alex's as she prolonged the sweet torture. "Soon, baby...soon." Conner felt Alex's legs tremble as the first teasing pulses traveled up her body. She brought her hand up and gently caressed Alex's hip, sending her even higher. She waited until she heard Alex gasp, then slowly slid three fingers inside her slick warmth.

"Oh God, Conner, take it...yes." Alex's hips surged forward, taking Conner's fingers deep. Conner resisted the urge to plunge hard and fast, knowing that the slow strokes would prolong the impending explosion. She didn't have to wait long before Alex pulled her up to capture her lips in a long, passionate kiss. "I love you, Conner. God, I love you so much."

Conner smiled and returned the gentle kiss as she rubbed her thumb quickly against Alex's hard clit. She felt the muscles surrounding her fingers spasm, squeezing her as Alex cried out, "Conner, yes...oh God...it's...so slow."

Conner sucked a hard nipple into her mouth and continued the slow, gentle strokes in and out while Alex rode the long wave through the orgasm. Suddenly, with one forceful thrust of her hips, Alex went rigid as the orgasm surged through her body. Throwing her arms around Conner's neck, she held on while the waves continued, and she felt herself tighten around Conner's fingers deep in her core.

Conner held Alex tightly as her breathing slowed. Only after she could no longer feel the aftershocks of their lovemaking did she pull her hand away, smiling as Alex groaned, "I already miss you."

"Well, tonight when we can finally relax, I'll make sure you don't miss me," Conner said before she kissed Alex once again.

Alex's face turned serious. "Promise me. Promise me that tonight you will come home with me and make love to me until the morning."

Conner knew what Alex was asking, knew that even though there were no assurances either one would ever come back home, the promise needed to be made if for no other reason than to give them faith that the mission was going to be a success. That they would not lose each other; that they would experience more mornings like this one.

"I promise you, Alex, I love you with my heart and soul. I'm coming home with you by my side, I promise." They consummated their promise with a lingering kiss.

Taking a deep breath, Conner glanced at the clock. "I guess we'd better get ready. It's almost nine-thirty." Conner pulled Alex's robe back onto her shoulders and retied the sash. "You go ahead and take your shower. I need another cup of coffee."

"What, I didn't wake you good enough?"

Conner stole a quick kiss as she turned toward the coffee maker. "Oh yes, you woke me just fine. You can satisfy my every craving, except my body's addiction to caffeine."

Alex laughed as she headed through the door. "Smart answer, Harris."

Alex took the expressway toward the city. The rush-hour traffic had thinned out, and Alex and Conner enjoyed the relaxed drive to the large room Donald had reserved earlier that morning on Baymeadows Road. He had purposely delayed revealing the meeting place to further ensure there was no breach in the security. As Alex parked in the garage, she felt a chill run up her spine when the memory of the previous day's explosion flashed through her mind. She shook off the foreboding feeling and pushed open the door, not wanting Conner to sense her uneasiness.

Donald answered when they knocked on the door of the eighth-floor room and waved them inside, closing the door behind them. Olivia, leaning against the headboard of one of the large beds, raised one eyebrow as Alex and Conner walked in. Alex dropped on the bed beside Olivia; Conner chose to lean against the nightstand between the beds, crossing her legs in front of her as she quietly studied her surroundings.

Donald was busy in the far corner, talking to three men Conner had never seen before. *Must be part of the special ops crew,* she thought.

Olivia elbowed Alex in the side and grinned. "Glad you could join us, Montgomery," she said in a whisper. "Have a late night?"

Alex looked over at Conner and winked. "As a matter of fact, we had a late night and an early morning, Olivia," she whispered.

Conner had to bite her lip to keep from grinning at the surprised look on Olivia's face. Obviously, she wasn't accustomed to Alex being so forthcoming. *Humph, now maybe you'll get the hint that Alex isn't available,* Conner thought.

Olivia glanced at Conner and smiled. "I'm impressed, Harris. Although from what I saw yesterday, it doesn't surprise me."

Conner felt her face turn a deep red, the heat slowly creeping into her ears. She was saved from the embarrassing moment by a loud rap on the door. Donald again answered and waved several more unfamiliar faces into the room.

After another ten minutes of quiet discussion in the far corner, Donald called the meeting to order.

"Listen up, everyone. I'd like to start by introducing the special ops team. As you know, I contacted Ned Owens at Quantico and asked for twenty of the best people he has for this operation. He could only send us ten, but they're the best in their field, and we're lucky to have them."

Donald continued by introducing everyone. Gabe Watson, Jeff Goldberg, and Richard Blake were known throughout the bureau for their marksmanship. Dennis Andrews, Victor Garrett, Tony DeTomasso, and Eric Quincey were all recon specialists, and all held black belts in various martial arts. Chuck Bannister, Len Willis, and David Seay were all members of an elite special ops team specializing in hostage rescue.

When Donald was finished, he saw a thin smile cross Alex's lips. He returned her gaze and saw her dip her head slightly in acceptance and gratitude. *Finally, I've done something right.*

Alex had worked with Blake and DeTomasso and knew them to be the best in their field. She was impressed with the team Ned Owens had assembled; he obviously was as ready for this circus to be over as she was.

In minutes, maps were pinned to the walls and folders passed among the members. Alex summarized the investigation, from her first day on the case through the explosion, José's death, Olivia's involvement, and the information found at José's house.

Olivia had been quiet throughout the meeting and was startled when Donald asked her to explain the body mikes she had brought for them. She demonstrated how to place and secure the mikes, although most of the team had, at one time or another, worn such devices and didn't need much instruction or preparation.

She told the group that she had programmed the layout of the warehouse into a computer so that Peterson and Donald could monitor each team member's location from their surveillance site back on the boat, then added that she had returned to the warehouse earlier and shot darts around the building so they could monitor any movement or conversations around the perimeter.

Conner spoke up. "Exactly what are darts? I heard you mention that yesterday, but I forgot to ask."

Olivia looked at Alex and shrugged, giving Alex the floor.

"Actually, the darts Olivia shot in were developed several years ago during a surveillance operation." Looking at Olivia, she rolled her eyes. "Olivia here was getting impatient because we weren't able to pick up anything through the bugs in a house we were watching. Most of the conversations took place in the driveway, on the back porch, usually anywhere but inside the house. During the many hours we sat in the hot attic of the house across the street, Olivia worked on her darts. They're just like the ones used to tranquilize animals, only much smaller."

Alex looked at the other members of the team. "Anyway, to make a long story short, Olivia shot a few darts around the perimeter of the building, and we got the suspects on tape planning out a bank heist. Since then, we've used them when other means of surveillance didn't work, like now."

The schedule was set. Alex, Conner, and Olivia would meet the special ops team at 8:00 in an empty garage across the river and about half a mile west of the Container building. Donald and Peterson would dinghy to the boat at 7:00 and set up the communications equipment. They would perform a comm check at 8:15, and then they would wait.

Everyone had their orders, and they headed out the door. Olivia waited behind, asking to speak with Donald alone. Alex considered her ex-partner's request odd, since she and Donald had only met the previous night, but she shook off the uneasy feeling and asked Olivia to call her later in the afternoon. She and Conner headed to the field office to get the latest results from the lab concerning Donald's assault, then home to spend a few hours in the peace and quiet before they had to report for duty at the garage.

Chapter Eighteen

Alex walked into the quiet house, kicked off her shoes, and after grabbing a soda from the refrigerator, headed toward the deck. Conner came out a few minutes later and sat down in the lounger next to her.

"I wonder why Olivia wanted to talk to Donald alone?" Alex said, then took a long drink.

Conner crossed her ankles and shrugged. "I don't know, I was wondering the same thing." She looked at Alex and saw the frown that creased her face. "Probably just wanted to clarify something with the communications equipment."

Alex sighed. "Maybe, but somehow I don't think so. I think she's planning something, but I can't put my finger on what it is."

They sat quietly for a few minutes, each lost in her own thoughts, and then Alex gently grasped Conner's hand. "Let's take a walk on the beach."

Conner let herself be pulled up. Wrapping her arms around the taller woman, Conner lifted her head and pressed her lips to Alex's. The kiss was gentle and lingering, relaying the warmth and love the women had come to know with each other. "I love you, Alex." Conner's eyes were sincere and tender.

"I love you. Don't ever leave me." Alex's hold tightened around Conner's waist as they shared one of their last quiet moments before the mission.

Conner smiled up into Alex's somber face. "Never."

It was only one word, but the promise behind it caused Alex's heart to soar. "Come on, let's take that walk before I change my mind and ravish you right here."

Conner's brow furrowed. "Don't I get a choice?"

Alex pulled Conner out onto the sand. "No." She laughed and pulled Conner into her arms. "Well, not until we get home tonight, anyway."

They returned to the house about an hour later. As they climbed the steps to the back deck, Conner sensed a transformation in Alex. She looked into her eyes and saw the deep, dark eyes of the Shadow. Taking a deep breath, she slid the back door open and walked into the kitchen. "I'm going to take a shower and get ready."

Alex only nodded as Conner left the room. She walked into her office, sat down at her desk, and opened folder Donald had given them the night before. Something wasn't right in Alex's mind about Olivia; she had sensed it earlier that morning but forced it out of her head, not wanting to question the trust they had built over the years. However, as she sat reading through the list of names in the Hernandez organization, a thought crossed her mind. Searching the list of names, Alex's eyes suddenly stopped, and she felt her blood turn cold as she read the name "Angel Martin."

Alex stared at the name and closed her eyes in disbelief. *Angel Martin, the alias Olivia always used when she was working undercover. How could I have missed it? There has to be an explanation for this. I have to figure out if she is really working undercover, or if she has turned rogue.* Alex leaned back in her chair, processing the information. Her senses came on full alert as she felt Conner enter the room.

She closed the file and returned it to the filing cabinet. "I'll be back in a few minutes. I need a quick shower." Conner watched Alex leave the room and wondered why she was so distracted. Deciding that it must be part of Alex's Shadow persona, she went into the kitchen to recheck her gear before they had to leave.

Alex stood in the shower and let the warm water cascade off her body. She concentrated on relaxing her muscles, mentally preparing herself for the night's mission. The few hours that led up to a mission were always the hardest for Alex. Waiting wasn't something she did well. She quickly showered, stepped out into the cool air of the room and grabbed a towel to dry her body.

Looking at herself in the mirror, Alex regarded her reflection. Her body, defying time and her job, still looked firm and muscular. Although there were scars scattered along her back and legs from the previous year's raid, most were fading and would soon disappear. The one she wanted to remain was from a bullet that had penetrated her chest four inches above her left nipple. That scar she wanted to remember, and tonight she would get her revenge on the man who had put it there.

Alex heard a soft knock and turned to see Conner step through the door.

"Hey! What ya doing?" Conner smiled, knowing she would never tire of looking at Alex's body.

"Just looking at all the scars this old lady has on her body." Alex moved to pull the towel around herself, but was stopped as Conner reached for the towel and pulled it away.

"I love your body, Alex." Conner leaned to kiss the scar on Alex's chest. "Each scar is a reminder of how lucky I am to have you in my life."

She turned Alex around to face the mirror. "However, I don't intend on your getting any more. I love your body just the way it is." She lifted Alex's arms, wrapped the towel around her, and kissed her lightly on the neck, then wrapped her arms around her waist as they looked at their reflections in the mirror.

Alex swallowed hard, feeling the now familiar heat rise through her body. She smiled and caressed Conner's face. "You are so bad. Even at a time like this, you make me want to block everything out, take you to bed, and make love to you all night."

Conner grinned. "Yeah? Well we'll have plenty of time for that after tonight." She nipped Alex's earlobe. "Right now you need to hurry up and get dressed. We have a few bad guys to get."

Alex smiled as Conner released her, swatted her on the ass, and headed for the door. She turned just as Conner was closing the door. "Conner?"

The door swung open and Conner stuck her head back in the bathroom. "Yes?"

Dark eyes met blue. "I love you."

Conner took a deep breath and smiled. "I love you too, Alex Montgomery." She lifted an eyebrow. "Now, get dressed before I lose my resolve."

The women quickly gathered their things and headed out the door. Alex was driving north on I-95 when her cell phone rang. Flipping the cover, she saw from the caller ID that it was Sam. *Talk about bad timing*, she thought.

"Hello, Sam!"

"Hey, Alex. What's up? Kelly and I were just discussing the weekend and decided to call and remind you that you're coming over on Saturday for the barbecue. You do remember, don't you?"

"Uh, yeah. Is it okay if I bring an old friend? She doesn't know too many people in town and I thought maybe...Well, if it's okay with you and Kel?"

"Sure, Alex, bring whomever you like. Who is this *old* friend?"

Alex rolled her eyes. "No one scandalous, I can tell you that. Just my old partner from Chicago." Alex thought she heard Sam choking. "Sam, are you all right?"

"Yeah, I'm, uh, fine."

"Hey, if you'd rather I not bring her, that's fine."

"I just don't care for Olivia Morgan, Alex, that's all." Sam's voice was cynical and short.

"When have you met Olivia, Sam?" Alex was confused. She had never mentioned Olivia to Sam, at least not that she remembered, and couldn't figure how Sam would know her.

"I haven't met her, Alex. I just—well, look, I need to run. We can talk about this later, okay? Bye."

Alex heard the click as Sam hung up the phone. She flipped her cell phone shut and placed it back on the console. Shaking her head, she tried to push the conversation out of her mind. *I can't think about that now. I have to focus on this mission.*

Conner saw the odd look on Alex's face. "Are you okay?"

"Um...yeah. Sam was just acting strange, that's all."

Sam hung up the phone and sat back in the recliner, thinking about Alex's former partner. *When the hell did she surface again?* Years ago, on a cold December evening when Alex and Kelly were both away on business, Sam and Feryle had decided to go to Antonio's for dinner to pass the lonely hours. Feryle had been distracted throughout the evening, and Sam had finally asked what was bothering her. She sat, shocked, as Feryle told her about her trip to San Diego and the woman she'd met there.

Feryle told her how she had awakened the next morning nude in her hotel room, remembering the mysterious woman and what they had done. After considering everything, she had decided not to tell Alex about the terrible mistake, thinking it unlikely that she would cross paths with the nameless woman ever again. That assumption had proven false when, planning an aerial tour of a property for some developers, she and Alex had visited Olivia's office. Now she asked Sam what she should do. Not only did Alex and Olivia know each other, they had once been very close. Feryle didn't know if she could live with herself, knowing that she had slept with Alex's ex-partner, even if she had been drunk and manipulated.

Sam and Feryle had talked well into the night, with Sam finally convincing her that the meeting in San Diego probably wasn't accidental after all and that telling Alex was what Olivia probably wanted in the first place. Feryle had finally agreed and decided to put the incident behind her.

Sam took a long pull from her beer, got up, and walked to the window. *What the hell are you after, Olivia Morgan? Whatever it is, you had better not hurt Alex.* Sam shook off the bad feeling that had washed over her and headed to the kitchen to start dinner. Kelly was coming home early tonight; she would talk to her about it and figure out what they should say, if anything, to Alex.

Alex and Conner pulled up at the empty garage at 7:15. They were almost an hour early, but neither woman could sit at the house any longer and they decided to use the extra time to prepare for the rest of the team's arrival.

They selected weapons, including stun guns, ammunition, quick cuffs, tear gas grenades, and a few other items before walking back toward the window. Alex picked up her binoculars and looked toward the warehouse. "We have movement."

Conner brought her binoculars up to her eyes and watched as a small sports car drove toward the warehouse. A lone figure stepped out of the car and walked the short distance to the door. "What the hell is she doing?" Alex didn't realize she had spoken aloud.

Conner looked at Alex. "Who? Do you know that person?"

Alex caught herself. "Um, no, I just meant the person looked like a female. I wonder what they're up to?"

Conner held Alex's gaze, knowing she wasn't telling her everything. Before she had an opportunity to delve any further into the subject, the rest of the team started to arrive.

Alex quickly made use of the interruption and headed over to greet the other members. She pointed out the equipment Donald had left for them and started pinning the maps and floor plans on the wall. By 7:45 everyone had safely arrived at the dark garage, except Olivia. A half-hour later, Alex heard Donald's voice over the earpiece tucked into her ear, telling everyone that he was ready for the comm check.

Once they had completed the task, Alex asked Donald to call her cell phone. A few moments later, the phone vibrated against her leg.

"Montgomery. Yeah, hold on a sec." Alex walked to the far side of the garage and turned her back to the group. "I just saw Morgan go inside the warehouse. Donald, what the hell is going on?"

"Shit." Donald hesitated. "Listen, Alex, I couldn't tell you before, but Olivia has been working this case since you were hurt last year. She's been inside now for over six months, and—"

His explanation was cut off by Alex's seething voice. "And what, Donald, you couldn't trust me, is that it?"

"Alex, please, let's not go into this now. Just know that she is one of the good guys and allow her some space to work. This can't be communicated to the rest of the group. It will only give them a false sense of security. We can't risk that. I need everyone alert and on their toes." Donald let out a long harsh breath.

"Oh, I'll give her plenty of room, Donald, since you don't seem to think I can handle the situation." Furious, Alex had to concentrate on keeping her voice down.

"This isn't about you, Alex, it's—"

Again, Alex cut him off. "Yeah, I know, Donald, it's all about you and always has been. Well, I only have one thing to say: fuck you, Donald!" She snapped the phone shut and looked back to see the rest of the group watching her.

Alex met their stares, then walked slowly back to the window and picked up the binoculars, searching the area of the warehouse. David Seay stepped over beside Alex and looked out the window. "Was that phone call something we need to know about, Alex?" he asked in a low voice.

"No, just a personal disagreement between Donald and me." Alex glanced at Seay.

"Then you need to put it out of your mind and focus on the mission."

"It's over, okay?" Alex's eyes bore into Seay's, and she could see that her point had been made. She turned to the rest of the group. "We need to get into place; it's almost 9:00. Does everyone remember their assignments?" Alex made eye contact with each member, then walked slowly to the map. "Okay, Andrews, DeTomasso, and Garrett, take off and let us know when you're in place."

The three men hurriedly gathered their equipment and quietly left the building as Alex returned to the window to watch. *I'm coming for you, Malcolm. I hope you're ready to die*, Alex thought as she looked for any signs of movement around the warehouse and Colorado Container buildings.

Conner stood off to the side watching Alex, trying to figure out what had happened during the phone call to upset her so much. She could see Alex's jaw flex as she peered through the binoculars. Before she had a chance to speak to her, she heard Andrews's voice whisper through her earpiece.

"Crab pots set. Let's move on up the river."

Alex watched as the *Shady Lady* slowly crept forward, stopping closer to the far shoreline. Donald had turned on the running lights, not attempting to hide their presence, as one of the men on board leaned over the side of the boat to look as though he was setting a crab pot. Alex turned back toward the rest of the group, "Watson, Goldberg, Quincey, head out."

While the men headed out the door, Conner took up the spot next to Alex by the window and raised her binoculars to watch the buildings. Glancing back over her shoulder, she saw that the others were on the far side of the room. "So, are you going to tell me what's going on between you and Donald?" Conner could see the muscles in Alex's hands tighten around the binoculars, and then she heard an exasperated sigh.

"Olivia's already inside," Alex whispered.

Conner could hear the anger spill into her voice. "What do you mean, she's inside?" Her question was louder than she intended, and she quickly lowered her voice, along with the binoculars. "What the hell is she doing?"

"I'm not sure. Donald seems to think she's on our side, but I'm not so sure anymore. Stay alert in there. I have no idea what she is up to, or what will happen." Alex raised the binoculars just as she heard Goldberg's transmission.

"Okay, boss, this one's set. Move on up."

Alex was impressed with the team so far. She knew they were out there, and she still couldn't see any movement. She watched as the *Shady Lady* eased closer and stopped once again about 100 yards from the end of the dock. "Bannister and Seay, head out."

Alex and Conner continued to watch the surrounding area. Soon, Bannister voiced the go-ahead, and once again Alex saw the *Shady Lady* pull closer. She could clearly see Peterson leaning over the side of the boat, positioning another crab pot.

Things were going well. Everyone was in successfully; there were four remaining members. Alex set the binoculars down on the table and turned toward Blake and Willis. "All right, guys, I'm going to tell you something even though I have been ordered not to. Morgan is already inside. Donald seems to think she is one of us. I'm not so sure. Don't go in there gunning for her, but don't let your guard down, either."

Blake looked at Alex and growled, "If she's one of us, then why didn't she say anything this morning at the hotel?"

"My thoughts exactly. Just be on your toes, and let's keep it clean." Alex watched as Blake, Willis, and Conner looked uneasily at one another. "We are the only four that know about this. Keep it that way. I don't want any confusion once we get in there, got it?"

Everyone nodded their agreement as Alex picked up the binoculars from the table and headed for the door. "Let's move."

237

Chapter Nineteen

Alex's team crossed the river in a small inflatable dinghy. When they reached the other side, Richard Blake pulled a stiletto from his boot, and in one quick motion, sliced a long slit down the side of the dinghy. Conner took a long, slow breath as their only means of escape via the river deflated before her eyes. She glanced at Alex and saw that she too was watching before snapping her head to the side, silently ordering them to move out.

The four stealthily moved through the darkness, entering the warehouse property through a narrow opening created by the first team. Silently, they moved closer to the warehouse, using hand signals and experience to guide their progress.

Alex couldn't force away the uneasy feeling that kept creeping into her stomach. Things had gone extremely well so far, almost too well. As she knelt behind an old rusted oil drum to watch the warehouse for any signs of movement, Alex decided she had to make a committed decision about Olivia. She knew she was only endangering the rest of the team with her uncertainty. Either Olivia was part of the team or part of the organization, but which was it?

A movement caught Alex's eye, and she watched as a tall figure moved from the building and out onto the concrete drive, stopping within the amber circle created by a halogen floodlight on the side of the building. The person pulled a pack of cigarettes from the left breast pocket of their coat and Alex watched as the small flame created by the lighter illuminated Olivia Morgan's face.

Olivia took a long drag of her cigarette, then blew out a stream of smoke before running her left hand through her long dark mane. She then stretched her arm above her head, fist clenched in a tight ball. At the peak of the stretch, she opened and closed her hand four times, letting her fingers spread apart in the dim light. *Well, I'll be damned*, Alex thought as she read the silent hand signal from her ex-partner, *she is one of the good guys*.

Alex smiled and turned to give a thumbs-up to her team. She heard Conner's sigh of relief in the darkness and quickly glanced over and gave a quick nod. Alex knew she had only one transmission to Donald before the frequency was silenced. She motioned to Willis, giving the go-ahead, and listened as he spoke through the tiny microphone taped to his collar.

"Got this one set, boss. Let's have a beer."

Alex watched as the dark figure on the boat moved into the cabin, then the running lights were shut off and all was dark except for the dim lights peeking through the portholes. She turned back toward the warehouse and saw Olivia talking with another person, a large male with what appeared to be an Uzi slung over his shoulder.

Olivia pointed toward the Container building and the man walked away. Alex hoped Olivia was dispersing the armed men to ease the FBI team's forward movement. Alex looked around and motioned the group to move out. They dispersed quietly, each member going in a different direction to allow a wider coverage area. All was quiet for a few minutes, and then Alex heard a muffled thud, followed by a click in her ear.

The click was Blake keying his microphone, indicating a takedown. They had agreed upon the unique communications signal earlier in the day, and as Alex watched the warehouse, she saw Olivia turn her head in Blake's direction. Olivia was apparently listening to their signals through her earpiece, and as she turned back to the door, she looked up toward the roof. Alex headed toward a shadow on the left side of the building.

Conner lay in the grass and watched Olivia as her head angled up toward the roof. Conner then made her way toward the rear of the warehouse and shimmied up a drainage pipe, stopping just short of clearing the parapet wall of the roof. She listened for any movement, then eased a small mirror over the edge. Swiveling it, she could see three men on the roof, one on the opposite side from Alex and two kneeling behind the parapet toward the front. There was a large exhaust fan approximately ten feet in front of Conner, and she eased herself over the wall and moved quietly until she was securely crouched behind it.

Conner looked toward the side of the building where Alex had headed, but didn't see any indication that she had cleared the roof. She picked up a small pebble and threw it several feet away, near an air-conditioning unit, and watched as the guard near the side wall jerked his head around. As he made his way toward the sound, Conner used the time to move from around the fan, where she again waited.

She heard the guard approach and eased the stun gun from her belt. She watched the guard's shadow as it came closer, and a quick glance around the other side of the unit confirmed that the other two guards were still standing quietly at the front wall. Just as the guard rounded the A/C unit, Conner pressed the stun gun against his neck, and he fell limp into her arms.

She quickly stuffed a gag in his mouth, and using flex cuffs, she bound his hands and legs behind his body and rolled him onto his stomach, then strapped his hands to his feet. By the time she had completed the task, Alex was on the other side of the building, hiding behind another exhaust fan.

Alex gave Conner a thumbs-up, then heard the quick click in her ear, indicating the takedown. Alex pulled the Taser gun from the holster on her hip and held it up to Conner, getting a quick nod in return. The two women eased their way forward.

Once they were positioned, Conner glanced over toward Alex. Alex held up three fingers and silently counted down. When her fingers formed a fist, they both pulled the triggers on their Tasers. The men fell hard onto the gravel rooftop, and both women sat silently for a few seconds, listening for any sounds that would indicate their cover had been blown. Hearing none, they quickly bound the two guards and carried them to a dark shadow in the corner. Conner keyed her mike twice as Alex quickly calculated the results. With the three guards down on the roof, the one Blake had taken out and six others she had heard, there were ten guards remaining.

Alex signaled Conner to head for the access door and covered her as she made her way across the roof before following. Once they were beside the door, Conner raised her Sig while Alex snatched the door open.

Moving through the door, they saw a dim light coming from the bottom of the stairs and quietly made their way down, stopping every few steps to listen. Once at the bottom, they peered around the corner and Alex held up two fingers. They reloaded the Taser guns and eased out into the hallway.

"Hey guys," Alex whispered.

The guards brought their weapons up, turning quickly toward the sound, but didn't have a chance to fire as darts hit them both, center chest. Alex and Conner moved quickly to prevent the dead weight of the men from hitting the ground and causing any noise. Pulling the guards into a side room, they quickly bound and gagged them and headed back out the door, clicking the mike twice on the way.

Hernandez watched Olivia closely as she walked toward two guards and spoke to them in a low voice before turning and strolling over to where he was sitting.

"Where did you just send my two best guards, Captain?" When they were around others, Hernandez always addressed Olivia with the military rank he had given her, although he was more relaxed when they spoke in private, especially when they were in bed.

Olivia met his cold glare. "I couldn't raise Saul out in the field, so I sent them out to have a look." She shrugged. "Probably nothing, but I don't want to take any chances. Where's Thomas?"

A thin smile formed across Hernandez's face. "Oh, he's around somewhere."

From the corner of the room, Alex and Conner listened to the exchange. Alex could feel the cold sweat that had suddenly covered her body when she first eyed Hernandez slowly trickle down her back. Her eyes bore holes in the man as she struggled to control her breathing. Her gut instinct was to raise her Sig and take him out right then and there. *I have waited so long for this moment, Malcolm.* She jerked as Conner placed a gentle hand on her arm. Looking into Conner's eyes, she could see the concern they held. She nodded and quietly inhaled, forcing her body to relax and focus. *Okay, Montgomery, stick with the plan.*

That one moment of hesitation was all it took. While the two women were distracted with each other, a dark figure eased forward, smiling as their bodies stiffened when he cocked his gun. "Good evening, ladies, so glad you could join our little party."

The two women slowly turned and Conner's mind reeled as she looked into the face of the man before her. "Seth!"

Seth's mouth widened in a malicious sneer. "Hey, Conner. You know, I never did get a chance to thank you for keeping Magnum while I was away on...vacation."

Conner lunged toward Seth, but was pulled back by Alex. "You sorry son of a bitch."

"Now now, Conner. It really doesn't become you to speak such foul words, my dear." Seth pointed the gun at Alex, knowing Conner wouldn't attempt anything daring. "Now, why don't you hand me your weapons, very carefully, and then we'll go join the guest of honor?"

Olivia took a long drag off her cigarette as Seth marched the two agents into the center of the warehouse. "What do we have here, Thomas?"

"Just a couple of rodents I found in the hall, Liv. This beauty here is Alex Montgomery—the Shadow is what they call her." Seth heard a low chuckle from Hernandez, who was sitting at the desk in a dimly lit corner, enjoying the introductions. "And this little spitfire is Conner Harris, my esteemed partner *against* crime."

Seth gave Olivia an amused look. "What, Liv? Did I finally get a little information before you? I'm disappointed, you know; I thought you would have done your homework. Hard to believe you're not familiar with these two."

Olivia walked over to the two women, stopping directly in front of Conner. "Nope, not this one. I'll have to make sure I get familiar, though;

she's very cute, Seth." Olivia raked her eyes over Conner's body before reaching out to grip her chin in her hand. "Very cute indeed."

Conner jerked her head away and glared at Olivia. "Fuck off."

Olivia raised an eyebrow and smiled, cocking her head sideways. "Ooh, and such a little fighter."

Alex heard Seth's snorting laugh behind her. "Yes, Liv, my dear, and just your type too. I know for a fact she likes tall, dark, sexy women."

Olivia's eyes became hooded as she moved closer. "Hmm. Well now, we just might have to get better acquainted a little later."

Conner remained silent and glared back, refusing to give Olivia the satisfaction of humiliating her. She could see Alex's muscles flex as Olivia grabbed the front of her shirt, pulling her roughly against her chest, and growled, "You'd better be nice, blondie. I'll be the closest thing you have to a friend before the night's over." Olivia then planted a rough, hard kiss on Conner's lips, taking her completely by surprise.

It took Conner only a second to regain her composure, and she quickly bit down hard on the intruding lip. Olivia jerked away, bringing her hand up to wipe away the blood that Conner's teeth had drawn. "You bitch."

Conner's head snapped to the side with the force of Olivia's blow, but she quickly faced her again. "That's what you get for not asking politely."

Olivia glared at Seth as he roared in laughter. "My, my, Conner, I would have never guessed you were such a live one." He looked at Olivia. "You're going to have some fun with this one, Liv."

"Yes, I certainly intend to have a grand time." She turned and faced Alex. "Take her to the office and tie her up. I have a few more pressing matters to take care of right now."

Conner felt the gun pressed against her spine, and as Seth pushed her forward she heard Olivia call, "Seth, be nice and don't hurt the poor girl. I certainly don't want you to ruin all the pleasure I'm going to have later tonight. It's been a long while since I've had a chance to saddle-break one like her." The sound of Olivia's roaring laughter followed Conner as Seth shoved her through the doorway of the office, making her lose her footing. "When this is over, you'll pay for this, Seth, I promise."

Leaning against a metal desk in the center of the room, Seth glared at her. "I'm sure you'd like to try, but unfortunately, when this is over, you'll be leaving in a body bag. I don't think I have anything to worry about."

Conner had eased herself into a sitting position against the far wall. Looking around the room, she tried to find something to use as a weapon. "Why?"

Seth raised his arms in exasperation. "Come now, Conner, think about it. Not everyone has the privilege of coming from a rich family like you," he snarled.

Conner's eyes widened. "If you needed money, Seth, all you had to do was ask me. God, Seth, you've been like a brother to me. I would have helped you."

Snarling, Seth knelt in front of her. "Yeah, right, little sister. You mean to tell me if I had come to you and confessed that I had gambled away my life savings and owed my bookie 200 grand, you would have bailed me out? I don't think so." He leaned in until Conner could feel his breath on her cheek. "Not the great, noble Conner Harris. I'm sure you would have run straight to Cappy."

"I would have helped you, Seth." Tears stung Conner's eyes. "So how did that lead to all of this? You telling me you trust Hernandez more than you trust your own partner?"

Seth stood and walked back toward the desk. "It's not about trust, Conner, don't you see? It's about survival." Seth raked a hand through his hair and Conner could see the stress in his face. "Hernandez came to me and offered to pay my way out if I would do him one little favor— keep an eye on you. After Montgomery's girlfriend got killed and you decided to play the *white knight*, you started getting too close for Malcolm's comfort."

"So how did that get you here tonight?"

Seth's malevolent smile sent chills up Conner's spine. "Money, my dear Conner, something you don't have many concerns with. Malcolm made me an offer I couldn't refuse, making more money in a month than I could make a year on the force. He gave me wealth...freedom. All I had to do was keep an eye on you and anyone else that got in his way and deal with them appropriately."

"You mean murder them, right?" Conner could no longer keep the venom from her voice. "You're pathetic, Seth."

Seth lunged off the desk. Before Conner could react, one hand was around her neck and the other held a gun against her temple. "Don't preach to me, Harris. I may be pathetic, but tomorrow I'll still be alive and well. Sorry, I can't say as much for you." He pulled a set of cuffs from his pocket. "This discussion is over, Harris. Don't move or I'll blow your righteous brains out, right here."

Conner seethed with anger as she stared her partner down. "You don't have the fucking guts." Conner felt the explosion in her head. The darkness begin to envelop her, she and fought to remain conscious as the pain ripped through her body. She felt herself sag as the darkness wrapped itself around her mind.

When she regained consciousness, her left arm was wrenched behind her back, then her right, as Seth snapped on a set of handcuffs. He rolled her over and moved on to her feet. When he took his eyes off her for a split second, reaching for a length of rope, Conner reacted. Her foot snapped Seth's head back as it made solid contact, and he fell back onto the floor, howling in pain as blood gushed out of his nose.

"You fucking bitch." He turned onto his side, trying to stand up, when another stabbing pain hit him in the ribs, sending him back to the floor in agony. He quickly crawled out of Conner's reach, retrieved the gun that had fallen from his hands, and pointed it at Conner.

"I should kill you right here." He took a labored breath. "But I'm going to enjoy seeing what Olivia has in store for you later. She's a real rough bitch, Harris, and I can't wait to see her break you." He pulled the straight chair from behind the desk. Still aiming the gun at Conner, he walked closer. "On your stomach, *now*."

Conner rolled over and felt the legs of the chair trap her legs. "Glad you learned something from me."

"Shut the fuck up." Seth quickly tied Conner's feet together. "You make one move and you're dead." He turned and walked toward the door, jerking it open. Taking a deep breath, he turned back to her, and with a small hint of remorse, said softly, "I'm sorry it had to end this way, Conner."

Alex glared at Olivia as Seth shoved Conner toward the office door. A wave of guilt surged through her body as she realized that she had trusted Olivia even when all the evidence pointed toward her involvement in the Hernandez organization. Now they were in a tough situation, one Alex didn't know if she would be able to get them out of. Her head snapped to the left as she heard Hernandez's dark, smooth voice from a few feet away.

"Please, Alex, come and join me, won't you?"

Olivia pushed Alex toward the desk in the dimly lit corner of the warehouse, then pushed her down into the chair facing him. "Hello, Malcolm. Long time no see." A thin smile crossed her lips. "How's the leg?"

Hernandez sat forward in the chair, placed his elbows on the desk before him, and glared at his nemesis. "Yes, Alex, it has been a long time." Completely ignoring her question, he smiled and continued, "May I offer you a glass of wine?"

"No. Thank you."

He leaned back in the chair, took a sip of his wine, and regarded Alex with probing eyes. "Well, since you won't allow me to be a good host, maybe we should just get down to business, then."

"Yes. Let's."

Hernandez reached into his breast pocket for one of his imported cigars and took his time lighting it while he considered his options. After sucking in a long draw, he blew out a stream of pungent smoke. "You have become quite a nagging problem for me, Alex. What will it take to make you go away?"

Alex regarded him with flat, dark eyes. This man had almost destroyed her life, and now the only salvation she had been able to find was being held captive in the office, out of her reach. "Seeing you taken out in a body bag would be the only thing that can make me go away, Malcolm."

Alex heard footsteps behind her and tuned to see the guards they had taken down earlier enter the room, followed by Seth. Now that these five were back on their feet, there were thirteen guards, Olivia, and Hernandez to contend with. "What is it that you want?"

Hernandez smiled, knowing he had the agent right where he wanted her. "Call off your team. I want them all to walk up to the building, lay down their weapons, and walk out the far gate. I have a very important meeting in a little over an hour, and I don't want any unnecessary distractions."

Alex smirked. "Sorry, Malcolm, that's not going to happen. You might as well admit defeat. You're trapped in here. If you think the FBI is going to let you walk away simply because you happen to have two of their agents held captive, you're more stupid that I thought."

A small thin smile crept across her face. "Listen, I'll even give them the instructions myself." Dipping her head, she spoke in a strong, clear voice. "Garrett, you're in charge. No way are you, under any circumstances, to surrender your weapons to this piece of—"

Hernandez was out of his chair and in front of Alex before she could finish. He grabbed her shirt and ripped it down the front, exposing the small microphone attached to her chest. Ripping the device from her skin, he threw it on the floor and stepped on it, crushing it. Before Alex could pull her head back, Hernandez's heavily jeweled hand struck her face, tearing a long gash down her cheek. He glared at Olivia over Alex's head. "Check the other one."

Seth moved toward the office and was stopped by Hernandez's raging words to Olivia. "This is your mistake, Captain. You clean it up."

As Olivia walked toward the office, she hesitated for a moment to look back over her shoulder. When she saw that Hernandez was watching her movements closely, she opened the door and stepped into the darkened room.

Flipping the light switch on, she found Conner slumped in the corner with her right eye swollen shut from the brutal blow Seth had delivered earlier. She knelt down in front of Conner, and grasping the cloth of her shirt in both hands, she tore it open, sending the buttons flying. Olivia refused to make eye contact with Conner as she ripped the microphone from her chest and crushed it beneath her booted foot. Only when Conner whispered her name did the guilt run through her soul.

"Why, Olivia?" Conner could barely form the words through the pain.

"Be quiet." Olivia's voice was flat and emotionless.

"She loved you, trusted you. Why?" Conner pressed.

Olivia made the mistake of looking into Conner's eyes. Tearing her gaze from Conner's, she practically ran to the door but stopped short of opening it. She tore a hand through her hair, took a ragged breath, and then turned once again toward Conner. "You love her, don't you?"

Olivia's face was blurry through Conner's one good eye. She nodded and smiled. "Yes, Olivia, I love Alex—more than life itself."

Even through the pain, Conner's eyes lit up as she spoke Alex's name. Olivia slowly walked back toward her and knelt down close to her crumpled body, reaching out to touch the smooth skin of her chest.

Conner felt something cold pressed against her skin, then watched as Olivia slowly walked to the desk in the dark corner, opened a drawer and placed something inside. Conner jumped as the desk drawer was slammed shut and Olivia stormed out of the room.

Donald Fairfax and Jack Peterson sat in the cabin of the boat listening as the confrontation in the warehouse played out and the tiny dots representing the other members of the team blinked on the screen as they moved closer to the warehouse.

"Fucking asshole. If I ever get my hands on the piece of shit, I'll kill him." Never had Peterson dreamed that the rogue was Seth. "Okay. We have to think here. If Seth is the rogue, then what is Frank Bivins's role in all of this, Donald?"

Donald took a ragged breath and watched his comrade closely. "Bivins was a setup, Jack." Before he could react, he was pulled out of his chair and slammed against the wall of the cabin.

Peterson's eyes bore into Donald's. "A plant? You're telling me you knew about this all along?"

"It was classified information, Jack. I couldn't tell you."

Peterson pulled Donald away from the wall and slammed him back again. "I'll give you a little classified information, you son of a bitch. If anything happens to Alex or Conner in there, I'll kill you myself."

Donald's eyes held Peterson's in a hard stare. "Sit down, Jack, and I'll fill you in."

Donald shrugged Peterson's hands away, walked to the cooler, and pulled out two bottles of water. He opened one and handed it to Peterson, then sat down heavily.

Leaning against the far wall, Peterson waited impatiently for Donald to begin. "Well?"

Donald swept his hand over the day-old beard on his face and said, "Remember when Bivins came to Jacksonville a couple of years ago?" Peterson nodded. "Well, he came from Colorado."

"How did you know all of this? I'm the one who hired him, remember? He works for me!"

"Actually, he works for me too, Jack. Bivins was a detective in Denver and accidentally ran across a vein of the Hernandez organization while working a drug case out there. He knew it was a big case for the FBI, worked his way into the setup, and *then* contacted the local field office. Graham Richardson, the local man out there, let him into the bureau on the condition that he maintained his cover as a bad cop. He didn't want anyone in the organization to think Bivins was FBI; it would scare them away from him." Donald took a long pull from his water bottle and glanced at the screen, giving Peterson a little time to absorb the information.

Peterson sat down. "Go ahead."

"Anyway, Bivins worked his way in, but the head honchos in Colorado never quite trusted him, so they sent him to Jacksonville. I guess they felt like he wouldn't cause any problems if he were located somewhere away from his family and known associates in the police force. Anyway, after he was settled in, he contacted me by way of Richardson, and we met. I put him on as a special agent, Jack, specifically to work this case."

Donald took another long pull from the bottle and glanced back at the screen. All of the agents were positioned near the warehouse, waiting. "The Hernandez organization wanted an inside man in your department so they sent him in. He went, you hired him, and his cover was complete."

Peterson raked his hand through his hair and growled, "So he was working for you all along. You didn't think you could tell me this before now?"

"No, I couldn't. I had orders from higher up. My hands were tied, Jack. Alex was the only agent we've had who ever got as close as Bivins did. Actually, Alex was deeper, but when she was injured last year, we had no choice but to turn to Bivins. His contact with our office was José Gonzolas."

"Well, José's dead, Donald. Has Bivins contacted you since the explosion?"

Donald looked away and exhaled. "No, we haven't heard from him. I can only hope he's in that warehouse somewhere, and still on our side."

"What do you mean, hope he's still on our side?" Peterson was once again pacing the narrow lane in the cabin.

"He's been avoiding everyone for a while—missing meetings, delaying the transfer of information. Right now, I honestly don't know for sure whose side he's on."

Stopping in front of Donald and glaring, Peterson shook his head, the veins in his throat bulging. "Great, this is just fucking great, Donald. My best detective and your best agent are in there, and you're telling me you don't know whose fucking side anyone is on! You'd better be glad you don't work for me because I'd fire your sorry ass right now, then I'd beat the shit out of you for putting them in the middle of this cluster fuck without giving them all the facts!"

"I don't blame you, Jack. If I were in your shoes, I'd feel the same way."

Peterson pulled a service revolver from his pack and stuck it in his belt. "Well, you can sit here and feel sorry for yourself all night if you want to, Donald. Personally, I'm going to get those two out of there, with or without your help." Peterson turned and climbed through the companionway, leaving Donald staring at the blinking screen.

Conner lay in the dim room trying to comprehend what Olivia had just done, but her mind was foggy and she couldn't stay focused on her thoughts. There on her chest lay the key to the handcuffs. Now all she had to do was figure out how to get it from there to her hands. Her head pounded and she closed her eyes. *Tired, gotta rest.*

The sound of the office door opening pulled Conner from the haze. A searing pain tore through her head as the fluorescent lights flickered on above her head. She slowly turned her head to look at the guard, getting only a glimpse before shutting her eyes against the pain.

"Well, well, what have we here?" He knelt beside Conner and ran his hand down her neck, picking up the small shiny key. "Someone leave you a little present, Harris?"

Conner closed her eyes again, trying to block out the glaring lights. "Fuck you." *Garlic, he always smells like fucking garlic.*

Bivins stood and walked by her. Leaning against the desk, he pulled a pack of cigarettes from his pocket, lit one, and slowly inhaled before blowing out a thin stream of bluish smoke toward Conner. "Looks like you got yourself in a little bind here, Harris."

Conner kept her eyes shut. "Fuck you."

He snickered. "That bump on your face cause your limited vocabulary, or are you just not very talkative tonight?"

Conner refused to respond and lay quietly, listening to him tap his foot on the floor as he finished his cigarette. When she heard footsteps stop near her head, she opened her left eye and saw his black boot. Slowly, he knelt beside her again and ran his hand across her neck. "Tell me what you want, Bivins, then get the fuck away from me."

Bivins looked over his shoulder toward the door, then back down at the battered cop. Leaning close to her ear, he whispered, "Believe it or not, Harris, I'm one of the good guys. All I want is for you to get to the roof, give your team a signal, then find a hole to crawl into until all this is over. You're in no condition to help with this, so stay out of my way, Conner. I'll make sure everything turns out all right—I promise."

Conner opened her eyes a few moments later, found herself alone in the room, and realized she must have passed out again. She turned her head to the side, and although the pain continued to sear her brain, it wasn't as intense as it had been earlier. She looked down at her chest and panicked when she couldn't find the handcuff key. The movement made her realize that the handcuffs had already been unlocked. She sat up, rubbing her wrists, but hearing footsteps approaching the door, she stopped and fell back, covering her hands with her body.

The footsteps entered the room, paused, then continued, finally stopping next to Conner's head. A boot lightly kicked her shoulder, and Conner opened her eyes to see Olivia standing over her. "You lose something?"

Conner looked confused for a moment before she realized what Olivia was referring to. "Um, no."

Olivia removed the cap from a bottle of water and gently lifted Conner's head. "Here, drink this." She held the bottle to Conner's lips as she eagerly drank. "Slow down, I'm not going to take it away from you."

Conner relaxed her head into Olivia's hand. "Why are you doing this?"

Olivia raised an eyebrow. "What? This?" She lifted her head indicating the warehouse. "Or this?" She lifted the bottle of water.

"Both." Conner lifted her head back up and Olivia helped her drink more water.

"I'm doing this because it's my job." She gently lay Conner's head back down. "This," she looked at the bottle, "I'm doing because, believe it or not, I care about you."

Conner looked at Olivia, not knowing what to feel or say. Before she had a chance to gather her thoughts, Olivia stood. "I need to get out of here. Be careful." She leveled a final glance at Conner and walked out the door.

Conner waited a few moments, listening for any signs of movement beyond the door, then slowly sat up and untied the bindings around her ankles. A wave of dizziness rushed through her as she stood and made her way across the room to the desk. Pulling the drawer open, she found a Sig lying beside two extra clips. Quickly tucking the clips into her pocket, she headed toward the door.

She struggled to keep the dizziness and nausea at bay as she stood by the door. She turned the knob slowly and cracked the door just enough to peer out. Seeing no one, she eased into the hallway, closing the door behind her, remembering too late that she had left her vest inside She crept to the opposite end of the hall to the stairwell that led to the roof. Staying on the inside edge of the steps, she slowly made her way to the top of the stairs, feeling a cool blast of air as the door pushed open easily in her hands.

Looking around for guards, she slipped toward the back side of the roof, staying low so as to avoid attracting any unwanted attention. When she reached the parapet wall, she peered over. Seeing no sign of the guards, she crawled over the wall and gripped the same pipe she had used to access the roof. She quickly slid down the pipe and hit the ground hard, her head vibrating with pain. Not knowing where her other team members were, she headed in the direction of the boat. *All I have to do is get to Jack.*

The pain resonated through her head with each step, and she kept up a mantra on her trek across the warehouse grounds. *Get to Jack, get to Jack, get to Jack.*

"Very clever, Alex, very clever indeed." Hernandez removed the diamond-studded ring from his fingers, and using Alex's shirt, polished her blood off the gleaming jewels. "It seems we now have a dilemma on our hands."

Hernandez returned to his seat behind the desk and regarded Alex with keen eyes that sparkled when he next spoke. "Liv, darling, I think it's time to show Agent Montgomery the little surprise I have for her tonight, don't you?"

Alex turned toward Olivia and saw a moment of uncertainty in her face, and then returned her stare to Hernandez. "What little surprise would that be, Malcolm?" Alex continued to watch Olivia and felt a stabbing pain in her gut when her ex-partner refused to make eye contact with her.

"Liv, why don't you go retrieve our little package?" Hernandez waited silently until he heard footsteps draw near. His face broke into a malicious grin as he watched Alex's face pale when she saw who entered the room. "Alex, my dear, you must remember that I am always prepared for the unexpected." His laughter echoed off the concrete walls of the warehouse.

Alex lunged from the chair and was over the desk with her hands around Hernandez's neck before any of the guards could react. "You fucking bastard. I'll kill you."

Hernandez rubbed his throat as the guards pulled Alex away and pinned her back into the chair. "My, my, Alex, I thought you would be delighted to see your sister after all this time. Karen, Mrs. Fairfax, please join us for a glass of wine."

Olivia pulled a chair up on each side of Alex and motioned to the women to sit. Karen rushed toward Alex and fell into her arms. "God, Alex, are you all right?"

Returning her sister's embrace, Alex kissed her cheek and whispered, "Yes, baby, I'm fine. Now just do what they ask, okay?"

Karen nodded and sat in the chair next to Alex, but did not let go of her hand. Catherine sat on her other side, carefully scanning the room, as Alex turned back toward Hernandez.

"You see, Alex, the tides always have a way of turning in the blink of an eye. One moment you're floating on a peaceful sea, the next you're swept away in a violent vortex. One must always be prepared for those changing tides—and the consequences of being caught unprepared." Hernandez chuckled as he sat with his hands interlocked behind his head. "I do believe it's time for you to make that call now, Alex."

"I don't think so. As I told you before, it's not an option."

Hernandez stood and walked around the desk. Taking Alex's chin in his hand, he leaned close to her face. "I think your sister has been through enough the past year. I would hate to have to kill her now and see all her suffering be for naught."

Alex tore her face from his hand, "Fuck you, Mal—"

Karen cut her off before she had a chance to finish. In a quiet voice she spoke to Malcolm Hernandez for the first time. "Mr. Hernandez, I'm not sure what your little game is here, but I can tell you this. Obviously, my sister believes that bringing you down is the right thing, otherwise why would she have given up as much of her soul as she has to this case?" Glancing at Alex and Catherine, she saw the shock on both their faces.

"I stand by Alex's decision, and if my dying is what it takes to get you off the street, then so be it. Death can't be nearly as bad as what she and I have had to live through this last year." Karen held his stare, never wavering or blinking.

So, which one of your guards would you like to have the honor, Mr. Hernandez?" Karen dared another glance at her sister. "Personally, I think it should be Olivia, since she knows both of us so well. What do you think, Alex?" Karen sat back and smiled as the color drained from Hernandez's face.

Chapter Twenty

"Hey, kid, you okay?"

Conner blinked several times, trying to bring Peterson's face into focus. Suddenly, through the fog, she remembered why she was trying to reach him and struggled to speak. "Help...Alex. Warehouse...roof...clear."

Peterson felt Conner's body relax in his arms, and he gently laid her back on the ground. He pressed the mike on his chest and directed the special ops team to switch to the secure channel. While he waited for each member to call in, Peterson thought about the situation. They had the Hernandez group pinned in the warehouse with no method of escape. There was no guarantee that Hernandez wouldn't harm Alex, but Peterson found it hard to believe that he'd be so stupid as to throw away his only bargaining chip.

After all of the team members had called in, he directed everyone but Bannister, Garrett, Seay, and Willis to meet him at the dock. Then he stood Conner up, pulled her arm over his shoulder, and headed over.

When Peterson arrived with Conner, Donald was waiting, dripping water on the weathered boards under his feet. Peterson raised an eyebrow at Donald's appearance and gently sat Conner on the deck. He took off his jacket and draped it over her shoulders.

Conner's eyes widened, and as she stood up the pain ripped through her head. "Alex—she's in there. The roof...go now."

Peterson pushed on Conner's shoulder, easing her back down. "Easy, Conner, everything's under control. Just relax." He looked up at Donald for the first time. "Gather everyone up, will you, Donald?"

Donald moved toward the team that was gathering at the edge of the dock. Peterson had left before he could catch him, and after hearing him break radio silence to call everyone together, he had no other way to reach the shore except swim. He was now out of breath and facing the special ops team. They looked at him with questioning eyes, but knew to stay quiet.

Peterson joined them a few minutes later, Conner beside him. Through her pounding headache, she forced herself to focus on what had to be done. "Someone hand me a floor plan."

The group gathered around as Conner pointed out Hernandez's location and the probable locations of his men. With disappointed yet angry eyes, she informed them of Seth's involvement, as well as Bivins's and Olivia's. "Seth's definitely turned, but I think Bivins is okay. As for Olivia, well, I think she's struggling with something, but I believe when things start going down she'll be with us."

Peterson sat stunned for a moment as he absorbed the news of Seth's betrayal. "Well, Harris, looks like you're the only one around here that I can trust. Okay, listen up. Here's what we're doing."

As Peterson made the assignments, Donald hung in the background, defeated. He knew the mistakes he had made in the case were probably going to end his career, and he resigned himself to letting Peterson call the shots. As Peterson finished talking, the team looked toward Donald with expectant eyes. "You heard the man, get going," he said, his voice harsher than he had intended.

Peterson turned to him. "Why don't you take Conner back to the boat and put a call in for the paramedics and backup."

Conner stood slowly. "No, I'm going back in with you." Before Peterson or Donald had a chance to disagree, she added, "I know the way in and out, and Alex, she's in there. She wouldn't leave me, I'm not deserting her either."

She walked toward the warehouse, calling over her shoulder, "You coming, Cappy, or am I going to have to do this all by myself?"

Peterson shook his head. "Right behind you, squirt. The dinghy is in the grass over there. I'd take that if I were you, Donald. You're too damn old to be swimming." With a sad smile, he turned and trotted off to catch up with his spitfire officer.

Donald quickly motored back to the boat, where he called for backup and a medical response crew. After he gathered his extra gun and ammunition and was on his way back to the dinghy, a thought crossed his mind. Returning to the cabin, he grabbed his cell phone from the desk and punched in a number in Miami.

Conner led Peterson back to the warehouse, where they met up with Garrett and the other three special ops members. Peterson quickly gave the men their orders and motioned for Bannister, Garrett, Seay, and Willis to follow them to the roof.

Conner led the way to the back of the building. "There's only one way into the warehouse from the roof. We'll enter by way of the stairs, two at a time. Captain, you and Seay give us two minutes, then follow us down, then Willis and Bannister."

Conner waited for an objection from Peterson, but when none was forthcoming, she continued, "When you get to the bottom of the stairs, the hallway leads directly into the main warehouse. There are crates stacked along the aisles that will give you some cover, but the guards will probably be in there as well, so keep your eyes open."

"I want us to get into a position to reach Alex, then we'll give the signal to the men outside." Peterson eyed the lead team for any questions, and then nodded. "Let's move out."

Conner let Garrett lead the way. Once he was safely on the roof, she followed and took up the watch position while the other members ascended the wall. They made their way to the door and as Conner looked back at Peterson, he winked and gave her a thumbs-up. "Let's knock 'em out, kiddo."

Conner returned the smile before slowly opening the door and easing into the darkened stairwell. A chill ran through her as she thought back on her previous descent of the stairs and the events that had ensured. Shaking it off, she crept down the stairs with Garrett following close behind.

When she peered around the corner, she found the hallway deserted, and she edged toward the door of the office. She and Garrett maneuvered further down the hallway and into the main warehouse. They took a position near the hall so they could monitor the others as well as the adjacent area. Conner watched the darkened lane until she saw Peterson and Seay emerge two minutes later.

Peterson took Conner's place as lookout and Conner, Garrett, and Seay spread out through the warehouse. Conner watched as a shadow fell over the gap she had ducked into. She froze as the guard walked by, then stopped a short distance from her. He lifted his head as if straining to hear, then turned and once again started in her direction.

Conner pulled the stun gun from her belt and waited until the guard was directly beside her before she pressed the device against his back. He collapsed into her arms, and she pulled him into the gap. After gagging and binding him, she moved out in search of the next guard.

The team outside listened as the clicks continued to sound over their earphones. So far, seven guards had been disabled, leaving only six armed guards, Olivia, and Hernandez. Andrews motioned to his men to move out. Three would enter the building from the roof as the initial entrance team had done, and he and the other two members would enter straight through the front door.

Andrew's pulse quickened as the minutes ticked off and more adrenaline rushed through his bloodstream. The time was near. Some would live—and some would die. The question that loomed large in all their minds was, who?

Karen thought back over that fateful night at the warehouse. Almost a year had passed since she'd received a call from someone warning her to stop Alex from going to the raid that night. After trying unsuccessfully to reach her sister on her cell phone, Karen panicked and drove to the warehouse herself. Just as she drove up, all hell had broken loose.

The confrontation had just begun. Karen raced back to her SUV and hid in the back, tucking between the camping equipment she had left there from a weekend trip.

She heard and felt the impact of several bullets as they penetrated the exterior shell of the truck and tore into the tent and sleeping bags. One of the bullets tore through her leg, and she screamed in pain. Two of Hernandez's guards heard the scream and pulled open the door of the SUV. One of the burly men crawled into the driver's seat, the other into the back, and the truck sped off in the direction of the warehouse.

They were just outside the city limits of Jacksonville when the truck slowed down and pulled to the side of the road. The driver got out, opened the back hatch, and hauled Karen out into the ditch. With a calm, calculating expression, he fired a single shot before jumping back into the truck and speeding off.

She lay there, bleeding and afraid, wondering if that was how she would die, when a car stopped alongside her. The driver jumped out and ran to her while his wife called 911. Soon the area was lit up with flashing lights, and Karen felt herself being lifted onto a gurney. Only after she had been placed into the safety of the ambulance did she let herself relax into the warm, soft comfort of unconsciousness.

She awakened two days later to find herself in the hospital. There was no phone in her room, and neither the nurses nor the guard posted at her door would answer her questions about the raid. She was told that someone from the FBI would be by to see her soon. She waited for six more hours before Donald walked in, looking tired and stressed. One look into his eyes and Karen knew the news he brought wasn't good.

He sat on the bed and held her hand as he recapped the events of that night. All he told her was that Alex was alive and getting the best care possible. It was another three weeks before Donald dropped by the house early one morning and sped off with her to visit Alex.

Donald had tried to prepare her for seeing Alex for the first time. She had sustained three gunshot wounds, any of which should have been fatal, and numerous injuries from flying debris as the warehouse had exploded. Alex had been in a coma since being transferred to the facility the day after the raid, and the doctors, although optimistic, couldn't say for certain if she would ever regain consciousness. The only thing they could say was that Alex's will to live was stronger than that of any other patient they had ever seen, or any medicine they could prescribe.

When Karen entered the room and saw Alex, she gasped. Alex was shadowed by numerous pieces of equipment monitoring and measuring her vitals and delivering fluids and medications. Karen sat beside the bed, holding Alex's hand for hours before Donald entered the room and told her they had to leave. She kissed Alex on the forehead and whispered in her ear that she loved her before quietly leaving the room.

Donald took a roundabout route back to Jacksonville, and on the way home, he explained very delicately how her life would change. She had identified Malcolm Hernandez as one of the men in the truck, and because she was the only surviving witness who could testify, Donald was placing her in protective custody.

After arriving back in Jacksonville, he gave her only six hours to pack and close up the house before whisking her away to an unknown destination. She spent the first three weeks inside a safe house, not knowing where she was, and then late one night she was moved to yet another unknown destination.

For the last year, Karen's life had been a series of moves. She had never known from one day to the next where she would sleep, and it had become almost more than she could bear. The only thing that kept her going was Donald's news that Alex was recovering and his assurances that their continuing investigation into the warehouse raid would lead to Hernandez's arrest. He kept promising that one day the nightmare would be over.

Donald's stomach lurched as he listened to the agent on the other end of the line. Apparently, their careful planning had failed, and someone had followed them to Miami, where Catherine and Karen had been kidnapped as they were strolling through the neighborhood.

"Why the hell didn't someone notify me?" Donald was furious as he listened to the agent's reply. "Who told you not to contact me?"

Donald sat down heavily in the chair and took a deep breath, trying to focus. "Have you received any communications from the abductors since they were taken?...You tell Assistant Director Albertson that I would like to speak to him as soon as possible."

There's only one person who would want Karen. As Donald hurried across the river in the dinghy, he thought about the possibility of Karen and Catherine being in the warehouse. As he jumped from the craft and sprinted across the open field, his one and only thought was of saving the three women being held captive by Malcolm Hernandez. He never saw the sniper on top of the Colorado Container building, nor did he immediately feel the bullet that penetrated his back. All he heard before stumbling to the ground and falling into the darkness was the loud popping sound of the rifle, followed by his own voice as he screamed out Catherine's name.

Dennis Andrews heard the crack of the rifle just as he rose to move toward the door. He saw someone running toward him, then heard a desperate scream as the figure fell to the ground. Looking on top of the Container building, he saw one of the guards watching the fallen figure. Andrews knew the wounded person had to be Donald.

He tapped Gabe Watson on the shoulder and pointed toward the Container building. Watson immediately spotted the guard and in one smooth motion raised his rifle to his shoulder and fired one shot. The guard fell, and Andrews took off running in Donald's direction while Watson covered him from the warehouse.

Andrew reached Donald and quickly accessed his condition. His pulse was weak, but he was alive. Using as much care as possible, Andrews lifted Donald onto his shoulder and hurried back across the field to the warehouse.

Watson felt a lump in Donald's pocket as he carefully laid the man out on the ground. Pulling out the cell phone, he placed a call to the agent at the command center, gave him Donald's location, and told him to forward the message to the backup team and rescue unit as well. He and Andrews then moved back toward the door to join Quincey, and they waited for the signal to storm the warehouse.

Catherine caught a movement to her left and slowly turned her head to see a woman peering around a large shipping crate. The woman slowly help up a single finger and made a circular motion. Taking advantage of Hernandez's shock over Karen's declaration, Catherine softly touched Alex's leg. When Alex looked at her, Catherine moved her eyes toward the woman in the shadows and heard a soft gasp.

Conner repeated the motion with her finger, telling Alex that they had the area surrounded. She tipped her head toward Hernandez, and Alex interpreted that to mean she wanted some sort of distraction. She was about to make a move, but froze as Seth moved from the shadows to put his gun to the back of Karen's head. Hernandez walked slowly toward Olivia, pulled his own gun from his jacket, and fired a shot point-blank into Olivia's chest.

Alex's body jerked as she watched her ex-partner and friend fall to the floor. A dark red stain spread across Olivia's white shirt as blood flowed from the wound. Alex couldn't tell if she was alive, but doubted she could have survived a shot from that range.

"I guess you'll have to choose another executioner, Alex. I'm afraid Liv is unavailable at the moment." A dark menacing smile crossed Hernandez's face. "I haven't trusted her for quite some time now." Turning toward Karen, he added, "Thank you, Ms. Hilliard, for clearing up that bit of confusion."

Karen sat in shock as she stared at the man in front of her. Guilt surged through her body as she realized her words had caused Olivia's death. "You son of a bitch."

Conner and Peterson watched as the scene unfolded in front of them. They both heard the crack of the rifle fire outside and knew something had to be done, and quickly. Malcolm Hernandez was swiftly coming unraveled. They had to make their move now, before anyone else was killed.

As Conner contemplated her next move, Frank Bivins emerged from the back of the room and walked toward Hernandez and Seth Thomas. "Get her out of here, Seth. You know how Mr. Hernandez dislikes blood." Bivins moved behind Karen as shots echoed throughout the warehouse.

When Malcolm Hernandez turned to flee, Bivins raised his gun from Karen's head and pointed it at his back. "Freeze, Hernandez."

Hernandez slowly turned to face his most trusted guard. "Not you too, Bivins? And to think, you would have made such a great soldier."

Alex took the opportunity to pull Karen and Catherine out of their chairs and push them toward Conner. "Cover them," she shouted as she turned back toward Bivins.

Alex could hear scuffling sounds from around the warehouse, but the gunfire had stopped. Peterson held up a hand, ordering everyone to stand back and allow Alex to handle the situation.

"Good evening, Agent Montgomery." Bivins smiled. He pulled a Glock from behind his back and passed it to Alex. "I think I'll allow you the honors. You've worked hard for this collar, take it."

With her left hand, Alex took the Glock from Bivins, never taking her eyes off Hernandez. A rage welled up from her gut as she walked toward him. She raised the gun to his chest, her hand shaking and her finger tight on the trigger. She had waited so long for this moment, and now that it was here, all she wanted to do was pull the trigger and watch him die. Her rage surged even further as she saw a smile cross his lips.

"You know you won't pull the trigger, Alex. It's not in you to kill a man in cold blood. I'm unarmed, totally defenseless."

Alex stepped closer. "You're never defenseless, Malcolm. We both know it. But no, I won't kill you. I want to see you rot in prison the rest of your life. I want to know that every day I live, you'll be penned up like an animal in a cage. I may even come by to see you on occasion, just to watch as your miserable life wastes away behind bars and to remind you each time that I put you there."

Alex stepped closer. "For now, I'll settle for this." She brought her right hand up hard and smiled as Hernandez's head snapped backwards and he fell back onto the desk. She quickly turned him over and pulled his arm behind his back. Reaching out behind her, she felt the cold metal of handcuffs as Bivins slipped them into her hand. Alex smiled as the ratcheting sound echoed through the warehouse when she cuffed Hernandez's hands behind his back. She pulled him up and turned him around once more. "Oh, I almost forgot, Malcolm. This is for Feryle."

Hernandez screamed as Alex's knee made solid contact with his crotch. She let go of her hold on his arm and watched as he fell to the floor retching. She bent down to lean in close to his ear. "Well, Malcolm, how does it feel to be unprepared? Looks to me like you're the one caught in the vortex now." Alex smirked, and as she stood up, she caught sight of Seth running across the warehouse floor.

Everything seemed to move in slow motion as Conner watched the scene unfold before her. One moment Alex was cuffing Hernandez, the next Seth was running with his gun pointed at her. Conner pushed off the wall and tore across the warehouse. "No!"

Alex saw another movement to her right and saw Conner rushing toward her. A scream pierced the shock-induced quiet of the warehouse. Alex heard the gunshot at the same moment Conner leaped toward her, and she felt the hard impact as Conner's body crashed into hers.

Seth's attack had taken Bivins by surprise, and as he raised his gun to return fire, a second bullet from Seth's gun pierced the base of his throat. Bivins pulled the trigger, then the gun slipped from his hands. As he collapsed to the floor, he heard a multitude of gunshots echo around him. He lay on the cold concrete floor, staring at the ceiling, as the mayhem continued.

Although he heard screaming, he couldn't make out the words as the darkness began to overtake his vision, and he felt a thick stream of blood run down his neck and pool behind his head. He tried to focus on the noise and activity around him, but felt a chill as his body responded to the loss of blood. Slowly he surrendered to the overpowering need to sleep, closed his eyes, and let the darkness encompass his soul.

Peterson saw Seth at the same moment Conner did and ran toward Alex. When the shots exploded from Seth's gun, he brought his own up to return fire. He felt a blistering pain as Seth's third shot pierced his arm. Helplessly, Peterson watched Seth turn and run into the shadows.

The warehouse was suddenly overrun with federal agents and police, and Peterson felt someone pull him to a crate and sit him down. His head snapped up when he heard a primitive howl from across the room. Holding his injured arm, he raced across the floor to see Alex cradling his best detective in her arms.

A flood of guilt washed over Peterson as he watched the blood saturate Conner's white shirt. From where he was standing, Peterson couldn't tell where the bullet had entered her body. He knelt beside Alex as the paramedics converged on them. "Alex, let her go. Come on, babe, let the paramedics do their job."

Alex cradled Conner in her arms, rocking her gently as Peterson tried to remove her hands. Alex didn't hear any of them as she looked into the pale lifeless face of her lover. "Come on, baby, wake up." Alex stroked Conner's hair, her panic rising with every second. "Conner, come on now, please wake up."

Peterson pried Alex's hands from Conner's body and pulled her away. "Alex. Alex!" Peterson pulled Alex to him. "Alex, you have to let them work." She finally fell back into his embrace, tears pouring from her eyes as she watched the paramedics work on Conner.

Alex felt the room spin as she saw one of the paramedics look at the other and shake his head. "No, Conner!"

The anguished scream echoed throughout the building and Alex began to fall. Two strong arms wrapped around her body as she sank to the floor, oblivious to everything except her pain as Karen held her and let her cry. Minutes seemed like hours to Karen before Alex was finally placed into the ambulance.

The pain Alex felt was not in her body but in her soul. She lay on the stretcher, staring at the ceiling of the ambulance as the flashing lights flickered across the landscape. The paramedic leaning over her spoke, but she didn't absorb his words. From somewhere in her mind, she watched as he inserted a needle into the IV tube and pressed the plunger. Soon her world turned gray, then black, and she let herself fall into the abyss.

When she woke up, Alex looked around the room, taking in the equipment and monitors hanging from the walls. Turning her head, she saw Karen asleep in the chair beside the bed and felt her sister's fingers interlocked with her own.

When she tried to move, her body screamed its objection. The bullet that had passed through Conner's body before entering hers had shattered her shoulder. She felt numb and empty as the events of the previous evening returned to her memory. A single tear slipped down her face as the image of Conner's lifeless body reappeared in her mind, and she closed her eyes, allowing the darkness to return.

Alex woke to a light tapping sound from across the room. Karen rose sleepily from the chair beside the bed and walked over, spoke quietly to the guard, then pulled the door open further to let Peterson enter.

Alex watched Peterson as he crossed the room. His injured arm was in a sling, and his face looked tired and pale. He had just come from Conner's memorial service and even though all he wanted was a very stout drink and a quiet place to think, he had promised Alex he would drop by afterwards.

"Hey, Jack." Alex saw the tears he tried to hide and reached out toward her friend.

Peterson bent down, allowing Alex to embrace him. He was ashamed of his weakness: even in her loss, Alex managed to draw courage and strength from deep within herself to comfort him.

He pulled back from the warm embrace and sat on the edge of the bed. "Hey, how are you holding up?"

Alex looked out the window and shrugged. "I really don't know. I don't feel anything right now, except empty. You look tired, Jack. How are you?" They had talked a few days earlier, and Peterson had told her about Conner's insistence on returning to the warehouse without her vest. He had completely broken down, crying as the guilt once again consumed him.

"I was so concerned about getting Hernandez that I let her to talk me into something I never would have allowed." Alex had held him as he sobbed in her arms. Conner was a lot more to Peterson than just his best detective; she had been his friend, and in a sense, a daughter. Alex wasn't certain he would be able to recover from the loss.

"I'm hanging on. We have a few leads on Seth Thomas from the other guards we brought in that night. He supposedly has a hideout down in Mexico, so we're focusing our efforts on tracing him down there. We used Hernandez's fingerprints to make a positive ID on him. I have to hand it to Bivins, his last shot took most of Hernandez's face off. We all knew it was him, but the positive ID made me feel a lot better."

Peterson looked into Alex's eyes, saw nothing but an empty abyss, and wished he could make this moment easier for her. Alex had waited far too long to put an end to Hernandez. She had lost so much during this case, and even knowing the man was dead wouldn't bring any happiness back into her life. Losing Feryle, and now Conner, was just too much. He watched as Alex wiped a single tear from her face, then walked to the window and gazed out, giving her time to regroup.

"So, Jack, when are you going to give me the entire story about Friday night?" She had asked several times over the last couple of days, but Peterson had always hesitated, telling her to focus on getting better. The excuse was wearing thin now, and she was determined to get some answers.

Karen walked to the bedside table. Picking up her purse, she said, "I think I'll go down to the cafeteria and get a cup of coffee, give you two some time to talk."

"Thanks, Karen." Alex turned back to Peterson, silently challenging him to try to slip away again. With a heavy sigh, he detailed the events as they had played out that night.

Alex sat quietly and listened. So much information had been kept from her during the investigations. Information that, had she been aware of it, would have made a difference in how she had planned and approached the raid. If Donald lived, he would certainly have a lot of explaining to do. The FBI had lost three men during the raid: Frank Bivins, Eric Quincey, and David Seay. Donald and Olivia were both in the intensive care unit, barely holding their own. It would be days before either would be out of the woods, and even longer before they could be questioned and debriefed.

Peterson and Alex continued to talk until he noticed the fatigue in her face. He said his good-byes and promised to come by the next day and give her whatever updates they had on the case. He kissed Alex lightly on the forehead and touched her cheek with a callused hand before turning and walking out the door.

For the first time since her arrival at the hospital, Alex found herself alone. She looked out through the window and thought of Conner, the happiness, although short lived, they had shared—and of the life they had promised each other. Her heart ached, and she freely let fall her tears of loss and sadness.

Karen approached the door and heard the sobbing inside the room. Her first instinct was to rush through the door to comfort her sister, but she stopped short, knowing Alex would force the tears back once again. Karen's heart broke as she heard her sister's wails, and she slowly sank to the floor beside the door.

Chapter Twenty-One

Alex sat on the back deck watching the sun rise over the horizon. The high tide had washed the beach clean, and the seagulls were gliding and dipping as they hunted for their morning meal. Most mornings Alex found herself here, watching as the sun rose, sleep once again only a distant memory for her. Between the half-empty bed and the frequent nightmares, she chose instead to take several naps during the afternoon and evening, leaving the darkness of the night for her waking moments.

During the last week, she had taken several midnight walks on the beach, often stopping to sit in the cool sand and watch the stars. She had found comfort in the memory of sitting on her grandmother's lap in the back yard. They would look up into the vast darkness of the sky and see the twinkling stars, and her grandmother would tell her their names.

As Alex had sat watching the previous night, she chose the brightest one she could see in the darkened sky and christened it Conner. She found herself now searching the same spot in the sky for the star, knowing that in the light of day its twinkling light would be shining over another hemisphere, but somehow she drew comfort from just knowing it was there, somewhere.

She laid her head back on the chaise lounge and was just dropping off to sleep when the shrill of the phone broke the silence. She reached over with her good arm and looked at the caller ID seeing, once again, that it was Olivia. She set the phone back down on the deck and closed her eyes, trying to shut out the memory of her ex-partner.

Sam had insisted that Alex come and stay with her and Kelly during her recovery, but Alex had held her ground, determined to go home after she was released from the hospital. Sam had made her usual daily visits, bringing enough food to feed a small army, and they had spent many hours talking. It was only a week ago, during a conversation about Olivia, that Sam allowed her temper to flare, and in the heat of her anger she had told Alex of Olivia's trip to San Diego and her encounter with Feryle.

At first, Alex was hurt and shocked by Feryle's betrayal. But as she thought about Olivia and her actions, she acknowledged that Olivia was the one who deserved her disdain, not Feryle. Slowly she rose from the lounge, holding her shoulder as she did, and made her way back into the house. Walking into the bedroom, Alex looked at the neat stack of Conner's clothes that Sam had washed and folded. A tear crept from her eye and slid gently down her face as she eased her way into the cool, empty bed. She lay there for a long while, staring at the ceiling, thinking about Conner and all they could have shared, until finally she drifted off into a restless sleep.

Olivia placed the phone down in its cradle and sat staring at it. She knew Alex was home from the hospital; Donald had told her as much the last time she'd spoken with him on the phone. She walked to the refrigerator and pulled out a cold beer, then walked onto the tarmac and watched as jumbo jets took off for destinations unknown to her. She momentarily thought about packing a bag, climbing in the helicopter, and escaping for a while, but she knew that running would never be the answer.

Olivia sat down in the lounge chair she usually used for sunning on slow days and let her head fall back, thinking about the events of the last few weeks. She had been safely tucked away during her recovery, as had Donald and Alex. However, now that everyone was out of the hospital, she wondered if the nightmare was truly over.

Donald had told her that Malcolm Hernandez was dead. Even so, Olivia knew that an organization of that size never died—and that the throne would be filled by the next in line, with a good possibility that their previous grudges would survive the changing of the guard. What she was having a hard time figuring out was who the new kingpin would be. Unconsciously, her hand came up to rest on the long scar along the midline of her chest as she thought about how close she had been to dying.

She knew it was a miracle she was alive, even more so that she was sitting here in the sun only four weeks later. *I let my fucking guard down for just a minute, and now I'll never be able to show my face again around the bureau. I'll never be able to live down getting shot point-blank in the chest with my gun holstered.* Once again, she felt the pressing need to speak with Alex and headed back to the office. She dialed the number she had memorized and waited as the phone rang several times. She listened to Alex's low sultry voice for a moment after the answering machine picked up before replacing the receiver. Growling, she snapped a pencil in half and threw the jagged pieces across the room, then jerked up from her chair and headed to the door. *Well, Alex, if I just show up on your doorstep, you'll have to talk with me.*

Donald sat staring at the computer monitor. He could hear Catherine moving around the kitchen as she prepared dinner. He read over the words on the screen, then printed the document. After tri-folding the letter, he slid it into a plain white envelope and stood up.

Walking into the kitchen, he crept behind Catherine and placed a gentle kiss on her neck. "I finally finished it. I'll be back soon, okay?"

Catherine looked deeply into her husband's eyes. "Are you sure this is what you want to do, Donald?"

A sad smile crossed his lips. "It's the only thing I *can* do Catherine, the only right thing to do."

Pulling Donald into her arms and placing a light kiss on his lips, she whispered, "I'm behind you one hundred percent, whatever you decide to do." Looking away, she added, "Donald, I do think it's time you took care of the other matter as well. It's not fair to you or Alex to keep going this way."

"I know. I just need to make sure Seth is out of the picture first. I promise you, it will be soon." Donald pulled away, picked up his keys, and walked out the door.

Catherine turned back to her dinner preparation and was deep in thought when she heard the piercing scream. Dropping the knife on the counter, she ran through the door, heart racing, and then stopped short as she took in the sight before her.

Alex woke with a start and sat straight up in the bed. She took a deep cleansing breath as she wiped the sweat from her face, then threw the covers back and pulled herself up, heading to the bathroom. Splashing cool water over her face, she pondered the dream that had plagued her for weeks.

The vision that unfolded within the dream was surreal as she watched, as if within another body, as Conner leapt across the warehouse. Alex massaged her side, still feeling the impact of Conner's body against hers. She watched as they crashed to the floor and heard her own voice cry out as she saw the bright red spot expand across Conner's shirt. She could see the paramedics kneel beside her lover, and Donald as he pulled her away. It was when the paramedics shook their heads that she always awoke, drenched in sweat and gasping for air.

She dried her face with a towel, then headed back down the hall to the kitchen, knowing sleep would be impossible. Alex set the coffeepot to brew and walked into her office. Sitting down behind the desk, she flipped the switch and waited as the computer booted.

Connecting to her office computer, Alex pulled up the latest reports from the database, reading each one carefully and pondering what Seth's next move might be. She was startled as the loud knocking on the front door echoed through the house. Easing out of her chair, Alex looked through the front window to see who it was. When she saw Olivia's car in the driveway, she moved away from the window and crept down the hallway to the foyer. Leaning against the cool wall, she listened to Olivia yelling through the door.

"Alex, I know you're in there. Please, open the door. We need to talk."

Squeezing her eyes shut, Alex once again felt the anger surge through her body. She listened as Olivia continued her pleas, then tore herself away from the door and walked back down the hallway into the bedroom, where she sat on the side of the bed until Olivia finally gave up and drove away. Alex fell back on the bed, exhausted from the unexpected intrusion, and fell into another disturbing dream.

The room was cold and impersonal, the furniture obviously mass-produced. From her viewpoint in the corner of the room, Alex watched as the two naked forms on the bed moved together, their cries of passion sending chills throughout her body. Olivia entered the woman beneath her, and Alex heard the fevered cries as her orgasm exploded throughout her body. The only features Alex could see were the woman's hands as she raked her nails down Olivia's back, raising long red welts.

After a few long moments, the two naked and sweating bodies stilled, the only sounds the heavy rasping breaths coming from the satisfied lovers. Olivia slowly pulled out of her lover, and Alex heard a longing moan from the unseen woman beneath Olivia. She watched as the fingers that had so recently ravaged Olivia's back now gently made their way up her body and into her soft, dark hair. She pulled Olivia into a passionate kiss that was only broken as their need for air overtook them. The woman whispered softly into Olivia's ear, saying "I love you," then kissing her once again. The kiss continued for long moments until Olivia finally broke it and rolled onto her side, revealing the woman beneath her.

Olivia released a boisterous laugh as Alex's eyes fell on the woman beside her. Feryle laughed as she turned into her lover's arms, tucking her face into the crook of Olivia's neck. When she once again turned toward Alex, it was Conner now laughing with Olivia. Alex felt herself swirling in the powerful vortex as the scene continued. Finally, it was Alex's own cries of pain that broke her free of the horrible dream. As her heart pounded in her heaving chest, the tears began their assault upon her face.

Donald placed his gun, badge, and the envelope on the desk. Assistant Director Albertson slowly opened the envelope and read the letter of resignation Donald had prepared earlier in the day.

His eyes met Donald's and in a low growl, he ordered his agent to sit. "Just what the hell is this supposed to be, Fairfax, some kind of escape for you?"

Donald sat down and shook his head. "No, Robert, it's not an escape." He ran his hand over his face. "Just accept it for what it is and let's get on with it, all right?"

Albertson looked down at the letter and then back at Donald. "I'll not accept this until the case is officially closed. One thing I've known about you your entire career, Donald, is that you're not a quitter. And I refuse to let you start now." He dropped the letter in his pending box. "You want to resign, fine. You get your ass out there and find Seth Thomas for me. Then, if you still want to throw your entire career away, I'll start the paperwork."

Donald's eyes flashed anger. "I can go over your head, you know."

Albertson met the infuriated stare with one of his own. "Yes, you could, but you won't. Now get this mess off my desk and get to work."

Donald held Albertson's eyes for a moment then, taking a long slow breath, he rose and reclaimed his gun and badge before walking out the door.

Assistant Director Robert Albertson watched his agent and friend leave the office. Donald had made some serious mistakes on this case, it was true, but Albertson refused to believe that he had lost the talent and passion required to be an effective agent. He took the envelope out of his pending box and reread the letter of resignation before placing it back in the envelope. He rose, walked to the credenza across the room, and watched the letter turn into confetti as it passed through the shredder.

Driving a short distance away from the house and turning down a deserted beach access road, Olivia parked the car facing the main road and shut off the engine. Reaching over and pulling the receiver from the floorboard, she flipped the power switch on and listened as she cycled through the frequencies for each of the bugs in the house. Olivia didn't hear any sound f until she switched to the frequency for the bug in the bedroom. Alex's gasping sobs filled the car, and Olivia felt her chest tighten as she listened to the ravaged cries.

She sat for almost an hour listening to her friend cry. The sobs slowly faded into soft whimpers. She was about to turn the receiver off when Alex's voice echoed through the car. "You'll pay, Olivia. One day

I'll make sure you pay for trying to take Feryle away from me. One day, you'll pay for Feryle and Conner both." A wrenching chill ran up Olivia's spine. Even though she couldn't see her face, Olivia recognized the voice of the Shadow.

Donald drove along I-95 with no destination in mind. The fresh air blowing through the window always seemed to clear his head. After driving for half an hour, he realized he was only a few miles from Alex's. Pulling the phone from his pocket, he punched in the numbers and waited.

When Alex answered, Donald could hear the fatigue and pain in her voice. "Hey, kiddo, I was in the neighborhood and was wondering if you're up for a little company?"

"Donald, you're never accidentally in my neighborhood, but yes, come on over."

Exiting onto the JTB Expressway, Donald pushed the gas pedal a little harder as he sped toward Alex's. He knew there was a lot of explaining to do; however, he was finding it very difficult to decide when, where, and how to begin. Pulling into the driveway, he took a deep breath. As he was walking up the steps of the front porch, the door swung open and Alex stood back to let him enter. Donald stood awkwardly in the foyer, looking at Alex.

Alex closed the door and turned toward him, noticing his discomfort. "Come here, you." Opening her arms and pulling Donald into a warm embrace, she kissed him on the cheek. "How are you feeling?"

Returning the embrace, Donald released a pent up-breath. "I'm doing good. How about you?"

Alex shrugged. "I don't really know. One minute I'm fine, the next...well, not so good." Taking Donald's hand, Alex pulled him toward the kitchen. "Let's sit on the deck and have a beer."

"After the day I've had, a beer sounds good."

Alex pulled two bottles from the refrigerator, then led Donald onto the deck. They sat for a few minutes, watching the beachcombers and letting the beer do its magic. Donald was the first to break the silence. "Alex, I know I made a lot of mistakes on this—"

Alex interrupted him. "Donald, we all make mistakes. You did what you thought was best under the circumstances. On some things you weren't given a choice, I know that. I also know that you would never intentionally put me, or Conner, in harm's way." Feeling tears brim her eyes, Alex self-consciously looked away.

Donald let her regain her composure before leaning over and taking her hands in his. "I love you, Alex. It kills me to see you this way. What can I do to make it better?"

A single tear streaked down Alex's face. "I wish it were that easy, Donald, but it's not humanly possible for me to have what I need."

Donald knelt in front of Alex and pulled her into his arms. "Alex, anything is—" His words were cut short as his pager beeped. Looking at the display, he stood and headed for the door. "I need to use your phone for a second. I'll be right back."

Alex used the time Donald was talking on the phone to compose herself. She took a long pull on the beer, emptying the bottle, then set it beside her on the deck. Standing up, she headed to the kitchen for another just as Donald finished his phone call. Seeing the excited look on Donald's face, she couldn't help but say, "Looks like that was good news. Anything I should know about?"

In two steps, Donald was beside Alex, giving her a warm hug. "Sure is. That was AD Albertson. Seth Thomas was just apprehended down in Mexico."

Alex could feel her pulse quicken at the news. All she wanted was five minutes alone in a room with Seth Thomas, then the FBI could have him. Five minutes to dole out her revenge for Conner's death.

Donald broke into her thoughts. "Sorry, but I need to be going. Robert wants me to go down there myself and bring him back."

Raising her eyebrows in a silent question, Alex smiled when he took the hint and asked her to come along. "Okay, Donald, I'll meet you at the airport in two hours."

Donald headed for the door. "Don't forget to leave your Shadow at home, Alex. We need to play this one by the book, all right?"

Smirking, Alex followed along behind Donald. "Party pooper. Okay, I'll be good." She shut the door behind Donald and stood in the empty foyer, contemplating the sudden turn of events. After a moment she shook her head and walked to the bedroom.

She quickly packed a bag and headed out the door. Driving down I-95 toward the airport, Alex remembered that Sam was coming over for dinner. Picking up her cell phone, she punched in the number. Sam answered on the second ring.

"Hey, Sam. Look, I'm not going to be able to make dinner tonight. I have to go out of town unexpectedly. I'll call you when I get back, okay?"

"Whoa, wait a minute. Where are you going?"

Alex couldn't help but grin. "Donald just got word that Seth Thomas has been apprehended in Mexico, and we're going down there to bring him back."

"Damn, Alex, can't you let someone else do this? You just got your cast off yesterday, for God's sake."

Alex took a deep breath before she spoke. "Sam, honey, we'll be fine. It's a simple prisoner transfer."

"That's exactly my point, Alex. Let someone else go. Stay here, please."

"I can't, Sam. This—this is the last thing I can do for Conner. I'm bringing her murderer home." Alex's voiced cracked as she spoke. "I'm going to make sure he gets what he deserves, Sam. He won't get away with killing Conner."

Her voice grew strong and dark. "One way or another, he will pay."

"Just be careful, and call me the minute you get back."

"Okay Sam, I'll call as soon as I get back, promise. Oh, and can you do me a favor? Call Karen and let her know I'm with Donald. She went to Cedar Cove yesterday to see the family, and I don't want her to worry."

"Yeah, I'll call her, you coward. Be safe."

Alex growled through her chuckle. "Yeah, yeah, I'm a coward, but you love me anyway. Thanks, Sam, see you soon." Closing the phone and tossing it back in her bag, Alex steered toward the exit for the airport.

Donald arrived home to find Catherine asleep on the sofa. Bending down and placing a light kiss on her lips, he woke her. "Hey, sexy woman."

Wrapping her arms around Donald, she pulled him down into her arms, then gently nipped him on the neck and murmured, "Hey you. Wanna snuggle?"

Feeling his heart beat faster, Donald pulled away and sat down beside her. "As much as I would like to, I can't. AD Albertson paged me a little while ago. They caught Seth Thomas down in Mexico, and Alex and I are leaving in a couple of hours to go bring him back."

Catherine's face darkened. "Donald, can't someone—"

"Yes, I'm sure someone else could, Catherine," Donald said, cutting off his wife's protests. "But I need this chance to show Alex that I'm not such a fuck-up. I want to do this, Catherine. We both know how important it is to get him back here safely."

Catherine sighed. "Okay, you're right, as usual. Just promise me you'll both be careful."

Glancing down the hallway, Donald asked, "How's she doing?"

"She came in a few minutes ago and went directly to her room. She's sleeping now, I think. She doesn't think Alex will ever forgive her for this."

Donald planted a long kiss on Catherine's lips. "Alex has been through a lot lately. She'll get it all sorted out in time. Mark my words, she'll forgive her."

Catherine helped Donald pack and saw him to his car, then walked slowly back into the house. Looking out the kitchen window, lost in her thoughts, Catherine was startled when she heard the voice behind her.

"Where's Donald off to?"

Spinning around, Catherine put a hand to her chest. "Damn, you scared me. He, uh, he and Alex are leaving for Mexico. Seth Thomas has been caught. They're going down to bring him back."

Alex arrived at the airport before Donald. She went into the charter office to make sure everything was okay and running on time. The FBI had sent a plane down to take them to Mexico, and Alex gazed out the window to the tarmac, watching as a crew checked and refueled it. She thought back over her conversation with Sam. *You're right, Sammy, I am a coward.* Alex couldn't face calling her sister and telling her she was once again on the case. She was lost in her thoughts when Donald walked up behind her.

"You okay, Alex?"

Alex jumped and turned to glare at Donald. "Well, I was until you scared the hell out of me. We ready to go?"

Trying to force back the smile that threatened to break across his face, Donald put his hand on Alex's back and led her outside. "Everything's ready, let's get this show on the road."

They boarded the plane and waited until they were cleared for takeoff. Alex looked out the window as the landscape disappeared below her, wondering what lay ahead of them. She finally reclined her seat and fell into a restless sleep as the plane flew over the Gulf of Mexico toward Acapulco.

Blue smoke curled from the cigarette and drifted out the window as the man sat in the parking lot and watched the plane take off. He sat watching until it was completely out of sight before throwing the butt on the ground and starting the motor. Slowly, he pulled the truck into the long-term parking garage and parked at the far end of a crowded lane. He grabbed a single duffel bag from the back and quickly made his way to the Delta ticket counter, where he purchased a one-way ticket to Acapulco, Mexico.

He hurried through the terminal, knowing the plane would be leaving in less than fifteen minutes. He knew he couldn't take a chance on missing this flight. He arrived at the gate just as the gate agent was about to close the door, and was breathless as he dropped down into his seat. Pulling a folder from his duffel bag, he opened it and thumbed through the pages. Satisfied that everything was going as planned, he closed the folder, returned it to his bag, and lay his head back for a much-needed nap. A smile crossed his lips as he thought about what the next few hours would bring. *Finally you are within my grasp, Shadow.*

Chapter Twenty-Two

The plane landed in Acapulco a little after six in the evening. As they taxied to the terminal, Alex looked out the window and felt a lump form in her throat as her emotions turned melancholy. It was just over a year since she had last been to Acapulco. She and Feryle had spent two weeks there on their last vacation walking hand in hand on the beach, dining at the most romantic restaurants, and savoring every moment of the romantic bliss. Now as she looked out at the skyline, Alex once again felt the emptiness within her heart. The last time she had taken in this romantic city, her heart had soared with delight; now all she felt was a hollowness in her chest that threatened to overtake her soul.

Taking a deep breath, she chastised herself for her mental weakness. She had to stay focused and alert. This case wouldn't be over until Seth Thomas was back in Jacksonville and behind bars. And she intended to make sure he paid for murdering Conner.

Turning to Donald, Alex noticed how tired he looked and silently wondered if he were up to the mental and physical stress of their mission. "I can't wait to get settled and take a long hot bath. How about you? Got any hot plans for tonight?"

Donald stretched as much as he could, given the small space, then yawned. "I think the first order of business is getting to our rooms for the night, then having dinner. I'll call the local precinct when we get to the hotel and see what their timetable is for tomorrow. Other than that, I have no plans, um, unless you're up for something."

"No, I'm beat. I think I'd like to make an early evening of it too. Hopefully we can pick Thomas up first thing in the morning and be home by mid-afternoon."

In the taxi on the way to the hotel, Donald looked at Alex with concern in his eyes. He had been acutely aware of Alex's nervousness throughout the flight. Her behavior during the afternoon was extremely out of character for the usually calm, cool, focused agent, and it had only seemed to worsen since their arrival in Acapulco. He knew Alex wasn't one to burden anyone with her personal problems, even friends, but

Donald decided to open the door and allow her the opportunity. "Are you all right, Alex?"

Alex shrugged, "Yes, I'm fine."

"You've seemed a bit distracted today, want to talk about it?"

"Maybe later. I'm just tired and need a shower to wake me up." Alex realized she was being overly emotional and mentally reprimanded herself for what she considered a weakness.

Just as she was regaining her normally stoic composure, the taxi came to a screeching halt just outside the glass doors of the hotel. The bellhop opened the door, and Alex stepped out into the cool, salty air. She took a deep breath, then walked with Donald into the elegantly decorated lobby. For a moment, Alex felt light-headed as her mind flashed back to images of her last trip.

She didn't realize she had stopped walking until Donald placed his hand under her elbow, looking at her with deep concern. "Alex, are you sure you're okay?"

Alex closed her eyes, tears stinging her lids. Nodding to Donald and giving him a weak smile, she said, "Yes, I'm fine. It's—it's just that Feryle and I stayed here, and—um, forget it. Let's go." Turning, Alex quickly made her way through the lobby toward the registration desk. She was only a few feet from her destination when she felt Donald's hand on her arm.

"Damn, Alex, why didn't you say something earlier? Come on, let's go somewhere else."

Planting her feet, Alex pulled Donald back. "No, Donald, it's all right. I'm fine. We're tired, hungry, and we're staying here."

She dragged him the rest of the way to the registration desk, then said, "I'm going to get a drink. Join me when you're done here, all right?"

Donald joined her a few minutes later. The alcohol had allowed Alex to make some progress in calming her nerves and she was feeling somewhat more relaxed and in control as they left the bar. As they walked toward the elevator, Alex again sensed she was being observed. Looking around, her eyes met the registration clerk's, and Alex saw her smile as a solitary eyebrow rose in response. Alex quickly looked away, but she felt the piercing eyes burn into her back as she and Donald walked across the lobby and into the elevator.

Alex let the warm water cascade off her body. Even though the FBI plane was more comfortable than a commercial airliner, she felt an all too familiar tightness in her aching muscles. She knew from experience that her recovery process would be long and tedious. Her arm was still weak and pale from having been in a cast for several weeks.

She had just rinsed the shampoo from her hair when she heard knocking at her door. After turning off the water, she quickly dried and walked into the bedroom. As she walked to the passageway between the rooms, she saw Donald asleep on his bed. Shaking her head, she turned to walk back into the bathroom when she noticed the envelope that had been slipped under her door. She picked it up and sat on the bed to open it. Pulling a sheet of hotel stationary from the envelope, she read the note.

> I wanted to make sure you had everything you need. Please give me a call if I can assist you in any way.
> Alicia
> Ext. 8472

Alex felt a chill course up her spine, realizing Alicia must be the registration clerk. Walking back to the bathroom, Alex tossed the note in the trash, wondering if she were getting too paranoid. *Paranoia has been one thing that's kept me alive thus far. No, I'm not being too paranoid, maybe I'm not paranoid enough.* Twenty minutes later she quietly knocked on Donald's door, opened it slightly, and found him still asleep.

Grinning, Alex couldn't pass up the chance to tease her friend. They had been through a lot in the past few weeks, things that had shaken them to the foundation of their friendship, and Alex was anxious to restore the comfortable banter between them. Slowly, she crept over to Donald and bent down near his ear. She gently stroked his chin and breathlessly whispered, "Come on, lover boy, I'm hungry."

Donald slowly opened one eye and smiled as he peered at his friend. "You'd better be glad I'm not a bad boy, or you'd find yourself in one hell of a predicament right about now, Alex Montgomery."

Alex laughed and sat on the end of the bed. "Yeah, right. You'd be too afraid I'd beat the hell out of you if you tried to make a move on me."

Donald sat up and began pulling on his shoes. "Well, besides the small issue of preserving my life, I'm well trained and whipped. You have nothing to worry about from me." Chuckling, he turned to Alex. "Now, the lady down at the registration desk is another story altogether."

Donald noticed the dark look that shrouded Alex's face, and his tone softened. "Hey, I was teasing. Are you okay?"

Alex nodded, then ran her hand through her hair. "Yes, I'm fine. I just had a personal visit from Ms. Friendly. Luckily I was in the shower and didn't get to the door in time, but she left me a note."

"What did the note say? If you want to make a complaint, I'll be more than happy to go with you."

Walking back into her room to retrieve her wallet, Alex waved him off. "It will be all right, Donald. Forget it, let's go eat, I'm starving."

Alex was looking out over the ocean, waiting for Donald to return from the restroom, when she heard a quiet voice beside her. "Hello, I see you decided to dine at El Pescador. Is everything to your liking?"

"Yes, thank you." Alex's words were clipped, almost unfriendly.

"If I might, I would like to suggest the smoked salmon. It's divine." The woman's eyes swept over Alex's body. "Forgive me, I haven't introduced myself, I'm Alicia. Alicia Vergara. I am the hospitality coordinator here at the Hyatt Acapulco."

Her lips curled at the edges, hinting at a smile. "Please, let me know if I can do anything to make your stay more pleasurable." One eyebrow lifted as the woman's smile became wider, inviting Alex to read whatever she wished into the message.

"I'm afraid we're in Acapulco on business and won't have time for—"

"Is everything all right?" Donald interrupted. He looked up into piercing dark brown eyes and saw loathing thinly disguised behind the smiling façade of Alicia's face.

"Yes, everything is fine. Ms. Vergara is the hospitality coordinator for the Hyatt and just wanted to make sure we were happy with our accommodations."

"Oh certainly, Ms. Vergara. However, I'm afraid we'll be too busy to partake in all you have to offer in the way of amusement. Agent Montgomery and I are here on business. Hopefully, we'll be leaving in the morning." Donald watched as a faint look of agitation crossed the woman's face, then was once again hidden behind a forced smile.

"I'm sorry to hear that. Maybe on your next trip you'll have more time to spend enjoying the local attractions. It was nice to meet you both. Enjoy your stay at the Hyatt."

She turned and quickly walked out of the restaurant. Pulling the cell phone from her pocket, she quickly glanced over her shoulder before punching in the number.

"Yes."

"It's Alicia. Their plans are to stay for only tonight. They're leaving in the morning."

"Well, we'll just have to change their plans, won't we?"

"Look, I did this for you, we're even. *We* are not doing anything. You want more information, then get it from someone else. Leave me the hell alone." The woman's voice seethed with anger.

"Now now, Alicia. I think you owe me a hell of a lot more than this little favor. After all, your brother is safe because of me." His voice took on a threatening tone. "I'm sure you wish that to remain so. Yes?"

Releasing a frustrated sigh, she growled into the phone, "Yes, of course I do." She could almost feel the smile cross the man's face on the other end of the line.

"Good. Now be a good girl and meet me at the villa. We have a few plans to make tonight."

She heard the click. "You'll pay for this, Papa. One day I will stop you and your evil ways." Walking across the lobby, she grabbed her purse and keys and walked out into the cool night air.

Looking at Alex, Donald tried to keep his voice from revealing the concern he felt over Alicia's appearance. "What was that all about?"

Shaking her head, Alex gave him a puzzled look. "She's the hospitality coordinator here, it's her job to make sure the guests are happy and comfortable. I think I was just being a little overly paranoid earlier." Their conversation was interrupted as the waiter brought their salads. Once he had made his exit, Alex turned back to Donald and smiled. "Come on, enjoy your dinner, and then let's take a short walk and head upstairs."

Donald wasn't sure if Alex was trying to convince herself or him, but he smiled and nodded. "Okay, you're right. I think we're both a little on edge."

They finished their dinner, then took a stroll along the beach, enjoying the cool evening air. The wine had worked its magic, and both were feeling more relaxed and at ease. *I might even get some sleep tonight*, Alex thought as they waited for the elevator to deliver them to their floor.

Reaching Alex's door first, they said good night, and Donald waited until he heard the click of the lock before entering his own room. He took a quick shower, then crawled into bed and was instantly asleep.

Sleep came quickly for Alex but was sporadically interrupted by the now common nightmares. She glanced at the clock, noticing it was only five a.m., and groaned. Knowing more sleep was out of her reach, she tossed back the covers and headed for the bathroom. She donned the sweats she'd thrown into her suitcase, wrote a quick note to Donald and slipped it under the adjoining door, then headed out in search of the hotel gym.

Alex burnt off her frustrations for an hour as she completed a modified cardio and strength routine, then headed back for a quick shower. Entering her room, she turned on the shower, and knowing

Donald would be up, she knocked on the adjoining door. The door opened almost immediately, and Alex was surprised to see Donald already dressed. "Good morning. You hungry?"

"Yeah. I was just about to give up on you. Did you have a good workout?" Donald looked Alex over and frowned, seeing her clothes soaked with sweat. "Never mind. By the looks of you, I can tell you did. Go get dressed, I'm starved."

Alex laughed at Donald's frown and reached out for him. "Don't I get a good-morning hug?'

"Hell, no. Not until you're clean. Now go, do whatever it is you women spend half your lifetime in the bathroom doing." Donald smiled as Alex turned and closed the door. He sat down at the desk and picked up the phone.

Catherine picked up on the third ring. "Good morning to you too, lover. I missed you last night."

Donald smiled into the phone. "I missed you, too. We're about to go pick up Thomas, then head out. We should be home sometime in the early evening. Just wanted to let you know so you could be naked and waiting when I get home."

Catherine growled. "You are so bad, Donald Fairfax. There is nothing more I would like to do just that, but remember, we do have a house guest."

Donald laughed at Catherine's obvious frustration. "Oh, and speaking of our house guest, I'm dropping Alex by her house when we get home. Why don't you two meet us there? It's time those two straightened things out."

"You're sure? You don't need to push this, you know."

"I'm sure, Catherine. They have to see each other eventually, and I can't think of a better place for that to happen than at Alex's house, with both of us nearby."

"We'll be there. And Donald, be safe. I love you."

"I love you too, sweetheart. See you tonight."

Donald had just hung up the phone when he heard Alex's soft tap. Opening the door, he grinned. "Much better, stinky. You ready for breakfast now?"

Alex slugged him in the shoulder and walked past him into the room. "Very funny, smart ass, and yes, I'm famished. Let's get this show on the road so we can get back home."

After waiting for over half an hour at the local police precinct, Alex and Donald were finally led into what appeared to be an interrogation room. There they waited for another half-hour before a large, burly man in a captain's uniform entered.

The man introduced himself as Captain Cortez and asked Alex and Donald to sit. "I'm afraid there is going to be a little delay before we can release the prisoner to you. It seems some of the paperwork has been misplaced, and it will take most of the day to straighten it out."

Donald released a frustrated sigh. "Captain Cortez, I'm afraid I don't understand. When I called last evening, I was told everything was in order and that the prisoner would be released to us this morning."

Cortez watched as the frown deepened on the agent's face and held up his hand in resignation. "I am truly sorry, Agent Fairfax, but this was something no one expected." Standing and walking to the door, he called back over his shoulder, "I'm sure by tomorrow morning, everything will be in order and you can be on your way."

Donald and Alex watched as the door closed behind the captain, then looked at each other in confusion. Shaking her head, Alex stood and reached for her jacket. "Damn. One more night won't kill us, Donald. We've waited a month for this. Why don't we enjoy the day, have a nice evening, and try this again in the morning, all right?"

Donald decided not to make a fuss about it. "Okay. So what do you want to do with our afternoon on the taxpayers' money?"

Alex grinned as she slid her arms into her jacket. "Let's go sightseeing. I think it's time we both had some fun."

Looking at Alex skeptically, he opened the door for her. "And just what are we going to go see?"

Grinning over her shoulder, Alex walked out of the room. "You'll see. Come on."

She waited while Donald called Catherine to inform her of their delay, promising their plans were still on for the following evening.

"They'd better be, because I've already spilled the beans."

Donald chuckled. "No need to worry, honey. Everything's going as planned. Talk to you tomorrow...Okay...I love you, too...bye." He hung up the phone and turned to Alex. "You ready?"

They stopped by the registration desk on their way out of the hotel and secured their rooms for another night, both relaxing when neither spotted Ms. Vergara. Donald hailed a taxi, and they were soon off.

To Donald's surprise, they pulled up to the San Diego Fort. He glanced at Alex and saw the big grin on her face.

"What? Did you think I was going to drag you around shopping all day?" Taking Donald's arm, Alex pulled him from the taxi. "Come on, I know old forts and museums are your favorite."

Shaking his head, Donald smiled at Alex. "You sure know how to make my heart go pitter patter, don't you, girl?"

Alex treated Donald to a long lunch at Planet Hollywood before they headed out for their last stop of the day. She smiled as they stopped in front of the Mercado Municipal. "Didn't think I'd let you escape a little shopping, did you?"

Donald snorted and pulled himself from the taxi. "Damn, you women must have some kind of shopping radar implanted in your brains." He tried his best to snarl, but could only laugh when he saw the almost happy look on Alex's face. "All right, you bought me lunch and took me to the fort. The least I can do is walk around the rest of the afternoon while you shop."

Rolling her eyes, Alex marched ahead of Donald. A labyrinth of stalls, the old Acapulco marketplace was filled with vendors selling wares ranging from hand woven baskets to onyx chess sets.

When they headed out to hail a taxi, Alex couldn't help but chuckle at the difficult time Donald was having with the bags.

Shoving the bags in the back seat, Donald dropped into the taxi. "Don't even start."

Alex bit her lip, trying not to laugh at everything Donald had bought. She looked across to his bags, then down at the single package in her lap. "I didn't say a word." Mumbling under her breath, she added, "Women's radar, yeah right."

"I heard that." Donald growled but was thoroughly enjoying the teasing banter. He'd only intended to make one small purchase for Catherine, but before he knew it several hundred dollars' worth of items were in his possession, and he now had to pay an even higher price by being teased by Alex.

When they reached their rooms, Alex took several of Donald's packages from his hand so he could unlock the door. Walking him into the room, they spotted the rolling table sitting beside the window at the same time. Tossing the packages onto the bed, Donald walked over to the table and picked up the small envelope that stood beside a very expensive carafe of red wine. He read the note, sighed, and shook his head. "Seems our hospitality coordinator feels bad that our stay was extended and sent up some wine and cheese to make us feel all better."

Alex smirked. "Well, as long as she didn't add it to the bill, we'll take it." Picking up the bottle, she noticed it was the same vintage they had shared the previous night with dinner. "Very perceptive woman, Donald. At least she has great taste in wine."

Dropping down on the bed, Donald kicked off his shoes. "Well, it's fine with me. As much as we've eaten today, I don't think I'm up for a large meal. As far as I'm concerned, this can be dinner. Is that all right with you?"

"It's more than all right. I'm going to change. Want to see if they have any good movies on the television?"

"Sure, sounds like my kind of night." Donald picked up the remote and began flipping through the channels while Alex took a shower and changed.

When she returned, Alex selected an action movie, knowing Donald liked them, then settled down on the bed and stretched out.

Donald handed Alex a glass of wine, and she said, "No thanks. I think I've had my quota for the day. I think I'll stick with a safe beverage tonight, but I will take some of the cheese and crackers."

Donald placed the platter between them on the bed, and they munched quietly as the movie started. About halfway through the movie, Alex looked over at Donald and noticed he had fallen asleep. She quietly eased herself off the bed and turned the volume down, then padded back to her room.

She was glad she had decided to pack a book and settled down between the sheets to read. After an hour, she felt her lids grow heavy. Deciding not to pass up a chance for a little sleep, she closed the book and turned off the light.

Her eyes flew open an hour later, and she sensed another presence in the room. Forcing her body to relax, she listened and waited. She could hear the rustling of clothes as the figure moved closer, and all her senses went on full alert. The figure moved near enough for Alex to feel the heat radiating off her body, but she kept her eyes closed even as she got a faint whiff of a familiar perfume.

Her mind was reeling as she tried to figure out why Alicia Vergara would be in her room in the middle of the night. At the sound of a quiet click she felt her muscles tense and almost allowed herself to react, but quickly recognized it as the phone being taken off the hook. Focusing on the movement around her, she listened as the figure punched in several numbers.

"Yes, it's me. They are both unconscious." The woman was silent for a few moments, then Alex heard her growl into the phone, "I told you it would work. The rest is up to you. I'll stay until you get here, then I'm leaving." Seemingly as an afterthought, she added, "This makes us even, Papa. I'm through with you and your evil life."

Alicia replaced the receiver, then locked the door that opened into Donald's room. Walking to the window, she looked down at the ocean below, wishing she could fall into the water and become lost to her family and its evil ways. She had worked hard to overcome the influence of three generations of her father's family. Her heart ached for the freedom she knew she would never truly have. *Not as long as Papa is still alive.*

Tears stung her eyes. Looking out into the darkness, wishing for a life of normalcy, she didn't the subtle movements behind her until she suddenly heard a mechanical click, followed by hard, cold steel pressing against the back of her head.

"Who the hell are you and what the fuck do you want?"

Chapter Twenty-Three

"I'll only ask you one more time. Who are you?" Alex held the Sig level with the woman's head.

"My name is Alicia Vergara, and I am the hospitality coordinator for the Hyatt—or after tonight, I guess I can say former coordinator."

Alex motioned with her head for the woman to sit as she slowly backed toward the adjoining door. Flipping the lock, she pulled open the door to find Donald asleep. "What did you give him?"

Alicia spoke so quietly Alex had a hard time understanding. "It was only a moderate-strength sedative. It will wear off in a couple of hours."

Alex called out to Donald and saw him stir, then turned back to Alicia and growled, "Why? Who are you working for?"

Letting herself fall back in the chair, Alicia groaned, "Agent Montgomery, I'm not working for anyone. I was forced to do what I did tonight in order to keep my brother safe."

The confusion was evident on Alex's face as she watched Alicia. After calling out to Donald once again, she walked to the closet and pulled a set of handcuffs out of her duffel bag. She tossed them to the woman and ordered her to cuff herself to the headboard.

Alicia stood from the chair and obediently slid onto the bed and cuffed herself. She turned back to Alex and looked at her with sad eyes. "I'm sorry if I have caused you any trouble."

Alex relaxed her grip on the Sig as she walked back to the door separating her room from Donald's. He was sitting on the bed, obviously very groggy, rubbing his face. In a command voice, trying to break Donald from his drug-induced stupor, she yelled, "Donald, go to the bathroom and drink some water, wake yourself up, then get in here. We have a little unexpected company and more on the way."

Donald shook his head, trying to clear his thoughts as he stood and walked across the room on wobbly legs. "What's going on, Alex?"

"It seems Ms. Vergara here spiked the wine she sent up earlier. Good thing I passed on it, or we'd both be sitting ducks for whoever is on their way to see us."

Donald's eyes focused on Alicia, and his mind cleared as the adrenaline surged through his body. He stalked closer. "Ms Vergara, do you mind telling me what the fuck is going on here, or do I call the police right now?"

The woman shook her head and glanced at Alex. "I'm afraid the police can't—or won't—help you with this, Agent Fairfax. You're still here in Mexico because some important paperwork was misplaced, am I correct?"

Donald and Alex both felt chills run up their spines. Alex was the first to recover, and the anger in her voice mirrored the anger surging through her body. "Are you telling me the police helped set us up?"

Alicia shook her head. "No, no. Please sit and stop pointing that thing at me, and I'll tell you everything I know."

Donald and Alex listened as the story unraveled, small pieces fitting into place bit by bit until the puzzle was complete. When they heard a light tapping on the door, Alex held her finger up in front of her mouth, and Donald slipped into his own room. Alex quietly uncuffed Alicia and pushed her toward the door. Leaning in close, she whispered, "You open the door, get him inside, then get the hell out of my way. Do you understand?"

Nodding, Alicia walked to the door, opened it, and peered out. Alex could hear voices but couldn't make out what they were saying. Praying that Alicia wasn't double-crossing them, she waited in the darkened bathroom. Her muscles tensed as she saw the slash of light cutting the darkness of the room grow wider and then disappear as the door closed.

Taking a deep breath, she readied herself, hoping Donald was holding up his end, and flipped on the light while at the same time leveling the gun at the man's head. "Aren't you a bit out of your neighborhood, Papa? The slums are further down the street."

The man whipped around to see Alex's gun leveled at his face. Smiling, he pierced her with a cold stare. "Agent Montgomery. Why don't you put your little toy away? My bodyguard is just outside the door, and I don't think he will appreciate your inhospitality."

Just as the words left his mouth, Donald pushed a beefy-looking man through the door. "Is this the guy you're talking about? I'm afraid he's going to be a little tied up for a while. Looks like you're on your own, Mr. Sarantos." He ordered the man to the floor and cuffed his hands behind his back.

Alex waited for Donald to finish, then motioned for Sarantos to sit in the chair next to the window. Donald took the set of cuffs from Alex and secured Sarantos's hands behind his back. After both men were safely situated, Donald sat on the bed and faced Papa Paul. "Your daughter has been filling us in on your plans, Sarantos. And I'm not really liking what I'm hearing."

Sarantos glared at his daughter, wishing his hands weren't cuffed. *I should have been harder on you, Alicia.* "My daughter is a weakling and can't be trusted by either of us, I'm afraid." Glaring at her with disdain, he continued, "Alicia has her mother's disposition. Much too tenderhearted."

"Donald, I'm going to call Robert. I'll be back in a few minutes." Alex walked to the bed and un-cuffed Alicia's hand. "Come with me."

Alicia stood and followed Alex into the other room, rubbing her wrists as she went. As they entered Donald's room, Alex motioned toward the chair. Alicia sat quietly while Alex picked up the phone and asked the operator to connect her to the American embassy in Mexico City.

After concluding her conversation and hanging up the phone, Alex looked at the woman sitting across from her. "You said earlier that you were forced to participate here tonight. Is that correct?"

"Yes, of course it is." Letting out a long breath, Alicia continued, "I know you don't believe me, but I never wanted to see you harmed. You have to understand, once Papa sets his mind to something, nothing changes it. After you humiliated him last year, you're all he has talked about. Revenge for Papa is always sweet, and more often than not, deadly."

"I can't make you any promises. However, if you agree to work with us, give us information that we can use to put an end to your father's empire, I'll do everything I can to see that you're protected."

Alicia's eyes brightened and for the first time in years, she saw a way out. "I'll do anything I can to help." Her gaze fell to the floor as tears welled in her eyes. "I know I have no bargaining power here, but can you see what you can do to help my brother?"

Alex shrugged. "I can't promise you anything, Alicia. I don't know who your brother is or what role he's played in all of this. I'll do what I can for you, that's all I can promise right now."

Nodding, Alicia accepted Alex's terms. "I'll help you. All I ask is that you try. Hector is a good man, Agent Montgomery."

Alex, Donald, and Robert arrived at the police precinct a little after noon. To their pleasant surprise, Captain Cortez wasn't available. Instead, they were met by another, more cooperative officer.

"Hello, I'm Captain Rodriguez, I'm terribly sorry for the inconvenience you have experienced while in Acapulco. I assure you, the matter is being closely investigated." He smiled. "I won't delay you any longer. I'll go retrieve your prisoner now so you can be on your way."

Donald looked at Alex and noticed that her knuckles were white from gripping the arm of the chair. He placed his hand on hers. "You ready for this?"

Alex blinked, trying to hold back the tears that threatened to flow. "Yes. Just do me a favor, Donald, don't leave me alone with him." She looked into his eyes. "As much as I want to kill him with my bare hands, I also want him to live a long, miserable life in prison."

Donald gently squeezed Alex's hand. The door to the interrogation room opened, and Captain Rodriguez roughly shoved Seth Thomas into the room. Donald stood behind Alex as the captain pushed Seth down into a chair directly across from her. Donald knew that if Alex could maintain her composure for those first few moments, everything would be okay. Watching the two intently, he tensed as a smile crossed Seth Thomas's face.

"Good afternoon, Agent Montgomery." Seth smiled as he watched Alex's face turn red.

Forcing herself to remain calm, Alex nodded and returned his stare. "Seth."

Captain Rodriguez stepped back from the chair. "Agents, your prisoner. I'll have some of my men accompany you to the airport. Have a safe trip." He turned and walked from the room.

Donald and Robert each took one of Seth's arms and lifted him from the chair. As they were turning to walk out the door, Seth looked at Alex once again and laughed. "Alex, I was so hoping you would be here for this. Too bad Conner can't be here with us."

Alex's hands clenched into fists. "Yes, it is, but I choose to believe that she knows I'm here, eager to take you to prison." She smirked as the smile faded from Seth's face. "I wouldn't have missed this for the world, seeing you thrown in prison for the rest of your life."

Seth laughed and leaned forward against Donald and Robert's firm hold. "Yes, but what makes it better for me is knowing you'll be living in your own little hell right along with me."

Donald and Robert lost their grip on Seth's arm when Alex lunged at him, shoving him against the wall. With one hand around his neck, she used the other to pummel his face. "You son of a bitch, I'll kill you—"

Donald grabbed Alex, pulling her off while Robert restrained Seth.

Wiping his bloody nose, Seth grinned. "I think I've just become a victim of police brutality." He looked smugly at Donald. "I'm filing charges."

Donald looked at Robert, then Alex, before facing Seth. "Damn, Seth, I don't know what you're talking about. I'm sorry the door hit you in the face. We'll try to be more careful from here on out, okay?"

Donald and Robert led Seth out of the room with Alex following along behind, struggling to regain her composure. Captain Rodriguez looked up when he heard them coming down the hallway and gave Donald a questioning look.

"You really need to work on that door, Captain Rodriguez."

A knowing smile crossed the captain's face. "Yes, Agent Fairfax, I'll see to it. It's been a problem in the past."

They said their good-byes and headed for the airport under the escort of Captain Rodriguez's officers. Donald finally relaxed as they settled in the plane and the wheels left the ground. The trip had taken several unexpected twists and turns, but overall they had come away with more than they bargained for.

Alicia was sitting alone, looking out the window. Donald made his way through the plane and took a seat beside her. "You doing okay?"

She gave him a sad smile. "Yes, I'm fine. All of this seems a little surreal to me. Yesterday I was frightened for my life, today I'm on my way to finding a new one. I know you think my motives are skewed, but I do want to help. I've seen too many people hurt or killed by my father. It's time to put a stop to this evil. I want to start my life anew and finally become the person I've only dreamed about."

Donald tilted his head and returned her smile. "Well, you have that chance now, Alicia. What you do from here on out is completely your decision. I have a feeling that you're going to make the right ones and have that life you've always wanted." He stood up. "Get some rest. I'm afraid you have a long evening ahead of you."

Alex watched as Donald spoke quietly to Alicia. They were sitting several rows ahead, and she couldn't make out what was being said, but from both of their expressions, she knew it was a good conversation. A few minutes later Donald joined her.

"How's she doing?"

Donald shrugged. "She's fine. I'm sure she's confused and frightened, but I think she'll do the right thing and give us the information we need to nail this bastard once and for all. What about you? You doing okay?"

Looking away, Alex felt a slow heat rise in her face. "I'm sorry I lost it back there, Donald. I just wasn't expecting him to be so smug."

Placing his hand on Alex's arm, Donald smiled. "No problem. You couldn't help it if the door got stuck, so let's not worry about it anymore, okay?"

Shaking her head, Alex gave him the first real smile he had seen all day. "You got it. Oh, did you call Catherine and let her know we'll be late?"

Donald fought to contain a grin. "Yes, I called. I told her we'd be tied up at the office for most of the night but that I'd get home as soon as I could." Donald stood up. "By the way, tomorrow we're having a barbecue at your house to celebrate."

Alex looked up at Donald, surprised. "My house?"

"Yep, your house. You have a beach and the better grill. Catherine's making all the plans, so just be there, ready to celebrate." He walked toward the back of the plane before Alex could question him further. Finding an empty row, he stretched out across the seats, deciding to get in a short nap before they reached Jacksonville.

Alex watched Donald walk away. He and Catherine had been beside her almost the entire time since Conner's murder. Smiling sadly, she decided that a barbecue was the least she could do for them. Laying her head back, she closed her eyes, hoping that she could rest a little before arriving home and spending the next several hours at the office.

The plane arrived in Jacksonville a little after nine o'clock. The tarmac was crowded with police cars when they arrived, with Jack Peterson in the lead. There were been a few tense moments as Peterson and Seth faced one another on the tarmac, but Peterson kept his cool and backed away from the prisoner, not wanting to do anything to jeopardize the case. Seth was placed in an unmarked FBI car, and the group swiftly drove away.

The car came to a halt just outside the jail. The officer driving the car waited for the overhead doors to rise so he could pull into the prisoner bay. After a few minutes, a voice came over the radio, telling him that the mechanical doors were stuck and they would have to bring their prisoner in through the side door. The officer rolled his window down when he saw Captain Peterson walking toward him. "I don't like this, Captain."

Peterson looked around and noticed the other officers had exited their cars and were waiting for his orders. "I don't either, but we'll have to make it work." Raising his hand and waving two of his best officers over, he turned back toward the officer in the car. "Okay, let's go."

From the back of the vehicle, Seth looked around. There were too may men around to try and make an escape. He twisted his legs and rose from the car as one of the officers grasped his arm. Walking toward the side door, Seth felt his gut knot at the thought of what a future inside prison held for him. He knew it would take little time before he found himself beaten, raped, and more than likely killed within the walls of this building.

Not allowing himself time to think, he jerked away from the officer. They had made the mistake of cuffing his hands in front, and in the second it took for the officer to react, Seth had the officer's gun and was now pointing it at his head. "You tell everyone to back off or I'll blow your brains out right here."

Alex stood motionless as Seth's eyes locked on hers. "Montgomery, in the car."

Donald raised his hands to stop Alex, but Seth quickly turned the gun on him. "I wouldn't do that if I were you, Fairfax. I'm outta here, and if I have to kill you or anyone else to accomplish that, then so be it. It's your choice."

Alex glanced at Donald. "It's okay. Take it easy. I'm going." She sat down in the driver's seat, looking at Seth for further instructions.

"Move the car over here," he ordered.

Alex started the engine and backed up to get as close as she could to the men. Seth ordered the officer he was holding hostage to unlock his cuffs and leg shackles. For a split second, Seth's attention was focused on his hands and not Alex. Using this to her advantage, Alex prayed the officer could react quickly enough. She jammed her hand on the horn at the same time she floored the gas petal. The officer jumped to the side just as the car descended upon them.

Seth's eyes widened in horror as he realized too late what Alex was doing. Before he could roll away, the car made contact, crushing his legs between the car and the wall. He looked up to see Alex sitting dazed behind the wheel. He had kept his grip on the gun and smiled as he raised the barrel toward the windshield. A grin crossed his face the instant he pulled the trigger.

Alex could feel someone lightly slapping her face and struggled to comprehend what was happening. Opening her eyes, she tried to focus on Donald's face.

"It's over, Alex." Donald smiled. Although she was still dazed, he knew she would be okay. "Sit still, the paramedics are on their way."

Alex blinked several times before she realized Donald was talking to her. She rubbed her head. "What happened?"

"Don't worry about that now. I think you have a minor concussion." Donald winced as Alex frowned when he placed his handkerchief against her forehead. "I'm sorry, kid. Just try to relax, you have a laceration on your head."

Alex closed her eyes, feeling tired. *Donald. Donald will take care of everything.*

Chapter Twenty-Four

Catherine was making dinner. She knew Donald would be late but wanted to have something to eat when he got home just in case. She was thinking about the next night's barbecue when she heard her name frantically called from the other room.

"Oh my God, what happened?" Catherine reached for the remote, turning the volume up.

"It's Alex. Catherine, we have to go, she's hurt."

Catherine held up her hand. "Hold on. I'm sure Donald has his cell phone with him. Let me try to reach him first." She rushed to the kitchen, pulled the phone off the base, and dialed the number as she returned to the den. "Donald? What is going on? We just saw the scene on television." Catherine could hear the siren as the ambulance sped to the hospital. Trying to stay calm, she sat down on the sofa.

"I think everything is okay. Seth Thomas tried to escape and Alex stopped him. I don't think it's anything serious, just a mild concussion."

"We'll meet you at the hospital." Catherine was already searching for her keys when Donald's voice stopped her.

"No! You two stay there. Everything is under control. Alex is going to be fine. We still have some loose ends to tie up. You stay there for now, you hear me?"

Catherine sighed, "Okay, we'll stay, but you call us the minute you know anything, all right? I love you. Bye."

Donald sat in the ER, waiting for word on Alex's condition. He'd made several calls and confirmed that Robert had taken Alicia to a safe house, where she was secure, and Seth Thomas had been officially pronounced dead. Donald smirked. There had been ten officers at the scene, and every one of them had gotten at least one round off before Seth had a chance to take a second shot. The only thing Donald regretted about the outcome was that they would never really know just how deeply Seth was entrenched in the Hernandez organization, or how much he knew about Sarantos.

He looked up as the doctor approached him. "Agent Fairfax, I'm Dr. McLeod. Agent Montgomery is going to be fine. She is one lucky woman; the bullet only grazed her head, and she has a concussion from hitting the steering wheel. She'll have a headache for a while, but other than that, she'll be fine."

Donald released a relieved sigh. "Great. Can I see her?"

Smiling, the doctor turned and walked toward the doors leading to the treatment rooms. "Sure, come on, I'll take you. I want to watch her for another hour, then if everything is okay, you can take her home."

Donald stopped as he entered the room, taking a minute to look at Alex. She was lying on the stretcher, her eyes closed, and Donald could see the fatigue clearly etched across her face. Walking to her side, he gently took her hand in his. "Hey there."

Alex cracked one eye and squinted up at Donald. "Hey."

With a teasing smile, he placed a gentle kiss on her forehead. "I can't seem to keep you out of hospitals. How're you feeling?"

Reaching up, Alex touched the bandage on her head. "I have a horrendous headache. When can I get out of here?"

"Soon. The doctor wants to watch you for a while, then I'll take you home." Squeezing her hand, he stood up. "Get some rest. I'm going to make a few phone calls, then I'll be back to break you out of here, all right?"

"'Kay." Closing her eyes against the glaring lights, Alex drifted back to sleep before Donald released her hand.

Standing there, he watched as Alex's breathing took on the cadence of sleep. Leaning and kissing her cheek, he whispered in her ear, "This will all be over soon, I promise."

Heading to the cafeteria, Donald pulled the phone from his pocket as he walked along the deserted corridor and punched in the numbers for home. "Hey, sweetie, just wanted to give you an update. Alex is fine. She has a mild concussion and a laceration on her forehead, nothing serious. The doctor said I could take her home in an hour or so."

"That's great, Donald."

"I'm going to take her home and stay the rest of the night. She's still a bit confused, and I don't think she needs to be alone."

"You stay with her. She needs you right now." Catherine's voice dropped. "I miss you."

Donald smiled as he heard the deep growl in his wife's voice. "I miss you too, and I intend to show you how much tomorrow night when I finally get you alone again."

"Me too. So I guess the barbecue is still on?"

Donald watched as the vending machine filled a paper cup with hot coffee. "Absolutely. I'll call you in the morning, but plan on being there around noon." He lifted the plastic door and retrieved the small cup.

"Bring me some fresh clothes, too. I desperately need a shower and a change."

They said their good-byes, and Catherine walked back into the den. "You ready for tomorrow?"

"Yes. More than ready."

Smiling, Catherine took the soft hand between her own as she spoke. "Then I suggest you go get some sleep. Looks like you're going to have a long day tomorrow."

"Thank you, Catherine. I couldn't have made it through this without you and Donald. I...I..."

"You're welcome. Now hit the sack."

Rummaging through Alex's purse, Donald found the key, unlocked the back door, and led Alex into the house. Still unsteady on her feet, she held onto his arm as he led her to the bedroom. He hesitated as she sat on the bed, not knowing how much help she needed or wanted. His concerns quickly dissipated as she lay back on the pillows and instantly closed her eyes.

Donald lifted Alex's legs onto the bed and slipped off her shoes before pulling the cover across her body. He looked around the bedroom, for the first time noticing the absence of any pictures or personal reminders of Conner. Looking at the sleeping woman, he remembered how Alex had responded to Feryle's death a little over a year earlier.

Alex had survived that collapse of her world by burying all of her emotions and any reminders of the pain. Sighing heavily, Donald walked over to the window seat. As he glanced about the empty room, then back to Alex, he spoke softly to himself. "Seems like you're using the same defense this time around, kiddo."

After easing the shoes and socks off his aching feet and removing his tie, he piled several pillows on one end and lay down, looking out toward the ocean waves. He knew how much he missed Catherine if they were apart for only a few days and couldn't imagine the pain Alex had endured the last few weeks. As Donald lay in the darkness, he felt an overpowering need to hold Catherine. As he closed his eyes, a single tear slipped down his cheek. *Tomorrow, Alex, I promise tomorrow will be a better day.*

Alex woke as the sun broke through the morning clouds. Turning over to face the window, she saw Donald asleep in the window seat. She sat up in the bed and threw back the covers, realizing she was still in the clothes she had worn the day before. Standing up slowly, she brought her hand up to feel the bandage across her forehead and winced at the pain. Although it had lessened, she still had a dull, aching headache. Padding to the bathroom, she found Donald had placed her medication on the sink. She shook one of the pain pills into her hand and popped it in her mouth before walking to the kitchen to start the coffee.

Donald opened his eyes as his senses took in the scent of freshly brewed coffee. Groaning, he sat up and stretched his aching muscles before trudging into the bathroom. He smiled when he returned to the bedroom a few minutes later and saw Alex. "Good morning."

"Good morning, sunshine. You look like hell." Alex chuckled but quickly brought her hand up as a sharp pain coursed through her forehead.

Growling, Donald took the cup of coffee Alex had placed on the dresser. "Serves you right for making fun of an old man." He took a satisfying swallow of the hot coffee before looking back at Alex. "But I'll forgive you this time, since you brought me coffee."

Crossing the room to the window seat, she tossed the cushions off and lifted the top. Digging through the storage area, she came up with a bundle of clothes. "I love you, Donald, but you're in bad need of a shower. Here, take these. They may be a little snug, but they'll sure smell better than what you have on." Smiling, Alex flipped her hand, shooing him out of the bedroom. "I put clean towels out in the guest bath. If you need anything else, just help yourself."

Donald took the offered clothing and headed across the hall. He turned on the shower and looked in the mirror while waiting for the water to heat. Dragging his hand across the stubble on his face, he noticed the long creases that had somehow managed to creep into his face over the last year. He brushed his teeth and then stepped into the shower. Leaning against the cool tile wall, he let the warm water soothe his aching muscles. *I hope after today, Alex, things will be right with us once again.*

He toweled off and dressed, and as he was walking into the kitchen his cell phone rang. "Fairfax."

"Good morning."

A grin crossed Donald's face when he heard Catherine's voice on the other end of the line. "Good morning to you. Is everything set for the barbecue?"

"God, yes. We've been up for hours. Please don't tell me there's another delay. I don't know if either of us will survive it."

Chuckling, Donald looked out onto the deck to make sure that Alex wasn't within hearing range. "No. No more delays. I'm going to get her down to the beach so you can get in the house. Make an appearance on the deck when the coast is clear and we can come back, okay?"

"You got it. I'll see you soon." Catherine's voice again took on a low tone. "Donald? Just so you know, I love you."

"I love you, too. Now hurry up, I'm starving."

Dropping the phone onto the counter, Donald slid open the glass door and walked out onto the deck to join Alex. "You feeling better?"

"Much better, thank you." Turning to Donald, Alex lifted an eyebrow and grinned. "Damn, I never realized what a nice butt you have."

Donald could feel his face turning scarlet. "Stop it. I can't help it if these clothes are too tight."

"I kinda like 'em, Donald. Gives you that dark, sexy FBI agent look."

"You're a pervert, Montgomery." Kicking off his shoes and looking out at the beach, Donald grabbed Alex's hand. "Come on, take a walk with me. I need to feel sand between my toes."

Alex followed Donald down the steps. "What about Catherine, don't you want to get home to her?"

He shook his head. "No, don't you remember? We're having a barbecue here today. She'll be here after she goes by the market."

Alex stopped and turned toward her friend. After giving him a warm hug, she looked back into his eyes. "Well, it seems like you have my day all planned out."

Grinning back at Alex, he wiggled his eyebrows. "I definitely have your day planned, my friend."

Alex punched Donald in the arm. "You're up to something, Fairfax. Spill it."

Grabbing Alex's hand once again, he headed off toward the beach. "Me? Up to something? Alex, you know me better that that."

Alex glared back at Donald but couldn't hide a smile. "Well, just remember what happens when I'm surprised. I don't like 'em and I can't be held accountable for my actions."

They walked a long while, lost in their own thoughts. They passed several couples holding hands and quietly chatting along the way, and Alex wondered if she and Donald looked like one of them. The air was cool, and Alex snuggled closer when Donald wrapped his arm around her.

Donald broke the silence as they neared the house. "There she is now." He raised his hand in the air, waving as Catherine walked onto the sand.

Catherine opened her arms and pulled Alex into a warm hug. "Damn, you scared us last night. How are you feeling?"

"I'm fine, just a slight headache." Alex returned the hug and laughed as she looked at Donald. He was standing beside them, looking dejected.

"Hello! What about me?"

Both women laughed as he pouted. Wrapping her arms around Donald's neck, Catherine whispered, "You'll get your welcome home later, big guy." After planting a small kiss on his lips, Catherine squeezed between him and Alex. Taking their hands in hers, she led them back toward the deck. "I've got all the makings for a mega barbecue. You two sit and enjoy yourselves. I'm going to start lunch."

Alex and Donald sat on the deck talking about the case and Sarantos's upcoming extradition to the United States. After a while, Donald excused himself and walked into the kitchen. "Is she ready?"

Catherine turned and looked at her husband. "As ready as she'll ever be. Go get her."

Walking down the hall, Donald lightly tapped and then opened the guest room door. "Come on, I think It's time we get this over with."

Sitting on the deck, Alex couldn't help but wonder what Donald and Catherine were up to. She was standing to go into the house to find out when she stopped suddenly. Her heart raced as she looked into the face she'd thought she would never see again.

"Hello, Alex."

Alicia Vergara sat on the sofa in the safe house drinking a cup of coffee, thinking about the previous night and the unending barrage of questions she had endured. Laying her head back on the soft pillows, she wondered what would happen to her father now that she had supplied the authorities with the missing pieces to the puzzle.

She knew Agents Fairfax and Montgomery couldn't make her any promises, but she also knew that almost anything would be better than returning to her previous life. *Maybe this will allow me to finally break free.*

She stood and walked down the hallway to the bathroom. After turning on the water in the shower, she stripped off her clothes and stood under the warm spray.

The man moved warily through the trees until he was within range of the guard sitting outside the front door. After crouching for a moment to be sure his approach had not been detected, he lifted his gun and smiled as the silencer eliminated almost all of the sound as he fired. He waited until the guard's form slumped over before making his way slowly to the house.

He could hear noises coming from the back deck and stood at the front door listening for any other sounds from within the house. Easing the door open, he crept inside and looked around. He moved silently and quickly on hearing a noise at the other end of the hall. Stopping at the door he eased it open, crept in, and quietly closed the door behind him.

Alicia quickly turned, trying to cover herself as the shower door flew open. "Hector! What are—" Her words were silenced as the bullet entered her head.

Hector Sarantos watched as Alicia's head snapped back, a slow trickle of blood running down the front of her face as her naked body slid down the wall, leaving the tile cracked and smeared with his family blood. Muttering darkly under his breath, Hector sadly watched the life drain from his sister, the only person who had truly loved him. "Sorry, Alicia, but you knew Papa would never stand for your betrayal."

A wrenching ache encompassed his heart as he looked down upon his dying sibling. She had almost managed to escape the greedy claws of their father, but he, the only son, had never had that chance. His fate had been sealed even before his birth. Death would be his only escape—a death he would welcome in time, but not before his own plans were complete. With one last look at Alicia, Hector turned and made his way back out of the house and into the thick cover of the trees.

Alex stood stunned. "Olivia. What are you doing here?" Alex turned her glare toward Donald as he walked onto the deck. "Donald, what the hell is all this about? Do you think this is some kind of joke?"

Donald looked into Alex's eyes and could see the anger and pain buried within. "No, Alex, it's no joke. The two of you have a few issues to settle, and it's time you did it. Catherine and I will be inside if you need us."

Alex turned away from her ex-partner and friend. "What the hell do you want with me, Olivia?"

Olivia gripped the railing of the deck. *Maybe this wasn't such a good idea. Maybe I should have just let Donald handle this himself.* "I want to explain a few things to you. I'm not asking for anything from you, Alex, just a few minutes of your time, then I'll go."

Releasing an exasperated breath, Alex fell back into her chair. "Fine. Say what you have to say, then leave."

Sitting across from Alex, elbows on her knees and looking at the deck, Olivia took a deep breath and began to relate the story, hoping that it would somehow bring her a little peace. "After Jen was murdered, my life was in shambles. I still don't know how I got through that time, but one thing I do know is that you were a big part of my surviving. After the case was over and we became partners, I found myself falling in love with you. Everything was coming back to center for me and I thought maybe—well, I don't know what I thought. Anyway, when you transferred to Jacksonville, I found myself lost again."

Standing and walking to the railing, Olivia looked out over the water. "I allowed myself to turn into the type of person I've always hated. After a while, I knew I had to get out of Chicago. So I came here. I guess I was hoping to reconnect with you and, well, maybe see if something would develop between us here. When I got here, I looked you up. That's when I found out you were with Feryle. I did a little checking and found out she was going to San Diego on business. I followed her there with the intention of seeing what I was up against."

Turning toward Alex, she saw the dark brooding eyes of the Shadow cutting into her. "I swear, Alex, I never meant to hurt you. I was desperate. You were the only escape I had from the hell I was living in. I needed you and wasn't really concerned for anyone else's feelings. I had hoped that after it was all over, Feryle would confess to you. I knew how much weight you put in loyalty and knew you wouldn't stand for her betrayal."

Olivia moved back to the chair and sat down heavily. "When nothing happened, I realized that Feryle hadn't told you. A few months later, when the two of you came into the office, I could see how afraid she was that I would say something. Once I saw the look on your face, I knew I could never let you know. I'd never seen you look happier. I knew then that my chances of ever having you were gone."

Alex watched as Olivia struggled with her words. A part of Alex wanted to comfort her old friend while another wanted to choke the life out of her. "Olivia why are you—"

"Please, Alex, let me finish. Anyway, after that day, I fell back into my own little world. I kept in touch with the bureau and did some small freelance work when they needed it. I found out you were working the Hernandez case and decided I wanted to get involved. Help you. I infiltrated the organization after you were injured last year. I guess the bureau saw me as the perfect plant; I had no family or friends, nothing that would threaten the case or my focus. I was already well involved by the time you and Conner came to the office. I guess you could say I went a little crazy again when I found out you and Conner were together, but you have to believe me, Alex, I wouldn't have done anything to hurt either of you."

She stood up. Looking down at her old friend, she sighed. "I know you won't ever forgive me, Alex, and I don't expect you to. I just wanted to explain it all." She watched as a myriad of emotions flashed over Alex's face. Knowing there was nothing more she could do or say, she simply placed her hand on Alex's shoulder and squeezed gently. "I have something for you. I'll be right back."

Alex sat, trying to assimilate all the information Olivia had just dropped on her. Her emotions were shattered, and all she wanted to do was be alone and try to work through her feelings. Wiping a tear from her face, Alex looked at Olivia as she knelt down beside her.

Placing a small bundle in Alex's lap, Olivia smiled. "Here, maybe this little guy will help bring back some of those wonderful memories you've shared with Conner."

Alex looked at Olivia, not fully understanding. "Where did you..."

Olivia gave Alex a sad smile. "One of the investigators found him when they were going through Seth's house. Donald's allergic to cats, so I told him I'd keep Magnum until you were back on your feet. I remember Conner talking about the little furball, and even though she didn't want anyone to know, we all knew she loved the little guy."

Alex picked Magnum up and cradled the cat in her arms. "Thank you, Olivia. I-I don't know what to say."

Olivia nodded, then stepped back to lean against the railing. "I know it's not the same, but I thought having him would make you feel closer to Conner."

Alex stared up at Olivia, not knowing what to say or how to respond. Before she found the words, Olivia continued, "I *am* sorry, Alex...for everything. Take care of yourself, Alex."

Olivia quietly walked back into the house, stopping beside Donald and Catherine. "Thanks, Donald, for giving me this time. I really appreciate what you've done." Looking back through the glass door, she watched as Alex gently stroked Magnum, tears streaming down her face. "Take care of her, okay?"

With one last look, she turned and made her way out the front door, down the steps, and down the street to where she had parked the car. Reaching into her pocket for the car keys, her fingers circled the tiny bugs she had removed from the bedroom while Catherine, Donald, and Alex had been on the beach. Looking at them with disdain, she tossed them into the woods.

Watching as they scattered into the underbrush, she reflected on her similarly scattered life. She closed her eyes and sighed heavily, and after dropping down into the seat and starting the car, she pulled into the morning traffic. Heading nowhere in particular, she drove north on I-95. Now was the time for her to search, seek and heal. Time to start again.

Chapter Twenty-Five

A lex gently smoothed the fur on Magnum's back as she sat on the deck, looking out over the water. Tears stung her eyes as memories of Conner flashed through her mind. She was grateful that Donald and Catherine were in the house; she didn't have the strength to talk at the moment.

She sat for a long while, lost in a thousand thoughts until she heard the sliding door ease open. Donald scratched Magnum under the neck before dropping down in the chair across from her.

Alex attempted an evil glare. "So this little guy was the surprise you had for me."

Sniffing, Donald looked down at the little cat. "Everyone thought you'd like to have him." Raising his eyes to look at Alex, he questioned his decision. He could see the tears forming in her eyes and wondered if this was too much, too soon. Pulling a handkerchief from his pocket, he wiped his eyes. "Alex, if you'd prefer not to keep him, I'm sure Greg would take him."

Alex pulled Magnum closer. "No. I do want him. I just—well, it's just difficult right now." She looked into the kitchen. "Where's Catherine?"

Donald's face contorted as he released a roaring sneeze, "Damn cats." Wiping his eyes, he sniffed and looked back at Alex. "She had to go to the market. Seems like we thought of everything except food for this little guy and some allergy medication for me. She'll be right back."

Alex laughed as she watched Donald's suffering. "Um, I'll go put him in the bedroom." Alex began to stand but was waved back down by Donald.

"Hell no, you won't. That's the first real smile I've seen on your face for a while. A little sneezing never hurt anyone. Cleans out the sinuses."

Alex shook her head, smiling at Donald's obvious need to ease her pain, and remained seated. They sat silently, lost in their own thoughts for a few moments, until they heard Catherine call out from the kitchen.

Donald stood and held out his hand for Alex. "Sounds like we're needed in the galley."

As they walked into the kitchen, Catherine turned and grinned as she spoke. "Well, what do you think of your surprise?"

Alex raised Magnum up, kissing him on the nose. "I love him. He reminds me of Conner. Bullheaded and persistent." A sad look crossed her face. "I just wish Conner were here to help me take care of him."

"Well, I guess you have nothing to worry about, Agent Montgomery."

Alex's world started to spin as she tried to comprehend what she was seeing. Leaning casually in the doorway stood Conner, flashing that crooked smile she knew Alex loved.

Donald held onto Alex's waist as she started to sway, and Catherine took Magnum from her arms. Conner walked up to Alex and gently cradled her face in her hands. "God, I've missed you so much." She then leaned in and placed a tender kiss on her lips.

Alex was speechless as Donald and Catherine stood by, grinning. Donald kissed Alex on the cheek and hugged her tightly. "Now *that* was really the surprise."

Conner wrapped Alex in her arms and led her over to a chair. "Alex, baby, are you all right?"

Alex blinked, focusing on Conner's face. "Oh my God. Where...when..." Her eyes met Donald's and she saw pure joy in his face. "You knew?"

Catherine pulled on Donald's arm. "Come on, hero, you need to take your wife for a walk on the beach and give these two a few minutes to say hello."

Alex was struggling with her thought processes even as Conner led her into the front room and pulled her down onto her lap. Alex's mind went into overload when she felt Conner's soft lips capture hers. Throwing her arms around Conner's neck, she fell into the passionate kiss, her head spinning as a myriad of emotions passed through her.

Pulling back for air, Alex kept her tight hold around Conner's neck and looked into her eyes. "I saw the paramedics, heard them say you were dead."

Conner held Alex close as she took a deep breath. She knew all the information would be hard to absorb at once; even she had trouble believing it all. "We have Jack and his quick thinking to thank for that. The first group in was the special ops team. Once Jack realized Seth had escaped, he had them get me out and into protective custody. I was never dead—well, close, but not quite." Conner leaned in for another kiss.

"Anyway, Jack arranged for me to be taken to a hospital in Colorado as soon as I was stable. I was there for almost four weeks."

Alex couldn't believe she was sitting in Conner's lap. Tears streamed down her cheeks as she gently stroked her lover's face. "I didn't want to live without you. Didn't think I could." Alex kissed Conner again, savoring the taste she had yearned for so badly the last few weeks. "Where have you been since you got out of the hospital?"

Conner grinned and nipped Alex's nose. "I've been with Donald and Catherine. Jack wanted me to be close but somewhere Seth would never look for me, in case he found out I was alive." Conner looked deeply into Alex's eyes. "Donald loves you. He feels terrible about everything that's happened between the two of you. Please give him the chance to make it up to you."

Alex claimed Conner's lips with her own. Before either realized it, the kiss had deepened, and they both felt the familiar surge of heat as their passion rose. Tearing her lips from Alex's, Conner took a deep breath. "God, I want to touch you. I've needed you for so long."

A ragged breath escaped Alex's lips as her hands wandered down Conner's chest. She moaned when Conner grabbed her hands and lifted them to her lips, "Um, we have to remember we have guests, but believe me, later I won't be stopping you, Agent Montgomery."

"Oh God, I want you so much." Alex stole one last kiss before rising and taking Conner's hand. "Let's go find those two before I change my mind."

Walking out onto the deck, Alex saw Donald and Catherine's grinning faces. She crooked her finger, "You. Come here."

Donald stood and walked toward Alex and was stunned when she grabbed his face and planted a kiss on his lips. "That's for bringing Conner back to me." He grinned proudly at Alex, just before he bent over in pain as she buried her fist into his stomach. As he struggled to breathe, she growled into his ear, "And that's for keeping her hidden from me, you lug."

Catherine and Conner howled with laughter as Alex led Donald back toward the chair and dropped him unceremoniously down. He rubbed his stomach and looked up at the smiling woman. "Damn, Montgomery, remind me never to piss you off. That hurt."

Conner came up behind Alex, wrapped her arms around her, and peered over her shoulder, smiling at her new friend.

Catherine walked over to her husband and smacked him on the back of the head. "Oh, quit whining, Donald. You're such a baby." Leaning down, she kissed him on the top of the head. "Now get up and light the grill, we're hungry."

Still rubbing his stomach, Donald stood and walked toward the kitchen. "Try to do something nice, and where does it get me? Sucker punched and smacked in the head. Damn, you three are hard to please."

The three women laughed, and Conner yelled out just as he reached the door. "Hey, Donald, anyone ever tell you that you have a cute ass?"

Donald glared at the three laughing women before snarling and walking into the house to change his clothes.

Donald had the grill fired up and the four were sitting on the deck talking over the events of the last few weeks. When the doorbell rang, Alex looked at Donald with suspicious eyes. "God, Donald, I hope you don't have any more surprises for me today. I'd hate to have to kill you."

Donald curled his lip at Alex as he made his way toward the glass door, chuckling as he spoke. "Just one more, Alex, then we're done for the day. I promise."

Alex turned toward Conner, and her questioning look was met with a shrug. "Don't look at me."

Alex sat, waiting pensively, until she heard a familiar voice echo through the house. Rising, she met Peterson at the back door and immediately drew him into a hug. "How can I ever thank you for this?"

After returning Alex's hug, he leaned back and looked into her eyes. "Just promise me you two will take good care of each other. That's thanks enough for me."

Alex kissed Peterson's cheek, then stood aside as Conner hugged her friend and captain. "I owe you big time, Cappy."

Rolling his eyes, Peterson laughed. "You want to pay me back, then don't get shot again. Too much damn paperwork."

Conner knew this was the closest Peterson would come to sentiment and lightly slugged him on the shoulder. "You're such a softy, you know that."

Looking over at the grill, he said, "No I'm not a softy, just hungry. Where's the food?"

It was after seven when the house emptied and Alex and Conner were finally alone. They lay on the sofa, holding each other contentedly as the room darkened with the setting sun. Turning, Conner slid on top of Alex and each felt the other tremble as their bodies reacted to new but very familiar sensations. Conner traced Alex's eyebrows as she looked longingly into the dark eyes gazing back at her. "I missed you so much, baby."

Alex's lips found Conner's. Their tongues probed, searched, and tasted the familiar sweetness as they slowly began to rediscover each other. Soon their breathing and heartbeats quickened to match the surging flow of blood coursing through their bodies. Alex gasped as Conner's hand slipped beneath her t-shirt, her nails sending rippling spasms throughout her body. A low growl escaped Alex's lips as Conner continued to caress her, slowly inching her way up Alex's firm stomach.

"Oh, baby, I've missed you." Alex arched her back as Conner's hand found her breast, her thumb tracing the outlines of the sensitive nipple.

Conner smiled into the kiss, relishing her lover's response. So many nights during the last few weeks, she had imagined this moment. Now that it had arrived, she was determined to make it as slow and wonderful for Alex as she had imagined. "You feel so good. I've missed you." Tugging the shirt over Alex's head, she dropped it beside them on the floor, then dipped her head and took the hard nipple into her mouth, gently running her tongue over the hard peak. "I've missed this. I've missed you."

Conner could feel the muscles in Alex's stomach spasm as she gently made love to her. Kissing her way back to Alex's mouth, she was consumed by the warm fire surging through her body. Hands searched and tongues mingled as their passion continued to grow higher. Tearing her lips from Conner's, Alex smiled as she took in a rasping breath. "I want to make love to you in our bed."

Understanding the sentiment, Conner smiled. "*Our* bed?"

Alex traced the line of Conner's jaw and then lightly kissed her chin, "Yes, our bed. I want you with me every night...forever."

Conner helped Alex stand, then encircled her within warm arms, "That's exactly where I intend to be."

With gentle hands, Alex led Conner down the hall and into the bedroom that had for too long been empty and lonely. Stopping beside the bed, Alex turned Conner toward her, reached for the buttons of her shirt, and began slowly unfastening each one. The room was in shadow except for the fading light coming through the windows facing the sea as she opened the last one and slowly slid the soft fabric from Conner's shoulders. She gazed longingly at the firm taut breasts, the nipples hard and erect, aching for her touch. Gliding her hands up Conner's arms, Alex cradled Conner's face within her hands. "You are so beautiful."

Tracing the taut muscles in Conner's neck with her fingers, Alex slowly lowered her hands to rest on the firm muscles of her chest before kissing the top of the scar that ran the length of her torso. Cupping each breast in her hands, Alex growled as Conner's head dropped back, exposing the soft enticing skin of her neck. Leaning in, Alex gently kissed the pulsing artery of her neck and felt the increasing heat between her own legs.

Conner's breathing increased as each kiss brought Alex closer to her aching nipples and she released a deep growling moan when she felt Alex's lips close around the hardened peak.

"Ah, yes." Arching her back and pressing herself deeper into Alex's hands, Conner felt every nerve ending in her nipples respond to Alex's gentle sucking. Lowering her own hands, she unsnapped Alex's jeans and heard a low growl against her chest as she slowly worked the zipper down. With a single finger, Conner lifted Alex's face and bent in for a gentle kiss. She could feel Alex tremble as she traced the fullness of her lips with her tongue. She knelt, and looping her thumbs into the waistband, slid the jeans over Alex's hips, tracing the newly exposed skin with her tongue. "God, how I've missed you, Alex." Looking up she found Alex's eyes following her path.

With an impish smile, she wrapped her arms around Alex's legs to cup the firm, muscular hips as she worked her way back up Alex's body, stopping just below her navel to lightly nip her tender skin. Using her tongue, Conner traced a path to Alex's chest, where she took the hard nipple in her mouth and felt Alex's legs tremble. Turning Alex around, Conner gently lowered her onto the bed, looking down at the undeniable beauty of her lover. Sliding between Alex's open legs, Conner seized Alex's lips with her own. "I've missed kissing you...tasting you."

Gasping, Alex tore her lips from Conner's tugged the drawstring on Conner's sweat pants and then pushed them over her narrow hips, moaning at the discovery of soft skin beneath her fingers and the realization that Conner had nothing on beneath the sweats. She cocked her eyebrow at Conner. "Trying to tease me, Harris, or do you just like going commando?" She brushed her cheek over the smooth skin of Conner's stomach, then ran her tongue around the edge of her navel.

Conner's fingers feathered through Alex's hair. "You know I like to tease you, and I know you like it."

Looking into Conner's eyes, Alex could see her passion mirrored. "Oh, I definitely like it." Lifting Conner's legs, she placed first one and then the other on beside her so that Conner straddled her lap, her slick wetness bathing her legs. Lying back, Alex pressed against Conner's hips, bring her closer. "Come here. I need to taste you."

Conner's breath quickened as she eased her way up Alex's body, and she cried out when she felt her tongue slide between her warm wet lips. "Yes, baby...oh, Alex."

Conner's hips and legs were trembling as Alex smoothed her tongue along the hard shaft of her clitoris. Looking down into Alex's eyes, Conner tangled her fingers in Alex's silky hair as her heart melted at the sensual sight. "I love you so much."

Alex's hands firmly cupped Conner's hips, moving her so that Conner's hard clitoris glided slowly back and forth across Alex's tongue. Feeling the surging wetness between her own legs, Alex dropped her hand and slid a finger between her swollen folds, releasing a deep moan as her hard, aching clitoris pulsed. She let her fingers dance across the hard shaft for a moment before pulling her hand away and bringing her fingers up to trace Conner's swollen lips.

Conner took first one finger, then another, and sucked Alex's juices deeply into her mouth. "Oh, baby, you taste so good." Conner's hips moved faster as Alex's tongue pressed harder against her clitoris, making her body shake with the rising passion. "God yes, baby. Lick me."

Alex could feel Conner getting close, and she backed off just enough to slow the surging storm between her legs. Her lover groaned above her. "Please Alex, I need you now...I need you inside me." Alex's silent reply was to rake her nails gently down her lover's back.

Conner's hips bucked harder against Alex's tongue as she felt the beginning pulses of her orgasm. Alex released the hard clitoris, licked her lips, and then turned to gently bite Conner's thigh. "Behave. I've missed you and I intend to savor every drop of you."

Alex pushed two fingers deep into Conner; at the same moment, she closed her lips around the hard, pulsing shaft. When her legs gave way under Alex's sensual touch, Conner fell forward, catching herself with her arms, but she felt herself lose control as she watched Alex's fingers pumping in and out of her wetness. And when Alex looked into her eyes and began to slowly stroke her tongue along the length of the hard distended shaft, Conner felt the orgasm explode through her body.

Alex felt the muscles tighten around her fingers and knew Conner was lost in the release of her orgasm. Looking up into Conner's eyes, she pumped her hand harder, taking her lover over the edge.

Conner lost all sense of time and space as the spasms ripped through her body. Her hips bucked against Alex's warm, soft tongue as each spasm surged through her body. "I-I love you, Alex...God, I love you."

Conner rode the consuming wave as Alex gently, tenderly sucked her pulsing clitoris until finally she collapsed beside her, gasping for breath. Rolling over, Alex wrapped one arm around Conner's shoulders and leaned down to tease her lips in a slow, lingering kiss. As their lips met, Alex felt the muscles squeeze her fingers, still pressed deep within Conner. She held her close as their tongues tasted each other's sweet juices until Conner again lifted her hips, taking Alex deeper into her.

Tearing her lips away from Alex's and gasping for air, Conner grabbed Alex's hand. "Damn, woman, are you trying to kill me?"

Kissing Conner's nose, Alex smiled. "Not a chance, Harris. I'm keeping you around for at least the next fifty years." Sliding on top of her lover, she bent her head and placed gentle kisses along the scar that bisected Conner's chest. A tear fell from her face as she looked into Conner's eyes. "Please tell me this isn't a dream and I'm not going to wake up tomorrow and you'll be gone."

Alex's pulse raced as Conner's fingers played across her back. Bringing her hand around to gently lift Alex's chin, Conner tenderly kissed her lips. "I promise, baby, it's not a dream." Rotating her pelvis, she rolled over, taking Alex with her, and then slid her thigh between Alex's open legs. Feeling Alex's warm wetness caress her thigh, Conner moved down Alex's body. "I'm going to show you this isn't a dream."

Sliding lower, she captured one hard nipple and sucked it between her lips before releasing it and looking up into Alex's hooded eyes. "I'm real." She shifted, licking the valley between her firm breasts. "I'm staying."

Moving over, she captured the other hard nipple between her lips and sucked it deep into her mouth until she felt Alex's hips thrust against her stomach. Lifting her head, she smiled up into her lover's face and slid lower until reaching Alex's stomach. Stopping only for a moment to flick her tongue into her navel, she slid lower still until she was nestled between Alex's legs.

Conner could see Alex watching her every movement. "And I'm going to show you just how much I've missed you, Alex." She sat back on her knees and let her eyes roam across the hard firm muscles of Alex's body. Her hands feathered down Alex's legs, causing sensual waves along the defined muscles. Her fingers traveled across the soft sensitive bottoms of Alex's feet before beginning their journey higher, closer to the warmth she knew was waiting, aching for her.

Conner stretched her lean body between Alex's legs and gently nipped the soft flesh of her thighs before running her cheek across the trimmed wet curls. Alex's eyes closed as the warmth of Conner's love spread throughout her body, and she moaned as Conner slowly separated the swollen lips, crying out as Conner's tongue, in one long, slow stroke, embraced the sensitive clitoris hiding below.

Alex felt the electrical shocks reverberate throughout her body. She pressed Conner closer. "Oh baby, yes...God, I've missed you." Alex's body responded instantly to Conner's teasing touch, and she knew she wouldn't be able to hold back the thunderous orgasm for very long. She desperately needed to come, to feel the surging release that only Conner could make her feel, yet she didn't want the incredible feeling to end.

Having Conner make slow passionate love to her was something she had thought she would never feel again, and she wanted to delight in the amazing beauty of it all.

Alex's body, its need too great for release, surged on as Alex felt the rising pressure build. "I want you inside me, baby." Alex's hips thrust against Conner's tongue and all thought fled from her mind as she felt Conner's fingers glide slowly into her, reclaiming her body. "Yes, that's it baby, deeper."

Alex felt the explosive wave as it centered around Conner's fingers and spread rapidly throughout her body. "I'm coming...Conner...yes." Alex's world exploded as Conner drove her deeper and harder while at the same time stroking her tongue lightly across Alex's clitoris. Alex reached out, and pulling Conner up along her body, held on as the orgasm pulsed through her, sending unyielding ripples up her spine and through every nerve ending in her body.

Conner held onto Alex as the waves crashed. "That's it, baby, let it go. I've got you." Kissing Alex's lips, Conner continued to slowly slide in and out of her as she gently stroked the pulsating shaft with her thumb. After long, delicious moments, Alex's spasms began to slow, and Conner felt her collapse into the mattress. "God, Alex, you're so beautiful. I love to watch your face as you come for me."

Struggling to breathe, chest heaving and lungs burning, Alex tenderly stroked Conner's face. As the emotions she had buried deep inside escaped from her soul, tears flowed down her cheeks. "Please don't ever leave me." Pulling Conner closer, embracing her with weakened arms, Alex spoke in a voice that was choked and broken as tears of unparalleled joy cascaded down her cheeks. "I love you so much, Conner."

Conner held Alex as their tears blended and fell together onto the sheets. "I love you. It was so hard for me to stay away. I can't even imagine what I would have felt like in your place." Conner gently captured Alex's lips and tasted the salty evidence of their shared release of well-dammed tears. "It's over, baby. Hernandez and Seth are both dead. Sarantos will spend the rest of his natural life behind bars. It's over. Nothing—*nothing*—can get to us now."

They lay together, arms and legs intertwined, soothing the pain of the last few weeks away until at last their breathing became slow and rhythmic as they fell into a peaceful sleep.

Chapter Twenty-Six

The sun peeked softly through the window as Alex slowly awoke. During the night, she and Conner had slept, legs and arms intertwined, each needing the reassurance that the last few hours had been real.

Alex opened her eyes and watched as Conner lay in the crook of her arm, her breathing softly caressing Alex's breast. Turning onto her side slowly, so as not to wake Conner, she kissed her sleeping lover's soft lips and heard the wonderfully familiar growl. "Wake up, sleepyhead."

Conner burrowed deeper into Alex's arm, her muffled voice still hoarse with sleep. "No. Sleep...more." She slid her leg over Alex's and turned, burying her face between Alex's warm, firm breasts.

Groaning as Conner's thigh brushed against her still-aching clitoris, Alex closed her eyes and relived the wonderfully sensual reunion they had enjoyed just a few hours ago. Unable to control her growing hunger, she ran a hand down Conner's leg, pressing it tighter against her quickly hardening clitoris, and released a primal moan as she felt her own wetness bathe her lover's thigh.

Looking down into Alex's eyes, Conner was overwhelmed with love for the woman who only a short time ago had sped into her life and stolen her heart away. She gently brushed Alex's lips. "I love you so much, Alex."

Alex's body reeled with the electrifying charges Conner sent through her. Knowing she couldn't hold back any longer, she drew Conner to her, capturing her lips with her own. At the touch of Conner's tongue on hers, Alex exploded into orgasm and she felt Conner follow her over the edge, their cries muffled as their mouths hungrily devoured each other. In complete harmony, they rode the wave as it brought them slowly back to reality.

Chest heaving and heart racing, Conner fell into Alex's arms. Tracing the line of Alex's jaw, she looked deeply into Alex's dark eyes. "I love you too much to ever be away from you again."

Alex's hands glided over the firm muscles of Conner's hips before coming to rest solidly around her waist. She could still feel the muscles tremble. "I love you, too, and we'll never be apart again, I promise."

"Good, then you'll like my surprise."

Alex lifted a solitary eyebrow at her grinning lover and tickled Conner's ribs. "Oh? And just what kind of surprise would that be, Officer Harris?"

Conner tossed back the covers and slid out of bed, making a long, sensual show of stretching her muscular body as she strolled across the floor to the bathroom. Never looking back, but knowing Alex was watching her every move, she drawled over her shoulder, "I suggest you get your lazy butt up if you want to find out."

Turning at the bathroom door, Conner crooked her finger, beckoning Alex to follow. "First we need a shower, then we need to pack. I'm taking you on a long cruise to Blackbeard Island."

"Pack? A cruise? What about Donald? The case? We can't just leave, can we?"

Conner stepped into the shower, and pulling Alex in behind her, backed her against the cool tile wall. Cupping Alex's breasts in her hands, she tugged on the quickly hardening nipples. She captured one of the taut peaks between her lips and sucked it deeply into her mouth. Hearing Alex's moans, she released the rigid nipple and moved toward the other. "Sometimes, Agent Montgomery, you talk too damn much."

The End

About The Author

KatLyn, who is a native of the South, currently resides in North Central Florida. KatLyn's is a simple philosophy: "I love strong-minded women who have a desire to refine the attitudes of the world with subtle words and an astute sense of direction without feeling the need to censure those opposed to their views. After all, it's those very closed-minded attitudes that made this biased world what it is today."

She makes her home in Gainesville, Florida with her partner Denise and their cats Lucky, Paris, and Colby.

When she's not writing, KatLyn can be found spending time with her family and friends or indulging in her passion for playing the guitar and writing musical compositions.

Other Books Available From
StarCrossed Productions

Safe Harbor, second edition
Radclyffe

A mysterious newcomer, a reclusive doctor, and a troubled gay teenager learn about love, friendship, and trust during one tumultuous summer in Provincetown. Reese Conlon, LtCol USMCR, is the new sheriff who has heads turning amidst speculation as to who will be the first woman to capture her attentions. Dr. Victoria King has been betrayed by love once and refuses to risk heartbreak again. Brianna Parker, the teenaged daughter of Reese's chief, fears her father's wrath when he learns that she loves another girl. As these three women struggle to live and love in freedom, they risk their hearts and souls to give one another a *Safe Harbor*.

Tomorrow's Promise
Radclyffe

Adrienne Pierce, buffeted by fate and abandoned by love, seeks refuge from her past as well as her uncertain future on Whitley Point, a secluded island off the coast of Maine. Tanner Whitley—young, wild, restless—and heir to a dynasty, desperately tries to escape both her destiny and the memories of a tragic loss with casual sex and wild nights, a dangerous course that may ultimately destroy her. One timeless summer, these two very different women discover the power of passion to heal—and the promise of hope that only love can bestow.

Beyond The Breakwater
Radclyffe

In *Beyond the Breakwater*, the sequel to *Safe Harbor*, Sheriff Reese Conlon and Dr. Tory King face the challenges of personal change as they define their lives and future together. Tory's pregnancy forces her to examine her personal needs and goals while Reese struggles with her escalating anxieties over conditions she cannot control. Twenty-year-old Brianna Parker makes a sacrifice for love that threatens not just her happiness, but her life, when she returns home as the newest member of the sheriff's department. A life-threatening accident, a suspicious fire, and the appearance of more than one woman vying for Bri's attentions makes one Provincetown summer a time of transformation as each woman learns the true meaning of love, friendship, and family.

Love's Tender Warriors
Radclyffe

Drew Clark, ex-Marine and martial arts master, is the new instructor at the Golden Tiger dojang. Intense and aloof, she hides dark secrets and unhealed wounds beneath her warrior's exterior. Sean Gray is the young psychologist and senior student who threatens to bring down the barriers Drew has erected around her heart. Battle hardened and world weary, Drew discovers that Sean wields a weapon she has no defense against—tenderness. Together, two women who have accepted loneliness as a way of life learn that love is worth fighting for, and a battle they cannot afford to lose.

Above All, Honor - Revised Edition
Radclyffe

In an all new, expanded edition of the first in the Honor series, *Above All, Honor revised edition* introduces single-minded Secret Service Agent Cameron Roberts and the woman she is sworn to protect—Blair Powell, the daughter of the president of the United States. Cam's duty is her life and the only thing that keeps her from self-destructing under the unbearable weight of her own deep personal tragedy. However, she hasn't counted on the fact that the beautiful, willful first daughter will do anything in her power to escape the watchful eyes of her protectors, including seducing the agent in charge. Both women struggle with long-hidden secrets and dark passions as they are forced to confront their growing attraction amidst the escalating danger drawing ever closer to Blair.

From the dark shadows of rough trade bars in Greenwich Village to the elite galleries of Soho, each must balance duty with desire and, ultimately, chose between love and honor.

Honor Bound
Radclyffe

Secret Service Agent Cameron Roberts made a promise to Blair Powell, the president's daughter—not to place her own life in danger protecting Blair—but a request from the commander in chief forces her to break her word. In this sequel to *Above All, Honor* revised edition, Cam places duty before love and accepts reassignment as the chief of Blair's security detail, despite knowing that this decision may destroy their tenuous new relationship. As the rift between them widens, more than one woman is happy to offer Blair the company that Cam cannot. Amidst political intrigue, an escalating threat to Blair's safety, and the seemingly irreconcilable personal differences that force them ever further apart, these two unusual women struggle to find their way back to one another.

Love's Melody Lost
Radclyffe

A secretive artist with a haunted past and a young woman escaping a life that proved to be a lie find their destinies entwined.

Victim of a terrible accident, famed composer and pianist Graham Yardley loses her sight, her heart, and her soul. Wealth and fame mean nothing after the devastating loss of her beloved music; her life is reduced to silence, darkness, and bitter regret. In a bleak mansion atop windswept cliffs, she withdraws from the world, her once consuming passions now a source of anguish and fear. Then Anna, a lost woman seeking a place in the world, comes into her life and awakens feelings Graham thought were dead forever. A fragile melody of love is played between these damaged souls, a song made sweeter and stronger by the day...but will their blossoming romance be destroyed by an outsider's greed or will it succumb to the discord of Graham's tormented heart? Can Graham find happiness with Anna, caught up in the fiery overtures and darkly gothic strains of...Love's Melody Lost?

Love And Honor
Radclyffe

US Secret Service agent Cameron Roberts has more than one secret that could destroy her career, not the least of which is that she's in love with the president's daughter. Blair Powell, the first daughter, returns the feeling despite her ambivalence about Cam's role as her security chief, particularly in the aftermath of an assassination attempt that nearly cost Cam her life. In this third book of the Honor series, Blair and Cam struggle to protect their relationship from intensified media exposure even as they are unwillingly drawn into a shadowy conspiracy that puts Cam's career and the president's political future at risk. When Cam's previous lover resurfaces to offer support and solace, the president's daughter and her security chief are faced with difficult choices as they battle a tangled web of Washington intrigue for...love and honor.

In Pursuit Of Justice
Radclyffe

Detective Sergeant Rebecca Frye and Dr. Catherine Rawlings return in the sequel to *Shield of Justice*. Barely recovered from a near-fatal injury, Rebecca insists on returning to duty even if it means temporary assignment to a Federal task force led by a Justice agent with an agenda that may be more than meets the eye. Joined by a troubled young rookie and an enigmatic computer consultant with secrets of her own, Rebecca's obsession with finding her partner's killer and her involvement in the multi-jurisdictional investigation of an international child pornography ring threaten both her life and her new relationship with Catherine. Even Catherine's professional assistance and personal devotion may not be enough to save their love.

Visit us at www.StarCrossedProductions.com

StarCrossed Productions Order Form

Name:			Date:	
Address:				
Apt, Ste:				
City:			Email:	
State:	Zip:		Phone: ( ) -	

Name, address and zip code, **must** match exactly with the information you have on file with the credit card issuing bank in order to be processed. Non-matching information will result in a denial of your transaction and delay the processing of your order.

Check One	Mastercard _____	VISA _____	AMEX _____	
Card Number				
Card Code			3 digit number on back of card	
Expiration MM/YY				

Title	Price	Quan	Total
A Matter Of Trust - Autographed	$18.95		
A Matter Of Trust - Unsigned	$13.95		
Above All, Honor - Autographed	$22.50		
Above All, Honor - Unsigned	$17.50		
Honor Bound - Autographed	$21.95		
Honor Bound - Unsigned	$16.95		
Honor Series - Autographed	$42.45		
Honor Series - Unsigned	$30.15		
In Pursuit Of Justice - Autographed	$19.95		
In Pursuit Of Justice - Unsigned	$15.95		
Justice Series - Autographed	$35.95		
Love & Honor - Autographed	$22.99		
Love & Honor - Unsigned	$17.99		
Love's Melody Lost	$22.50		
Love's Melody Lost - Autographed	$17.50		
Love's Tender Warriors	$16.99		
Romance Set (Includes both of the above titles)	$32.50		
Safe Harbor - Autographed	$22.50		
Safe Harbor - Unsigned	$17.50		
Shield Of Justice - Autographed	$18.99		
Shield Of Justice	$13.99		
Storm Surge - Autographed	$22.99		
Storm Surge - Unsigned	$17.99		
Tomorrow's Promise - Autographed	$22.50		
Tomorrow's Promise - Unsigned	$17.50		
		Subtotal	
		Shipping (See rates below)	
		FL residents add 6% Sales Tax	
		Balance Due	

Shipping Scale		
Location/Method	First Book	Each Additional Book
US Priority	$6.00	$1.50
US Economy	$3.50	$0.99
Canada/Mexico	$7.50	$1.00
All Other Int'l	$10.00	$1.50
Sets count as 2 books for shipping purposes		

Credit Card Orders may be faxed to: (352) 337-6669 or mailed to the address below.

We accept checks drawn on US Banks (Will be held for 7 days or until bank clearance), US & International Money Orders, or Cashiers Checks.

Please make payable to StarCrossed Productions

Mail Orders To:
StarCrossed Productions
Attention: Sales Department
PO Box 357474
Gainesville, Florida 32635-7474